A GREAT PLACE
for a
SEIZURE

a novelory

by
Terry Tracy

novelory [nov • el • o • ry] *noun* (1) A fusion of the terms "novel" and "short story" to describe a series of linked stories that may stand by themselves as individual tales and/or come together as a novel, when read in sequence. (2) A term, coined by Terry Tracy, to identify a species of literature that reflects a 21st century IT-induced mind-set of tight schedules, rapid communication, and the desire to have all things at once. (3) a gimmick.

Example: ***A Great Place for a Seizure*** by Terry Tracy is not the only **novelory**, but it is the first of its kind to be identified as such.

For media inquiries: tftpdb@yahoo.co.uk

A Great Place for a Seizure is available as an eBook, compatible with KINDLE, as well as other eBook readers. The e-Book is text-to-speech enabled.

| First Printing | April 2011 |
| Second Printing | October 2011 |

CreateSpace
Published in the USA

ISBN: 1453834702
ISBN - 13: 9781453834701

To QCL

TABLE OF CONTENTS

*In our sleep, pain which we cannot
forget falls drop by drop*

upon the heart until, in our own despair,

*against our will, comes wisdom
through the awful grace of God.*

Aeschylus
Agamemnon
458 BC

⌘   ⌘   ⌘

Is your cucumber bitter? Throw it away.

Marcus Aurelius
Meditations
180 AD

⌘ ⌘ ⌘

1. THE LIBRARY

September 1982

SHE HAD SEIZURES SHE FORGOT AND WANTED TO FORGET, BUT SOME NEVER LEFT HER. Unwanted, a word or a scent could throw her back into those haphazard moments. But there were times she wanted to remember. Like a child who collects random treasures in a shoe box, she wanted to own those curious fragments of her life; for inside the memory of a single seizure, events and impressions that occurred years ago came alive again in seconds.

Mischa awoke slowly and searched her mind for a reason to get out of bed. Her eyes surveyed the floor, strewn with yesterday's clothes. They settled on the crimson Oriental rug. Its strict geometric pattern led to a row of knots whose tangled threads ended in a jagged fringe. Reminded and disturbed, her mind began a frenzied search, sifting and scattering minute details of memories. She bolted upright and pressed her hands against the sides of her head to make it stop. If she were going to remember, she wanted it whole, not in pieces. Of those shattered bits, one would be enough to retrieve the memory. A number stood out from the clutter: 823. She exhaled and fell backward.

She looked above her and there were faces looking down. She closed her eyes. *Who are they?* Mischa opened them to see fluorescent bars of light overhead, one after another, pointing her down an aisle lined with bookshelves. She closed her eyes and felt like a plane running down a bumpy runway, ready for takeoff. She felt breezes. *But how am I moving?* Mischa opened her eyes and saw branches, leaves, and sky. She closed her eyes and felt that she was inside again. She heard a manic siren and a voice that spoke in a machine-gun rhythm.

"Female...teenager...seizure...grand...mal...Jefferson...Library...witnesses...three to five minutes...no status epilepticus...oxygen loss...stabilized...no signs of drugs or alcohol...regaining consciousness...on the road...there in five minutes."

1

Mischa eyed a man at her side holding a rectangular plastic bag. Clear liquid splashed inside from one corner to the other as the ambulance jarred left and right, making its way between cars. She saw the tube that dangled from the bag and followed its path down to a needle inserted into her forearm and covered with white tape smudged with blood. A smiling woman leaned over her. Little crystal balls dangled from the ends of the woman's braids and swung back and forth like a beaded curtain. *She has a crooked tooth, just like mine,* Mischa thought.

"Wha...wher...wha...where...?"

"Honey, you had a seizure. Don't try to talk. You're on the way to the hospital. Don't worry, baby, just hold my hand."

Mischa looked at the woman's hand. Her glossy red nails were perfectly manicured. Mischa felt the calloused palm against hers and finally felt at ease. *Her hand is so friendly, so rough and so friendly. Her voice is so smooth, so...I can't...can't...deal with this. I think...I think...I'll sleep.*

⌘ ⌘ ⌘

Mischa judged her mother's mood by how the rosary beads swung from the rearview mirror. Sweeping arcs cut short by erratic, sudden shifts signaled frenetic driving and a very bad mood. Today the rosary beads told Mischa to stay silent and let her mother speak. While she spoke, Mischa heard occasional words: *dry-cleaning, father, car wash,* and *conference.* They were still ten minutes away from the library and it had reached an even eight. Mischa had been counting the number of times her mother asked, "Why do you always wait until the last minutes to start your school assignments? *Por qué?*" Her mother's mantra for scolding was a question oft-repeated, without expectation of an answer. It was always asked in English and punctuated with "why" in Spanish. Mischa ignored the sound of her voice, but remained alert to the pauses. In those, she would insert the two words meant to pacify her mother.

"Yes, Mom."

"Mischa, are you listening to me? I asked you, what do you wants for the dinner?"

Mischa stared out the window to watch the Rhode Island suburbia whiz by. It was typified by the flat expanse of gray sidewalks and black parking lots in neighborhood shopping malls. The white houses were individualized only by the colors of their shutters and doors; either black, dark blue, dark green, or dark red. Like matchboxes lined up, with an inch of space between each one, they belonged in the backdrop of 1950s advertisements for family cars. The leaves were the only real show of beauty. The trees along the road were a pageant of warm amber, with blazes of crimson and bolts of gold. Even the dried ones, on the cusp of flying off the branches, seemed more genuinely alive than their surroundings. On lawns, responsible neighbors were raking fallen leaves and putting heaped armfuls into overweight trash bags.

"Mischa!" Mrs. Dunn grabbed her daughter with a look.

"Yes, Mom?" Mischa knew she had been caught, but her wide eyes tried to look innocent.

"I have asked you twice, what do you wants for the dinner? I go through the trouble of making home-cooked meals. I cannot think what you do. We all sit down together, not like some American family that microwaves their food and eat in different parts of the house, *la casa*. These American mothers take their food, *esa comida*, from a cardboard box. Together we eat, *una família*, like a family. They are homemade and you never appreciates them!" The martyr argument, she knew it was futile to respond. As the library parking lot came into sight, Mischa broke into a relieved smile.

"Thanks, Mom." She stepped out of the clumsy, clunky brown station wagon and slung her backpack across her shoulder. She regretted having made her mother angry, now that she needed a favor. She leaned down to speak to her through the car window. Her mother could distinguish the difference between a semi-tone of respect or disrespect in her voice. Mischa knew that she had to strike the right note.

"*Por favor, Mamá*. Please, Mommy, let me skip dinner, please, just for tonight. I need to finish this paper. I can't get this done if you pick me up in one hour."

The car drove off and Mischa swaggered toward the library's main entrance, impressed by her own powers of persuasion. She saw the victory as a good omen. She reveled in the fact that it had cost only two instances of "you're right, Mom" and she was not forced to deploy "I was wrong." Too much use of the latter phrase, like radiation, had long-term implications.

So maybe I procrastinated a little. Well, perhaps maybe a little too much, she thought as she walked. She justified it to herself with her motto, "Pressure is a wonderful muse." It sounded grandiose, even silly, but she liked it. She took it out in situations such as these, like a shiny penny rubbed smooth with hope.

The automatic glass doors swung open as if to welcome a conqueror. Mischa adjusted her glasses, ready to begin the expedition. When she entered she saw busy librarians shelving and stamping. Students with armfuls of books, a testament to hours of research, walked past with purpose and intent. Her confidence, so buoyant only moments ago, plunged.

At the far end of the library were the binders that held the transparencies cataloging the library's collection. A few feet away from them were only six microfiche machines and an expectant line, another reason to despair. Then she saw her.

"Sophie!" Mischa waved across the library and ran between irritated looks from the other library patrons.

Maria Sofia Marina Lopez was her real name, but she preferred Sophie. Her parents were Bolivian, but she was born in the United States. People often asked Sophie, "Where are you from?" It always stung her when she replied "here" and the person insisted, "No, I mean, where are you from?" Sophie tried to make herself look more American, but the several do-it-yourself perms and dyes to lighten her inky black hair had never worked. At school, when Sophie saw one of her blue-eyed idols, a look of envy stole into her kind brown eyes.

"*Hola, chica!*" Mischa gave Sophie a hug and a quick kiss on the cheek. "Oops. Gotta be quiet. I just got a dagger stare from that librarian, Mrs. Wart-on-the-Nose." When Mischa looked at Sophie, she found comfort in her chocolate-tinted Andean profile. It was a face from home that reminded her of the churches and markets in Chile.

"What are you doing here, Mischa?"

"A paper for lit class. I haven't even read the books. What's your assignment?"

"Sister Eleanor put me in the Latin American group. We had to write something about the magical surreal or magic surrealism. I don't understand. And you, *y tú?*" Sophie asked.

"I've never even tried to understand it. The titles are weird enough. I'm in the English literature group. I have to compare some book by Jane Austen to some book by Virginia Woolf. I can't remember the titles, but I think they're women's names. Ah, here they are."

She took a crumpled piece of paper out of her pocket.

4

"I gotta go Mischa, there's a machine free." Sophie hugged her good-bye.

Twenty minutes later, when Mischa returned with her transparencies in hand, there was still a traffic jam at the microfiche machines. People looked at their watches and tapped impatient feet. As she waited in frustration, she recalled the promises made by Mrs. Wart-on-the-Nose.

"Everything is going to be better. You'll have instant access to all our books. Look here, just place a transparency under the glass. Think of each microfiche machine as a slide-show projector. Switch on the light and pres-to! A hundred book titles, authors, or subjects all at once! No walking back and forth to the card catalogs for little cards in tiny drawers. All you have to do is move the transparency to the right or left, up or down, and you can find the exact book title you want. Isn't technology wonderful?"

Finally first in line, Mischa's eyes ran back and forth to be certain she caught a machine as soon as it came free. Sophie had already left. When Mischa saw a man grabbing his notebooks to begin his search through the shelves, she walked over briskly to begin her search. *Let's start with Virginia. Gosh, what was the title? Mrs. Dalton? No. Mrs. Dallon? Mrs. Dalloway! Got it!* Mischa grabbed a blunt pencil lying in the plastic tray. *Why don't they sharpen these things?* She pressed the pencil hard and saw herself writing the call number on a scrap of paper, and then stuffing it in her pocket. At the machine beside her sat a woman in a strange cream woolen sweater. Mischa fixated on the design on the front; three pea pods lying next to a cobalt blue bowl filled with peas. She studied each of the peas, small green crochet balls that popped out of the sweater. The lady returned Mischa's curious stare with a glare. Mischa heard the crack of hard candy in the lady's jaw and smelled a cherry-flavored cough drop. *Stay still, stay.* She muttered with annoyance as her fingers tried to adjust the transparency that slanted and slipped between the slides. *I guess...I guess...I should...I should...* She looked up and saw herself suspended from the ceiling. Mischa saw herself raise a finger to touch a ray of dusty light that bounced off the glass. Her body began to descend and bend and twist into a tight knot that rolled slowly into a dark tunnel. Gaining speed as it rolled, the knot transformed into a smooth ball, rolling faster and faster, until finally it hurled itself forward and crashed against a wall of light.

2. THE HOSPITAL

Her nose twitched at the smell of disinfectant.

"Mischa, it's Dad. Mom is here too. Don't try to get up. The doctors want you to stay here for a while. You...you...you had two seizures today."

Seizures? Her head felt like it had exploded. It had never hurt like this before. She wondered whether it had grown larger just to accommodate that amount of pain. When she looked around questions ran through her head. *How did I get into this hospital gown? Where are my clothes? Where are my shoes? Why is there blood on the hospital gown? Where am I bleeding from?* She tried to lift herself up.

"Why can't I get up?" She tried again. "Why can't I get up!" she shouted. Mischa turned her head to see the rest of her body bound in white canvas straps. "Why do I have straps around me? Get these straps off me!" When her father ran to her side, she saw the helplessness in his eyes and forgot her fear in sudden pity for him.

"Mischa, dear, you were at the library. You had a seizure there, and then you had one here. They bound you to the bed so that you wouldn't fall out." Mischa laid her head back and took a deep breath. A knife sliced through her skull when she exhaled. *No more questions. Too hard to understand. No more. Sleep. Sleep. I'll close my eyes and this will go away.*

She awoke when she heard a metal platter fall and teeter as it rocked back and forth. She looked through the slits of her almost-closed eyes to see that the hospital had not gone away. *It's all here. I'm still here. What happened? Why? How?* The heavy thud of the headache inside her skull made it difficult to move. She remained still and her eyes darted around the room. Her parents were seated in chairs against the wall, silent and unaware that she was awake. They sat slumped, like children in a principal's office, cowed in shame and fear. Her father kept pushing his thumbnail into the narrow fissure behind the nail, slowly and steadily tearing the finger away. He had drawn blood from one nail already; there was a thin red line beneath it.

The thumbnail continued its tender torture, moving mechanically from one nail to another and then back again.

The sight was at once distressing and familiar. *When did I last see him do that?*

⌘   ⌘   ⌘

"We've got to get out of this country!" He punctuated that statement with a slam of the newspaper on the breakfast table and then said, "I want to go back to the United States." The first time Richard did this, Mischa and her mother were stunned. Her father had never raised his voice before. They had just heard him shout for the first time, but it wasn't at them. It was at Chile.

Life had worsened since the coup d'état. General Augusto Pinochet inaugurated his regime by bombing the presidential palace, La Moneda on September 11, 1973. The military moved swiftly to dissuade dissent and silence any opposition. Between September 12 and September 23 the International Red Cross reported that the armed forces had imprisoned approximately seven thousand people in the National Stadium in Santiago. After a few months, that make-shift prison camp had held captive twelve thousand, some witnesses reported twenty thousand.

Under the watch of guards with rifles, men and women were crowded into the stands, in the damp hallways, on the bleachers, beneath the bleachers, on the field, and in locker rooms, dressing rooms, and twisted corridors. Hearing the screams and the pleas followed by a sudden silence was torture enough, but there was more. Executions, electrical shocks, shackles, humiliation, rape, repeated rape, mock executions, filth, and isolation, barely describe the experiences within those walls. Interrogations occurred in the sports facility's administrative offices. Beatings and torture took place throughout, but the most methodical and cruelest forms were committed inside the bunkers at the cycling track.

The brutal killings occurred in the showers and baths. Heads were repeatedly rammed with rifle butts against white ceramic tiles. At night the showers were turned on and buckets of water were thrown at the walls and on the floors. The bodies disappeared, but the smell and the cracks remained.

People "disappeared" from the streets, abducted by soldiers and policemen. Thousands disappeared. They had protested, handed out political pamphlets, had written a newspaper article with negative allusions, or belonged to the wrong political party. Sometimes they were activists. Sometimes they were journalists or academics. Sometimes they were university students with long hair presumed to be sympathetic to the leftists. Other times they were merely in the wrong place at the wrong time. Soldiers, secret security forces, and police, uniformed or not, took people off the streets, into cars, and then to cells or graves. They were called *los Desaparecidos*, the Disappeared ones.

Over the years, the National Stadium became a sports arena again and the General built secret detention and torture centers around the country in order to disperse political prisoners. Of those detained, thousands were tortured; another few thousand were tortured and then executed. Their bodies were dumped into mass graves in isolated areas, like trash. Looking into the eyes of a survivor, it was difficult to judge who was the more fortunate, the living or the disappeared.

Intimidation made the air heavy. Conversations in Chile, in public, followed a polite protocol, sterilized of politics. People spoke in secret to those they trusted. But sometimes even those they trusted turned against them. Founded and unfounded paranoia spread. Opinions disappeared. Books were burned in fear and in silence. As time went by, even the most outspoken became quiet. Opposition to and criticism of the General seemed to disappear.

When photographs of the General in his gray uniform appeared above the blackboards in the classrooms, the parents said nothing, to protect themselves from a child's indiscretion to repeat unguarded comments. Ignorant and innocent, the children still played in the parks, where vendors roasted and sold caramelized peanuts. Their laughter consoled and reminded adults of life before the coup.

When Mischa's father exclaimed his intention to leave Chile and return to the U.S., Mischa thought it curious that his voice was so angry and solemn. For her, the thought of leaving Chile was exciting. She was a child, too young to understand politics. The United States was the land of color and sun. Vacations at her grandparents' house in Miami were visions of pink houses with palm trees, sky blue pools, neon green Slurpees at the 7-Eleven, and best of all, Krispy Kreme doughnuts. The morning after they arrived from Santiago, Mischa and her grandfather made their ritual visit to the Krispy Kreme on Route 1.

As a child, she pressed her nose against the window to watch the doughnut machine. Thick rings of dough dropped into a pristine metal vat of bubbling oil. They rose to the surface, like magic, transformed into floating pillows. A metal arm pushed the doughnuts onto a black rubber moving belt. Next, a waterfall of white icing fell onto the hot doughnuts and melted to a transparent glaze. When they left the shop, her grandfather let Mischa cradle the green dotted box filled with warm newborn doughnuts.

Mischa remembered her frustration as she waited years for that impending move to America. She lost hope. Her father's pronouncements lost their association with Krispy Kreme doughnuts, and this custom of slamming the newspaper on the breakfast table became a meaningless and irritating habit. Her mother always registered her disinterest with an immediate request to pass the marmalade. Mischa would oblige, and the two went about their breakfast as before, while Richard stewed in his opinions about the state of the country.*Now I remember.* Mischa finally placed the image of her father tearing his nails. It was in Chile, the night Mrs. Alvarez cried in their living room. Cristina tried to comfort her with a slice of the Sunday flan and gently stroked her back, but Mrs. Alvarez would not stop sobbing.

"It has been a week. He has not come home. No one has seen Tito. It's not a woman, it's not a student. I would have known by now. People gossip. They would have told me if he were having an affair. He never came home on Wednesday. He never came home."

"There is an answer to all this. I am sure there is an explanation. He will come home," Cristina said.

Mrs. Alvarez hung her head. Then, she looked up at Mischa's father and shouted at him in accusatory anger. "Why, Richard? Why? He's your friend. Tell me why! Tell me! Why should my husband care about politics? He is a professor of English literature! Why did you not stop him? Why? Why did he have to go to a protest in a shantytown? We're eating. We have what we need to survive. Make him stop! Why does he protest? Why did you not stop him?"

Mischa had never seen an adult cry. She was embarrassed to be there, but too self-conscious to stand up and leave. Her father sat on the moss green velvet chair across from Mrs. Alvarez. Unable to answer or even look at her, he stared down at their Oriental rug. His thumbnail dug into the crevice of one fingernail after another, slowly tearing the skin from alongside the nail until he drew blood. Mischa sat on the floor next to his chair and saw the thin red lines gradually emerge behind each nail.

By the next morning those lines had dried to black. At breakfast, Mischa studied them while she crunched her toast and drank the warm milk made with cinnamon and a spoon of coffee from her mother's cup. Without ceremony, her father stood up to make an announcement in a firm voice.

"We're leaving Chile. It's too dangerous. I'm going to find a job in an American university." Mischa waited to hear the slam of the newspaper, but there was none. Her mother said nothing, but tilted the coffee cup to her lips and took a quiet sip. Mischa smiled and imagined doughnuts once again.

⌘　⌘　⌘

It's just like that night in Chile. He's doing it again, that thing with his nails. She looked over at her father as he stared at the floor and continued his mild mutilation. Her mother stared ahead with empty eyes. Her purse sagged on her lap under her elbows.

A hand pulled back the curtain dramatically. As he entered, the doctor's unbuttoned white coat billowed behind him, like a cape on a superhero.

"Hello! Well, let's see what we have here," he said with exaggerated cheerfulness.

"Why do I have straps around me?" She felt her voice quaver.

"Miss...uh," he began, then took the clipboard off the foot of the bed and read her name. "Miss Dunn. Let's see here. You've just had two seizures. This is to keep you from falling out of bed in the event you have another one. But I guess we could put up those rails at the side. Yes, I think that will be good enough." He put his head through the slit in the curtain and called for a nurse.

"Hey, Sandy, can you give me a hand? Take these safety restraints off this young lady."

As the nurse bent over to undo the canvas straps, Mischa smelled wisps of peppermint from the chewing gum she held tightly in her jaw. The nurse moved down her body, removing the straps from across Mischa's shoulders, stomach, hips, and thighs. The doctor continued as the nurse silently walked in front of him to return to her previous task.

"Miss Dunn, you had two grand mal seizures today." He looked to her mother and father and asked, "Does she have a history of seizures?"

"When she was three, she had a fever that ran very high and then it broke when she had a convulsion," her father explained.

Why didn't he ever tell me this before?

"Mr. Dunn, I know this is difficult, but let me try to explain."

Her mother interrupted, "Excuse me, it is Dr. Dunn."

The doctor smiled with relief. "Well then, this will go quickly. I recommend a CAT scan, followed by an EEG, and an appointment in Neuro, with perhaps an MRI to follow. What are your thoughts, Dr. Dunn?"

"No, no, no." Mischa's father looked at his wife, irritated that she had derailed the conversation. "I'm not a medical doctor. I'm just an academic. Call me Richard."

The doctor looked at Mrs. Dunn, annoyed, and then he turned to the patient. "Miss Dunn, how old are you?"

"Fourteen."

"Let's see now. Miss Dunn, have you been taking any drugs?"

"No," Mischa replied defensively.

"Do you drink?"

"I do not drink. I do not do drugs. I never have. Why are you asking me?"

"Miss Dunn, sometimes seizures are induced by drugs and alcohol intake. It's a perfectly normal question. I have to examine all the possibilities." The doctor looked to her father again. "Has she had any traumas to the head? Was she ever in a car accident? Did she suffer a concussion as a result of a serious fall?"

Her father shook his head no. Her mother stared into space.

"Does anyone in your family have epilepsy?" the doctor asked Mischa.

Epilepsy? Mischa thought. She knew what the word meant, but had never heard it spoken out loud. Her father replied by again shaking his head.

"Miss Dunn, just tell me what happened. Start with the library," the doctor said.

Mischa recounted the day from the moment she left her mother's car.

"Then, as I was sitting at the machine I felt like I was outside my body, like my senses were mixed. I saw colors and I felt light. There were green peas and the smell of a cherry. It was hot. I really can't explain it. Then I was in the ambulance."

The doctor motioned to the nurse to take her parents away and pulled the curtain closed.

"Miss Dunn, we're alone. Your parents are not here. I'm going to ask you again and I want an honest answer. Are you taking any drugs, and have you ever taken drugs?"

"I don't even know where to get them. Why do you keep asking me?"

"When you've had two seizures in one day and describe a psychedelic experience of hot peas and cherries, then it's a pretty reasonable question. Give me honest answers and they can help us explain these attacks. I'll be referring you to a neurologist to make the final diagnosis, but strictly speaking, after more than one seizure a person is considered to have epilepsy. You've now had three in your lifetime. But perhaps we're getting ahead of ourselves. The neurologists will have to consider some form of treatment. I'm going to schedule tests for next week."

Epilepsy. The word hung in the air and Mischa stared at it.

"Miss Dunn, how long were you on the microfiche machine? Miss Dunn?"

Epilepsy. Epilepsy. Epilepsy? She felt as if that word had contaminated the room and if she stayed much longer she would get worse. *I have to get out of here. I just have to get out. Now.*

"Miss Dunn?"

"Sorry, Doctor, what was it?"

"I asked you, how long were you on the microfiche machine?"

"Probably about five minutes, maybe even less."

"Did you move the transparency?"

"Of course I did. That's how you look for books," Mischa replied with adolescent arrogance. The doctor glared and Mischa glared back.

"Have you ever used the microfiche before?" he asked.

"Yes. When I go to the library I often need to find books." The doctor glared again and Mischa stared straight back. *You don't like attitude, well, fine. I don't care. You just accused me of getting drunk, taking drugs and lying.*

He looked down to the clipboard and scribbled. A serious, authoritative voice replaced the fake cheerful one. "We'll keep you under observation overnight and do the tests next week."

"What's happening to me?" Mischa cringed when she heard her voice quaver. *That's not me. I don't talk like that.*

"That's really for the neurologist to say. My guess is that the flashing lights of the microfiche probably set off the seizures. Let's just do those tests. If it's a symptom, maybe the direct cause can be addressed and you won't have any more attacks."

Attacks? It's like I didn't fight back. This isn't my fault. I wasn't attacked. It just...it just happened. Her tongue felt as if it were covered in cotton balls and had been stabbed with a pin.

"What's wrong with my tongue?"

"It's probably swollen. You must have bitten it during one of your seizures," he replied matter-of-factly as he filled out a form on the clipboard.

Your seizures? What does he mean "your seizures"? My seizures? MY seizures? Why "my" seizures? I don't want seizures.

"It's typical for a seizure. The swelling will go down. I'll get a nurse to bring you a cup of ice." The doctor pushed open the curtains and said, "Mr. and Mrs. Dunn, you can come back now."

⌘   ⌘   ⌘

The next morning, Mischa changed into her clothes. She felt the back of her head; underneath a mat of tangled black hair her fingers rubbed a tender bump. She started to dress and felt a crinkled scrap of paper in the pocket of her jeans. On it was the number 823.912. The first two numbers were neatly written in pencil, but the rest were in a child's distorted handwriting. It was the call number for the book she was looking for yesterday. Or was it the day before? *Was it Mrs. Dalton or Mrs. Dalway?* Frustrated, she crumpled the paper into a tight pellet, tossed it at the wastebasket, and missed.

"Miss Dunn?" A polite knock on the door followed.

"Yes?"

"Your parents are in the hospital lobby. All your forms are done. You're free to walk."

"I'll be out in a minute—just dressing."

When she came out her parents stood up. At first hesitant, they walked over to hug her. The three descended in the elevator without a word. She wondered what they had said to each other the night before. Emotionally exhausted, they crossed the parking lot in silence, each alone in his or her own mental space. The radio announcer's polished tone introducing the next symphony was the only voice in the car. Her father's hands manned the steering wheel, and the steady swing of the rosary beads offered the most comfort she had felt since those rough, friendly hands in the ambulance.

The days that followed merged, as one hospital appointment followed another. There were waiting rooms, old magazines, strange machines, clip-boards, and nurses calling out her name. She went to the hospital for a test and returned to her room to curl under the covers and sleep. She woke, she stared at the walls, she slept, she went to the hospital, and she slept. She stayed in her room and ate the meals she found on the night table. In the mornings her mother knocked on the door and reminded her of the test for the day.

"Mischa, we have to leave for the hospital in an hour. Remember? It's the computed-axial-tomo…*ay, no lo recuerdo*. I can't remember…ah…CAT scan. *Eso es. Mi amor*, my love, start getting dressed."

Her mother drove the car slowly as a symphony played on the radio. Mischa turned to the window and stared numbly at the passing scenes.

"*Mi amor,* you could be stunning. Do you know that? You have my black hair and your father's green-brown eyes. I call them frog pond eyes. They say hazel here, no? They are beautiful. You are beautiful. Really, *bella*, if you lost a little weight, fixed your hair, no boy could ignore you."

"I want boys to ignore me. Stop it, Mom. It's embarrassing. I don't want to talk about this."

"That will change, *mi amor*. You will need a husband. Your breasts will grow. You do not want to be like your Tia Teresa. She never married. It is so sad. *Que triste. So sad.*"

Mischa rolled her eyes. Cristina always referred to Tia Teresa as if she were the patron saint of spinsterhood, a martyr that served as an example of 'what not to be' for the women in her family. Her mother invoked Tia Teresa whenever Mischa expressed disinterest in her own appearance, boys, or marriage. *That was a totally weird conversation. Why bring up boys now? Why talk about my hair? That's all she cares about, finding a husband, getting a husband, catching a husband. Why? How does that apply to now? It's the only thing she can think of. Everything will be solved with a rich husband. That's it. The future is all about that. You want to talk about the future? Fine, let's talk about the future. What's going on now? No husbands. Now. Me. Seizures. Me. Now.*

"What's going to happen to me?"

"You'll survive. We survived Chile. We survived the move to America. You'll survive this." Her mother replied so swiftly and certainly that it startled Mischa.

Has it really been five years since we left Chile? Survive? Why use the word "survive"? It was great! An entire other world had opened when they moved to the United States. At least that was Mischa's memory. She had always thought of herself as Chilean and American. Their move was a chance to discover her other half. The anger from a few minutes ago left Mischa. She looked at her mother, who concentrated on the road ahead, and for the first time Mischa considered how her mother must have felt when they moved. Cristina left her family, her friends from childhood, her homeland, and more.

Cristina Isabel Márquez-Dunn wore her sleek black hair in an elegant bun. It was a chignon, she told Mischa. Her mother spoke five languages. As a daughter of a Chilean diplomat, she had lived in Paris, Buenos Aires, Rome, and Bonn by the time she was fourteen. Her mother's family owned a hundred-year-old vineyard that produced award-winning wines. But in the 1970s, in the United States, when people saw her mother and heard her accent, they presumed Cristina was illiterate and impoverished.

Cristina was invisible to the other mothers waiting for their kids in the school parking lot. Those mothers were dressed in bright polyester colors. Their hair was blonde and light brown. They had highlights and perms. They smoked cigarettes and stood together in tight circles.

An attractive woman, Mrs. Dunn had cared about her appearance before, but in the U.S., it became her obsession. She did not just dress for the day; she had outfits.

Cristina's dresses, her shoes, her coats, and her scarves were carefully chosen for the season and occasion. She even wore calf-leather driving gloves. Cristina did not depend on her husband's paltry academic salary. She lived off her generous inheritance.

When those thin, fair-haired shopgirls looked past her when she entered, Cristina gained their attention by politely insisting to see the more expensive items behind the counters. Mischa remembered the purchase of The Purse. The shopgirls were rude as Cristina browsed through the thickly perfumed boutique. They might not have been able to guess her origin, but they supposed it was a third-world country. Their eyes roved and judged her silently as Cristina walked around the store. She was dark. She had an accent. She could not speak English well. She was not an American. Cristina had to walk up to the shopgirls to ask for their attention. They did not come to her, as they did when taller, whiter women beckoned them with a finger and a low voice.

The shopgirls looked over her shoulder with suspicion when she touched the merchandise. They rolled their eyes when she examined a price tag. They began to speak in hushed voices behind her back.

There seemed to be an unspoken protocol for those deemed more trespasser than customer, for Cristina received the same treatment in every elegant boutique. But it was particularly bad that day, in that shop, with those girls. That was the day Mrs. Dunn bought The Purse, the one that said, "You can't afford me. I'm worth more than three months of a shopgirl's salary."

With a look of some incredulity, the shopgirl took her mother's credit card. The girl's cynical eyebrow settled back down when the authorization rattled out in seconds. She gave a surprised glance to her colleague, who rushed to her side to begin the ritual wrapping of a purse worth nearly one thousand dollars. They began to call her mother "Madam." They tried to make chatty small talk to amuse her. Cristina remained regally silent as they placed The Purse on a nest of white tissue inside a round box, the soft color of a ripe apricot. The boutique's shopping bag, which by itself was a declaration of luxury, was held open by one shopgirl as the other carefully placed the box inside. When a woman in a fur coat beckoned from across the room, one of the shopgirls said, "I'll be with you in just a minute. I need to attend to this lady first."

In the miniature ceremony of the transfer of a purchased luxury good to a worthy customer, Mischa saw an almost imperceptible bow from the fair-skinned blonde when she gave her mother the silk ribbon handles of the shopping bag.

Mrs. Dunn carried The Purse with pride. In times of distress, she clung to it. Mischa looked down as it lay on the car seat between her mother and herself. Mischa had also come to see The Purse as a shield of dignity.

Its presence, as they drove to the hospital, reassured her as much as it did her mother.

After one week of medical tests, Mischa arrived at the appointment to see the neurologist who would interpret the results and give her the diagnosis. In the waiting room there was a man in a wheelchair with bandages wrapped around his head. He mumbled and no one paid attention, not even the woman next to him who idly turned the pages of *Good Housekeeping*.

A girl in her twenties stumbled and staggered around the waiting room. The girl's mother, well groomed and gaunt, followed her in and out of the row of chairs, and kept her voice low, but insistent. She tried to persuade her to return to her seat. So innocent and unaware, the clumsy girl yelled, "Hello! Hello!" and poked the shoulders of waiting patients when they didn't respond. At first, some would make a polite reply and smile with charity. But when the girl came around again, and again, their teeth began to clench. They grew visibly irritated. The girl had a bright smile. Her greeting was filled with goodwill, but they grew tiresome of her. The scene became embarrassing for everyone but the girl. Her mother, so anxious and so helpless, finally persuaded her to sit and the young women sat next to her and purred calmly as the mother rubbed her back and stared with exhaustion at the carpet.

At the entryway to the clinic's examination rooms, a nurse appeared and called out, "Dunn? Mischa Dunn?"

Mischa stood up and walked over. *Again with the gum. What is it about nurses and mint gum? Why isn't it strawberry or grape? Why must it always be mint?*

"The doctor will be with you in a sec. Just take a seat in here." She pointed into a small room with an examination table in the middle. After ten minutes of casually studying the medical posters Mischa saw the door swing open.

"Hello. You must be"—he looked down at his file to see his patient schedule—"Mischa Dunn." He extended his hand to shake hers. "So I guess you're getting the day off from school today?" He smiled as if he had colluded in scheduling the appointment during school hours. Mischa transmitted the universal signal to skip the small talk by remaining silent and impassive. The doctor acknowledged the transmission and set the test results on the desk.

"So, let's go over your case together."

3. THE SEINE

WHEN IN DOUBT, WITH REGARD TO THE CAUSE OR TREATMENT OF A PATIENT'S SEIZURES, SUMMARIZE THE FIRST CHAPTER OF AN EPILEPTOLOGY TEXTBOOK. Mischa began to believe that was the first lesson all neurologists had been taught in med school. She couldn't remember the number of neurologists she had been through, who, instead of giving a direct answer, rambled on, conveying relevant and irrelevant facts in the attempt to fill twenty minutes of airtime during an appointment.

But this neurologist was different. Despite his receding hairline, Mischa found him attractive. He was younger and more articulate than those who had preceded him. He held her attention, but not entirely.

"Now, a seizure may involve the whole brain, and the term for this is *generalized*, or it might involve part of the brain, *partial*. Mischa, you have classic tonic-clonic seizures. At least, that is what we can conclude from the witness accounts."

Witnesses? Why witnesses? I didn't commit a crime.

He went on to explain seizure categories. "In this genre of petit mal seizures there is the 'absence seizure,' otherwise known as the 'atonic' seizure, and the 'myoclonic.' Those seizures often go unnoticed. In an absence seizure a person may 'go blank.' A myoclonic seizure is an abrupt jerking of one or more limbs. Again, these can go on for only seconds and often go unnoticed. These are categorized as *petit mal*, or 'little bad' seizures, if you want the literal translation."

Why couldn't I have those types of seizures? The gin-and-tonic type. Shaken, not stirred. Wait, that's a martini, isn't it. That's it, I want martini seizures.

He explained that Mischa was having the *grand mal*—"big bad"—seizures, otherwise known as "tonic-clonic" seizures. He went on to describe what she knew so well—the yelling, the biting, the falling down, the writhing, and the loss of oxygen.

Mischa was familiar with the different terms, but she had not yet formed an opinion on them. Today, she decided that she preferred the French names. They were more human, even funny. While he continued, she heard them in her head with a French accent. She thought of the anonymous French neurologist who must have come up with the classifications.

She imagined someone like Toulouse-Lautrec, with a bowler hat and walking cane. He had just returned from a corner cafe. He had ordered an espresso, but had been having difficulty deciding whether he wanted a *petit* or a *grand* slice of lemon tart with a tiny violet, crystallized with sugar, perched on top. When he returned to his office, he would have looked down at his notes. He would have concluded that some seizures were bad and some were not so bad. Mischa imagined that he would have exclaimed, "*Eureka! Pour quoi pas 'petit mal' et 'grand mal'? C'est magnifique!*" Then he would have looked at the clock. It was three in the afternoon. It had been a hard day's work. It was time to go home. Mischa chuckled to herself. She grasped at anything to make herself laugh.

The doctor saw her eyes glazing over. He knew the look well from his Monday morning lectures at the medical school. He thought maybe this was too much information for her to handle.

"Mischa, I know this is a lot to absorb. Do you have any questions?"

Caught in her daydream strolling down the Left Bank, she tried to feign attention with a question.

"Why me?" She cringed with surprise and embarrassment. She had never said it out loud. The doctor sighed slightly. He paused to consider his response. These were difficult moments in any doctor's career, when they had to tell patients that their lives had changed irrevocably.

"Honestly, I don't know if we'll ever be able to tell you. Many times the cause of epilepsy goes unknown. Your tests show that you have not suffered from a brain injury such as a blow to the head, an infection, a tumor, or any other structural abnormality. That is the good news. All the tests confirm that you do not use drugs. Another test showed that you did not respond to flashing lights, so we know that photosensitive epilepsy is out. Genetic factors may also be attributed to epilepsy, but your records show no family history of epilepsy. What's left is the fact that you did have a febrile seizure when you were a child. That may have set a pattern in the brain for seizures and it was triggered, but that notion is not completely accepted and it's still debated among neurologists. Many believe that febrile seizures have nothing to do with the onset of epilepsy in later life."

It was a straightforward medical answer to a question that was embarrassingly existential. He had ignored her sudden outburst of emotion. She was grateful for the lack of pity in his response. She focused on medical questions.

"Why didn't I start having these seizures before?"

"Seizures are brought on by a trigger, such as lack of sleep, significant stress, flashing lights, a smell, or a sound. Technically, Mischa, any human can be provoked to have a seizure, often through sleep deprivation, drugs, and extreme physical or even emotional stress. Some people are more prone to seizures than others. Epileptics are characterized by a 'low seizure threshold' and are therefore more vulnerable to these triggers. We still don't know your trigger."

"When will it end? When will these seizures stop?" *That bordered on existential.* She regretted it for a moment, but then decided she was not embarrassed.

The doctor hated these moments, when he had to make patients realize that they were facing a lifetime condition, an incurable lifetime condition. No matter how softly he spoke, how sincerely he looked into their eyes, or how many times he personalized the conversation by saying their first name, these were among the worst moments in a doctor's career. He was already thirty minutes behind on his appointments for the day.

"Mischa, epilepsy is a condition that is managed through medication. There is no cure for epilepsy. It's something like diabetes or cancer. We can minimize the danger posed to patients with medical treatment, but it remains a constant factor in their lives. It's likely that you will be taking anti-convulsant medication for the rest of your life. We'll have to figure out which medication works best, and the correct dosage. That will come over time, Mischa. For now, we just need to start you on something as soon as possible. We have to stop these seizures. There are minimal side effects to most medications, but they all have them."

"What side effects?" she asked.

"Well, there can be weight gain, forgetfulness, fatigue, gastric problems, skin problems, hair loss, head-aches, and tremors. Sometimes there are mood changes, such as clinical depression, anemia so the patient should be monitored closely. Bleeding gums, acne, sometimes hallucinations. It's too early now, but considering that one day you may want to have children, you'll have to think about the effects of medication on the fetus and potential complications. Well, anyway, there are a series of them, and different medications result in different side effects. People react very differently.

21

We're looking for a medication that has the fewest side effects." He emphasized, "Our goal is seizure control."

He walked over to a shelf. "Here is the pamphlet I promised. You've asked some good questions. I have to say, you are probably the most articulate epileptic I have ever met. The ones I've dealt with have had the mental capacity of a ditchdigger. Here's your prescription. We'll start you out on that and see what happens."

Inside, the doctor recoiled. He could not believe he had compared her, albeit favorably, to a ditchdigger. It was only thirteen hours into his shift. To atone for his remark, he decided to give her an extra five minutes.

Mischa was still talking. "I still remember the first seizure. Before it happened, I had this odd sensation. I felt like a…knot…on a smooth surface. I felt as if my senses were mixed and I could see heat and touch light, and then I collided with the light. A woman next to me wore this strange sweater with peas and pea pods on it. I was observing the smallest details. It was weird. Everything was magnified. I have so many memories of that tiny bit of time. I must be speaking nonsense."

The doctor had never heard any epileptic try to explain an aura. His other epilepsy patients were barely literate.

"Mischa, why isn't that in your record?"

"After the first seizure, when I described that feeling, the doctor accused me of taking drugs or getting drunk. I guess I never really felt comfortable enough to talk about it again, until today." She continued to explain what she had felt and he listened to her closely. He had read accounts of patients' descriptions of their auras, but this was the first time one of his patients had tried to explain it.

"Mischa, what you experienced prior to the seizure was an aura, which sometimes accompanies an epileptic seizure, especially temporal lobe seizures. This is the most fascinating aspect of the condition. The aura is a presentiment that some epileptics have before a seizure, a warning. It is a subject of art and religion. Some of the most renowned epileptics have been inspired by their auras—like van Gogh, Dostoyevsky, and Saint Teresa of Avila."

"So does that mean I'm looking at a career as a painter, a writer, or a saint?"

Though surprised by her ready sarcasm, he engaged. "Depends how good you are." He smiled and winked, and thought, she's clever. She doesn't have the brain of a ditchdigger, and she's pretty. It is a shame she's epileptic.

"Mischa, once you become aware of that strange feeling, your aura, and can recognize it, then you can get yourself to a safe place. You can minimize the physical danger, like falling down the steps or on a hard surface, and find a safe place for a seizure. Some choose a corner. Warn someone nearby, tell them what is about to happen, and then stay there until the seizure passes. Gosh,"—he looked down at his watch—"I'm already so behind with my patients. On your way out, make an appointment for three months from now. Good luck." With a quick handshake, he left the room.

Mischa sat there for a few minutes longer and stared at the pamphlet, "How to Survive with Epilepsy." She wanted to tie it to a brick and send it crashing through the window into the hospital parking lot, but she folded it and put it in her pocket.

4. THE HOCKEY FIELD

SAINT MARY IMMACULATE ACADEMY FOR GIRLS, BAPTIZED MAMA MIA BY MISCHA AND HER FRIENDS, WAS A MODEST REDBRICK BUILDING ON THE OUTSIDE, WITH THE AESTHETIC NATURE OF AN INSANE ASYLUM ON THE INSIDE. Crucifixes were strategically placed on walls painted robin's egg blue. Three-foot statues of the Virgin Mary, standing barefoot on bouquets of roses, stood in alcoves that studded the hallways, often placed between a fire extinguisher and a bulletin board. The plaster figure factory that had manufactured the Virgins decided that a woman from the Middle East, somewhere at the beginning of the first century, was blonde and pale. No doubt they had intended to give the Virgin Mary a mother's benevolent gaze, but the painters missed by a millimeter or two and her sky blue eyes were disproportionately large. As a result, the Virgin had a stare that was both dazed and confused. It was a look entirely consistent with her surroundings, so the blunder went unnoticed—a lost opportunity for irreverent jokes.

The student population at Mama MIA, standard issue for a Catholic girls' school, was comprised of Nerds, Sluts, and Saints. By the outside world's standards the Sluts were typical, well-adjusted teenage girls. They discussed parties, boys, and fashion. In conversations around cafeteria tables, the other tribes referred to those weekend events as "pits of debauchery." They were not sure what debauchery meant, but they had a feeling it had to do with boys and so it was wrong. No one remembered who, but someone started using the phrase and the others followed. It made them feel intelligent and better than the Sluts.

The navy blue plaid skirts were the best indicator of tribal affiliation. The Nerds wore them at regulation knee-length or slightly below. The Sluts wore them four inches above, and the Saints wore them four inches or more below. There was a correlation between skirt length and knowledge of sex. The longer the skirt, the more naive the girl. These rigid tribal structures impinged on the free flow of information that normally occurs in high school. The tampon epiphany in the bathroom was the closest Mischa ever came to discussing sex in high school.

"Watch it, Sophie! *Chica*! Ugh, you were just about to step on...holy shit! What the hell is that?"

"Don't tell me you don't know. Mischa, you're joking." Sophie was incredulous.

"I'm serious, I haven't a clue," Mischa said.

"Honestly?" Sophie realized Mischa's complete sincerity. "*Chica*, it's a tampon, for periods. Haven't you begun?"

"Yeah, a few years ago. But I use something else."

Sophie's voice softened when she saw Mischa's cheeks redden.

"I'll make a go at Tampon 101. It's a cylinder of pressed cotton. A girl puts it inside her and it absorbs the blood. They're a lot better than pads. My sister made me believer."

"Inside? But it's so...so big!"

"Oh my God! Mischa, if I didn't know you, I would think you've been locked up in a room since birth. *Chica*, a few things a lot larger than a tampon are going to be coming in and out, unless you join a convent. Hell, who knows, maybe it would still happen in the convent." Sophie grabbed paper towels from the dispenser. "Really, girl, you're scaring me. If you stay this clueless, the first guy who shakes your hand in college is going to get you pregnant." Sophie let the paper towels drop from her hand to the floor. "We'll cover it and the janitor can take care of it."

Mama MIA lacked the most common tribe in high schools throughout the United States. There were no Jocks at Mama MIA. The track record of its three athletic teams—field hockey, tennis, and soccer—proved it.

Mischa and the other Mama MIA Nerds joined the athletic teams in order to check the "extracurricular activity" box on college applications. In the guidance counselor's annual freshman orientation lecture, she told the girls they had a better chance of getting into a good school if they appeared "well-rounded," and encouraged them to join the teams. The Nerds obeyed. The Sluts were too busy. After school, they raced to Cardinal Newman Academy for Boys to watch football, basketball, or baseball practice. The Saints, who wanted to be nuns or missionaries, were in prayer groups or volunteering at a local charity. It was the Nerds who bore the cross of representing Mama MIA in sports. It would not have been so bad were they not also burdened with Mama MIA's ridiculed reputation as an easy win among all the schools in the county.

Friday, October 22, was the day of the game: Saint Agnes Anglican School for Girls versus Saint Mary Immaculate Academy. Mama MIA was the away team, playing on Saint Agnes's well-manicured hockey field. For the entire game—actually, every game—Mischa was terrified of the ball. She played left wing, but hung back when her teammates went up the field. She prayed that no one would pass the ball to her, and no one blamed her, since they all did the same.

A Mama MIA hockey player with a ball found herself surrounded by the other team. The experience did nothing to encourage a Mama MIA player to hang on to the ball. When it came, she hit it in any direction, just to get rid of it. No one wanted to be a star. The goal was to leave the field without injury.

The girls on the Saint Agnes field hockey team were Wagnerian. They were big, they were blonde, and they were Protestant. Two years before, they had won the Rhode Island State Championship. The last time Mama MIA played them, they lost to Saint Agnes zero to seven. The varsity goalie, Cindy, who was in a lesbian relationship with the junior varsity goalie, probably had saved them from the shameful defeat of zero to twelve.

Mischa watched the coin toss with her stomach tightening. When the captains returned to their positions and the whistle blew, Mischa's thoughts raced frantic. *Oh no, oh no, oh no, not me, please, not me... Agh! She's hitting the ball at me! I stopped it! Where do I hit it? Holy shit, they're coming at me!*

Blonde braids and ponytails whipped her face. *I MUST get rid of this ball.* Mischa hit the ball and a Protestant intercepted. Sophie stopped the Protestant and took the ball. Mischa's happiness over her friend's show of athletic prowess suddenly evaporated. *Damn it! Why hit it back to me?* The herd stampeded toward Mischa. *Holy shit!* Mischa stopped it and passed it back to Sophie, who passed it to another Mama MIA teammate. Mischa watched in pleasant surprise. *That looked like a real maneuver! God, I need a rest. They can take it up the field.*

"Dunn!" Coach Robinson yelled. "Get up there!"

Damn it! She didn't want to be the one that caused Coach Robinson to go into premature labor, so Mischa ran up the field, sweating and panting. She panicked when she saw the hard yellow ball propel toward her. A Protestant intercepted and Mischa sighed with relief. A minute later, out of nowhere the ball came back. *Again? Oh no!* The Protestants rushed toward her. *God, what huge thighs they have! How does a girl get such huge thighs?* Mischa hit the ball. *Oops.* One of the Protestants intercepted her pass. They raced down the field; one, two, three passes and the Protestant who stole the ball drove it into the goal. The immense blonde with the braids lifted her hockey stick into the air like a spear, acknowledging the cheers from onlookers.

Cindy, the Mama MIA goalkeeper, glared at Mischa. Her look made it clear that she wanted to whack Mischa with a hockey stick. Mischa glared back. *"Ya think you wanna a piece of me? You wanna piece of me? Yeah, Cindy, if I had a goalie helmet, leg guards, a face guard, elbow pads, a chest pad—and by the way, my padded bra does not count—then I might be brave, too. I don't like being trampled by the Protestants, so go to hell!"* Of course she would never say that to Cindy, but Mischa liked to imagine she was capable of such mafia bravado. The referee blew the whistle.

Holy shit! Here comes that goddamn ball again. Why is that blade of grass blinking? Why are so many blades of glass blinking? Why is there glass on the grass?

The ground felt soft and cool beneath her. Her brain felt mashed, like grass pressed into mud. She decided to stay still and keep her eyes closed until she felt strong enough to raise her head. Coach Robinson directed a girl to get a sweatshirt and knelt on the grass next to her. Mischa could feel Coach's pregnant belly, like a water balloon, press against her forehead when she placed the sweatshirt underneath her head.

When Mischa heard a collective roar from the crowd, she chuckled. She knew that Saint Agnes had scored another goal. First, it was more likely, and second, no one from Mama MIA came to cheer them. *Who would give a shit, considering the way we play? Remember, this is all for my college application.* She knew her brain had returned. She felt sarcastic again.

As she lay there with her eyes closed, she considered a potential benefit of the seizure. *Maybe Cindy will show some mercy. Maybe she won't "accidentally" trip me in the parking lot.* After a game, everyone knew to watch out for Cindy and her hockey stick. A lot of Mama MIA hockey players had scabs on their knees.

Two days later, when Mischa entered Madame Poulet's homeroom, everyone stared, which was to be expected. The seizures she had during practice didn't get much attention, but Mischa was realistic. She had a grand mal seizure during the most theologically important game of the season; of course it would be news. Sophie and a few other friends ran up to hug her. The rest of the class looked on silently for a few minutes as she took her seat. She was accustomed to the looks that said, "Oh God, is she going to have another one, here, in front of me?" or, "Is she dying?" or, "Thank God I don't have it!" or, "I hope I can't catch it."

Mischa was certain she would have met with the same reaction anywhere. Mama MIA was odd, but there was no one to blame. It's just the way it was. When she had one or two seizures in a month, Mischa wanted to return to school as soon as possible. After she had a succession of seizures, she had to be absent for a few days of extra sleep, followed by medical tests and a visit to the neurologist. The hockey field seizure was the third one that month. After her mother drove her home that day, she called for an appointment.

⌘　⌘　⌘

The hospital technician had made an obvious effort to put his patients at ease. Mischa wished she could have complimented him on his effort, but she was taken aback by the tackiness of the converted laboratory. Ponds, lilies, and ladies with white parasols from Impressionist posters were scattered on the walls that were painted a soft jade. He had even decorated the window into his monitor room. On either side of the window, satin ropes with gold tassels held back lavender chintz curtains. Delighted to introduce a patient into his world, the technician pushed a button to welcome her with a flush of elevator music.

When she looked to her left, she saw what looked like a lost prop from a science-fiction movie.

"It's brand-new," he said proudly, pointing to the massive machine. He ran his hand down the side of the gleaming white tunnel like a showroom model. "You're so lucky. The hospital acquired this MRI just two months ago! Before, you would have had to travel five hours for the nearest one."

Mischa tried to hide the extent of her disorientation by engaging in conversation. "What does MRI stand for, anyway? If I hadn't read it on my appointment sheet, I would have thought I was here for a 'ma-rye' scan. I'm thinking of going to a deli and asking for a tuna fish on ma-rye."

"It is a complicated name. MRI is short for Magnetic Resonance Imaging. It's something like an X-ray. I'll be taking pictures of your brain. I won't bore you with details. Get your doctor to earn his paychecks. Ask your neurologist to explain it when you see him. If you're still confused, call the nurse for an appointment and I can give you a small tour. I'm filled up today and already behind, so I don't have time to chat. Here, put on this apron, dear."

"What is this?" She was annoyed that her witty banter had gone unappreciated.

"It's to protect you from the radiation from the machine, like cancer and other stuff. The apron is filled with lead so it's heavy. Here, hold this." He gave Mischa what looked like a garage door opener on a key ring. "Here's a panic button. Just press it if you want to get out of the tunnel."

"Why would I need that?" Mischa asked with some insolence, still annoyed.

"It's not that strange, dear. Some patients get nervous in an enclosed space. If you do, I can get you out in seconds. Take it or leave it. It's just a precaution. It makes some people feel more relaxed. Now, lie down on the table." The technician entered the small room next door and stood above a control panel behind the rose-patterned chintz curtains. He spoke through a microphone, "Okay, Mischa, I'm going to put you in the machine now. Stay very still."

As the engine rolled the table slowly into the tunnel, Mischa felt as if she were entering a time capsule. Once inside, she found the dark enclosure strangely comforting. She fell asleep as the machine whirred and clicked.

Two weeks after the hockey field seizure she was waiting in another doctor's office. She had now had five neurologists since her first seizure. She was running out of hospitals in Providence, and this would most likely be the last one, no matter what he concluded. The first appointment was always long—about forty-five minutes—but after five months, they turned into no more than twenty-minute updates, little more than face-to-face greetings. They ended with the doctor making a quick scribble for her next installment of anti-convulsants—sometimes the same ones, and sometimes new ones. They prescribed pills of different sizes, same sizes, different colors, different shapes, and yet they were all the same to her. They were daily reminders of powerlessness. They were the irritating scabs that people picked when they asked after a seizure, "Did you take your medicine?"

5. THE CHAPEL

THE TEACHERS WHO INTERESTED THE NERDS MOST WERE THE ONES WHO BROKE THE MOLD. Madam Poulet was clearly the most eccentric and most sophisticated teacher at Mama MIA. In the first weeks, everyone made the initial mistake of pronouncing her name as PULL-et. She was an American, born and bred in Ohio, but Madam Pu-LAY had deluded herself into thinking that she was French, so she spoke English with a slight accent. She was tall and thin, with red hair which was cut into a graceful wave that brushed her shoulders. In autumn and winter she wore cashmere, and in the spring and early summer she was a display of vibrant silk blouses atop black pencil skirts and stilettos. She was a faint breath of elegance amid the navy blue polyester plaids and acrylic sweaters.

Every student was assigned a homeroom and Mischa was in Madam Poulet's class. For four years of high school, she saw Madam Poulet every morning after the bell rang. During those thirty minutes of homeroom, Madam Poulet would take roll call and read the school announcements. For the remaining time, she would play Edith Piaf at a low volume while the Sluts gossiped, the Nerds studied, and the Saints drew their chairs into a circle and said a rosary.

Mischa always walked to her favorite seat in the first row, first chair. That's all she wanted out of homeroom, to be close to the door. She wanted to smell the incense. Madam Poulet's classroom was across the hall from the school chapel. On Mondays the smell of incense was diluted by the lemon disinfectant, leftover from the weekend cleaning, but by Tuesday incense was the smell of morning at Mama MIA. A priest came from their brother school to say the seven a.m. daily mass for the nuns. The leftover smell of incense reminded Mischa of this asylum's link to gold-encrusted altars, Gothic arches, marble Madonnas, silver baptismal fonts, jeweled vestments, and stained glass windows; all that was extravagantly exquisite about Catholicism.

The incense imparted some dignity to the school—at least that corner of the school. It was the scent and the atmosphere of a bewitching traditional

Latin mass. It smelled of burning leaves mixed with lavender oil, nutmeg, and cloves, blended with Chanel No. 5, the perfume her mother gave her when she turned fifteen.

As much as could be said against it, the Catholic Church had an understanding for sensual ritual. For millennia it had used this wisdom of the senses to captivate followers with fascinating frescoes, transcendent domes, glamorous vestments, and the grandeur of ringing bells. Mischa's theology was thin and her interest in the readings or the gospel was nonexistent. The rich smell of incense was Mischa's strongest attraction to Catholicism. When she was little, it was the votive candles that had just burned out. She quietly escaped from the pew and rubbed her fingers into the soft, warm wax before her parents rushed to retrieve her.

Some mornings she would see Sister Clarence Marie leaving the chapel with her rosary. Mischa had taken one class with her. They had never had a real conversation, and yet she was Mischa's favorite teacher. The other teachers left Sister Clarence alone and she didn't seek their company.

Sister Clarence radiated a solemn dignity. She was the most respected teacher at Mama MIA, a master at the humble craft of touch-typing. She could have passed for Humphrey Bogart. Put him in a wimple, throw away the cigarette, fedora, and Ingrid Bergman, and you had Sister Clarence. In the unwritten teacher biographies that students shared, Sister Clarence had a PhD in English literature from Smith College. It made sense. Timed typing assignments in class were poems by Tennyson, Wordsworth, and Byron. The girls knew Sister Clarence was in a bad mood when she passed out poems for typing assignments that were written by some woman no one had heard of, Sylvia Plath.

Not only had the school administration relegated her talents to a low-end subject, they had left her to teach on manual typewriters that belonged to the era of typing pools made up of women with straight backs wearing tight-waisted skirts. But Sister Clarence took pride in her mundane craft and cherished each machine. Between classes she was often spotted cleaning the fifty-year-old relics with a worn felt cloth.

Even her choice of wearing the crucifix differentiated her from the other nuns. The cross is an abstract reminder of sacrifice. The crucifix is the depiction of the figure of the body nailed to the cross. Sister Clarence entered the convent at a time when Jesus Christ—crowned with thorns, dripping with blood, and writhing in pain—was the focus of prayer. She wore a chain around her neck, from which hung a crucifix four inches in length and two inches across.

Wearing traditional robes, immaculately starched, Sister Clarence was magisterial, and her attire proclaimed that she had, without regret, clearly chosen to live away from the outside world. The other nuns wore ill-fitting secondhand clothing with self-righteousness, to prove they were still keeping to their vow of poverty despite the fact that they were not wearing robes. To the students, they were embittered women clad in elastic-waist skirts, wrinkled shirts, and polyester jackets, rejected by the world. They wore crosses the size of kitchen scissors and their hair looked like it had been cut with them.

One morning Madam Poulet came to Mischa's desk and whispered in her ear that Sister Alice had summoned her. When Mischa arrived at the principal's office the receptionist showed her in. Mischa took a seat in one of the chairs across from Sister Alice, who was wearing a beige sweater dotted with hundreds of tiny fuzz balls.

"Mischa, I want to talk about your plans for next year. I think you should pull out of the race for student body president. You are epileptic and that would interfere with the job. I don't think you could handle the pressure."

It was infuriating, but oddly refreshing to confront such open prejudice. It confirmed what she had felt, but had tried to dismiss as paranoia.

"No, Sister, don't worry, I can handle it."

"I spoke with your parents and they don't think you should run either."

In her gut, she knew that Sister Alice was bluffing. Mischa could hear her voice quaking when she replied. "I know my parents, and if you should ever—ever—happen to speak to them, they would tell you that they support my decision to run. I would like to be excused now."

Sister Alice's face showed no shame at having her ruse exposed, only irritation at Mischa's impertinence. With a nod, she approved Mischa's request.

Mischa felt her hands tremble as she walked back to Madam Poulet's classroom. At the end of the hallway, instead of taking a right, she found herself walking into the school chapel. She sat in a pew, with her head in her hands, staring down at the kneeler. A few minutes later a pair of polished black shoes under a long black robe came into view. She looked up to see Sister Clarence with rosary beads in her hand. Mischa realized that she must have already been in the chapel.

Sister Clarence put a gentle hand on Mischa's back and said, "We don't ask for these burdens, but they are given to us."

In that moment, Mischa felt as if a whole day, an entire week had passed, yet it had only been an hour since the bell had rung. Her weary eyes were filled with tears. She refused to let them fall, but against her will, they trickled down slowly.

"Sister, it's true, I didn't ask for it, but it's not a burden. It's a problem. It's my problem and I need to solve it myself. There's no one else." Mischa wiped her eyes with her sleeve.

"Why not pray?" Sister Clarence offered.

"Prayer just isn't working for me anymore. It's not God. It's just me. I'm the one with the answer."

When Mischa heard her words—unexpected and uncensored—come out of her mouth, she anticipated a steely reprimand for confessing agnosticism. Instead, Sister Clarence gave a submissive nod to Mischa and returned to her pew.

That night Mischa told her parents about the incident with Sister Alice. They confirmed that they had never spoken to the principal. Her father declared that he would go to the school and demand an explanation.

"No, Dad, I have to deal with this myself," she said as she left the room, leaving him wounded, denied the chance to be a hero.

6. THE MONITOR ROOM

As she waited for the neurologist, she wondered when she was going to be able to forget. She didn't want reminders that she had epilepsy. It was her last year of high school, and she had hoped she might get a lucky break and the seizures would subside. There was no reason for this to happen, just blind optimism. She had been accepted to university early, so she was expecting to coast along for a few months like Sophie and the other girls who had gained early acceptance. Instead, the seizures increased and left her emotionally and physically exhausted.

The doctor marched into the room with a confident smile. "Hello, Miss Dunn. So, how have we been since we met in…uh…let's see here, in February? Tell me what's happened."

"I've had four seizures in the last six weeks. The worst one was two weeks ago while getting a Slurpee in a Seven-Eleven."

"Do you remember anything about the seizure?"

"I think it was lime-flavored."

"So, your aura was comprised of a sensory perception of limes?"

"No, it was the Slurpee. It splattered on my face when I hit the floor."

"Miss Dunn, I don't think your current medication is working."

She nodded her head solemnly. *So, Sherlock, is this the kind of deductive reasoning that got you through med school?*

"Miss Dunn, I think we should do another EEG. You've done a few before, but during an EEG, I would like to catch you actually having a seizure. It will give us more precise information about your condition. We'll have to induce one. We'll take you off your medication and keep you on the EEG for forty-eight hours or more. Check with the nurse at reception. I think we can schedule you for this Friday."

Mischa and her mother returned home that day, silently in the car, with Cristina's favorite purse between them. When they arrived home, they both automatically walked to the kitchen unaware of the other's intention.

"Where's my blue plastic cup?" Mischa asked indignantly as she searched the cabinets above the counter.

"*Mi amor*, my love, I have no idea. Look for another. There are many glasses in the cabinet above you."

"I want my blue plastic cup."

"I said there are other glasses. Get another one."

"No! No! I said I want my blue plastic cup. I want it now."

"Mischa, why? What is this, this blue cup?"

"I want my blue plastic cup. I always drink from my blue plastic cup during the weeks that I'm having seizures, in case I have a seizure when I'm drinking. I don't want my teeth to bite into glass. I don't want to massacre my mouth." Cristina stood still for a moment, in surprise, sympathy and the sudden realization of how her daughter's life was so different now. Even a glass was dangerous. Cristina had to find the blue cup.

"*Mi amor*, I'm sorry. I'll look." She went on a frantic search through the kitchen shelves, drawers, and cabinets and then ran through the rooms of the house until she found it in the bathroom. She smiled and ran victoriously down the steps with the cup in hand. Mischa received it with little ceremony, filled the glass with tap-water, gulped the water down and slammed it on the counter. She walked past her mother and out of the kitchen. Cristina stayed still and looked at the seemingly insignificant cup on the counter. She gathered her keys and her purse from the kitchen table.

"Mischa, I'll be out shopping. I forgot to pick something up."

When Mischa opened the cabinet that night, and looked for her blue plastic cup she found it alongside ten plastic cups of blue, green, yellow, and pink, small, and medium, and large.

The last EEG was two years ago. She still remembered the comb handled by fingers with three-inch nails that dug into her scalp each time the technician cleared a spot for an electrode. This technician had smelled vaguely of rotten fish, but Mischa hadn't minded. The woman's steady progress had assured Mischa that she was in the hands of an experienced professional. She had parted Mischa's hair methodically, and with admirable precision and speed had placed the electrodes equidistant from each other around Mischa's skull.

This time, the technician showed Mischa back to her hospital room for the night and hooked her to the machine, showing her the moving graph of thin spikes and dips. The screen looked like an expensive stereo system showing the beat and pace of the music, but instead, it was the electrical activity of her brain. For a few minutes after the technician left, Mischa acted like a chimpanzee, entertained by the immediate effects that speaking, moving, and blinking her eyes had on the rapid spikes and the dips. The novelty wore off when Mischa recalled the sober purpose of the test, so she put herself between the starched white sheets of the hospital bed.

In the corner of the room, a video camera hung from the ceiling. She had stopped taking her medication as the doctor had ordered. The technician was hoping to induce a seizure by keeping her up all night. He would check on her periodically, offer movies, and operate flashing lights for intervals of a few minutes. Mischa was always ready to sleep and doubted that the test would work.

She opened her eyes. *I knew it. I can sleep anywhere, anytime, no matter what the movie or magazine. Maybe I can convince them that we can come back next month. I can't be bothered. I don't want to stay here tonight.*

The smell of rotten fish invaded her nose. In her mind's eye, she saw an image of a woman in a tailored black suit wearing a yellow corsage and three-inch blood-red high heels. Mischa looked to the left and saw her mom and dad, red-eyed and slumped in their chairs. She supposed that they had stayed overnight, but remembered that the plan had been for them to go home after they had their dinner in the hospital. She hadn't seen them enter. At first confused, clarity came through the pain of a headache's merciless assault. She felt as if her head were covered in glass and a spike heel was digging itself into her skull, crushing and twisting glass shards and splinters into her brain.

"She's awake. I'll get the doctor," said her father, and he left the room. Her mother stared silently at the floor.

When the doctor came in, he was effervescent. "Well, well, we've had success! You had a tonic-clonic seizure and it's recorded on video."

Mischa looked at him blankly, trying to understand why her seizure was making him so happy.

"The EEG shows a slight abnormality in the temporal lobe. Not a lesion like a tumor, but one that indicates the origin of your seizures. In short, Miss Dunn, you have temporal lobe epilepsy." The patient's flight of mind had gone unnoticed and he continued merrily. "You see, physically, the seizures begin in your temporal lobe. Those are the parts of the brain that roughly sit above and behind your ears. The auras you report are another indicator that they are complex partial, yet they 'generalize' rapidly. This means that the seizure, which is like a spark in the temporal lobe, turns into a firestorm that spreads all over your brain."

"What is the spark?" Mischa asked.

"That we don't know. You've been told, and it's true, that you don't have any lesions or tumors. There has never been evidence of injurious drug or alcohol use in your past tests. You did not respond to the flashing lights. An immediate reaction to that would have indicated that as a trigger and classify you as a photosensitive epileptic. You had been under observation for only five hours. You told me that you had a good night's sleep the night before. Therefore, we know that it was not triggered by sleep deprivation. I'm sorry, Miss Dunn. We might never know the trigger." His voice was despondent for a moment, but then he considered the bright side. "But now we know that the medicine is working marginally, since the seizure occurred thirty hours after stopping your medication. Of course, since you are still having breakthrough seizures, this means that the medicine is not completely effective. After all, we're at such a high dosage with this one. You told me that your memory is starting to suffer and your gums bleed, so maybe it's time to move on to something new."

Mischa wished she could get some aspirin for the headache that was splitting her skull. She tried to interrupt, but the doctor was in raptures.

"I recommend observation on your part to help us figure out what the trigger might be. There is always the option of brain surgery, but let's stay with an anti-convulsant strategy for a little while longer. Tomorrow you can see the videotape of the seizure."

"Can I have some aspirin? I need the extra-strength kind."

"Of course. I'll have a nurse bring some in, along with your anti-convulsants so we can start you back on them. After all, we don't want another seizure."

Mischa thought she saw him almost skip, hop, and jump into the hallway.

Much of what he had said she had forgotten. Her head ached. That's all she thought about; there were sharp objects sprouting inside her head, and she wondered whether the pain was more like knitting needles or long nails.

The next day, a sunny nurse came into her room and drew back the curtains. Mischa winced as a wave of unwelcome light poured into the room.

"Miss Dunn, the doctor said that you wanted to view the videotape of your seizure. The technician is free. He asked me to take you up to the Monitor Room."

They went three floors up in the elevator and walked down the hall to a room that looked like a television studio. A tall rotund man with reddened cheeks and sagging jowls dressed in a tent of a hospital uniform stood to greet her.

"Hello, you're Mischa Dunn?" She nodded, and as the nurse left, he started to explain. "I have here a tape of your seizure from yesterday. Are you sure that you want to see it?"

"Yes." She was curious. It would be interesting. All these seizures, all these years, they were dark moments, hours for which she could not account. They were unknown fragments of her life. She wondered whether watching this video would help her recapture that time lost.

The technician showed her to a chair in front of a wall with several television screens. He directed her to look at the second one from the top.

"This is going to be difficult to watch. I just want to prepare you. Do you still want to see it?"

The second warning made her apprehensive. She nodded yes, though slightly less certain than before.

"Okay, Miss Dunn, I'm going to start by running the tape for about five minutes before the seizure, and then you'll see the seizure, which lasts for about three minutes. I'll let it run a few minutes longer so that you can see the doctor's and nurses' response. The screen above will be the tape of you and the monitor underneath will show a simultaneous relay of your EEG."

When he pressed the button, Mischa saw herself on the twenty-four-inch color screen, in bed, staring at the ceiling, and looking to the side of the bed to pick up a fashion magazine that her mother had brought for her. Mischa flipped through the pages. When her parents came into the room, she looked up and stared straight ahead. Her parents said hello and were walking to their chairs, talking about their dinner in the cafeteria. Her mother complained about the greasy fish and promised that she would make Mischa *pastel de papas*, her favorite dish, as soon as all this was over.

Mischa saw herself on the screen, ominously still. Her eyes stared at some invisible, distant object. When her parents took their seats next to the window, her father picked up his newspaper and her mother rummaged inside her purse to find her book. Mischa watched the on-screen Mischa emit a long, loud howl. As she looked at the screen, Mischa drew back in the chair, startled and frightened. On the monitor she saw the magazine that had been in her hands flip into the air. Her back arched as she banged her head against the bed. Her eyes rolled back and one arm repeatedly hit the edge of the night table. Watching the monitor, Mischa put her hand on her arm. *That explains the bruises.*

Mischa looked below the screen to see neon green spikes from the EEG running across the black screen frantically, barely able to keep up with the speed of the event. Some points were so steep and frequent that they were pressed together, no longer single lines. They formed a band of light beneath a jagged mountain range that represented the electrical storm inside her brain.

On the monitor, she saw her mother stand up and freeze; her eyes were wide and her lip curled in disgust. Her father paused, watching for seconds before running out the door, yelling for help. *Bang! Bang! Bang!* Her head hit the bed rails. All at once, Mischa's entire body was pulled in different directions. It continued its savage rage and her teeth tore at the air. Her face changed colors and turned blue. A doctor and two nurses rushed into the room. A nurse held her down as the doctor took out a syringe. Another nurse struggled to put an oxygen mask on her as he injected her. The fury of the convulsions gradually subsided, until her body was left jerking lightly and finally went limp. Her arm fell over the side of the bed.

Mischa's mother stood back with her hand over her mouth and her father held his wife in his arms. The doctor and nurses turned Mischa on her side, readjusting the mask, reading her pulse rate and oxygen levels. After some final checks, the doctor took a deep breath and told her parents to page him once she regained consciousness, and he lay her on her back again. The doctor and nurses left the room. Her parents brought their chairs next to the bed. Both put their hands over hers and began sobbing uncontrollably.

The video technician pressed the button.

"Miss Dunn, I don't think there's anything really left to see on the rest of the tape."

"I...I...I...guess not."

"Are you okay?"

"Um...uh...yes. Sure. Yes. Yes." She swallowed and wiped the corner of her eye with her hand. She realized that her parents had never seen her have a seizure before. And she had never seen her parents cry.

"Why don't I call the nurse to pick you up?"

Mischa nodded.

7. THE LIVING ROOM

November 1987

THEY MET ON ORIENTATION DAY. After she registered in the dormitory lobby, the resident adviser took Mischa up to her assigned room to meet Martha, her roommate for freshman year. Most of Martha's belongings were already unpacked. Her family had left New Haven early that morning and they were in Boston by afternoon. Martha's mother wore a lime green headband over her Doris Day-like hair and capri pants embroidered with pink tulips. She was the picture of New England preppydom. She laughed nervously as she rearranged objects and returned them to their original spot, only to find another object to pick up and do the same. Martha's father wore a blinding white golf shirt with a country club logo on it. Though he had a ready grin, his bright blue eyes were sharp and mean. At two in the afternoon, he already had a heavy stench of scotch about him.

After three months together, Martha and Mischa had an unspoken understanding that they would share a room and no more. Martha's side was dotted with various sizes of teddy bears wearing sweaters with college logos, while Mischa's side was adorned with fifteen or more Post-it reminders placed on the wall next to her bed, in no particular order. Everything about them—their housekeeping habits, choice of music, majors, clothes—predetermined the conclusion that they would be friendly, but not friends.

Sitting on her bed, unable to think of what to do next, Mischa could only hope that Martha would return soon. The lock turned and a finger flicked on the light switch next to the door.

"Mischa? What are you doing, sitting in the dark?"

"Curtis tried to kill himself."

Martha's jaw dropped. "Isn't that the guy you dated? The weird one on the first floor?"

"Yes."

"How?"

"With a razor across his wrists," Mischa replied, emotionless. It was a simple statement of fact. Martha's eyebrows furrowed as she tried to think of what to say next.

Okay, so he was...is...odd. Weird is too strong a word. Sounds a little too pejorative. Then again, I'm weird and I accept it. Okay, so Martha's not completely off base, he was weird...is weird...is...is. Curtis liked jazz. He liked Billie Holiday, but still he knew the lyrics to every Cole Porter song that Ella Fitzgerald had ever sung, and that impressed Mischa. He loved black-and-white movies. He could quote every line from *It Happened One Night*. Like some nervous tic, he made a point of quoting a line from that movie in every conversation. In the middle of a sentence he would change his tone, which signaled that the *It Happened* demon had taken possession and a movie reference was imminent. He even gave her a script of the movie that he had typed in high school. He thought that Mischa could learn the lines and they could parry back and forth. Curtis wanted to play Clark Gable to her Claudette Colbert. *Okay, so maybe he was weird.*

Curtis talked a lot about his friend from high school. He showed Mischa photographs of the two of them together. Curtis's favorite was the one of them dressed in vintage tennis garb holding wooden tennis rackets. She often wondered how Curtis and he had survived high school without getting beaten up. In the back of her mind she wondered if Curtis was gay, but had not yet come out, or perhaps was unaware of it himself.

They both loved Ella Fitzgerald, Benny Goodman, Glenn Miller, and Oscar Peterson. Who else could she talk to? Everyone else listened to other music. She felt like a fish out of water at college, but she was accustomed to being out of water. She thought he was comfortable, too. He never had to study much before exams and could write first-class papers in hours. *He was—he is, he is—funny, too.* Dark humor, very quick-witted, with word play and puns, that's how he spoke.

"Mischa. Come back to earth. Mischa, look at me." Martha stood in front of her while Mischa sat on the edge of the bed. "Who found him? Did you find him?"

"What? Me? Oh. No. His roommate did, Daniel. He came in and told me this morning. He went to the hospital with him. I don't know. I don't really know." She would never have imagined Daniel, so soft-spoken, slamming a door. His rage had been directed completely at her. *Why me?*

"So what are you going to do?" Martha asked.

"I thought of curling up in a fetal position in the corner."

"OKAY." Martha raised her eyebrows with concern and bewilderment. "Well, um, when did this happen?"

"This morning. His roommate told me around noon or something."

"It's past nine. Have you been sitting here, in the dark, all this time? What are you going to do?" Martha asked.

"Perhaps I'll move to the corner."

"Um...well." Martha never really "got" sarcasm, and after a while Mischa had stopped using it with her. She thought that one-sided sarcasm was cruel. Tonight she did not have the concentration to tailor her speech.

Like a commando on a mission, Martha went into action. She took a Diet Cherry Coke from the refrigerator and handed it to her. She made Mischa a ham and American cheese sandwich smothered with mayonnaise. Martha sliced the sandwich diagonally on her neon blue cutting board on top of the retro refrigerator, the color of a 1950s pink Cadillac. Had she put it in a Ziploc plastic bag, it would have been Mischa's childhood dream realized. In elementary school, Mischa always wanted that type of sandwich made on flat, unnaturally white Wonder Bread, just like the other kids. She hated her deformed sandwiches, made with homemade bread that her mother baked every Wednesday. Martha handed the sandwich to her on a plastic plate covered with bright yellow daisies.

"Eat something," Martha ordered.

They sat in silence and Mischa could hear her drink fizzing inside the can. She was stunned by Martha's kindness and obeyed her order by taking timid bites and chewing carefully.

"I'm going to Sigma Chi tonight. You are coming along," Martha announced. "You've got to take your mind off this. I don't want to come back to find blood on the sheets."

Wait a minute, was that dark humor? Is Martha being sarcastic?

"Martha, no, I couldn't."

True, there's no protocol for dealing with an ex-boyfriend's suicide attempt, but going to a party just doesn't seem right.

"Listen, Mischa, I'm not asking you. I'm telling you. I'm going to take a shower. We're leaving in a half hour, and you're coming."

Martha charged out the door in her purple silk kimono robe with her red Snoopy beach towel. When she returned, the smell of her peach shampoo filled the room. Martha went through her drawers and surveyed her closet while Mischa watched admiringly from her bed. Mischa's clothes were jumbled together, with no order to them, but Martha's organization was so clear that even Mischa knew what item of clothing Martha was going to get before she took it out. *Ah, she's going into the sweater drawer.* Martha took out her thin powder blue sweater with the deep scoop neckline and wriggled into it. The sweater shouted, "Look at these!" whenever it was accompanied by a push-up bra.

You know, I've never understood the desire to show cleavage. Then again, I've never had cleavage. How can I be such a catty bitch? I've got to stop it.

Martha squeezed the remaining water from her hair with the towel and threw it on the bed. "Well, Mischa, it's all over the dorm. Girls were chatting in the bathroom, trying to get the four-one-one on what happened."

"What?" asked Mischa.

"Information about the incident. Curtis. You. Get with it! Wake up!"

"Oh gosh, Martha, please, really, I can't leave this room." She curled up behind her pillow, against the wall.

"Look, Mischa, the resident adviser found me. The Dipshit told me if I don't stay with you, then, according to college regulations, she will have to stay with you. You need to be accompanied tonight."

"But I wasn't the one who tried to commit suicide!"

"You were 'peripherally involved', is what the Dipshit said. They are taking it seriously. So you and Daniel both have to be accompanied tonight. Unless you come with me, you'll be stuck with her, in this room, until I get back from the party. You choose. Me or her?"

"Not the Dipshit," Mischa said glumly.

"Okay then, get ready. I can style your hair, once I'm done with mine." With that, she pressed the button and the overpowering volume of the blow-dryer allowed Mischa to be free of conversation for a few minutes. When Martha was done, she came over to Mischa with a brush. "Turn around and face the wall so I can brush your hair in back." Mischa obeyed and shifted herself. "You know, I really love your long hair. That must come from your mother. She's Spanish, isn't she?"

"She's Chilean."

"Oh yeah, right, Chile. Well, I'll never find a conditioner that will make my hair glow like yours."

Martha found a tangle, and softly pulled at the strands of hair with her fingers until they came loose and she could continue brushing.

"So, Mischa, is your dad from Chile as well?"

"No, he's American, Irish American."

"That explains those green eyes. I thought Spanish people had brown eyes. Hey, I've got a green cashmere sweater. I can lend it to you tonight. It would look really nice on you, and would make your eyes stand out."

"Thanks, Martha. I'll just stay as I am."

This kindness was a side of Martha that Mischa had never seen. While Martha brushed her hair, it occurred to Mischa that perhaps they had bonded during those three months they had been living together. *That must be why I was waiting for her to return. Maybe Martha was nice all along, but she didn't fit my idea of a friend. Maybe I knew that I didn't fit Martha's idea of a friend. Maybe I'm just a pretentious bitch who shouldn't judge people by first impressions.* There might have been truth to all three, but the last one lingered longest in Mischa's mind.

"There you are." Martha put the brush down and smoothed Mischa's long black hair with a few strokes of her hand. "Okay, you're done. Let's get out of here. My sorority sisters will meet us at the frat house."

There was a palpable curiosity in the hallway. Mischa could feel it as she passed people standing in the doorways of their rooms or letting her by as she followed Martha. She wasn't the siren they had expected—the type worthy of making a young man desperate to end his life. Consequently, in the instinctive judgment of a crowd, she merited only second glances, not stares.

When they arrived at fraternity row, there was a mass of humanity outside the brick houses with five-foot Greek letters painted on their roofs and smaller ones nailed on signs on their sides: Sigma, Epsilon, Alpha, Kappa. Greek letters were prevalent in the crowd, printed on sweatshirts, huge plastic beer cups, and baseball caps, up and down the half mile of houses that comprised fraternity row. They passed four of them and came to the designated spot which, with the exception of the three Greek letters that signified its particular fraternity, seemed no different from all the other houses.

A concentration of people surrounded each beer keg and jostled to get to them. Huge colored plastic cups stood in tidy towers on folding tables or littered on the lawn. Mischa could smell the beer. It was on the grass, on people's clothes, on their breath. Guys and girls leaned against porch railings. There was laughing, shouting, giggling, and guffawing. Laughing frat boys, with beer spilling from jumbo plastic cups, had their arms around stumbling girls.

Even in my wildest "misfit fits in" fantasies I have never, ever wanted to be part of this world. I don't want to be with these people. My mother would be appalled if she knew I was here.

On the porch Mischa saw a bounty of potato chips, Doritos, and pretzels, and an array of iced, cake, sprinkled, and glazed doughnuts. She looked in the box and saw that the cold weather had cracked the icing. She stood by the Krispy Kreme doughnuts and alternated soft, sweet bites with salty Doritos. After two Coca-Colas, she was on a caffeine high, and in her own non-alcoholic way, felt she could finally join the party.

She stepped into the fraternity house, pushing and being pushed as people entered and exited. Going through the crowd, an occasional piercing blast of cheap perfume tickled Mischa's nose, but the overwhelming smell was a stew of stale beer, cigarettes, and sweat. The interior was a testosterone celebration, a guy's world. The walls were an homage to pubescence, a collection of souvenir rock concert posters taped on the walls alongside posters of supermodels in lingerie. Plastic blow-up girls in bikinis dangled from the high ceiling, and at the center, two of them, reached over pillows that also hung from the ceiling. Their fingers reached across and barely touched in one frat-boy's 3-D version of the Sistine Chapel.

I can't believe it, but I think I'd actually like to meet the guy who thought that up.

There were two lava lamps on mismatched side tables. The random surfaces were littered with copies of *TV Guide*, men's magazines, sports magazines, and rock fanzines. A few plastic palm trees dotted the archways, with Styrofoam tropical fruits still attached, resident remnants of a previous theme party. Dartboards graced one door and a basketball net was nailed to another. In the dining room, a pool table was in the center, surrounded by a few shabby chairs.

All the furniture was ripped and mismatched, evidence of its origins, from sidewalks in suburbia where people had deposited the pieces for garbage collection. They were treated like treasures, and the frat brothers who carried them in were greeted like triumphant hunters as they hauled in their captured prey of sofas and tables and chairs.

The furniture had been pushed against the living room walls and a sophisticated stereo system blasted music at such a volume that a person had to decide where to stand based on whether his or her eardrums could take the sound. Martha was on the improvised dance floor with her sorority sisters, balancing their beer cups while they danced and sipped. Fifty or more girls and guys were crammed together while they gyrated and flung their arms to the beat. Heads whirled and hips swiveled.

I think I'd rather see It Happened One Night *for the ninth time.*

"Come on! Mischa! Dance! It's Madonna!" Martha yelled.

"I LOVE MADONNA!" one of her sorority sisters shouted. The other two strutted their stuff, much to the delight of leering frat boys.

Why am I here? Why am I here?

⌘　⌘　⌘

"Where am I?" Mischa said. She saw Curtis's roommate at the foot of the bed and Martha sitting at her side. "What happened?"

"Mischa, you had a seizure. My sorority sisters and I took you out of the party. Don't worry. People just thought you were drunk. It was pretty funny. Right before the seizure you were dancing like a go-go girl."

"There's a chance that it could have just been the convulsions," Mischa said, hoping her modesty was intact.

"Whatever it was, the guys were looking. If you had started stripping they probably would have started putting dollar bills—"

"Shut the hell up, Martha!"

"Anyway, my sisters caught you when you fell. People thought you were drunk or drugged. The seizure was really quick. Some of the frat guys helped us carry you down the road. No problem."

Mischa looked over to the other bed in the room. It was stripped of the mattress and sheets. She smelled disinfectant. She saw Curtis's vintage movie poster of *It Happened One Night* and his tweed coat hanging on an oak clothes hanger from a hook. *This is his room. I'm in his room!*

"Why am I in here? What the hell am I doing here? Get me out of here!"

"Steady, girlfriend. We couldn't lift you up the stairs. Curtis's room is on the first floor and Daniel was here."

"Get me out of here!"

Daniel glared at Mischa from his desk.

"Get me away from here!" Mischa shouted. Then, in a stern voice and emphasizing each word, she demanded, "I...SAID...GET...ME...OUT... OF...HERE!"

Martha, calmly and equally determined, replied, "No, Mischa. We're waiting for the school medics. Don't worry, I'll tell them you have epilepsy."

Mischa was quieted by her surprise and her voice became politely quizzical. "How did you know? I was waiting to tell you."

"I was forewarned by the college. They wrote a letter asking me if I was comfortable having a roommate with a disability. The Dipshit told me, too. By the way, I'm not completely stupid. I saw your pills on the desk and they didn't look like birth control."

Disability? It's just epilepsy. It's just my seizures. I'm disabled? She had never really considered that before. Martha said it without hesitation; it was as if she had called Mischa's hair black.

The school medics came in and asked her questions for nearly an hour, all the while taking her blood pressure and temperature, examining her pupils, and doing a breathalyzer. They filled in their forms, took her name and Social Security number, and whatever else she was conscious enough to provide. They reinforced the requirement that Mischa would have to be accompanied for the entire night, and Martha assured them that she would stay with her. The girls finally went to their own room.

Martha and Mischa had an unspoken rule: they didn't play their music when the other was in the room. That first day of college, when they moved in and arranged their music, they saw the tapes on their shelves and knew it had to be that way. But tonight, Mischa didn't ask Martha; she just put the tape in the stereo at a low volume—*Ella Fitzgerald Sings the Cole Porter Songbook*. Martha changed into her aquamarine flannel pajamas with jumping purple cows. She fluffed her pillows, and took a book off the shelf and a Diet Cherry Coke from her pink fridge. Mischa didn't bother to change. She curled under the covers. She could still smell the beer and cigarette smoke on her clothes. Mischa rubbed her fingers, they had a thin film of stickiness leftover from the doughnuts. She stared a few inches in front of her at the white cinder-block wall until she fell asleep.

On Tuesday, Mischa came into the common room to find a first aid on epilepsy pamphlet on the announcement board. She wanted to smack the Dipshit across the face. There were smiley faces all over the pamphlet. Editorial remarks sliced through her thoughts as she read it.

FIRST AID for EPILEPSY

Epilepsy is a condition producing seizures. A seizure occurs when a surge of electrical activity affects part or all of the brain. A seizure can range from a momentary disruption of the senses, to short periods of unconsciousness (staring spells or fainting), to severe convulsions. When a person has two or more unprovoked seizures, he or she is considered to have epilepsy. Currently there is no cure for epilepsy, but there is something you can do about a seizure. Please read through and share with others.

SEIZURE FIRST AID

If you are with someone who has a convulsive seizure, you should try to:

1. Stay calm and remain with the person.

Yeah, try telling them that when someone is writhing on the ground like a demon possessed.

2. Time the seizure.

Uh, I don't think so. Getting out a stopwatch is not a first thought.

3. Protect the person from injury—remove any hard objects that are near the person.

True, this might be helpful. She could have had a lot of fewer bruises if someone had done that. She'd prefer to have someone do that than get out a stopwatch.

4. Place something soft under the head and loosen any tight clothing at the neck.

But this contradicts the first rule of first aid with seizures: let them have a seizure and don't touch them. But hell, if someone could have found a pillow for me, I would have accepted it if I could. Probably would have saved me from a few headaches.

5. Gently roll the person onto his/her side as soon as it is possible to do so and firmly push the angle of the jaw forward to assist with breathing. If breathing seems difficult, check the mouth to make sure that food or dentures are not blocking the airway.

So, how do you do this when the person is convulsing violently?

6. Establish communication with the person so you know he/she has regained consciousness.

I think that's common sense.

7. **Reassure the person and minimize embarrassment during recovery.**

Embarrassment? I'm unconscious; I have no idea what I did. What do they mean? Why should I feel embarrassed?

8. **Stay with the person until he/she recovers; this may range from five to twenty minutes.**

Make that one to two hours or more.

WHAT NOT TO DO:

Do not put anything in the person's mouth or between the teeth.

Agreed. Why is it that people think they have to put a spoon in a person's mouth? Where did that myth begin?

Do not restrain the person unless he/she is in danger.

Agreed.

Do not give pills, food, or drink until recovery is complete.

Agreed.

Mischa had an intense desire to scrawl all over the pamphlet. She would have put the "Do Not" section first. She would have cut the "embarrassment" commentary. She didn't understand where that had come from. She wanted to tell people herself, not have some goddamn pamphlet announce it on the dormitory announcements board. Mischa ripped it off.

The next day, Mischa felt guilty for having gone to a party on the eve of an ex-boyfriend's suicide attempt. She gave herself the excuse that there was no protocol for such a situation. She felt obliged to inquire about Curtis's health. It seemed like a mature response. She decided to visit his roommate, Daniel. As she stood at the door, for a minute she reconsidered and stepped back, but then moved forward and knocked.

Curtis opened the door. He wore an unforgiving short-sleeve shirt that allowed the white strip bandages wrapped around his wrists to be on full display. She wished that he had worn long sleeves so that she did not have to see them.

"Uh, hi, uh, Curtis. Uh. I was wondering how you were and was going to ask Daniel, but, well, it looks like you're, uh, here. I didn't expect you to be back just yet. I was just checking in, I...uh...guess." She stared at his bandages.

"I heard you had a seizure here." He spoke in a monotone. His eyes were emotionless gray stones.

"Well, uh, not exactly. You see, they brought me here after the seizure. Well, it looks like your room saw a lot of action that day. Ha-ha." *That was probably inappropriate.* She regretted the dark humor, but he brightened and laughed. She smiled with relief and wondered how long she could keep him happy. "When I woke up, Claudette Colbert and Clark Gable were looking down at me."

"There are worse things to have staring you in the face."

"Curtis, did you know that I have epilepsy?"

"Yes, you told me the first day we walked to class together. Did you know I suffer from clinical depression?" he asked.

"You never told me, but I could tell you had a screw loose." *He didn't laugh. Maybe that remark was less than appropriate. I should change the topic of conversation. Maybe we could go somewhere else.* "So, Curtis, uh, would you like to grab some lunch with me?"

"Sure." He picked up his keys and they walked outside. They didn't look at each other, focusing instead on the dry leaves that twisted down the street ahead of them.

"Why, Curtis?"

"Why not? The first person to ever say 'I love you' drops me a few weeks later. Why not, Mischa?"

What could she say? Her ideas of romance came from movies from the thirties and forties. That night, when he took her in his arms, under a tree in the moonlight, she said what she thought people were supposed to say in those scenes.

"Mischa, you should be careful throwing around words like that."

They walked into the university canteen. A wave of warmth and the smell of frying fat greeted them at the door. People from their dorm were seated at a nearby table. As they passed, the group went noticeably quiet. Mischa and Curtis picked up their plastic trays and studied the food set out on glass shelves. She slid her tray down the metal rails and walked along, selecting plates and bowls of chocolate pudding, lemon meringue pie, and green Jell-O. A mug of coffee and ice water topped off her selection. They took the first table they could find. As they set down their trays she could not avoid staring at his wrists. There was no need for discretion; she felt they had already crossed that line.

"How do they feel?" she asked.

Curtis looked down as if he were examining cuff links. "Not too bad. I can't type very well. Daniel is going to help me. I dictate and he types the paper. It's a good setup. I get a typist and a copy editor."

"I could do that, too." She was desperate to make any gesture of atonement.

"I don't think so." He forked mashed potatoes into his mouth.

"Okay, Curtis." Mischa searched her head for something to fill the silence. "Daniel was pretty furious at me that day."

"I don't blame him. You deserved it."

She took the punch. *Why fight a guy with slit wrists?*

"So, Curtis, have you seen *It Happened One Night* since you returned from the...uh..."

"Just once."

"We've got to get you out of that *It Happened* hole. There are loads of other movies from that time. Why not try *Arsenic and Old Lace?* It was also directed by Frank Capra. I think he made it about ten years later. *South Pacific* and *Arsenic and Old Lace* are my favorite movies."

"Isn't *South Pacific* a musical?"

"Yes, and what's wrong with that? Don't knock it. You should see *South Pacific*. It's much deeper than you think. The plot revolves around interracial relationships and the setting is World War II. There's a lot more to it than a baritone singing 'Some Enchanted Evening.' Rodgers and Hammerstein, 1949, way, way ahead of its time."

Curtis picked up his knife and a frisson of fear sped through her as she followed its path with her eyes. He gracefully scooped butter from the small plastic tub and spread it smoothly across the roll he had ripped open. Mischa took a deep breath to relax. As she tried to recapture her train of thought, she hoped her hesitation had gone unnoticed.

"Back to *Arsenic*, it's hilarious. I told you, it's in black-and-white, just like *It Happened One Night*. You see, Cary Grant goes to visit his two aunts, charming old ladies who rent a room in their house and select lodgers with certain traits: lonely and depressed men." *Maybe this isn't the movie to discuss.* She hesitated. Curtis looked to her. *I'm too far along.*

"Go ahead." He seemed to want to assure her that he had not taken offense.

"You see, the aunts decide to poison the old men with arsenic, mixed with elderberry wine, to free them from their misery. They have three nephews: a crazy schizophrenic that lives with them, Cary Grant, and a third one, who comes in later in the story. They ask their crazy nephew, who thinks he's Theodore Roosevelt, to dig the graves. They tell him that the corpses are malaria victims who were working on the Panama Canal. The best part is watching Cary Grant as he discovers a dead body and gradually realizes his aunts' twisted moral code that justifies their 'good deeds.' The aunts are sweet and gentle throughout the movie. They act without a hint of malice or guilt, but with complete goodwill. Despite all of Grant's questions and delicately phrased accusations of first degree murder, they are calm and dismissive. They explain that their work is merely charity, and suggest that Grant forget he even saw the corpse in a trunk in the living room. Meanwhile, they go about their business of frosting a cake and tidying up the house. The contradictions are overwhelming for Grant, who is constantly trying to reassure himself that he's right, that he is not the crazy one. You can see it in all of Grant's facial movements and body language. He's really a comic genius, it's just that—"

Curtis interrupted, "But, Mischa, they are burying the bodies in the basement, not calling the funeral home to take them away, so there is an element of deceit, which implies guilt."

"Not really. I think they justify the burials with an ethic of tidying up a mess and not making a fuss for others. Well, then again, maybe you're right." She was happy they had found a topic of conversation that did not involve their feelings.

"Okay, so anyway," Mischa continued, "Cary Grant's lost brother, the third nephew, shows up at the aunts' house. He is a murderer on the loose, traveling with a cohort and looking for a hideout. The unassuming abode offers the perfect spot. They also come to realize what the aunts are doing. When the third nephew and his cohort count the graves in the basement and compare them to the number of their murder victims, the aunts are up by one. It has a lot of slapstick and it's such a great mix. The movie revolves around Cary Grant's face. He is so dapper and handsome that I think people forget how great he was at slapstick, and—"

"I liked him in *The Philadelphia Story*," Curtis observed coolly.

"Yeah, I can see why. He had a bit of that Clark Gable personality from *It Happened*, that sort of rapid-fire response that you like so much."

"In that story, Katharine Hepburn was a little like you." He took another bit of butter and moved his knife toward the roll.

"How is that?" Mischa's voice flirted. She was flattered.

"She tells Jimmy Stewart that she loves him while she's drunk and walking in the moonlight. The next day she drops him."

"I don't drink."

He just wants to use me as a punching bag. I hate passive aggression. She wanted to stand up, shout at him and leave. *Aggressive aggression is so much healthier. Why don't you try it, Curtis! It gets it out of your damn system! Passive-aggressive people fester and simmer and then explode. They go postal with machine guns, or razors across their wrists! Okay, Curtis, so you want to speak passive-aggressive. Okay, damn it, I'm not fluent, but I can get by.* Mischa paused in thought to calm herself. *Speak slowly. Passive aggression is fifty percent tone and fifty percent content. Keep it nonchalant.*

"So, Curtis, why didn't you do it in a bath? I've heard that if you slit your wrists in a warm bath you don't really feel the pain and the blood flows out faster."

"I didn't want to make a mess." He shoved another forkful of mashed potatoes into his mouth and swallowed. "Anyway, we only have showers. Why would I want to re-create a scene from *Psycho*? You know I don't like Hitchcock. Back to you, Mischa, how many times have you said 'I love you'?"

He's so goddamn sublime. He's a master. She sipped the lukewarm coffee to calm herself.

"One time. Only once."

"Why me, Mischa?"

"Why are you asking me?" She gave up on politeness. Her voice made it clear that she was annoyed and wanted to end the conversation. She gave him an irritated look and returned to her coffee. She was ready to leave.

Curtis slammed his fist down with his wrist facing Mischa. The plates rattled and clinked in fear and Mischa shuddered. She could see a round brown stain showing through the gauze. The people at the tables surrounding them looked over. Curtis glared and they averted their eyes.

"Mischa, let's think about that one. I am asking why you said something, and then retracted it, which prompted me to make a decision to end my life, which was halted by the actions of a well-meaning but interventionist roommate. The least you can do is answer my question. I want to know. Why me? And why did you drop me? Looking at the circumstances, I think I deserve an answer."

Mischa studied her green Jell-O. It refracted the light, and the spoon behind it was larger for it. *I don't really like green Jell-O. Red Jell-O is best.*

Green Jell-O tastes a little too much like a fifth grade chemical experiment, but it does handle light interestingly. She could see the faint diagonal scratches left by the knife that had cut the Jell-O into cubes before these were placed in the stark white little bowl. She took another sip of coffee. *I forgot the milk. This is bitter. It's watery, too.* She didn't want to look at him. She didn't want to shrug helplessly. *It's true, he deserves an answer.* Her thoughts had barely congealed, but Mischa knew she had to speak before she lost the courage.

"Why you? I don't really know, Curtis. I never dated anyone before. I'm not accustomed to being with someone. I don't know what to do with a boyfriend. I thought that was what a girl said to a boy when they walked in the moonlight. I promise it was complete naïveté. I realize that I was stupid. Why did I break up with you? I think it was instinct. After a few weeks together I could tell that you were an emotional whirlpool." His eyes were angry and tense. "Curtis, I have my own issues, my own survival to consider. I don't have the energy to save you. I would have drowned in you."

When she stopped, he looked at her thoughtfully and his stare softened. "At least you're honest," he observed.

Is this the setup for another punch?

Mischa did not look at him as she spoke. Her eyes shifted to different objects on the table: the clean fork next to the mashed potatoes, the empty plastic containers of butter, and the uneaten cubes of green Jell-O. She peered at him slyly from the corner of her eye and wondered what he would do next. She decided that she would not fight back. She would let him have the last word.

"True. I don't delude myself." She looked into her mug to see how much coffee was left. Another thought locked away in her head suddenly escaped. "Sometimes it's a good thing, sometimes it's a bad thing, because I end up questioning myself, constantly."

"Something like Cary Grant?"

"Yeah, I never thought of that. Maybe that explains why that movie appeals to me. It's funny and dark, with a moral twist."

"That describes you entirely, Mischa."

He smiled for a moment and returned to his meal. He finished his plate in silence and she sipped the last drops of stone-cold coffee. They said good-bye at the entrance to the canteen. Mischa returned to the dorm and he walked the other way.

I probably shouldn't have said that thing about a warm bath.

8. THE CAMPUS

FROM SEPTEMBER TO DECEMBER, HER FIRST YEAR IN COLLEGE WAS SO DARK. There was so much death in such a short time. Curtis tried again and again and again. He chose a different way each time; drug overdose, hanging, and gas. After the second time, his roommate couldn't handle it. Daniel appealed to the college administration for other accommodations. After the lunch with Curtis, Mischa never spoke to him again, but somehow, someone always found her the next day and reported on his latest suicide attempt.

Then her mother died. For years, when Mischa looked back at those months in her life, the day skies were gray and the night skies were black. When memories of those seizures returned, there were no colors. There was so much pain.

It was early December when the department secretary interrupted Professor Dunn during his class. He looked at her quizzically as she walked across the room to the lectern. Then, she whispered in his ear that he had an urgent phone call. He turned to the students and excused himself for a few minutes. As he walked down the corridor to the secretary's office, she told the class that the lecture was over and dismissed them.

The secretary returned to her office and saw Professor Dunn's hands trembling as he tried to write an address on a notepad on her desk. His voice quavered as he asked the person on the phone to repeat the street name. When Richard insisted on knowing what had happened, the person refused to answer and only repeated the address of the hospital.

After he arrived, Richard found the hospital administrator waiting at the information desk as he had promised. He took Richard into a room and told him that he had been asked to come there to identify the body of a woman who might be related to him. Dr. Scaletta, his closest friend on the faculty, had accompanied him to the hospital. He stood outside the door.

The administrator explained to Richard that the female had been killed instantaneously in a car crash that morning. She had been driving a brown station wagon. The man read out the license plate number to him.

Richard squeezed his eyes closed and nodded in terrified recognition. When Richard Dunn left the room with a face of horror, shock, and despair, just the sight of him made his colleague shiver.

The hospital administrator walked them to the elevator and they descended to a windowless, stainless-steel-encased room, the morgue, where Richard identified his wife, Cristina Isabel Dunn. He reached out to touch the shoulder of her beige camel hair coat. He recognized so little of the body. Only the corner of her shoulder remained unstained, unmarred, and familiar. He had helped her put on this coat for years, and had patted her shoulders as she tied the belt tightly around her small waist. Cristina would tilt her head up to signal that she was ready, and he would kiss her forehead and step ahead to open the door for her.

He looked at the table next to her body, and there lay her wedding ring and her favorite purse. He stared in silence for a while—he thought it was just seconds, but twenty minutes passed—and the medical examiner stood back to give him some privacy. When the shock of the sight had finally been absorbed by his brain, he realized that he had to tell Mischa.

He could not leave this to a phone call. He must tell Mischa in person. He would have to fly to Boston today. His colleague from the university refused to let him travel alone, so the two left Washington National Airport five hours later.

When Mischa's father and his colleague arrived at her dorm they sat in the reception area. Mischa was still at dinner. She returned, walking through the hall laughing and talking with two of her friends. For some reason, she turned her head to the right and saw a familiar face across the room. *That's Dr. Scaletta. He must be up here for a conference.* Mischa thought she recognized the figure next to him. She walked over and looked more closely. She could not see his face, but his shape and clothes were immediately familiar. *Dad?* She was confused. He sat crumpled in the chair, motionless, with his head in his hands.

"Dad?"

He raised his head slowly, and she could see his bloodshot eyes and his face contorted in pain. Mischa's friends fell silent. Dr. Scaletta motioned for them to move on as Mischa walked over to her father haltingly. His eyes were glassy with tears. He had rehearsed so many versions of what he would say, but was uncertain which one would come out. He hoped that the words would leave his mouth in some gentle sequence, but there no such order.

"She's dead. Cristina's dead. Your mother's dead. Car crash. Today. I saw...I saw..." He almost collapsed to the floor, but Mischa and Dr. Scaletta caught him in time. Once they returned him to the chair, Dr. Scaletta excused himself and went outside. He could see Richard speaking, and looked away when he saw him fall into his daughter's arms. Mischa stared ahead blankly as she hugged her father. Thousands of thoughts tried to storm her brain, but only one, a refrain, stood like a wall against the onslaught, the first sentence her father had uttered: *She's dead.*

Mischa looked out the window of the airplane while her father slept. When she glanced over, she could read the emotional, physical, and spiritual exhaustion on his face. She recognized the utter surrender to unconsciousness, sleep for the sake of sanity. She tried to convince herself to accept what her mind was continually rejecting. It was still a thought process and her emotions had not yet registered the news. Her overloaded brain had prompted an emotional short circuit. Mischa was numb.

Her father had told her that it was a car crash. During the flight she wondered what had happened. It wasn't difficult to guess. She knew what must have happened. Her parents had left Providence when Mischa went to college. Her father was offered a promotion, to be the director of the Comparative Literature Program at Georgetown University in Washington, DC. Her mother was always a bad driver. She was unaccustomed to the highways and complained about driving around Washington. She had learned how to drive only after they came to the United States, on the wide suburban streets of Rhode Island with its courteous drivers. The aggressive driving and the traffic speed on the Beltway, the highway that coiled around Washington and offered a myriad of exits, always made Cristina nervous. They could have afforded a better car, but her mother insisted on keeping the old one, the car in which she had learned to drive. *That damn brown station wagon with those goddamn rosary beads.*

Mischa's father had moved beyond the shock and had begun to grieve. With the white-noise hum of the plane's engine, sitting next to Mischa on the plane, he closed his eyes. Half asleep, his mind leapt between thoughts of the past and future. The house, what was it going to smell like without her? She made it smell of warm baked bread and garlic. There was a smell of affection in the aroma of her food—the *pastel de papas*, the lasagna, and the beef bourguignon made with her family's red wine. The lunches and dinners were finished with flans, chocolate cake, or rum-soaked *pastel boracho*, the cake that Tito Alvarez's wife had taught Cristina to make, the one which left the dessert plate sticky with condensed milk.

What would tomorrow be like? For first time, he realized that in twenty-four years he had never been in the house alone for more than a few hours without her. He could not remember life without her. He could not imagine what life would be without her. It was too much to think about, and he pleaded and prayed for his mind to go blank so that he could sleep.

For days, as they made the arrangements for the funeral, Mischa was ashamed of her numbness. She even wondered if it was apathy. She wondered when her wall would fall and the waterfall of emotion would come. When would she understand that this was real?

They never had much to say to each other. *When did our silence begin?* Her mother would tell her what was for dinner and ask, "Do you have enough shirts for the week? Have you ironed them? What about your school sweaters, are they all washed?" The most existential discussion was the need for Mischa to focus on finding a rich man to be a good husband rather than a profession.

"You'll have to leave your job anyway to take care of the children. *Verdad,* it's true, *tienes que* get an education. University will be where you meet your husband. *Te prometo.* I promise that you will be unhappy if you never marry."

"I don't care, Mom. I'm going to have a career. I'm going have my own life. I'm not going to stay in the background. I don't need a husband."

"How can you speak like that? You will, you'll see. All your friends will get married and then you will know. *Mi hija,* you should learn to dress better. Okay, so you will get a job, but you will have to leave it to have children."

"Stop it. I don't care, Mom. I don't want to talk about this."

"Mischa, you are a beautiful girl. Look at yourself. *Mira, bella.* Take care of yourself. When you go to college, make yourself pretty. Don't worry, you will find a husband. And I will pray that he is rich."

Was it my emerging feminism, or adolescence? she wondered. *Was it the epilepsy?* Perhaps the silence started around the time of the first seizure. Her mother had no idea what to do. She was silent. She never spoke to her while they were in the waiting rooms, never spoke on the rides to the hospital.

The few times—Mischa could count them on one hand—that she made references, the words were "it" for the epilepsy or "them" for the seizures. *Could the silence have begun then? Was it typical adolescence, that tumultuous time for any mother and daughter when most rifts occur? Was the epilepsy AND adolescence a toxic combination for a mother-daughter relationship?*

They didn't talk to each other much at the dinner table, even though they all ate together almost every night. Her mother would begin a soliloquy while Mischa and her father ate quietly. Dinner was her mother's time to shine. Cristina had labored all day for the family. She believed that the other two had their time, their lives, outside the home. Dinner was her moment to place herself back in their lives and remind them that she was not a servant, not their cook or their gardener; that she had a life, and that she, too, had been outside.

Her father made encouraging monosyllabic remarks that assured her mother that she was not speaking into a lonely abyss. Perhaps he was listening, but Mischa barely paid attention. She occasionally caught phrases spoken by her mother.

"*Su hija* was just accepted to Princeton."

"He divorced *la esposa* and married the Italian au pair, Richard, can you believe it?"

"*No se como van a* survive on just one salary after she was just let go."

"I would never have guessed that he would defraud a company. *Es tan amable, siempre saluda,* he says hello to us when we walk by his house in the evening."

Mischa knew the monologue was drawing to a close when comments were made about the bargains her mother had discovered that week—oranges, boots, mangoes, photo frames, poultry, napkin rings, and lamp shades.

When did we last have a conversation? When did we stop noticing each other? Mischa could not hear the eulogy. Her father was slumped in the pew next to Mischa, digging into his nails, drawing blood from ones that had already gone black from being tortured the night before, even the day before, and the day before that. Mischa had seen him do it in Chile, when his colleague at the university disappeared and the man's wife came to the house. She remembered seeing him do it in the emergency room, after her seizures started. But she had never seen them like this before. The lines behind his nails were now thick bands of black dried blood.

Professor Dunn knew that he would be unable to deliver the eulogy. He composed it and asked his closest friend, who had accompanied him to the hospital and to Boston, to read it. Dr Scaletta came to the pulpit and adjusted the microphone. After a tentative tap, he explained that he was delivering the eulogy on behalf of Richard. He cleared his throat and, in a stilted voice, read from the papers that Professor Dunn had put in his hands just before the mass began. He spoke words that Richard had written the night before, alone at his desk. Poignant and passionate, the words were written in the sincere voice of a love letter. The private suffering of such a reserved man was laid bare. In the church, their friends were made aware of the great depth of their love, which from the outside had seemed so ordinary. As the pallbearers took up the coffin, Mischa walked next to her father. She knew that the woman in the coffin was her mother, but she had never known the person.

As they rode to the graveyard in the back of the undertaker's limousine, Mischa remembered a casual conversation with her father. It was an exchange that had recurred in her mind for years, lightly knocking at her subconscious until now, when she finally understood its significance.

She remembered being in the car with her father. He had been driving her to Sophie's fifteenth birthday party, her *quinceañera*. On the ride over, Mischa had asked an obvious question for the first time.

"Why did you and Mom choose to live in Chile? Why didn't you just come back to the United States right after you were married?"

"I had a good job teaching at the University of Santiago. We had a good life in Chile and Cristina had family nearby. Also, we married a year, or maybe two, before the U.S. laws against interracial marriage were struck down. The U.S. civil rights movement was big news around the world and your mother heard about a certain court case on interracial marriage. When I raised the idea of moving to the U.S., she refused to go to a country where our marriage might be considered illegitimate."

"Illegitimate?" Mischa asked.

"It wasn't every state that had those laws, just a few in the South. Cristina was angry. Frankly, I can't imagine that anyone would have taken those laws seriously, but the news about the case bothered your mother."

"You're kidding. I never heard of this," Mischa said, incredulous.

"Haven't they been teaching you about the civil rights movement in school?"

"Yes, but I never heard of this."

"I knew it. I told your mother you should be going to a public school, not that Catholic one. Well, where to begin? There were some states that had laws against interracial marriage that dated from the nineteenth century. The Supreme Court ruled them all unconstitutional in 1967. The name of the case was memorable, *Loving v. Virginia*. God, what a decade for the United States.

"Anyway, a married couple—a white man, Richard Loving, married to a black woman, Mildred Loving—brought the case to court. By the way, I want you to look this up and we're going to talk about this again. If they're not going to teach this to you, then we're going to fill in the blanks with a trip to the library this weekend.

"Returning to the story, your mother told me that she would not live in a country that would not accept us as a couple. That was why you were raised in Chile. But, once Pinochet started cracking down, I convinced your mom that conditions in Chile were worse and the situation in the U.S. had improved. I promised that we would stay on the East Coast, away from the South and in a more cosmopolitan environment. Brown University was looking for a professor of Russian literature and we ended up here. Rhode Island isn't very cosmopolitan, but it's not the South and it's not a military dictatorship, so your mother compromised and we moved. I think we did okay, especially when you consider…"

Her father continued, but Mischa could not hear him anymore. *Interracial?* The word blazed like a lit candle in a dark room. *I'm interracial? Mom and Dad are an interracial couple?*

Her father was oblivious. He innocently fell in love with a woman from another country, another race, and married her without any consideration of prejudice. *Thank God for people like Dad and Mr. Loving.* But he never felt the pangs of difference that Mischa and her mother felt. They did not tell him, nor did they speak of it to each other. A random thought burst into her head. *Is this why we both loved* South Pacific? Every so often her mother brought the 1949 musical home from the video store. *Come to think of it, that's my favorite memory with Mom, sitting on the sofa together with popcorn and hot chocolate, watching* South Pacific. *Dad was never there, it was just the two of us.*

When they arrived at the grave, Mischa looked around at the familiar faces, from dinner parties, Sunday mass, and coffees. There were neighbors who would offer her mother rides when the car—that car—was in the shop. When they all came back to the Dunn's house after the burial, many of the women were in the kitchen making coffee and setting out pastries. Mrs. DeKorsy had brought her almond cookies. Mrs. Lane always gave them a loaf of lemon drizzle cake at Christmas, and there, on a rectangular crystal plate, it was set out on the dinner table alongside Cristina's favorite, a basket of cranberry nut muffins from Mrs. Stucki.

Mischa wandered through the rooms and heard people talking about her mother. One member of the book club recounted how her mother's experience made the discussion so rich. They would never have read Latin American literature had it not been for Cristina Dunn.

There were women in her swimming exercise class who remarked to each other about how disciplined she was, and how she attended every single class. Each of them admitted to skipping a few classes, but they always knew that Cristina would be there when they returned. If they arrived early enough, they could count on Cristina to teach them the new exercise routines so that they were not left behind during the class.

Others remembered how Cristina had terrified the parish priest. She had suggested the creation of a parish soup kitchen, and when the priest rejected the idea, she organized a petition. The ladies continued trading anecdotes about the soup kitchen. One remembered fondly how homeless men and women asked especially for Cristina's carrot soup. The women laughed softly, and admitted to taking home a few bowls of her soup themselves. Then they grew silent, looked down at their plates, and one or two looked away as they bent their heads to wipe away tears.

Where are my tears? Mischa wondered why she still had not cried. She could not summon them. She overheard the conversations—one blended into another as she passed people, sat behind them, or stood near them— and she realized that she didn't know this woman they called her mother. Mischa could only remember discussions—short ones—about bothersome logistics. When she began high school, her mother always gave her ever-changing directives to eat or lose weight. Mischa was always told to dress better, that she didn't care how she looked, and she wouldn't find a husband if she dressed like that. They exchanged angry looks and impatient pauses. They gave each other dutiful greetings and aloof good-byes at the doorway.

Those pointless soliloquies at dinner, perhaps those were the only "conversations" she remembered. It wasn't the topics, but the style of them. The only exchanges she could remember had been about clothes.

Mischa would come home and sometimes find a blouse, a skirt, a coat, a vest, or a sweater on her bed. They were occasionally useful and pretty, but more often they seemed to her to be a veiled opinion and a suggested style change. When Mischa was in her adolescent phase of black, the items she found on her bed were grass green, raspberry red, and plum purple. When Mischa wore loose clothing, the items were tight-fitting. When Mischa wore boots and sandals, she found pumps and flats. Mischa would see them and then go downstairs to hear the inevitable "Did you see what I left you?" and deliver her "Yes, thank you," and a kiss on the cheek. The object provided material for that night's dinner table monologue. Her mother would explain where she had bought the item, the original price, the bargain price, the difficulty in finding it, and the comments by envious buyers who asked where she had found it. Her mother would follow with suggestions of how to pair the item with others in Mischa's wardrobe. "Yes, thank you," was all that Mischa ever replied. Mrs. Dunn heard nothing more than that, even when she noticed that Mischa wore her gift frequently. Her mother never heard her speak of it again, mention its usefulness, or tell how her friends wanted one just like it. All Cristina heard was the first "Yes, thank you."

When Cristina saw Mischa wearing one of her gifts, even when she was fifteen or seventeen years old, Cristina instantly returned to the memories of Mischa's smiles and excited hand clapping when she was overjoyed with a box of crayons, a dress, a storybook—one of the occasional surprise gifts that she gave Mischa. As a little girl, Mischa would hug her and excitedly kiss her several times, then beg her mother to play with her or help her put on her new dress. But when she grew older Mischa's reactions turned weary and cold.

These presents offered Mischa's mother the rare comfort of a common topic of conversation. At least Cristina had a few minutes at dinner when she could look directly into her daughter's eyes and engage with her, while her husband continued to eat, unaware and disinterested in the subject matter. Mischa's "Yes, thank you," followed by her kiss, was a brief moment of recognition for her efforts; it was an atom of affection unshared with Mischa's father, only for Cristina. It was not like the good-byes or the hellos when Mischa hugged her father a little more closely and then turned to her mother to give her a loose embrace and an air kiss. At least with the "Yes, thank you" and the accompanying kiss—sometimes a kiss on her cheek, not just the air—Mischa's mother could celebrate in having her daughter's undivided attention, if only for that moment.

A few days later, after the funeral, Mischa informed her father that she would come live with him in Washington, DC. When Mischa offered to transfer to Georgetown University and move home with her father, he was instantly grateful. He did not go through the false motion of asking her to reconsider. For the rest of her time in college she lived at home, cooking the dinners and riding with her father to the campus.

The other students had their independent lives, but living in her parents' house again, Mischa felt like a child and a mother at the same time. She could not leave her father, but she felt suffocated. The only part of her existence that seemed to breathe life into her was her seizures. They were her events, hers alone, and when she came back after a seizure to sleep, her father seemed to stop grieving for the night; the air was lighter. Mischa was the center of attention and he would care for her. By the time she graduated from college she had counted twenty-seven seizures. That was her routine. Before she left a place in life, she counted the number of seizures she had there. These simple numbers—twenty-three, nine, and now twenty-seven—were morbid mementos of places where she had lived.

While she was at Georgetown, she went through two neurologists by following her simple rule. Whenever a neurologist suggested brain surgery, it indicated that he—and invariably it was a he—had given up on her. She would look for another one, but they had all become pharmacists in her eyes. They prescribed pills, she bought them, and she took them. Sitting in the waiting room at the hospital one day, she realized that she had to move out and move on with life or these events—Curtis's suicide attempts and her mother's death—would define her forever. College had been a time for other people to experiment with freedom, but Mischa had been denied that experience. She was still a child. She decided that she would stay in Washington, DC, but move out of her father's house. She would find freedom in a room of her own.

9. THE CASTLE

November 1992

> *At a certain age, when a man is more than 40, but not much beyond 50, an inexperienced girl can be more appealing than a beautiful woman. It's that time when a man has lived his life, with success and disappointment, love and rejection. The attraction to a younger woman is a fundamental characteristic of the male mid-life crisis. With a girl he hopes to capture his lost youth. It is a craving that some men ignore, but others seek desperately to satisfy.*

THE ARTICLE, "EXPLAINING LOLITA," HAD CAUGHT HER ATTENTION AS SHE FLIPPED THROUGH THE PAGES OF A GLAMOUR MAGAZINE AT THE DRUGSTORE. *It makes sense. I can't imagine any other reason he would want to be with someone like me.*

Mischa was uncomfortably aware that she was virginal. She was invisible to men her age, who were instinctively impatient with her inexperience. Men her age didn't give her a second glance on the street. She knew it wasn't her looks. Her friends, who had boyfriends and were often the object of pick-up lines, were no more attractive than she was. But young men never tried to flirt with her while standing in line at a cash register or waiting at the bus stop. It was older men—they were intrigued. They would try to engage her in small talk. She noticed how they would stare at her longer than usual and would edge closer. Their attention made her cringe. She couldn't understand; it was as if these men could smell her naïveté. Young males had no time for it, but the older ones were captivated.

Mischa was still insecure about dealing with men of any age in any setting. Her eyes would shoot to the floor in anxiety when she spoke to a man. In her experience, she was little more than the student she had been at Mama

MIA. Her looks had improved since her time at Mama MIA, but after Curtis, there had been no one, and Curtis had lasted for only a few weeks. Mischa had no boyfriends. She didn't seek them and they didn't seek her.

"Mischa. Petra. Dunn. That's quite an exotic name." The Institute director took a paper off his desk and walked around to sit in the leather chair across from Mischa. He studied it briefly and then looked at Mischa, as if her face would provide some verification for the facts listed on her CV.

"Where does your name come from?"

"My father is a professor of Russian literature. He won the coin toss and gave me my first name. The middle one is from my Catholic mother, it's her family's patron saint, and the surname is Irish."

"Interesting enough. Your CV says that you are bilingual. Is your Spanish native?"

"Yes, my mother is—was—Chilean. I spent most of my childhood in Chile."

"Good. In this job you will have to operate fully in Spanish—speaking and writing. The president, or rather the ex-president, will be accompanied by two advisers. He prefers not to come to the Institute, so you will have his assigned office."

He continued to dictate her logistical arrangements. As she sat there in the director's office, she considered how the shelves of books went from floor to ceiling and encircled the room. Her books lay horizontal or stood vertical, with no rhyme or reason. On her shelves, philosophy and chick lit were interspersed with politics and history. Her favorites were mixed with failed purchases of books that she had stopped reading after ten or twenty pages. She wondered if the director's books were arranged alphabetically by author or by subject. Her runaway mind was pulled back by the director's sudden tone of sincere sympathy.

"Mischa, the president is a tired man. He has been through a rough time recently. Let me know if he needs anything. We want to make it easy for him."

"Yes, sir."

"Okay, why don't you go down and see my secretary."

This was too easy. It was confusing. She had simply sent her CV and asked if they might have a position available. After the interview, she realized that she must have been hired. The Woodrow Wilson International Institute for Scholars was prestigious. Scholars, statesmen, academics, and authors applied annually for fellowships to fund their biographies, studies, and novels. Each one was provided with a research assistant. Mischa had been assigned to a president who had just been ousted in a coup d'état. The director was a personal friend of the former president, who was in need of a safe haven.

At the first phone booth she could find, Mischa called her father, overjoyed that she had a job. Not only was she working for a former president, but for the one who had ordered the investigations into the military regime and set the precedent for trials of human rights violators. *Maybe one day this will happen in Chile.*

Her first duty was to collect her Library of Congress Research Card, as the secretary prescribed, so she skipped toward the white dome, giddy with her new job. *Incredible*, she thought, as she was walking down the Mall, a stretch of grass and walking paths between the Washington Monument and Capitol Hill. The dust hit her shoes as she passed mothers and fathers in sunglasses wearing T-shirts that read, "I love DC" and "THE WHITE HOUSE." Children were running with rocket balloons from the Air and Space Museum.

Mischa had moved out of her father's house two months before and had rented a room at 16th and S Streets. When she returned to the house she could now call home, she found Anne, the lady who rented out the rooms, inside her Fiesta Ware-filled kitchen, lined with colorful antique pottery she had collected from flea markets all over the U.S. The pottery was against the wall in dark oak cabinets, and Le Creuset pots squatted on the stove. She enjoyed the moments when she walked into Anne's house. It was filled with Victorian antiques, heavy velvet drapes, intricately carved mahogany chests, Oriental carpets, and a Georgian grandfather clock that rang with a deep, mellow chime. Dark portraits of Anne's White Anglo-Saxon Protestant forebears staggered up the stairs. The English antiques reminded her of her uncle's estate house on the vineyard. He was an Anglophile, as were so many Chilean aristocrats.

Anne's nineteenth-century Victorian Gothic town house was at the end of a row of terraced houses. It had a turret and looked like the corner of a castle. She was a widow, with one grown-up daughter, and she had an obvious talent for nurturing. She rented out rooms at the top of her house to young interns and professionals just starting out in Washington, DC. Anne was wealthy; she didn't seek the money, but their enthusiasm kept her young. Fledglings came in as interns and low-level bureaucrats, and then left her house once they had a paying job, inevitably visiting her later for dinner and drinks after they had become senior Senate aides, journalists for the *Washington Post*, deputy directors of think tanks, and government officials.

Mischa loved Anne's house. Every evening, she came through the door to hear a sweet chorus of crystals dangling from a petite antique pendant chandelier in a crown of gold filigree. A forest green Oriental carpet took her to a staircase heralded by mahogany pillars. Anne had a clear view of the entrance from the kitchen and greeted her with a hello and a warm smile. Mischa would smile back and wave before she ran up three flights of stairs to her sanctuary, the converted attic, with its arched ceiling, a table and a vanity/desk of heavy oak, and a brass bed. Finally, she had a room of her own. *Life suddenly feels good right now.*

When she walked into the former president's office at his home, she saw that he was not at his desk, but appeared sedated, in an armchair by a side table, under the glow of a table lamp. The curtains were drawn. When she looked closer, she could see that his eyes were vacant. He was despondent. One of his aides came forward to introduce himself. He was perhaps in his late forties and pudgy, with an abundance of soft white hair.

"We are so appreciative that you will help us in his research. This is my colleague. We are the president's political advisers."

The other aide was more than six feet tall, with curly black hair and brown Latin eyes. He radiated the confidence of a polo player, certain that he could get anything he set his mind to win. He was so glaringly handsome that it was difficult to look at him. She focused on the older adviser. The former president summoned Mischa to sit next to him and she walked over tentatively. He stood up to shake her hand and showed her to a chair beside his. When he was finished, he turned and looked to his aides to explain the nature of the research for the book the former president was going to write. They wanted to consider federalism and taxation, the growth of democracy, election observation, and global human rights trends. They were not quite sure of the direction, but were certain they would be able to work it out over the coming months.

"We are so grateful that you will be helping us. We would like to begin with human rights trends in Latin America, and then we'll move on from there," said the older aide.

Back on the street Mischa grabbed a taxi. She never understood the maps of Washington taxi zones, so when he told her it was ten dollars after they had driven for only five minutes, she stifled a sharp intake of breath. Mischa planned to move her things from a table in the Institute library to the office—her office. She hopped up the steps of the Institute and went straight to the secretary's office, where she turned in the taxi receipt and in return received the key to her office. Mischa would miss the easy access to the free tea, coffee, and muffins at the Institute library, but she was nearby. When she walked down it, she found the hallway deserted.

There was one open door and she stopped to introduce herself to her neighbor, but no one was there. There were just a few stacks of books, a computer, and pens and highlighters kept in a shiny copper cup. A few doors down she came to her office—her first office. Sunny and small, with only a desk, shelves, and a computer, its window looked out into the bright blue summer sky of Washington. She sat down and eagerly twirled around in the chair. She stopped suddenly when she heard steps. *My neighbor must be in the hallway*, she thought. Perhaps playing carousel in the office chair was not the way for a research assistant to be found by a Woodrow Wilson scholar. To be found busily arranging her office would be a more dignified sight. With the flurry of a girl arranging her new dollhouse, she began to unpack her favorite office supplies.

When she looked at the clean white walls she thought of brainstorming all over them with yellow Post-its. These sticky pieces of paper were not merely office supplies, but an integral element of Mischa's interior design. Her walls were filled with favorite quotes on Post-its more than five years old. They represented the very moment that she had come across the words. She would mark the page and run around her room to find a Post-it and a pen. Once transcribed, she stuck it to the wall. As it aged and its edges curled, she would secure it with tape. She had a collection of more than thirty. They had traveled with her from her bedroom when she was at Mama MIA, to her dorm in Boston, to her parents' home in Alexandria, and to Anne's room in Washington, DC. She now had another room of her own and another wall for her Post-its.

As she looked out her window at a cloudless sky, she was surprised to realize that she felt too warm. She saw the dome of the Museum of Natural History. Beneath it, tourists scurried up and down the steps like brightly colored ants. She was glad that she was inside an air-conditioned office on a hot and humid day like this. But gradually it began to get really warm. She put her hand over the vent and felt the ice-cold air. *Why should I be so hot?* Her senses ran between rapture and terror in seconds as she realized what was about to occur, but she could not stop it.

"Are you okay?"

She knew it had happened, but wondered how long she had been there. She had no idea who was talking to her. She kept her eyes closed while she concentrated on assessing her headache. She had begun to correlate the aftermath headache with the severity of the seizure.

"I'll be fine if you let me lie here for a moment." She opened her eyes and saw a tall man looking down at her. *He must be the one with the shiny copper cup. Perhaps twirling around in a chair might not have been the worst way to meet.*

"You had a seizure. I think you cut your lip. Here's a tissue," he said as he knelt down. He offered to call an ambulance, but Mischa assured him that this was normal; it happened regularly and she just needed to rest. He put his hand out to help her stand, and she noticed that her skirt had shifted upward and was showing a bit too much leg. She pulled it down, thankful that she had shaved her legs the day before. After a seizure, not only was the return of her sarcasm a sign that she was beginning to recover, so were petty vanities. She was either grateful or embarrassed about whether her socks matched, if she had worn a slip, or if she had shaved her underarms.

The gentle stranger was nervous and Mischa found herself doing what she always did. She tried to calm the witnesses to the seizure, while enduring a tormenting headache. When they were strangers, they had a look of trauma on their faces.

"Please don't worry. I'm okay. I suppose I should introduce myself. I'm Mischa Dunn and I have epilepsy." It was a line that she always used with strangers. The juxtaposition of a mundane introduction with the intimate confession of a serious medical condition was absurd and made people feel instantly at ease, especially when delivered with a sly smile. It made them laugh, and he was no exception.

"I'm Stanley Phillips. I'm your neighbor down the hall. Let me at least get you some water." He left and came back, genuinely worried, and gave her the paper cup. She hadn't realized how thirsty she was and drank it down in one gulp. He left swiftly and returned with a second cup. She did the same and he brought a third, at which point they both laughed and he, with evident relief, could tell that she was fully recovered.

"Thank you, uh…"

"Stanley."

"Please don't be insulted if I don't remember your name tomorrow. Well, if you'll excuse me, I think I'll wrap things up for today and take a taxi home."

"Let me take you down to the street at least." Stanley took her briefcase and they went down the stairs. Mischa wanted to avoid the reception desk. She could imagine that she looked haggard and it might invite questions. He flagged down a taxi and she took her briefcase and thanked him.

When Mischa came through the heavy oak door, she looked up to the gold filigree pendant chandelier, grateful to hear the cheerful greeting of tinkling crystal. She dragged herself up the stairs, threw her briefcase on the bed and lay down. Another seizure. How many since she had come to live with Anne? She could not remember; she did not want to count them now.

As she lay in bed, she could tell that her headache had completed its metamorphosis and now had entered the third stage. The first stage occurred while she was regaining consciousness and answering questions shortly after a seizure. It would last for a few hours. It was the repeated strikes of a hammer against her skull. Sometimes the hammer was muffled; sometimes it came down so hard that she thought it would crack her skull. The second stage was longer: the slow and constant squeeze of her brain in a vise. The first two stages were oppressive, but they were outside forces and therefore forgivable.

The third stage of the headache felt like a betrayal. Her brain transformed into a sadist and she fell victim to its creative cruelty. Random glass shards would spontaneously generate, at the front, the side, the bottom, on her crown. If she lay down, they were still, but remained in her head, instantly ready to attack at any hint of movement. It was painful when they were there, but it was worse when they began to leave, for each one possessed the intensity of a glass splinter piercing the skin.

In this stage, the pain was magnified and in slow motion. The exit of a single jagged shard was not the end, but the foretelling of the lacerating escape of hundreds, torn and pulled out, one by one. Lying in bed, she wished she could enter a dark room to howl and crush the glass into a fine dust. There was only one escape: to plead herself to sleep.

When she was shown into the former president's office, she saw him in the armchair, sitting in abject despair. His aide fluttered around him like a mother caring for a sick child. All the books, her background papers, and her research plans were toys meant to amuse the former president. When she came in, the Polo Player aide would rush to help her set them down on one of the towers of books that were slowly beginning to populate the room. He no longer looked at Mischa in a way that made her feel like easy prey, for she had become more of a visiting niece. The aides would try to amuse the former president by searching through the stack of books to read an interesting passage out loud. She joined their efforts to lift him out of his depression.

To the aides' surprise, the former president would respond with warm smiles of appreciation whenever she arrived. Mischa could only attribute it to the chipped tooth phenomenon. Over her lifetime, Mischa had chipped teeth during her seizures. One or two were evident, others were not so obvious. Despite all her mother's pleadings, she refused to have cosmetic dentistry, so she learned to smile in a way that did not show her teeth. But sometimes, when she was unguarded, she smiled widely and those imperfect teeth were on full display. People told her they liked her smile. She thought, after a time, that they appreciated the fact that she had submitted herself to undue ridicule for the sake of a smile.

When she came into his office, the former president gallantly walked over to give her a kiss on the cheek before returning to his armchair to hear a summary of her research efforts, like a patient grandfather. Mischa came to understand that they had no plans to write a book. She was just a prop, but she enjoyed the research and did not mind the theater of it all.

She alternated between the office and the Institute library, carrying her yellow legal pads and manila folders and roller ball pens. Stanley would come in occasionally when she was having her tea and say hello. Then, after an hour he would come in again, and she would smile. He seemed to tiptoe around her. His nervousness made her feel that she should reassure him. Perhaps he was scared that she would have another seizure. Perhaps he was concerned and wanted to check on her. Then he stammered a question one day.

"Mischa, would…you…like to…see a movie with me?"

"Sure, what's playing?"

"I think there's a movie theater in Georgetown. We could leave after work and grab something to eat at a restaurant on the way."

"That would be nice. Shall we go tonight?" she suggested, without hesitation.

He was taken aback by her spontaneity, but pleased. "Certainly. I think I'll be done by five, if that's okay with you. We can take a taxi to Georgetown."

She looked at him more closely now. Stanley was just one of many seizure witnesses over the course of her life. Her seizure witnesses were a class unto themselves. They were not individual men or women, but faces of kindness and sympathy. They helped her, they sometimes pitied her, and they made great efforts to show that they accepted her. She would show them that she could function normally, put them at ease, express her appreciation for their help, and continue on with her life.

But in the restaurant, as she looked at him she wondered, *Am I on a date? Am I on a date with a man over twenty years older than me?*

Removing him from that bland, genderless seizure witness category, she considered her history of dating. The first one had been to the high school prom with Sophie's rude and obese brother. Of course, those few weeks with Curtis before the suicide attempt were memorable for their aftermath. Then, there was no one. She was certain that she wasn't remotely in Stanley's league of attractiveness. He was tall, blond, calm, and confident; a professor of classics at Yale. Over dinner he explained that he had received a yearlong fellowship, but he planned to stay for only six months. He had to return New Haven for classes and personal reasons. He wasn't boastful; he was genuinely humble as he answered her questions about his career that included fellowships to Oxford, visiting professorships at Harvard and Stanford, and conferences in France and Australia. There was even a hint of guilt that these accomplishments had come so easily. No doubt he was the object of a few student crushes. He was so casual. She almost had to convince herself to be nervous with him, which was how she thought she should feel, because when she forgot, conversation came so easily.

The next day, when Mischa passed his office, he leapt up immediately, came to his door, and stammered another invitation. It finally struck Mischa that it wasn't a "being nice to the epileptic" gesture; he was actually interested in her. She had a hard time believing it because she had not even applied to an Ivy League university, knowing she would never be accepted. Finally, her most damning reason for why she would never have thought he would like her: *He belongs on a Beach Boys album cover. He is so...so...white. Why does he want to date me?*

They went to a movie again and to dinner afterward. She would ask questions about his work and he would answer. He was not patronizing. She did not feel stupid with him. The waiter brought a bottle of sparkling water. When he twisted the cap the water sprayed and Stanley's glasses were wet from the shower. His glasses were perhaps two decades out of style and looked as if they belonged in an early Woody Allen film, or even to Woody Allen himself. It lent Stanley an air of disinterest in the way he looked or the appearance of a lack of style. Mischa wasn't certain, but she realized that she had never really looked at him until that night, when he took off the glasses to dry them. She stared at the man's face—not the seizure witness, but the man sitting across from her. She couldn't hide her growing curiosity and confusion.

Why would a man who looks like THAT want to be with ME? Wait. Oh my God, I've never thought of it. He's a professor. Am I suffering from a Freudian complex? What is it? It's not Oedipus, Electra, something. Wait, wait, this is NOT my fault, I did NOT seek him out. I'm young enough to be one of his students. WAIT, am I some kind of sick academic fantasy? Is this what they do on a fellowship, date someone young enough to be a student? Didn't the Police do a song about this?

"Mischa, is anything wrong? Did you get wet, too?"

"No, no, no, I'm fine. I'm just trying to figure out what to order." She hurriedly picked up the menu.

Stanley put his glasses on again and laughed at himself, water splattered across his shirt, while the waiter hurriedly replaced the dishes and continued to apologize. Earlier, she had wanted to escape in a taxi, but his laughter had put her at ease again. She gazed at him and he could tell that she looked at him differently tonight.

There were more dinners and movies. She kept trying to justify his interest in her. Perhaps he was attracted by the almost forbidden nature of the relationship—the age difference. At night Mischa kissed Stanley's cheek when they said good-bye, the same way she always kissed Sophie and all her other friends. Mischa would walk to the Metro or take a taxi home. After a month Stanley invited her back to his basement apartment under one of those Victorian attached houses. He had rented it for the time he was in DC on his fellowship, and he apologized for its state. It was a cavern, ascetic and spare, with books stacked neatly against the wall. The shoes of passersby could be seen through the window to the street.

They sat on the sofa and he offered her a glass of mineral water. Stanley put the water on the table and came closer. He put his glasses on the table and pushed her hair behind her ears. Later, when she thought of that night—in hospitals, in the shower, in a train, in a car, in bed, or in the office—she would cringe from embarrassment, remembering how she had trembled.

As he held her, Mischa berated herself, *Why don't I know what to do next?* She had kissed only two men—or rather, boys—in her life. She was sixteen for her first kiss and nineteen for her second. Two lips facing two lips. Clumsy and awkward. She had seen more passionate, imaginative ways of kissing in the movies, but never thought they would happen in her life. Stanley put his hands around her waist and pulled her closer. Her stomach muscles tightened, but somehow she remained calm. He gently choreographed her movements, turning her head one way to glide his face under her chin. He took her unsteady hands and guided them to his back. She wanted to kiss him, but she stayed still.

"Hold me, just hold me," he said softly. Was it an hour, or maybe a half hour, she could not remember, but she removed herself from that trance to stand up and say in a perfunctory voice, "Stanley, it's been a lovely evening. I think I have to go home." Confused, but not irritated, he offered to take her back. She asked him only to accompany her to the street to catch a taxi. It was evident that she wasn't angry, and he wasn't offended. She decided it should end like that, tonight.

They met often in their offices and would walk to the Library of Congress or have lunch at nearby coffee shops. Mischa might spend the day at the library, but the next day she would be there and they might spend a few minutes in the Institute library with coffee.

Stanley asked Mischa home again one night after a concert. It was a query always made and the answer was never assumed. After a while, she would stand up gradually and that would be the signal for him to get her coat and accompany her to the street to get a taxi, where she would give him a kiss on the cheek before she stepped inside. One night, after they were on the sofa for far longer than an hour, Stanley asked if they could go to the bedroom. It seemed natural, so she followed. She sat on the bed, still in her black pencil skirt. He went around the side and started to pull back the sheets. She could not look at him directly; her eyes circled the room and settled on her toes.

"You're not going to believe this, but don't laugh. Stanley, I'm a virgin. And it's not that I'm not ready. It's that I don't want to, and I don't want it to be you." He was silent. He knew it wasn't a joke. The last few weeks had given him enough reason to believe her. Mischa wondered whether he was going to suggest that she go home. He didn't want to let her go, not just yet.

"Don't worry, we can lie here. We won't do anything you don't want to do."

Mischa tucked her chin into her chest. She was embarrassed, but proud of herself. He wasn't the one. She trusted her instincts. They had taken her this far, after all. They were the same ones that had told her that she would drown if she stayed with Curtis. But she did want to stay with Stanley for the night, so Mischa put her head on his shoulder and fell asleep in her pencil skirt, with his arms around her.

10. THE COLOSSEUM

AS HE LAY THERE, STANLEY WONDERED WHETHER HE WAS RIGHT TO STAY WITH HER. Maybe this was too much, too quickly, for her. Mischa was in her mid-twenties. He was in his mid-forties. That was a large age gap. He had never dated a woman so much younger than himself. Mentally and physically she was a woman, but sexually she was a child. This naïveté was disturbing, and yet, he had to admit, compelling. She didn't believe she was attractive; she didn't understand her leverage. There were no games and yet this innocence was incredibly seductive. He wondered how she had managed to stay this way throughout college.

As he lay there with her in his arms, he told himself to be careful. There were only a few months left in Washington, and then it was back to his real life. He had to handle Mischa with care. He could not give her any hope, but he did not want to let her go. It was all so exhilarating; he felt as if he were sixteen again. His greatest obligation to Mischa was to do her no emotional harm. He did not doubt that he was Mischa's first relationship.

When they came to the apartment, it was the only place where she would kiss him. She only held his hand when they walked in the street. When Mischa said good-bye she would kiss his cheek, but every time they crossed the threshold she was a little bolder, a little more passionate, a little more ready, a little needier. He was more aware. He could pace her and lead her by keeping her away or drawing her closer. They would make their way to the sheets, just lying together and kissing in a room hardly the size of a walk-in closet. Sometimes Mischa wished he were the one, but she pulled back. He was never angry or frustrated, and retreated at the slightest signal that he was too close or moving too fast. She never doubted that this would all end once he returned to New Haven.

Mischa did not know whether he had been a partner, a husband, a father, or a boyfriend. She was certain that he didn't live alone. There were small hints. The sheets and the comforters that he brought from home had a touch of the feminine: pastels, flowers, and curled patterns. They were chosen by a person with a certain taste. The ones he had bought for himself in DC were different. He had once said, "I'm not very good at this. I don't usually make the coffee." She left it alone and never questioned him. He was with her at a time when she wanted to be with him. She had no expectations for anything further.

One night, staring at the ceiling only three feet above them, Stanley said, "Mischa, I hope you don't take this the wrong way." He hesitated. "I was doing some research, just in my spare time, on epilepsy. It's not much. I was looking into the origins and its history, from a Western perspective. The word itself, epilepsy, is derived from the Greek verb *epilambanein,* which means 'to seize' and 'to attack.'"

Mischa looked over at him strangely, as it was an odd interruption. She was flattered by his interest.

He continued, "You see, the word *epilambanein* was used to describe the condition since these attacks were attributed to a demon or deity who 'seized' the person. I looked into its historical context in Ancient Greece, and also a little bit about the history of its pathogenesis and etiology. Anyway, I collected some of the research and put it together for you."

He left the bedroom and came back with a binder holding a collection of photocopied articles from academic journals and books. "I thought you would like them. It's a gift." It was not a bouquet of flowers, it was a more touching show of affection. They lay back on the pillows and looked through some of the articles as Stanley spoke.

"The condition was associated with Artemis. Do you know who she is?"

"Diana was the Roman goddess of the hunt and the moon or something, and I think she was derived from Artemis, the Greek goddess?"

"That's right. Artemis was a virgin goddess. Epilepsy was an affliction associated with her."

"Really?" She started laughing. "Stanley, is this a not-so-veiled reference to my status and a suggestion for a cure?"

"Please!" He laughed and pleaded, "Really, Mischa, you cannot believe that I would say something like that."

"I don't know," she smiled. "Maybe this kind of pick-up line works for classics scholars. Like, 'You remind me of a Greek goddess I researched for my dissertation,' or, 'I went to Delphi and the Oracle said we're made for each other.' Oh yes, and, 'Your Parthenon or mine?'" She was crying with laughter at her own corny jokes. "How about—"

"Wait, Mischa, come on, give me a chance. I haven't finished. The condition was also associated with goats. Hecate, who is the goddess of death, lizards, menstrual cycles, and garlic, was as much associated with epilepsy as Artemis. You could also say I'm comparing you to a clove of garlic. Oh, wait, here's a touch of the disgusting. If you ever saw an epileptic near the Colosseum, he probably wasn't there for the show. Ancient Romans were convinced that gladiator's blood was a cure. It's all in here, my dear—the good, the bad, and the ugly. I'm not giving you a line. Seriously. You can't believe that."

"Stanley, it's fine. Even if you call me a goddess of death, virginity, a lizard, or a goat, you have made me feel fascinating. Really, I love it. Thank you."

Mischa swept up from behind him, put her arms around his chest. She rested her chin on his shoulder to look at the binder. Despite the surroundings, Stanley was in his college lecture mode, concentrating on the papers and tying to make sure that the tabs matched the table of contents.

"The best books I found were Owsei Temkin's *The Falling Sickness.* Also, I found some different translations—rather, excerpts—of Hippocrates' *Diseases of Women.* I would really recommend them as a start, but even beyond Ancient Greece, there is a fascinating history to the condition. And it's interesting that you mentioned the Oracle at Delphi, because that was a woman who was believed to have breathed in a brew of special herbs in order to induce seizures for the sake of a prophecy."

He continued contemplating his research aloud.

"It was a condition suffered—I mean, several historic figures had epilepsy. Temporal lobe epilepsy, which is what you told me was your form of epilepsy, is really intriguing. Socrates, Fyodor Dostoyevsky, Lenin, Nobel, Saint Teresa de Avila, Julius Caesar, Saint Paul, Joan of Arc, and van Gogh are thought to have had the same type. The research is by no means exhaustive, but I thought you would like to see it."

He leafed through the binder and stopped every so often to confirm that articles were in the appropriate place. "So, Mischa, what do you think?" After a few minutes of silence he looked over and saw Mischa lying in his sheets. He dropped the binder on the floor and turned off the light.

Stanley left the Institute before winter. On a park bench where Mischa and Stanley said good-bye, he gave her a small Roman coin: *L Rutillius,*

Flaccus, AR denarius, circa 77 BC. She did not tell him that she understood the arrangement; she did not expect any letters or calls. She had had time with someone she trusted, so that when it mattered she understood how a relationship could work.

A few years later, Mischa was in Washington, DC, still renting a room in Anne's house. She had left the Institute to work for a human rights organization. When she came home after a protest rally, she saw a package addressed to her under the tinkling chandelier. The postmark was New Haven and Stanley's name was in the corner. She ran upstairs and tore it open in her room. It was the book he had been writing when he was at the Institute. On the title page he had written, *For Mischa, whose rare combination of intelligence, grace, and spirit I have had the pleasure to know.*

She had survived both Curtis and Stanley without resentment or unfulfilled wishes. Stanley was the first man to make her feel brilliant and beautiful. She considered herself lucky the day she left him. Those lonely, empty years in high school and college now appeared to be a combination of fate and good judgment. She leafed through the book, *Women and Power: The Matriarchs of Ancient Greek Tragedy* by Stanley Phillips. It was not for subway reading. It would end up in one of her horizontal piles of books that were used as bookends, but for now she put it on her night table and smiled when she turned off the light.

11. THE SUBWAY

THE BOOK DROPPED FROM THE MAN'S HANDS AND HE BEGAN TO JERK.
The sound of his teeth chattering uncontrollably was like a multitude of
knives tapping against plates. When his body slammed to the floor of the
subway car, an invisible force pulled at him frantically and his body was
contorted in violent convulsions. His eyes stared wildly, like a victim in a
horror movie who has seen his killer seconds before his own slaughter. He
might have been a pitiful figure but for his hands, which became claws,
ripping and slashing at some unseen prey. The whole event occurred within
five minutes, but each one seemed like an hour.

Mischa was transfixed by the man at her feet. As the other passengers
moved back in fear she stood there, over him, watching him. Gradually he
began to stop seizing, and like a fish just caught, he flopped and twitched
before he lay unconscious and still. Above the silence, a nervous voice
pleaded for help on the emergency subway phone. A woman passed Mischa
a tissue and she knelt down, put his head on her lap, and wiped the blood
and drool from his chin.

The blood that fell onto his yellow silk tie turned into brown stains
that continued to billow. On his shirt pocket his initials were embroidered
with precise black thread: JGR. His white shirt, which a dry-cleaner had
pressed impeccably crisp, was stained with bright red splotches. As she
examined his lifeless face she recalled the salty, metal taste of blood after a
seizure. *His tongue will hurt for days. He will be a walking migraine. This is why
people go speechless. This is why they look at me like that when I wake up. That's
what happens. He's…that's me.*

Mischa handed his belongings to one of the medics who carried the man
out on a stretcher. The barrister briefcase was made of expensive maroon
leather with the gentleman's initials, JGR, embossed tastefully in gold,
just above the clasp. After the subway doors closed, a robotic voice broke
the silence and announced the next station as the train rushed through the
tunnel.

People parted to allow Mischa to return to her seat. The space next to her, where JGR had been sitting, was left empty, though the car was full and people were standing. Shocking, frightening, pitiful, horrible, and disgusting were the words the passengers used to describe the event to others, after they left the subway.

Mischa sat still, trapped in her epiphany. The same lady who had given her the tissue for the man quietly passed her another tissue and pointed to the blood on Mischa's fingers. *Who would have known? He's just a white man in a dark pin-striped suit. Maybe he's a lawyer. This town is full of them. I would never have known.*

Mischa tried to remember a number from a pamphlet that a doctor had given her years ago. *Wasn't that the same neurologist who told me about Dostoyevsky and Van Gogh being epileptics? That was the same guy who said I was smarter than a ditchdigger. That man was probably smarter than a ditchdigger.* As much as she had wanted to throw away the pamphlet that day, she could not help but read it on the ride home. There was nothing to talk about with her mother. *Millions of people. Three and fifty. Three million and fifty million. That was it. Three million people in the U.S. have epilepsy. Fifty million people in the world have epilepsy. I'm just one. I just met another person with epilepsy. Maybe I've met others. I just never knew it. They never knew about me.* After five stops, she arrived at her destination. When the subway car doors opened Mischa knew she would never see him again.

Mischa considered herself lucky for tonight's dinner date. Sophie was always in a good mood, and could make her forget the events in the DC subway. Mischa obediently stayed on the right side of the escalator steps as it rose to the Dupont Circle and 16th Street exit from the subway. Washingtonians understood that the left side was the fast lane reserved for those who wanted to rush their trip on the escalator by walking. She was late, but she needed a few more minutes to compose herself before she met Sophie, so she stayed on the right.

It had been three years since they had graduated from university. Mischa had finished her college years in Washington, at Georgetown with her father, and stayed for her job at the Woodrow Wilson Institute. After that she began working in the Human Rights Advocacy Forum, a non-governmental organization (NGO) that had its headquarters in Washington, DC. Sophie had gone to study in Texas for college and law school. Mischa was afraid that the culture shift from the East Coast to the South would separate them. Mischa was scared that she would lose Sophie, since the American South was not merely geography, but a state of mind. When they spoke on the telephone she had detected a Texas drawl developing in Sophie's voice. She was relieved when Sophie came to DC to do her master's at George Washington University. They met at Zorba's on Dupont Circle every week for a gyro and fries. It was as if they had never parted since Mama MIA.

Over dinner they could fall into Spanish and exchange stories about hockey games, typewriters, and Sophie's despair at ever finding a boyfriend she would like and her parents would approve of. Her mother expressed her preference for someone white and Catholic. Her father preferred a Hispanic Catholic. Therefore, Sophie was on a quest for the lowest common denominator—a Spanish-speaking Catholic. Mischa could talk about her late mother and Sophie would listen with sympathy, not pity. It was that consideration that she appreciated most in Sophie. She understood that Mischa didn't want a shoulder to cry on, but someone to listen for a few minutes before moving on.

Mischa was happy to see Sophie's transformation after law school. Sophie's eyes no longer darted sideways when she saw a beautiful blonde girl. In fact, while they were sitting under the fountain at Dupont Circle one summer day, she looked around at the people on the grass and observed how white people resembled raw pastry dough. She told Mischa that, despite her father's white heritage, she should count herself lucky for having inherited more of her mother's features and color.

When Sophie arrived at her chosen university in Texas, she found herself at home. Hispanics were everywhere. Latin culture dominated the campus and the state. Mischa envied her experience. For Mischa, college had been an incubator. There had been no real growth, no awakening. She felt as if she had lived four years inside a plastic bubble.

When Mischa arrived at the top of the escalator, she found herself facing the Krispy Kreme shop pointing to Dupont Circle. She must have come out the wrong exit. She had meant to come out on Q Street. She crossed over the Circle, and looked at the homeless men playing chess against each other and against geeks with their sleeves rolled up and their ties loosened. It was a warm day, and already boys were lying on the grass with their navy blue blazers next to them. The girls were wiggling their toes in their hose, their sensible pumps thrown onto the grass.

On a mild summer's night, if you were a twenty- or thirty-something, Dupont Circle was the place to be. You could get drunk on Capitol Hill, but if you wanted a nice dinner and a walk, you went to Dupont. It didn't offer wild and raucous bars, but a polite good time. Office life was social life and a journalist could gather inside information just by eavesdropping on the conversations of relaxing policy wonks. Dupont was also the gay neighborhood in DC. DINK (double income, no kid) gay couples made the nineteenth-century brownstones elegant and edgy, with the dedication of parents decorating a nursery. In pursuit of DINK pockets, European bakeries, independent bookshops, exotic tea houses, coffee shops, boutiques, and ethnic restaurants were interspersed with embassies and law offices.

Even from a block away she could see Sophie gleaming and waving madly when she spotted Mischa waiting under the awning at Kramerbooks.

"You will never guess what happened to me today!" shouted Sophie with glee, as she literally jumped up and down.

"Tell me, I won't waste your time." Mischa was laughing and so happy to see her. The events of the last hour were already swept away.

"I jogged with the president!" exclaimed Sophie.

"What?"

"Mischa, can you believe it?"

Sophie told her that she was in the library that morning when the dean came to a table of students. He explained that he was a personal friend of the president, and the White House had called. They wanted to set up a photo opportunity with the press and needed some college students to jog with the president, just around the reflecting pool near the Washington Monument. The White House press office wanted to frame a health and fitness initiative that the president was set to launch that week.

"Sophie, this is incredible! You have got to be kidding!"

"NO! I promise! We were given one hour to change into sweat suits and come back to the library, and the Secret Service drove us to the site."

"Wait, wait, hold on. Sophie, you hate exercise. You don't jog, you don't go to the gym. You don't do anything physical. You didn't even vote for the president!"

"They didn't ask whether or not I voted for him. They asked if I wanted to jog with him. Hell, *chica,* I don't hold puritanical party views about fraternizing with the enemy. This is the president of the United States. We were told to wear dark solid colors. No bright blue or red—that was what the president was going to wear. I didn't have dark sweatpants so I ran in pajama bottoms, *lo puedes creer?* I still think he's a fool, but how could I have missed this opportunity? *Por favor,* come on, you probably would have jogged with Reagan in the same situation if you were asked." Mischa and Sophie had started walking to Zorba's, the favorite of interns and low-paid twenty-somethings.

"Okay, okay, so how many of you were running with him?"

"Five."

"Only five of you running next to the president of the United States?"

"Well, no, I was a little behind. The rest of them were too fast. The president might be overweight, but boy, he can run. I was out of breath and the Secret Service men offered to take me the rest of the way in the one of the four-by-fours that followed the president."

"No, Sophie. You are kidding me! You've got to be!"

"I climbed in, I just couldn't go any further. When we came closer to the White House I decided to make another go at it, for the last three blocks. Jimmy and Bob came to run with me."

"Excuse me, Jimmy and Bob? Sophie, you're on first-name basis with the Secret Service?"

"Yeah, well, but I didn't get their numbers. Anyway, I'm such an obese, out-of-shape idiot. Even after riding in the car, I was already out of breath after one block."

"Sophie...stop! Stop...I can't take anymore...wait." Mischa was crying with laughter so much that her stomach hurt.

"No, no, Mischa! It gets better! You will not believe this, but for the rest of the way, Jimmy and Bob, in their black suits and sunglasses, were running next to me, cheering me on, shouting, 'You can do it, come on,' and chanting, 'SO-PHIE! SO-PHIE! SO-PHIE!' Two other Secret Service agents were cheering me on from inside the four-by-four. When I got to the back gate at the White House, the president had already gone in. The other joggers were downing water and juice that some White House intern had brought out. Then the Secret Service drove us back to the GWU library."

"Stop, Sophie! You are crazy! How do these things always happen to you?"

"Don't worry, story's over. That was my adventure for the day. So what did you do?"

Their laughing descended from hysterics to giggles as they continued. It was their turn in line; Mischa and Sophie ordered a gyro, moussaka, and baklava to share. As they waited to the side, Mischa chuckled. She felt as if she had been on a rowing machine for the last ten minutes, her stomach hurt so much from contracting in laughter.

They took their trays outside. The place was already crammed with diners eating at the tables covered with blue-and-white checked plastic cloths. Sophie and Mischa dissected every detail of the story. People sitting a few feet away stopped talking, their forks hanging in midair en route from their plates to their mouths as they tried to hear more of the story. They were not really eavesdropping; Mischa and Sophie wanted an audience. After all, they were part of the DC scene of enthusiastic policy wonks, nerds with anecdotes that proved that they were only a few degrees of separation from the center of power.

12. THE OFFICE

August 1993

MISCHA CHOSE NOT TO DAMPEN THE MOOD THAT NIGHT BY TELLING SOPHIE ABOUT THE EPILEPTIC ON THE SUBWAY. On the walk home she could think of nothing else but JGR. For the entire week he invaded her brain. Every detail came under scrutiny.

Ditchdiggers do not wear pin-striped suits. Look at the quality of his suit and the briefcase; he must have had a job of some responsibility. Did his colleagues know about his epilepsy? He was wearing a wedding ring; how did his wife deal with his seizures? Did he have children; did they ever see him have a seizure? How long has he had epilepsy? How many seizures does he have a month? Is he epileptic or was this a first-time seizure? What does he do? How much does he earn? Did he throw away the shirt and the tie when he got home? What book was he reading? Did someone pick it up and put it in his briefcase or give it to the medic? Was the yellow tie a gift from someone, maybe one of his kids? Where was he from? Were all his attacks grand mal? Was it epilepsy, or perhaps the first sign of a tumor or some other abnormality? Could that have been his first seizure? Did he tell his family what happened or just call his wife from the hospital and tell her that he was working late? Will he be pestered with questions like, "Did you take your medicine?" Where does he live? What does the medicine do to him? What is he taking? What will he be thinking when he is alone in the hospital and realizes that he had a seizure? How long will it take him to regain consciousness? Will he try to remember where he was when it happened? Will he talk about it to someone afterward? Does he get mad at himself after he has a seizure? Does he try to forget them?

"Ground control to Mischa. Ground control to Mischa." Becky caught Mischa staring at her computer, while photographs of the Andes drifted across the screen.

"What? Oh. Sorry, Becky. Do you need something?"

"Where's the third funding proposal?"

Mischa sat up straight. "I'm working on the final one." She touched a key so that the draft would appear, but it was too late to look like a busy worker bee. After all, Becky had caught her in a daze staring at Mt. Illimani. "I put the other two on your desk so that you could run through them while I finish this one."

"I wanted to see them together."

"Sorry, I thought you told me to have them to you by the end of the day. I'm almost done."

"You're getting sloppy, Mischa. Father Roy Brady is coming in Thursday afternoon. He needs to see a draft of the proposal going to the Ford Foundation—human rights training for the military—the one you haven't done yet. Get on it. I want to be able to go through a few drafts before we give it to him."

As a team leader in the Human Rights Advocacy Forum, Becky worked for the masses yearning to break free from cruel authoritarian regimes, yet her standard tool for management was the humiliation of subordinates. Not only was Mischa made to feel like an idiot, but any small accomplishment was dismissed and attributed to Becky as an achievement in spite of Mischa.

The years in the Forum taught Mischa that not everyone working on human rights was nice. Frankly, she concluded, there were some real bastards. She wondered whether it was worse in the private sector. She thought it was probably the same; it was just that the self-righteousness and hypocrisy seemed to magnify the vices of office politics inside an NGO. The juxtaposition made it feel worse.

Mischa was a pathological office slob. Her desk was a mess, and though no one else knew where to find files, she could always pull the exact one needed. That ability was the single thread of credibility to make others see her mess as an enigmatic order. Her first real paying job was an inconvenient time to discover that she was a technophobe. She came close to anxiety attacks when the copier broke down. Mischa also kept deleting e-mails accidentally, and her computer files kept moving into other files inadvertently when she moved the mouse, suddenly disappearing from the list.

Mischa's counterpart on the South American team, Ricardo, was a technophile with a flawless filing system and a desk so clean it seemed to spit its tongue at her from across the room. Not only did her flaws magnify Ricardo's virtues, but his team loved him. He was the office puppy. Mischa felt like an abused pet. Out of desperation, Mischa asked Ricardo how he organized himself. She thought that maybe she could learn something. He gleefully took on this opportunity to display his genius and squeezed her in for a two-fifteen appointment.

In the midst of his explanation about the necessary ratio of distance between the computer, the in-box, and the phone, Mischa arrived at the diagnosis of Ricardo's obsessive-compulsive disorder. Recognizing this touch of insanity provided instant relief. Maybe this was what she had sought. She wanted to see his absurdity in freakish detail so that she would feel better for it.

His sermon on the virtues of Post-its segued into a paean on the merits of using pink, green, and yellow highlighters. Mischa sank deeper and deeper into herself. She looked at the calendar he showed her and could taste the sweetness of pink, the bitterness of green, and the tang of yellow. She started to taste them again, and put her hand forward to touch the colors as they swam from the paper toward her. They twirled like ribbons around her. They began to twist, then bind and gag, as she was dragged into a whirlpool of color and light.

She looked up and could see people going about their business. The scene was surreal. She stayed on the floor, closed her eyes, and decided to sleep. Mischa awoke to an aching back and a headache drilling her brain. She felt a throbbing in her arms, and knew they would turn black and blue within a day. There were books and boxes piled nearby. They had been on the shelf. She must have been in the way while she was unconscious; otherwise, Ricardo would have put them back on the shelves. A half hour or more passed before Mischa looked up again, barely opening her eyelids to see her office mates continuing as normal.

Maybe, Mischa thought, after all these seizures in public places, she had turned into an epileptic diva. She expected to be awakened to concerned, compassionate, sympathetic faces of people who would turn their jackets into pillows, hold her hand until she recovered, run to get her water, and help her stand up by offering their hands. The office knew that she had epilepsy, but she had never had a seizure in here before. She told them that she had tonic-clonic seizures, and gave them first aid information on how to react.

Mischa slowly stood up. One of the interns, who was in his second week, came over to help her. Ricardo said from his desk, "Hope you're okay. Let's take a rain check and I can explain my system next week."

Others suggested that she go home, smiled momentarily, and turned back to their computer monitors. She picked up her bags and went down to catch a taxi, counting the steps as she went so that she would not trip.

When Mischa arrived at home, she didn't even look up to see the tinkling crystal; she went directly to bed. She slept for three hours and woke up to cook her comfort food of noodles and butter. While waiting for the water to boil, she rang the neurologist's office. A patient had just pulled out at the last minute, so Dr. Golden had a free time slot for tomorrow. *What a thrill.* It was as if she had called the concierge of a five-star Michelin restaurant and acquired a reservation as a result of a last-minute cancellation. Usually, she had to wait two weeks for these ten-minute appointments. It was almost worthwhile having the seizure because she could get her prescription written faster. Maybe she could ask him for a few months' worth of medication.

Mischa was always nervous in her last month of medication and acquired squirrel-like habits of hoarding pills in different spots. She could always be assured that she had random pills running loose in the pockets of a few of her purses; she put some in the spice cabinet, and some in her jewelry box. She never wanted to have all those pills in one place or think that once she had come to the end of the bottle there was nothing left. The knowledge that there were always some, somewhere else, made her more comfortable. There were always a few pills around so that even if she forgot to get her prescription filled, she had about a week's worth of anti-convulsants in her home.

"So, what happened to you, Mischa? How are we getting along with seizure control?"

"I had a grand mal seizure. It's about the eighth one this year, I think."

"Perhaps we should start logging them. Did anyone witness it?"

"Yes, pretty much the entire office."

"Did you have an aura, any premonition that it would occur?"

"Yes, I did, but it was so close to the actual seizure that I couldn't do anything about it—like tell the person next to me or get on the floor or find a place to lie down. I was paralyzed."

"What is your aura like?"

"It has differed over the years. Sometimes, it's nausea and dizziness and sudden warmth. The more interesting auras are hard to describe and they vary. It's an acute awareness of the specific, a sudden obsession with detail.

I can see it, smell it, touch it, but I'm in one place. Then I'm usually overwhelmed by some object, often some form of light, and I feel powerless. But auras can be mundane as well. I have nausea maybe a day in advance, and it's the same kind of feeling as from eating bad fish or too much sugar, or having the flu. It's not exclusive to the epilepsy, so I don't take it as a signal."

"The auras describe the symptoms of someone with temporal lobe epilepsy."

"Yes, well, Doctor, that's in my records. That was what I was diagnosed with when I was fourteen, and there are a few tests in there that verify your observation."

He thought of her as another patient with an attitude. How many of these would he have to deal with in a week? Then he said, "Good point, Ms. Dunn. So, what did the witnesses see?"

"I called the office, and they explained that I screamed, fell to the floor, convulsed for about three or five minutes, and then I went blue."

"Where did you fall?"

"On my back."

"Did one side of your body move?"

"I don't remember, or rather, I didn't ask him." *What does it mean if one or all sides of my body moved?* "I was convulsing all over. No one really noticed."

"If we knew, we might be able to determine the origin of your seizures more precisely. I really think you should be considering brain surgery, but let me see your back."

She took off her shirt. *Thank God I wore a bra today.*

"Your back is entirely bruised, it's black and blue. And so is your arm."

"Yes. They told me that I fell from my chair in the office, hit the photocopy machine, and a box of print cartridges and some books fell on me, and my arm knocked against a bookcase. Anyway, that is what the guy told me."

He looked closely and lifted her arm. "Are you in a relationship with someone? Do you have a boyfriend or a husband?"

"No."

"Are you living at home?"

"No. Excuse me, what do these questions have to do with my seizure?"

"Your bruises indicate that you have been badly beaten. While you may have had a seizure, I need to examine all the possibilities."

"Dr. Golden, it's not that I MAY have had a seizure. Doctor, I HAD a seizure. Bruises? I've had bruises throughout my life. I've had scratches, torn tongues, broken wrists, twisted ankles, and black eyes. You name it. It's not a boyfriend, a husband, or a father, it's my epilepsy. MY seizures. I would like to have the prescription now."

"I'm just doing what is responsible. I am required to look into all possibilities, and these bruises are extensive. I don't think that one seizure could have caused them."

"Well, try falling down on a photocopy machine, then the edge of a bookcase, onto a concrete floor, and writhing about while office chairs and books fall on you, and you might understand."

"Let me take a look here at your current medication."

"Also, can I have five-month supply? I may not always be able to come back after sixty days and I like to have some backup."

"Sorry, the most I can give you is three months. That way I know that someone, or I, will see you in three months and check up on your condition."

That's precisely what Mischa didn't want to be bothered with. They never let her alone. *And yet they never do anything for me.*

She had showed up at the office after the doctor's appointment in hopes of going to the congressional hearing scheduled that afternoon, but Becky gave the assignment to an intern and told Mischa that they had a "human rights hero" visiting this afternoon. Mischa had to take care of getting the papers together for the meeting.

Human rights NGO employees were essentially bureaucrats. They organized protests and petitions, knew the names and direct numbers of aides to senators and representatives on the congressional committees, and became civil society representatives at the United Nations and other multilateral institutions around Washington, DC. They researched, wrote, and published the research papers on human rights abuse and took pride in being expert tacticians. Since protest signs and megaphones could never work alone, human rights bureaucrats worked on understanding the labyrinth, personalities, and leverage needed to make something happen in DC. They were not lobbyists for pharmaceuticals or arms manufacturers. Nevertheless, their tactics were the same, and sometimes lobbyists would watch and learn.

A fundamental strategy in raising awareness of an issue was finding a "hero" to put a human face on a cause: ending training for the El Salvadoran military, decreasing the drug budget to Colombia, improving labor rights in Peru. Some of these heroes were counterparts for the cause in their country, directors of non-governmental organizations such as advocacy groups, or lawyers who had put their lives on the line to organize a group to speak out on a particular injustice.

They were energetic leaders, articulate and brave, natural politicians. Sometimes their cause was a vehicle to exercise power and sometimes it was a genuine search for justice. Often it was both, and if they could get the Forum, Amnesty International, Human Rights Watch, or any other respected organization to take on their case, they became celebrated international heroes. By affiliating themselves with outside organizations, they won a protective shield—not bulletproof, but their adversaries, their governments, knew that if anything happened to them, their organization would have a direct link to Washington, DC. A senator or congressman asking for an investigation into the matter, sitting on a budget committee or taking a trip to the country, could wreak havoc on a development assistance package.

The most touching heroes were the reluctant ones, those who had not sought this high-profile role. A tragedy had brought them to take on this function: a son, sister, or brother had been the victim of torture, kidnap, forcible disappearance (*desaparecido*), or a target of an assassination. Sometimes they themselves had been the victim. These were people who had never expected to be in the international spotlight of human rights in foreign policy. They were engineers, archeologists, secretaries, doctors—from professions that were removed from politics, but circumstances pulled them into that world. Mischa would see them in the reception area, waiting and nervous, and uncertain of themselves. They had never come automatically after an incident. The reluctant heroes had tried every available means possible to peacefully make their case, discover the whereabouts of a loved one, or seek justice, but time and time again they had met a dead end. Exhausting all other means, someone had told them to come to Washington and contact the Forum. If their case was tragic, just, backed with solid evidence, and coincided with the Forum's agenda for change, the Forum would take it on.

The reluctant heroes had a dignified presence that none of the other advocates could match. Even in a cynical town like DC, their sincerity showed clearly and had immediate effect. These reluctant heroes suddenly found themselves giving speeches in Washington, DC, to human rights coalitions. They were speaking in protest rallies and human rights supporters would stand in line to shake their hand and tell them how much they admired them. They attended reluctant heroes awards ceremonies in Europe to celebrate their bravery, and met with senators who promised to raise the issue in their meeting with the president and other government officials. In their own country, these reluctant heroes were labeled troublemakers; they were under surveillance and often the recipients of death threats. Friends and colleagues feared guilt by association and so life became lonelier.

Father Roy was not a reluctant hero, but a self-anointed one. He was a human face for the cause of closing down the Institute for Training the Armed Forces of Latin America and the Caribbean, known as ITLAC. Father Roy's eyes were in a state of constant vigilance. He never turned his head or looked away when someone spoke; he stared straight at the person, seeking constant eye contact. He was a fanatic.

When someone turned his or her eyes downward or looked to the side, Father Roy would shift his body to regain that eye contact. It was uncomfortable, but also clear that you were in the presence of that indefinable phenomenon—charisma. This explained his fervent group of followers who joined him in acts of creative nonviolence.

In June he came up to do his annual rounds in Washington. The Human Rights Advocacy Forum was planning his appointments with policymakers and other human rights groups. Between meetings, he sat at an empty desk next to Mischa. When Becky went to lunch the day after he arrived, Mischa looked over to see Father Roy flipping the pages of a magazine in his hands back and forth. This was the moment to inquire, for she was curious about his imaginative protests. More than happy to discuss his efforts, he smiled and began his story.

He dissected the logistics of his plan. Some of the parishioners organized a glass recycling week and they collected hundreds of glass bottles. Father Roy noted how the dill pickle jars were the best ones, because they were the largest. "They finally collected about eighty of them. The parishioner who works at the slaughterhouse transported the blood in these ten-gallon ice cream tubs, leftover from church barbecues." Father Roy paused for a few seconds.

"Wait...what is it called? I forget now. A funnel! That's the word! You know, the kind of things people use to change the oil in your car. You see, getting the blood into those bottles wasn't that big a problem. It was just a waste of funnels. No one wanted to use them again so we threw them away."

Mischa nodded and kept her face impassive. *Proof positive. This guy is crazy.*

"Juan, another parishioner, got a job as a janitor on the base. I sponsored Juan as a refugee. He lost his family in the Village of Aguilares massacre. In fact, he was at mass on March 24, 1980, in the chapel at Divina Providencia. The mass where Archbishop Oscar Romero was assassinated. Juan was only thirty meters away from Romero. You see, Juan and I put a strategy together on how to gain access to the building. Once we were inside, the group of us, I think we were six that night, walked through the halls throwing the jars of blood on the pictures in the gallery of famous graduates, on the maps, and on the classroom doors."

Father Roy was passionate talking about the military instructors and their students, whom he saw as the next generation of human rights violators.

"You see, I wanted them to see, smell, and feel the blood. All these classes on how to fight an insurgency, what must be done in the name of national security, how to minimize collateral damage, are all so distant and theoretical at that school. It's just cocktail parties and Clausewitz at these war colleges. You know, if the students just admitted what they were learning and teachers just admitted what they were teaching, the course titles would be 'How to Murder the Innocent,' 'How to Suppress and Repress in the Name of Power,' and 'Collateral Damage: Justifications for Killing Civilians.' That's what's going on in the classrooms over there. That's the real story."

"But, Father Roy, there is no way they would let the officers go to classes with blood splattered on the walls. So how did you make your point?" *He might be sincere, but I think he missed his target.*

"Of course I knew classes would be canceled. Sure, it would be cleaned up, but a few of the officers would probably want to see the building out of curiosity. Those few teachers or students would tell the others and it would be worth it. But hell, we weren't just going to let it out by word of mouth.

We took photographs and I sent them to the press with a statement. I held a press conference the next day at the church hall."

His ego was now on full display. In this protest he was the star, not just an activist. With all the cunning of a slick PR man from Manhattan he made his observations on the media. She could see that beneath the Southern accent and under the collar was the heart of a sophisticated K Street lobbyist.

"I knew it would make a good story. You see, a protest like this would not be ignored. Local press would cover it, no question about it. Hell, if it was a slow day, I knew we had a chance at national press, and maybe with that the international press would pick it up. University radio stations were great. Today's students feel like they've missed out and their parents fought all the big battles with the civil rights movement. They're always looking for a cause, some way to change the world. If we could get the story onto some university radio, I knew we would have the start of a movement that goes beyond the state. So, in one night we made some little ol' training camp in the backwoods of Georgia infamous. There was poetry, symbolism, pragmatism, and strategy in that one act of creative nonviolence. Mission accomplished."

Mischa reassessed him. *He's not just crazy. He's a genius. These are the kind of people that change the world. The kind who think of ways to put cows' blood into pickle bottles.*

He observed that he was at a key stage in his plan to transform a media event into legislation. He needed to get congressional leaders onto the bandwagon. "I'm offering moral high ground, and if we can get some of these guys to jump on it, we're gonna close that place. So that's why I'm seeing some Congress people. That's why this hick-priest from Georgia is up here in the big city. Hey, Mischa, does Washington have any barbecue joints? It's summer and I need some ribs and corn bread."

Mischa wondered if this was a joke, but there was no body language to indicate irony. A man who threw cows' blood on walls genuinely wished to find a place that roasted cows in tangy sauces. "Certainly, Father, let me look that up for you." Becky had returned to lead Father Roy into a strategy session with the director. Mischa called Sophie. Her Texan-educated palate would probably have found a good barbecue place by now.

"Hey, Sophie. What about a date with a priest tonight?"

"*Chica,* what are you talking about?"

"We've got one of these human rights advocates making his rounds on the Hill and he wants to go to a barbecue place. He's one of yours—a Southerner—but he's a real one. He didn't just go to school there."

"Hey! Am I hearing some uppity Northern derision in your voice? Barbecue is the sacred food of hallowed veneration of my region—"

"Sophie, *chica*, what the hell are you talking about? For God's sake, you're from RHODE ISLAND! Just because you went to college in Texas doesn't make you a Southerner. Get rid of that fake drawl!" Mischa rolled her eyes.

"Okay, Professor Higgins. The best one is Pig in a Pit in Old Town, Virginia. They cater most of the Christmas parties for the congressmen from the South. After six o'clock, we can meet at the bottom of the escalator at Union Station. It'll be about a forty-five-minute ride on the Metro."

"Sounds good. Gotta go."

Father Roy came out of the meeting. Becky shot over to her desk and handed Mischa a list of Senate aides she was to call.

"Get the packages ready. They will include his bio, a press clipping, and a fact sheet on the ITLAC. You'll make calls tonight just giving a heads-up. Give me a first draft by COB tonight. We'll get the final draft by tomorrow at ten, and you should be faxing at one p.m., with calls made at three p.m. We're sending twenty faxes. I want at least five appointments for Father Roy by Friday. Call them, and then call them back. I want you to push the aides for liberal senators in particular. Also, I'm going to say this again, like I've said a hundred times: I don't want fax pages missing. No typos. I've seen a lot lately. And try improving your phone manner. The monotone way that you deliver our information makes you sound like some kind of call center operator. Remember, you're trying to convince these guys to give up a half hour in their schedule to meet with Father Roy."

"Sure," was all Mischa could muster in reply.

Becky turned and left. Father Roy came over, looking embarrassed for having witnessed the verbal beating.

"I found a barbecue place. If you're up for it, my friend and I will take you there for dinner. She lived in Texas for a while and is more than happy to go out for barbecue."

"I couldn't be happier—good company and good barbecue. Let me help you out with the package. I could at least do the bio."

Mischa pressed her lips together to mute herself. *No, Father, I think references to voices in your head or undercurrents of a messianic complex might set off alarm bells in any congressional aide.* She said out loud, "Actually, would you mind writing up the fact sheet? We find that our 'heroes' don't see themselves as such and they undersell. You'll see the drafts, don't worry."

Congressional aides were guard dogs. You had to get past them to get a meeting with a senator or a representative. An exclusive club of them had been on the Hill for decades. Any advocate of a human rights organization brought forward had to have an unassailable, honorable character. Writing the biographies was a craft. A bio had to have strategically placed words and phrases that made subtle references to the congressman's work or the lawmaker's background. The familiarity would prompt and enable the aide to ask questions and engage more comfortably: "You have one hundred refugees in your parish from El Salvador? What a coincidence, the congressman has about two thousand Salvadorans in his constituency." Or, "The senator just visited Honduras last month. How long have you had a partner parish there? Is that where you were born?" And, "Why, that's the hometown of the congressman's mother. By the way, we were thinking about having a hearing on this same issue. Maybe you could come in and testify?"

Human rights NGO personnel gleaned personal intelligence on the aides and traded it like spies among themselves. They used anything they could to strike familiarity, to demonstrate coincidence of cause between a man who throws blood on walls and one who casts votes in the U.S. Congress.

By five, all the papers and calls were done and they headed off to get barbecue.

They were about a block down from the office when Father Roy asked, "How do you like working at Human Rights Advocacy Forum?"

"I like the causes, but the office relationships can be difficult," Mischa replied.

"I see that," he said, and looked at her sympathetically.

"But I guess you find it everywhere. It's just funny, or maybe pretty sad, that in a human rights organization there's a lack of common courtesy or even kindness. You expect more from people that fight for peace and justice."

"You should see the office politics of a parish council. Inside the rectory it's no better. You get a priest who gives a homily on tolerance and patience at the ten o'clock mass, then comes back to shout at another priest for taking the sports section. Mischa, where is this barbecue place?"

"It's in Alexandria, Virginia. We're meeting my friend Sophie at Union Station."

Ring-ring-ring. Mischa's cell phone went off. "Excuse me, Father. Hey, Sophie, we're on our way. What? Jogging with the president again, are we? Don't worry, just give me the directions." Mischa wondered if Father Roy was going to ask her about the remark about the president that she dropped. It was the ego of a junior policy wonk on display. After a few minutes, she closed her cell phone and explained, "She's got to finish something at her office, but Sophie will meet up with us later."

"No problem. Just get me there. I want my ribs and corn bread."

The subway came and it was still early enough in rush hour that they could get seats. Mischa automatically went to the same seat in the car as the one chosen by the man who had had the seizure. Only at that moment did Mischa realize she had been choosing that same seat for the last week, every time she took the Metro. She had never told anyone what had happened.

"Father, a weird thing happened in the subway last week. I was sitting right where you are now, in another car, and a man next to me had a seizure."

"What did you do?"

"I have epilepsy, so I knew what to do. Someone else called the medics, who met us at the next station. It wasn't really the seizure that was so strange, but the reaction of those around us. Only two people helped me. The rest were frozen. There was such a look of revulsion and fear on everyone's face. I wondered if people look at me the same way when I have a seizure."

"They probably do."

Mischa turned, surprised by that frank, and rather unsympathetic, response.

"My sister has epilepsy too, pretty severe. The seizures cluster. She has about fifteen or twenty in a week, then she's fine, and then they come again. They've taken a toll on her. She lives in the rectory with me since our parents died a few years ago."

Mischa looked horrified.

"I don't mean to compare you to her. You have obviously made a life for yourself. She's different."

"What type of seizures does she have?"

"Both kinds, sometimes petit mal, but mostly grand mal. She may be having even more seizures. These petit mal ones, I guess they're called 'absence seizures,' may be happening more often than we realize. The doctors call them cluster seizures. Sometimes the housekeeper finds my sister and she looks as if she's meditating, but then when she comes to, she's exhausted. I guess she's had a storm going on inside her head. All we saw was the calm."

They turned the corner and saw a large neon pig flashing red and blue.

"Well, Father, I think we've found it."

When they came in it was packed. Beer, loud country music, pool tables, peanuts, and spittoons transported her to another frame of mind. Walls were covered with license plates from gun-toting Southern states: Alabama, South Carolina, Mississippi. There were black iron pots of barbecue sauce bubbling on a counter, and the wooden benches and tables were covered with newspaper.

"YEE-HAW!" Father Roy exclaimed. He looked up at the menu in awe. "CORN BREAD pudding! My mama used to make that stuff. I hope they use real cream. Well, whatever they use, I'm getting it. You gotta have some. I'm going to order three tubs—one for you, one for me, and one for me to take home for breakfast. Hope you're hungry! Let's see, I think I'll get one rack—no, make that two racks of spareribs, biscuits, okra, a gallon of mint iced tea, and corn bread pudding." He took his wallet out. "Mischa, let me take care of this one."

After telling Father Roy about the incident, Mischa's small obsession will JGR gradually turned into a stale curiosity. A year later, she heard that the military institute did close and Father Roy was unquestionably instrumental. When they announced the news at a human rights coalition meeting everyone rejoiced, and all Mischa could think about was cows' blood, dill pickle jars, and funnels.

He came up again to celebrate its closure and Mischa was happy to see him. She was in her final month at the Forum and his success was the perfect way to end her time there. After the meetings on the Hill, Father Roy found himself with an evening free. Mischa reminded him that it was her turn to buy the barbecue, and they made their way to Pig in a Pit.

Amid the spittoons and the country music, he asked, "So, what comes next, Mischa, after the Forum?"

"I found a job as a journalist in a small news agency in Guatemala. I need some time on the ground. I've been studying and working in Washington. After that, I'll head for grad school. I'm waiting for my acceptance, or my rejection letter, which should be coming any day now. My plan is to stay out of the country for the next few years. I need to get away from the DC Bubble. I need to see the real world."

"I was a parish priest in Antigua for two years. Guatemala is more than real. The violence suffered by the indigenous in that civil war is beyond the imagination. The mixture of tragedy and beauty in such a small country is bewildering. Watch yourself. Stay safe."

Before she left the Forum, the office manager took her out for lunch. She wanted to tell Mischa about a disagreement that occurred within the Forum when Mischa was hired. Midway through lunch, the office manager eased into her story. She told her how the director and the senior staff had considered exempting her from the organization's health insurance plan because of her "long-term medical condition."

Due to her epilepsy, the organization had to pay higher fees to the insurance agency to cover Mischa's medical expenses. The deputy director, alone with the office manager, stood against the rest of the staff and somehow they prevailed, though the odds were against them.

The deputy director was forced out in an office "putsch" a few months later. He had never earned the respect of the staff, since his position at the Forum was a condition of an extremely generous financial contribution from a family that could not find a place for their Grateful Dead-loving Communist-sympathizer son in their Fortune 500 Company. Though he was bumbling and nervous, the office manager always thought the deputy was a good man and she wanted Mischa to remember him in that light.

When they returned from lunch Mischa stared at her senior colleagues when they came into view. They caught her fierce glares. Confused and uncomfortable, after a few seconds they looked down and walked out of her sight. She wanted to stand up in the middle of the room and shout at them one by one. Inside she was teeming with insults.

So, what did you do today? Did you testify at some congressional hearing on the acts of some oppressive regime after you voted to refuse me health insurance? Did you just come back from giving a lecture on justice for human rights victims? Tell me, did you climb on your goddamn high horse and shout at some government official about U.S. foreign policy in Central America?

She wanted to wave their hypocrisy in their faces, but tomorrow was her last day at the Forum. In ten days, Washington, DC, was going to be part of her past. She took out her notebook with her scattered to-do list and scribbled, "Count number of seizures while at Forum."

13. THE KITCHEN

October 1994

CLARISSA AND CHRISTOPHER MADE A GLAMOROUS PAIR. Both were graduates of the London School of Economics. She was a BBC correspondent and he was the correspondent for *The Economist* in Central America. They had hyphenated last names, which meant nothing to most, but to the British expatriates in Guatemala, class-aware among themselves, they explained to the rest of them that Clarissa and Christopher were members of the British aristocracy.

Mischa met them at a going-away party for Alisa Moseley-Simpson, who was on her way to work in the United Nations Mission in Haiti. Mischa had only been in Guatemala for two days and Jill, her predecessor at the newsletter, thought the party would be a good way for Mischa to meet the other expatriates roaming around.

When Jill told her where they were going that night, Mischa was startled by the coincidence. Florence, her former colleague at the Human Rights Advocacy Forum on the South American team, had suggested that she contact Alisa. On Mischa's last day in the office, Florence took a card from her Rolodex, wrote down Alisa's address, and handed it to her.

"So, how do you know Alisa?" Mischa asked.

"My father had an affair with her mother," Florence said without hesitation.

"Oh."

"They were both economists with busy spouses. They met at a conference at Oxford University and hit it off, so to speak. In fact, it was a national scandal. Alisa's father was a rather prominent politician. Playing the cuckold is never a career enhancer and his wife's affair probably put an end to his chances for prime minister."

It was the first real conversation that she had with Florence, and by far the most interesting conversation she had ever had at the Forum. As Florence told the story of her family, she sounded like Alistair Cooke introducing a decadent plot in *Masterpiece Theater.*

"After that affair my parents divorced. My mother decided to take us across the pond and begin anew. My father and Alisa's mother ended their affair. My father continued to seduce one graduate student after another. I think Alisa's mother was a faculty chair at some university. She was rather beautiful. I wouldn't be surprised if she hasn't seduced a few students as well. I think Alisa's father is a BBC commentator, political thriller novelist, or some such. Well, enough family history. Alisa and I got along well. We're the same age, and at Oxford we were at the same college, Balliol. Look her up. Tell her we worked together."

It was a kind gesture on Florence's part, but as Mischa looked at Alisa gaily chatting with her guests, she thought it would be best to leave her to say her good-byes.

In her mingling, Mischa overheard a few people planning a trip to Mexico, in hopes of getting a glimpse of the insurgent Zaptista leader, *Subcomandante* Marcos. The guerrilla leader's speeches, poems, and communiqués were making him a Che Guevara of the 1990s, and one of men at the party was reciting, from memory, one of the *Subcomandante's* pronouncements to a small group:

"In the mountains of Chiapas, death is a part of daily life. It is as common as rain or sunshine. You don't lose your fear of death, but you become familiar with it. It becomes your equal. Death, which is so close, so near, so possible, is less terrifying for us than for others. So, going out and fighting and perhaps meeting death is not as terrible as it seems. For us, what surprises and amazes us is life itself. The hope of a better life. Going out to fight and to die and finding out that you are not dead, but alive. And, unintentionally, you realize you are walking on the edge of the border between death and life."

It was an impressive performance. There was a respectful silence when he finished. The guy chugged his bottle of Gallo beer, burped, and the girls giggled as they revealed their fantasies of the Balaclava-clad *Subcomandante* Marcos whisking them away to his guerrilla camp in the jungles of the Yucatan. The conversation turned from ideology to balaclavas and role play as foreplay. One had to respect the guy's adept adaptation of "what's that perfume you're wearing?" for his target audience.

Most of the crowd was European or American. They had an array of degrees—bachelor's, law, master's, medical, and doctoral—and worked either with the UN, human rights groups, the media, development assistance agencies, or universities. There were Palestinian kaffiyehs draped loosely around girls' necks, peace sign tattoos, Birkenstocks, and T-shirts featuring Che Guevara, Green Peace, and HIV-AIDS awareness. Name a cause for justice and someone was wearing it. There were no sequins. High heels were a no-no. The purses were woven, with wooden beads for snaps. The alternatives were canvas, jute, or backpacks. Even faded souvenir T-shirts from rock concerts, typical for that age group, were nowhere to be seen. It was a parallel international diplomatic community—just younger, more casually dressed, non-governmental, and anti-establishmentarian.

Jill introduced Mischa to Clarissa and Christopher as the editor who was going to take over from her at the newsletter.

Clarissa eyed Mischa up and down. "So you're the one who was duped into the job. I think the newsletter is likely to go bankrupt in three months. I hope you have something else lined up."

From the corner of her eye, Mischa spied Jill frantically signaling to Clarissa to stop talking. After a few minutes of polite exchange, Clarissa left for more red wine. Christopher stayed behind.

Mischa asked him a little about the crowd and his current assignments. They discussed a book written by his LSE thesis adviser on the 1954 Guatemalan coup. Clarissa suddenly appeared and took Christopher by the arm.

"It was a pleasure," she said to Mischa, and with a clenched smile she led him away.

It had been getting so tiresome for Clarissa. Lately, there had been an influx of available females in the expat community. At these times, Christopher was on the prowl as much as he was prey. Clarissa kept herself on alert for "whores," which she defined as any woman who clamored for Christopher's attention. After she found him inside a closet with Carmina, Clarissa had wished she could run away. That incident swiftly assumed the stature of a classic on the gossip circuit. It had happened nearly two years ago, but it was filed away in people's memories and recounted when someone new inquired about the intriguing duo. Clarissa recognized the signs of the telling of this particular tale. At a party she would see a clutch of people briefly glancing over at her. The storyteller would continue as they bent their heads forward, their eyes widened, and they laughed. Clarissa made sure that she was engaged in conversation by the time the anecdote was finished. She knew that the listeners would want to take another look at her, so she engineered a way to be out of sight by the time the group was laughing uproariously. Above all, she wanted to avoid being caught alone, sipping a consolatory glass of wine.

Clarissa wished that she could play around, but she was caught in a trap of unrequited devotion. She let her affection suffer one blow after another and she absorbed each one. She convinced herself that his adventures were merely a sport, not emotionally meaningful, but it was difficult to accept this unsavory weakness of her character. She took solace in the knowledge that Christopher was also trapped. He would always come back. Clarissa offered him comfort, habit, and convenience. He wasn't strong enough to leave her, and she held that over him. They were both victims in their own way.

Clarissa invited Jill and Mischa over for lunch the next week. She had no interest in a friendship with Mischa, but liked to keep herself apprised of new arrivals. She registered a slight degree of interest on Christopher's part for the new girl; therefore, it was worthwhile gauging her threat level. Jill was leaving the newsletter for a position as the Central America correspondent for the *Washington Post*. It was a recognized quantum career leap and everyone offered her endless congratulations. An invitation for lunch, in Jill's honor, was the perfect opportunity. It would be seen as a courtesy to invite Jill's successor.

Christopher and Clarissa lived in Zona 10—the wealthy area of the city. Perhaps, Mischa thought, she might get a few hours of air-conditioning. They would not be living in one of the rat holes like most of the young expatriates. Jill shared a two-bedroom apartment with another girl in a house converted into three apartments. Mischa lived around the corner, in a house of the same size that had been converted into six apartments.

The buses from Zona 1 didn't go to Zona 10, so Jill suggested that they take a taxi from the city center. That would probably be half a day's wages for Mischa, but she was curious about Clarissa. Christopher was a standard character, but Clarissa was provocative. They would never be friends, but Mischa would like to see Clarissa operate. She loved to observe personalities in motion.

When the taxi driver pulled up to the address, Mischa looked up to see a twelve-foot wall of gray cinder blocks surrounding the house, with barbed wire on top, and a jagged layer of broken glass to prevent intruders from coming over the wall. It was a common sight in good neighborhoods. They knocked on the black metal door that was barred shut. After ringing the bell, a Guatemalan man with shears greeted them at the door. *A gardener, they have a gardener?*

Mischa was stunned when they entered the enclosure. She felt as if she were Dorothy entering Oz. Inside the enclave was an enchanted cottage in the tropics. Clarissa came down the pathway to give them air kisses.

A terra-cotta roof overhung a white stucco house beneath a palm tree, heavy with clusters of green bananas. Mischa walked over to see the different fruit trees: mangoes, bananas, and tamarind were scattered throughout the garden. There were vines of tomatoes curled on sticks along the walls, with flowers and ferns. There was even a cactus garden in the corner, a small area of pebbles and sand around each plant; a piece of sculpture with needles of different sizes springing out in warning. Clarissa picked up some mangoes that had fallen and gave them to her.

"Rather you take them than have them rot on the ground. The gardener also takes them home, but his family is probably sick of mangoes by now. Take more if you'd like."

Mischa thanked her for those in her hands already. They were so plump and ripe that each of them had a trickle of sticky juice at the stem. Next to the mango tree was a fountain springing from a nest of pink azalea bushes. It was unreal.

They walked down a cobblestone path to a cottage surrounded by a patio of ice blue glazed tiles under beams of dark wood, which gave way to an open living room of glazed red pepper tiles. Trinkets from Latin America adorned the room. A black cast-iron chandelier hung over a rustic mahogany table in the dining room, which had a basket of mangoes in its center.

The gardener excused himself, and Clarissa went to the kitchen to get the drinks. She came out with *jugo de tamarindo* in a blown-glass pitcher and cobalt blue goblets. What looked like dirty pond water was the recognized "lemonade" of Central America. The drink was made from a tropical fruit—a plump brown pea pod that hung from the trees, like the ones next to their mango tree. The fruit inside the thin shell of the tamarind was dark brown, sticky, and tangy.

To make the juice, Guatemalans pulled the pulp off the seeds by placing them in hot water, and then added about twenty tablespoons of sugar and cold, hopefully filtered, water. Street vendors—it was always women who sold the food and drink—would have large plastic bowls of tamarind juice with metal ladles in them and a kitchen towel over the top to keep the flies away, with a few glasses standing nearby on a tray.

Customers paid a few centavos, eagerly drank the juice, and then would go on their way. The women washed the glasses in a little tub of water and placed them back on the tray. Their regular customers were the soldiers who stood at corners nearby or alongside them, holding machine guns. The country was still in the midst of a thirty-year-old civil war, and the soldiers were a common sight. People could forget consciously, but unconsciously the message of who was in control stayed in their mind.

Christopher walked into the room and greeted them with a smile. He said Mischa's name and asked how she was doing. Mischa realized no one had spoken her name since she arrived. It was, "Jill, does she want a drink?" or "Are you hungry for lunch, Jill? Is she too?"

Women can be sublime in their disdain.

Christopher had an article to write, so he excused himself and went into his office. Clarissa showed Jill and Mischa around the house while they waited for the *tamales* and *hilachas*, which the cook had made the night before, to warm up. For dessert, Clarissa promised baked plantains and mangoes covered with a Belgian chocolate sauce. She told them that she had purchased the dessert sauce just last week from a duty-free shop at Heathrow.

Mischa was visibly impressed with the place and complimented Clarissa appropriately. Jill, who had probably seen the house a hundred times, remarked gushingly on every room. She shrewdly noticed new trinkets or different arrangements of furniture. Clarissa received each of Jill's reverential observations with practiced grace. Mischa looked at Jill, with her avant-garde glasses and Frida Kahlo fetish. It was clear that she worshiped at Clarissa's temple, the alpha female among the cool expatriates. Clarissa had the clique survival skills to banish someone to social Siberia on the mere hunch that the person threatened her standing. Christopher would never be cutthroat. He would never need to be. Clarissa would be his guard dog.

"What a memory you have, Jill! You are absolutely correct, I just bought that *huipil*. We went up to Tikal on the last bank holiday. I love to call it Tickle. Anyway, a man on the road sold it for three hundred *quetzales*, something like ten pounds. He originally asked for two seventy-five, but I just couldn't do that to him. He's probably going to feed his family for five months on the sale of that *huipil*. It is beautiful." Clarissa looked at it in sincere admiration of the workmanship.

Huipils were part of the traditional dress of Guatemalan indigenous women. It was a blouse made from a rectangle of rough, thick cotton, often made of cloth that the women had woven themselves, with elaborate embroidery of colorful birds, fruits, flowers, and complex geometric patterns in vibrant colors. To the non-indigenous Guatemalan, the *huipil* was just a part of the other people's culture, not theirs. To the foreigner, the *huipil* was the resplendent emblem of Guatemala.

"Jill, I think I'm going to have a collection of *huipils*, and when we get back to London, I want to frame them and hang them in a hallway."

"Oh, that would be amazing, Clarissa! You could alternate them with the fantastic portrait photographs you've taken of indigenous women in traditional dress!"

"What a wonderful idea, Jill! You should be an interior designer!"

Mischa thought how she decorated her bedroom wall with a collage of quotes on Post-its. Jill and Carmina had posters. Clarissa and Christopher framed *huipils* and photographs.

As they sat down for lunch, Clarissa turned into the gracious hostess and inquired about Mischa's past and plans.

"I'm going to stay here for one year, then go to England for a graduate degree."

"Where?" Clarissa inquired.

"Cambridge. I decided to defer and come here first. My father thinks I am going to get lost in the jungle." Silence. Mischa also knew how to play the relay of information for greater effect. Give only a little information; wait for the question that signaled growing curiosity, and then reply. Regardless of where Britons are in the world, whomever they meet on the race or class spectrum, Mischa supposed that Oxford and Cambridge would win a few seconds of reassessment. In Clarissa's ranking of friends and useful acquaintances, Mischa knew that she was about as important as a flea. Now she saw Mischa as a little more than a flea, but not much.

For a change in conversation, Mischa moved on to Christopher. "So, how long have you and Christopher known each other?"

Clarissa looked to Jill. "Excuse me, what did she say? I couldn't hear her."

Mischa shortcut Jill, and spoke louder. "I asked, how long have you and Christopher known each other?"

"Oh well, we went to the London School of Economics together. Let's see now, we've been together for something like five years. Sometimes I can't even believe it. We decided to come here after our master's degrees. Everything worked out perfectly. You see, it always does for us."

Methinks the lady doth protest too much. Chica, from what I hear, it ain't so perfect.

Christopher had an eye that often roamed at expatriate parties. Tall, dark, and sullen, that last trait was unusually appealing to a woman, for if she were able to make him smile she felt triumphant. His meadow green eyes could make a girl wonder what it would be like to lie in the grass with him one afternoon or sometime around midnight. But he didn't rely on these attributes alone; Christopher was a cunning tactician.

From the crowd he would stare at the woman in conversation from a few feet behind. Once she noticed him, she became gradually disinterested in the discussion and returned his gaze. Finally, she would excuse herself and approach Christopher. He had not moved an inch; all he had done was stare. Once the target was next to him he struck up an immediate and disarming intimacy. He listened intently, drew close in conversation, lowered his voice, made a few strategic touches, and gently placed a wisp of real, or imaginary, hair behind her ear. His technique was studied, but subtle. He chose a target and then turned himself into her target and rested while she chased.

Most encounters ended abruptly with a visit from Clarissa making her territorial claim. If the girl didn't get the hint and leave immediately, Clarissa would take Christopher away. Despite his dusty jeans and wrinkled shirts, Christopher was urbane. Clarissa looked like she belonged on a country estate. *She would look good in riding boots. In fact, she would look good in a pile of manure.*

Mischa went to these parties for social interaction outside the small world of a newsletter about to go bankrupt. She didn't drink alcohol, do drugs, or disappear into closets or bedrooms. She was the odd one out on those matters, but hoped to shed those layers nerdiness. Pleased that she had found herself in this situation, Mischa looked around the room. She was certain that these parties were ten times more debauched than any of the ones in Rhode Island suburbia, the ones she had heard about in hallway conversations on Mondays at Mama MIA.

Mischa came to the parties early to catch people sober and before the drugs came out. She could have conversations then, but as their eyes became glassy she moved on. Sometimes she just sat silently in the corner, sober, taking in the crowd. Among the characters that defined those get-togethers was Jake, a wartime correspondent from the *Los Angeles Times*.

Jake had survived El Salvador; he knew the guerrilla leaders on a first-name basis and followed them into the villages and the jungles. Jake had even been shot. He would roll up his shirtsleeve to show his wound to anyone who wanted to see it. He also went around with a handheld tape recorder, the kind that journalists use for interviews or notes to themselves. He always had with him the tape of the moment he had been shot:

> *"We're moving forward. The guerrillas have taken out most of the battalion here in the village of San Miguel. This assault has lasted for more than five hours. The street is littered with the soldiers' bodies, yet the firefight is still intense. Here comes another barrage and it—oh FUCK! OH FUCK! FUCCCCCCCCCCKKKKKKKKK! I've been shot. Carlos, HELP me! Ayuda! Ayuda! Ayuda! Help! I've been shot! FUCK, FUCK, FUCK! Rip up my sleeve. I said RIP, damn it, PUTA! PUTA! PUTA! Wrap it around the arm, tighter… más, más, más. TIGHTER, TIGHTER. Stop the blood. Sangre, sangre, para el sangre. AGGGGGGGGGHHHHHHHHH! What the hell are you doing? Shoot the goddamn motherfucker. SHOOT HIM. My arm is numb, I can't move my fingers. FUCK! FUCK! FUCK!*

Click. Jake would turn it off, take a swig of whatever he was drinking, and eagerly await the listener's reaction, which inevitably kicked off at least an hour-long conversation focused on him and his exploits. If the listener was pretty and new to this group of expatriates, the "playing of the tape" would, on occasion, lead to their joint exit from the party.

Mischa was impressed when she first met Jake, but not attracted. He seemed little more than a stray dog in search of affection. At parties, whenever she saw Jake, he was holding that tape recorder in one hand and a drink in another, searching the crowd for someone new, man or woman, who would listen to his tale. If you were watching him from the start of the conversation you could almost time the point when he would pull up his shirtsleeve to show his wound and push the button to play the tape. It usually took about seventeen minutes.

Mischa saw a few more of these types, war correspondents. Not all had a battle scar and a tape recorder like Jake, but they had a look about them—the real ones, the ones who didn't just stay in the capital, but were covering the war on the front lines. The other foreign journalists were going to press conferences, reading the local newspapers, and interviewing aid workers and human rights observers who had been to the highlands. The safer journalists acknowledged their risk-taking colleagues with a degree of respect. Even those from well-established news agencies saw the freelancing, often financially strapped, war correspondents on a rung above them.

War correspondents often came to parties because they were a chance to unwind, keep up contacts with their unidentified sources, and be in the company of people with whom they were more ideologically sympathetic. These people, a class unto themselves, grow accustomed to the adrenalin rush of covering a war and find it hard to get back to Main Street, so they roam the world for conflict zones to cover.

They have seen blood splattered on floors and walls as a result of sub-machine guns, firing line executions, machetes, and assassinations. They have found tortured bodies and walked over corpses. They have visited mass graves and interviewed mothers who wailed in anguish. If these journalists didn't turn back when they first saw these scenes, it meant they had the courage to stay. The war correspondents were the ones who reported the stories that were catalysts for a United Nations Security Council Meeting or the resignation of a defense minister. In the morning, their reports were the ones on the desks of cabinet secretaries and White House aides. In all those places there would be a conversation that began, "Did you see the story in…?" and it would be their story.

On the basis of one story by a war correspondent, human rights advocacy groups could organize demonstrations on Capitol Hill. In their vision of themselves, war correspondents want to be the hero that breaks the story that ends the war.

But instead, many are seduced by the tragedy. Slowly, over time, some become voyeurs of horror. They are revolted and transfixed by their metamorphosis. The ones with enough survival instinct find their way back to Main Street, if not for the rest of their lives, then at least for some respite.

The ones who cannot find their way back still need to function and alcohol is the anesthetic of choice, as are a series of one-night stands in the expat community. Drugs are kept to a minimum, as these affect their writing and their deadlines. Jake was still lucid after downing three beers, eight tequilas, and five shots of vodka, but he became more boring.

When Mischa couldn't see anyone else who attracted her attention, her eyes always returned to Carmina. She was glorious; a raw Latin beauty. Carmina was a regular at these parties. She dressed in men's clothing as if to tease, but her curves were blatant. Mischa would stare in admiration; she had never seen anyone so beautiful. A perfect aquiline nose, high cheekbones, and reddish brown lips crowned with a beauty mark against milk chocolate skin. Her black eyes were deep set in brushes of eyelashes, and a waterfall of tight black curls ran down her back. It was pity, not goodness of character, which held Mischa back from envy. Carmina could not control herself and her most important commodity, her beauty. It showed in her eyes. A few too many men had plunged too many drugs and too much alcohol in expectation of her acquiescence. There were too many parties where Carmina ended up in someone's bed, then rapidly dressed to get back to the party, only to find herself in another bed, or the same one, with someone else.

Abe owned the house where most of the parties were held, as well as the bedrooms where Carmina slept. He was the son of two successful lawyers from New York City. He grew up in a Manhattan penthouse and wore a black dog baseball cap that implied a summerhouse on Martha's Vineyard. He was an alcoholic, but highly functional, like most of them. Though occasionally offensive, he was always generous. A trust-fund kid, he could afford to rent a big house, and his colleagues slept there rent-free, along with any visitor who might come and need a place to stay. When you could catch him sober in conversation, you could not doubt his dedication to human rights. He and the others were on a forensics team, employed by a human rights organization that was collecting evidence to try human rights cases in the international courts of justice. On occasion, some of the pioneer forensic scientists would drop in. These potbellied old men with scraggly beards had started the practice of applying forensic science to investigate human rights abuses in Latin America. Their work had brought down dictators and put torturers in prison, and they were gurus who now traveled the world training teams of men and women who put their own lives on the line in search of evidence. These elder forensic scientists were treated with reverence whenever they came to check on their disciples. They would find themselves surrounded while they told their war stories.

As a Jew whose relatives were victims and survivors of the Holocaust, Abe was especially drawn to the cause of finding proof of the genocide that the Guatemalan government denied throughout their country's more than thirty-year civil war. He and his colleagues were either on trips to the highlands digging up mass graves or studying and categorizing the bone and cloth fragments in the laboratory in the city center. It was difficult to be judgmental of them; the parties, the drinking, the drugs, and the sex were ways of leaving their work at the door. One or two of them would go overboard on occasion, but the others would rein them in and try to keep everything at the level of escape, not self-destruction.

Abe's most invaluable housemate was Gabriel, a suspected drug dealer and the de facto chef. Geographically, he originated from Spain, but he made it clear to every newcomer that he was not a citizen of that former empire nation, but a citizen of the Americas. Gabriel was the only reason that Abe's parties were not only drunken bacchanalia, but genuine culinary events. People came to drink and inhale, but they also came for the food, Gabriel's food. With a cigarette constantly clutched between his lips and his spiky salt-and-pepper haircut, he came out of the kitchen with quails roasted in thyme, paellas, freshly made ciabattas, mushroom cream fettuccine, and brie—yes, there was brie in Guatemala—melted and served with cranberry chutney. Thanks to Gabriel's jaunts to the more elegant parts of the city, near the embassies and the luxury apartments of the better zones, Abe's pantry was filled with the best of ingredients from European delis. On his way back from those places, Gabriel bought vegetables from indigenous markets.

As people got drunk at a party, the best place to be was the kitchen. After all, Gabriel had to be sober to cook. Mischa became his sous chef and learned how to cook. She had never wanted to learn from her mother; she thought it would chain her to a future as a wife and mother. But after a few years, she realized that her ignorance was not a badge of honor—just the shallow, temperamental response of a teenager. Mischa washed dishes in order to observe Gabriel more closely.

For Spanish tortillas, he advised that the potatoes and the onions be sliced thinly. The garlic must be crushed, not sliced. He could crack seven eggs with one hand and beat them with a fork at the speed of an electric mixer. The garlic, onions, and potatoes were mixed together gently and then poured into a black iron pan that was already burning with olive oil. Without the benefit of Teflon, only olive oil, he could flip the tortilla in the air and it would come out with a crispy golden sheen. They said Gabriel could cut cocaine well, too, but Mischa never played sous chef to that dish. Though he gripped an ever-present cigarette between his teeth as he chopped, blended, sliced, sauteed, and baked, he had a nervous tic that made him look as if he was perpetually suffering from nicotine withdrawal. After dinner, Gabriel would put away his trusty kitchen knife—a white-handled Swiss Army knife—which announced that the kitchen had closed. Abe and the others would give him a round of applause, and for the rest of the evening Gabriel reclined like Caesar on a sofa, while the others served him drinks, passed him joints, and introduced him to young and willing women.

One evening everyone was getting drunk a little too early. It had been a hard day at the office and an overseas visitor had brought a few bottles of whiskey from the duty-free shop. The party was deteriorating quickly. Mischa diligently washed the bowls and pans in the kitchen to get away from the crowd. When she looked into the room, it was filled with people. She saw Carmina, reckless, dancing on a table. Her hair swept the air wildly and her hips swayed as she spun. Men crowded around and she encouraged them to look. Someone threw her a broom and she made the most of the improvised prop. It was a scene impossible to ignore; Mischa was spellbound.

"Carmina is gorgeous. I've never seen a woman bewitch this many men all at once," Mischa commented.

"Carmina is dangerous, to herself and to others," replied Gabriel.

"Did you date her?"

"No one dates her, they just sleep with her. I've been with her more than once, and I can honestly say that when she is on a high—it's got to be coke, not weed—she gives a superb—"

"Stop. I don't need to and I don't want to know, Gabriel." Mischa punctuated the remark by hitting the garlic with the flat side of the knife, crushing it to Gabriel's specifications.

"Anyway, I don't know which way you swing, but there's a tip."

Mischa was silent, not wishing to engage. Again she slammed the knife and smashed another clove into a pearly pulp. Mischa reached for her drink by the side of the sink. She took a sip, and then looked into the glass. Was this her drink or was it Gabriel's? She was certain it was hers. Did someone spike it with rum? She looked over at the crowd in the dining room. It wasn't beyond this group, she knew. They knew she didn't drink, but it would probably be good entertainment to get her drunk.

Mischa felt as if she was rising above the floor. Then she fell, and felt smashed like a clove of garlic under a knife. She had never been conscious during a seizure. She did not know what was so different. Her teeth were chattering wildly. *Stop chattering, stop chattering, stop moving,* she thought. But she could not stop it. Only Gabriel was in the kitchen. Every bang against the floor was the strike of a concrete block against her skull. She closed her eyes and saw lightning. She opened them to see him drop his Swiss Army knife and put his arms under her head to keep it from hitting the floor. He yelled for help. She looked at his face and saw a cigarette gripped tightly in his lips. Despite the chaos, she hoped that an ember would not fall and burn her face. She grabbed his hand and heard him yelp in pain.

A few hours later, she awoke in a bedroom that stank of sweat, cigarettes, marijuana, and alcohol. Gabriel was sitting next to her and Carmina was stroking her head. There were maps and indigenous weavings nailed to the wall. She looked around to see posters of Patrice Lumumba, the Dalai Lama, Aung Sun Suu Kyi, and an autographed photograph of Golda Meir. When Mischa raised herself off the bed, the room twisted around her and she fell back.

An hour later, she could finally stumble to the door as Gabriel and Carmina let her try alone, but when she began to fall, they rushed to catch her. From the doorway, she looked into the living room and saw people around a candle sharing joints and telling stories. This group had seen much more freakish occurrences.

They inquired with kind curiosity whether she had recovered, and if there was anything they could do. It was not an extraordinary event. There were no stares and they returned to their joints and their stories. *That's probably why I keep company with these outlaws and delinquents, everyone's an outsider.* She walked to the kitchen, where she spat out what felt like a tiny jagged pebble in her mouth. She saw the chip of her tooth, lying in the swill of her saliva and blood. She turned the tap on full strength and watched the bit of tooth swirl down the drain. As much as she liked the group when they were sober, she had no intention of sleeping in Abe's den, and the two agreed that it was not the place for her to spend the night. When she found her purse and began to walk out, Carmina and Gabriel insisted on accompanying her home and making sure she made it to her bed.

She had thought Gabriel was a dishonest, self-serving bastard. Mischa slapped herself on her mental face for her puritanical opinions of Carmina. They were both good people and Mischa chided herself for her lack of judgment. It was always more complex trying to understand a person who had helped her after a seizure. Those first impressions always suffered.

14. THE MINISTRY OF DEFENSE

AFTER THAT NIGHT, MISCHA DECIDED TO STAY IN BED THE NEXT DAY. It would not be a tragedy if the newsletter went out late. The day after that, she decided to attend the press conference. It was a place to watch people interact—not as interesting as the parties—but the conferences were more like real-life events. She needed an injection of some normal day-to-day life amid the hypnotic lives of the expatriates. Mischa's ritual before these press conferences was to arrive early. She would stand at the corner across from the security-gated entrance, where a woman in a blue checked apron sold slices of mangoes sprinkled with salt and a crescent of lime tucked at the side in a plastic bag.

Mischa watched the journalists show their press IDs and have their bags searched. Once a few of her acquaintances had arrived, she felt comfortable enough to enter. She wasn't under pressure to report on the press conference in the newsletter, but she had a press ID badge, so there was no reason to miss out and stay at her desk at a financially imploding newsletter.

The dynamics were always interesting to watch. Unquestionably, and understandably, the domestic reporters were the most respectful of the spokesman giving the briefing. The foreign ones—like Clarissa, Jill, Jake, and Christopher—and others from Agence France Presse and the Associated Press, were much more aggressive. Since Guatemala was still in the midst of its civil war, press agencies chose to place their Central American correspondents in Guatemala City. When there were no natural disasters, peace negotiations, or elections for the correspondents to cover in other parts of the region, the correspondent stayed in Guatemala City. A press conference was always fodder for a story on the war or the impending peace negotiations, as well as a chance to show headquarters that they were doing a job, not getting a suntan.

It was entertaining to see the Defense Ministry spokesman balance his mood and his answers. The domestic journalists showed him respect in their tone due to his rank and status, but a subsequent question might come from a foreign correspondent that would be inquisitorial or sarcastic.

It was difficult for the spokesman to hide his anger when faced with the impudence, but he needed to cooperate with the foreign press. The suppressed rage and tension quaking in his voice made one frightened for his staff members, who were undoubtedly going to suffer the consequences of a bad mood afterward. Outside the press room, the journalists consulted with each other for a few minutes to corroborate facts before going back to their offices to file their stories. Clarissa offered to give Mischa a ride with Jill. With a good-bye and an air kiss she dropped Jill off at her office, and she and Mischa were left alone.

"I've been with Christopher for five years," Clarissa said, as she looked at the road and turned the steering wheel.

"Yes, Clarissa, you told me that once." Mischa furrowed her brow, not knowing where this conversation was leading.

"It hasn't been easy, but we're still together." Clarissa laughed nervously. "I remember there was this girl that liked Christopher. In fact, he started seeing her. I went to her apartment to visit but she wouldn't let me in. I just kept ringing her buzzer and yelling up at her window from the street, telling her to stay away from him. She never saw him again."

Mischa translated the anecdote in her head.

"Clarissa, let's just say, message delivered and acknowledged, and move on."

Mischa was flattered that Clarissa would see her as a threat, but perhaps this was a typical response to any woman who had spoken to Christopher for more than fifteen minutes. Mischa thought she would never want a relationship that incurred such paranoia and required so much maintenance. While they drove in silence, Mischa looked over at Clarissa, focused on passing another car. *Why does she put up with it?*

A few weeks later, Mischa was at a dinner at Abe's house. He had three people from the forensics team over, guys that stayed at his house intermittently. Two other stars from the expatriate clique had also dropped in, the guy who worked as the Reuters correspondent and the girl from the *Financial Times.* Carmina, Jill, and Christopher were there as well. While Gabriel was in the kitchen making paella, she and the other journalists were discussing the upcoming election. The forensics team was operating an assembly line, tightly wrapping crumbled bits of dried leaves in cigarette paper and placing them on a saucer. Abe uncorked bottles of Argentine and Chilean red wine. Mischa looked at the bottles and was startled by one.

It was the wine that her mother had served at Sunday lunch in Chile. The one at all the Sunday lunches and family gatherings in Chile.

The label on the wine bottle had the etching of the gate to her great-uncle's vineyard estate, Viña San Pedro. Her great-uncle had a crate of the wine delivered regularly to each family member, and no other wine was ever served in the family's household. Fatima, the family's cook when Mischa and her parents lived in Chile, always prepared roast beef, potatoes, and flan for Sunday lunch, along with ten other dishes and ten additional desserts. They always served her great-uncle's wine. Until she was older, Mischa thought every wine bottle label looked like the ones from Viña San Pedro. Those Sundays were always loud. The people and the house felt warm.

When Mischa's mother died, Cristina's family blamed her father. They had never liked him, and their anger grew once he had persuaded their beloved daughter and sister to move to the U.S. When Pinochet took over, Cristina's family was glad to see "that communist," President Allende, pushed out of government. Nevertheless, they made it clear to her that they were fearful that the Pinochet regime could misinterpret Richard's academic specialty in Russian literature and put the family at risk. If he were labeled as a subversive, the family might also be considered guilty by association.

At Sunday lunches, Cristina's family always made hints and sometimes overt suggestions for Richard to change his professional focus. They wondered if perhaps French literature, American literature, or Latin American literature would be a better career move. It was so much safer, they argued. It was that question, once asked by an innocent relative who had no idea of its significance, which drove Professor Dunn from the dinner table one day.

"And didn't I hear that a position opened for a professor in English literature at the university?"

Cristina followed Richard when he stormed out of the room. She pleaded with him.

"Richard, they don't understand. Richard, *por favor, mi amor*, don't take it the wrong way. They don't know what happened."

Deaf to her pleas, he slammed the door of the house. The dining room went silent as everyone looked at each other. They heard the start of a car engine. It only confirmed their opinion; this man did not belong in their family.

There was indeed a space for a professor of English literature; it opened when Tito Alvarez's clothes and his briefcase were found bloodied and torn on the steps, outside the Department of Literature. Professor Alvarez was never found—rather, his body was never found—but the message from the regime was clear: academics should teach, not protest. The other nine professors of literature, who had never shown an interest in politics, had an unspoken agreement to keep Professor Alvarez's office unoccupied. They never sought to replace him, nor did they offer another degree in English literature. It was their only show of defiance against the regime. It was not overt, but nevertheless courageous. But its double meaning saved them from a similar fate to that of Professor Alvarez. Through the eyes of a Pinochet supporter it was a timid concession. Whatever the meaning, all perceived what they wished; they found their peace and a way to move forward.

When Professor Dunn took his wife and child to the United States, Cristina's family viewed him as little more than a kidnapper. They knew that she would not have the benefit of a cook, or a gardener, or a maid, or even a driver. A middle-class life in the U.S. was far worse than an upper-class life in Chile. The women of her family bemoaned that the beautiful and intelligent Cristina would be reduced to a maid, taking care of her own house in "the United States of Suburbia," as Tia Teresa, the spinster, called it. The family marveled that Cristina would not even have a driver. She would have to learn to drive herself.

Cristina's family always raised the same arguments that they used to persuade Professor Dunn and Cristina to stay in Chile. They never worked on him; he felt guilty for the indolent life as a member of the elite in Chile, and was happy at the prospect of returning to a country where he would mow his own lawn and carry out his own trash.

For years after Cristina's death, her family still blamed Richard.

Mischa looked at that bottle from Chile, sitting on the table in Guatemala. She remembered that a bottle of her uncle's best vintage, 1958, always arrived in time for Cristina's name day, every July 24, the day designated for her patron saint. After her mother's death, a bottle never came. Her mother's name day became the anniversary of the day Mischa lost contact with her family in Chile.

She picked the bottle up and saw that the vintage was five years—no, she corrected herself—six years after her mother's death. She studied the pencil etching of the gate pictured on the label. She and her cousins had run races down the road and used the gate as the starting line. Sometimes they had used it as a goal for a soccer game.

"Can I get you a glass?" asked Abe. "It's a good wine. Strong, maybe a little too spicy, but typically Chilean."

"No, no, I don't drink. I was just looking at the label."

Mischa remembered that she wanted to ask Abe about the two men in suits, sitting in a car, just outside her house. "They were there last night, then again tonight when I came out on my way over here. What should I do?"

He was nonchalant, taking one of the joints from the saucer and lighting it. "I wouldn't worry. If you ask me, it's pretty normal. It's what happens with a lot of the human rights advocates that come down here, and journalists as well. It's just a message from the Ministry of Interior, you know, kinda like 'we're watching you.'"

Abe moved over to the sofa where Carmina lay. "Consider it the Guatemalan government welcoming committee." *Inhale.* "It's no secret. It's just an intimidation tactic. They do it all the time. Consider yourself one of us now." *Inhale.* "You can stay here if you want. We have enough rooms. They'll stop coming after about a week." *Inhale...puff.* "It's just a message, no cause for alarm." He blew the smoke into Carmina's face and she laughed lazily. Abe wanted his hands free. "Here, Mischa, have a go."

"No thanks," she said, missing the purpose of his offer.

"Mischa, would you put it on the table?" Abe asked, annoyed.

She took the rest of the joint and stubbed it out. Despite the two security men in the cars, she considered that staying in Abe's house with seven males prone to drunkenness, drugs, and random sex was not a reasonable alternative.

Christopher was seated nearby and overheard the conversation. "Why not stay with Clarissa and me? We've got a guest room."

A few days at a tropical cottage. Mischa had a vision of their fruit trees and their fountain. With less than a minute's consideration, she accepted the invitation. After dinner, Christopher followed her back to her apartment and saw for himself that the men were still sitting in the car. She packed her things and the two drove off in the Volkswagen Bug. When they arrived at the cottage, Mischa realized that they were alone.

"So where is Clarissa?"

"She left this afternoon. There was a plane crash in Costa Rica. She had to do a report."

"Ah, I see." Mischa's shoulders rose as she grew tense.

He walked over to the refrigerator. "I need a glass of white wine. A change of pace from all that red at Abe's house." He took a green bottle from the refrigerator door and turned to her. "I remember that you don't drink. We have some tamarind juice, would that be okay?"

"That would be fine, thanks. So, Christopher, what's the assignment of the moment?"

She stayed on the sofa. He came around the edge and sat at her feet on the floor. He was flirtatious. She curled her legs onto the side of the sofa to stay away. As he continued, she wrapped her arms around her legs until she was speaking to him with her chin resting between her knees. Hardly encouraging, she responded in a monotone voice, deciding to remain ignorant as he softly lobbed one sexual innuendo after another. It was difficult, for he delicately tailored his humor and conversation to her interests.

Mischa wasn't deaf to his charm, but she was a realist. It would be one night, and then back to Clarissa. The two had their unspoken arrangement. *Who knows, maybe Clarissa gives him "holidays," away from their relationship. Perhaps this is a negotiated settlement to keep him under control.*

Christopher edged closer. Those eyes were inviting and he was uncomfortably close. Any encouragement through body language, a calculated or miscalculated clumsiness, could lead to something else. Mischa reminded herself over and over, this was just a game for Christopher. *He's not interested in me, it's just the conquest. It's not me.* Her instinct with men was rarely tested, but she trusted what little she had. Around three in the morning Christopher finally gave up. He heaved a sigh, like a tennis player who had just lost a game, and pointed to the guest room behind the kitchen.

"You can sleep in there. Clarissa keeps the fresh sheets in the closet over there."

"Don't worry. I'll just stay here, on the sofa. This is more than comfortable."

He looked at her with a smile. "Mischa, darling, it's been a waste of an evening. I could have brought one or two of the other girls home with me and I would have had a lovely shag or even shags." he said good-naturedly. "My sweet, you are so excruciatingly boring." He stayed still and stared directly into her eyes for a few seconds to gauge her reaction.

Mischa laughed nervously. She thought it was the most sincerely flattering remark he had made all evening, but then she became flustered. She looked at him and realized that the match was not over. His sophisticated seduction technique had not worked, so Christopher was now offering an honest and direct invitation to a one-night stand.

She stuttered, "Why don't we...we...leave it at the fact that...well...I want to sleep by myself...here, right here, alone...on this couch...tonight. But I should...well...um...I guess...thank you and...I'll take it as a compliment that...that...despite my well-known status as a prude you would even want to try."

"Of course I wanted to try. Why not? Why climb Everest? Because it's there, my sweet." Like an athlete gracefully acknowledging defeat, he rose and with his back turned to her, waved good night as he left the room. Game, set, match.

The next morning, while he was still asleep, Mischa left a brief note of thanks on their dining room table. Mischa stayed with Jill and Carmina for the rest of the week, checking to see if the car with the two men was still parked outside her ground-floor apartment. While working on their computer she heard violent knocking at the door. *Is this what happens when Guatemalan security forces pick someone up for questioning?*

"Mischa! Mischa! Can you hear me?" *Ah, that lovely posh British accent.* It was Clarissa. Mischa was relieved. She laughed. *Is Clarissa really saying my name?* Mischa knew what this was about. She opened the door to find Clarissa's usually pale English face flushed red with anxious anger. *She must have seen the note.*

"Where did you sleep?" Clarissa demanded.

"Hello, Clarissa, how are you? I am fine," Mischa responded.

"Cut the humor. I want to know: where did you sleep?"

"I slept on the sofa. If you believe otherwise, talk to Christopher. Can I offer you a drink? I'm just about to make a pitcher of tamarind juice."

Clarissa turned and marched across the street to her Volkswagen Bug. No doubt she had found the note on the table. Mischa kicked herself for having sunk to such playground antics. She went back into the kitchen and stirred the murky water until the sugar dissolved. *What the hell, I'm not a saint.*

⌘ ⌘ ⌘

The day she left Guatemala, Mischa went to La Aurora Airport several hours before the plane was set to depart. The dead time before a flight always put her in a meditative state. It was a rare slice of time when everything that was to be done had been done, or at least it was too late to do anything else. It was a relief to arrive early and watch planes take off and land.

As she fingered her airline ticket, turning it back and forth, Mischa counted the seizures in Guatemala. The most memorable one was at the Ministry of Defense. *Was it at the entrance to the press room, or during the press conference?* She had forgotten to ask the witnesses. Out of curiosity, she usually asked for reports. Many times they were volunteered.

When she awoke from the seizure, she found herself looking up at flags of the different branches of the Guatemalan armed forces. She looked up at the walls to see photographs of the spokesman shaking hands with foreign dignitaries and military officials. There was one of him smiling with a group of Special Forces soldiers dressed in camouflage, posing with rifles at the sentry gate to a military training camp.

An army medic was next to her, checking her blood pressure while a headache raged inside. She thought about the floor in Washington, DC, at the human rights NGO. She looked up at the photograph above her. It was the spokesman smiling next to the defense minister, one of the architects of genocide in the Guatemalan highlands. Clarissa was a few feet away and in a conversation with Christopher.

"Clarissa, love, I've got to get back to the house and file the story. By the way, Jill is coming with me. The Internet in her office is down."

He looked directly at Clarissa. It was a challenge and a message. Clarissa paused and swallowed the sigh she might have made and the words she might have spoken. Jill looked awkward and expectant. As they left the office suite, Christopher gently guided Jill out the door with his hand pressed lightly against her lower back. Clarissa shut her eyes while she regained her composure.

"Why do you take it?" Mischa asked. She cringed as she heard a tone of derision in her voice, but after a seizure she had no social filter, no ability to nuance a phrase. Those were the first words that leapt to her brain.

"Because I'm besotted," Clarissa responded curtly. "Now, why don't you shut up? You have a bloody lip." Clarissa ordered ice water from the secretary across the room.

Mischa's tongue was a throbbing mass of ground meat, and she saw that she was drooling blood on her white shirt. One of the secretaries wiped her chin with a tissue as Clarissa looked around for a pillow for Mischa.

She didn't like me. She still doesn't like me. But here she is, next to me. She wondered how long the spokesman would allow her to sleep in his office suite, but she fell asleep anyway.

Mischa looked down at her plane ticket again, and flapped it against the palm of her hand rhythmically. Her last four years with human rights advocates and leftists had been a disappointment. They all wanted to change the world. Focusing on moral justice as a cause, many forgot to find it in their own lives. They were debtors living off credit earned from struggling for liberal rights, like medieval Catholics buying indulgences to wipe away their sins. They would lapse in their own lives and cheat on their partners, ridicule their friends, swindle someone out of profit on a drug deal, lie easily about anything, come down on their staff like a plantation overseer, or stay seated on the bus, while at their side an indigenous mother carried a baby and had two children clutching at her skirt. They were no better or worse than their counterparts to the right. But the hypocrisy made their fall from grace all the more painful in discovery, as if the ideals they fought for were sullied by their personal lives. Mischa could hear her own self-righteousness surge and she stopped herself. Sometimes these people who lived outside of social convention did achieve social justice, and it only happened because they fought for it, while others who dutifully came home to their husbands and their wives, who never had affairs, who never drank too much, who never tried drugs, sat by and did nothing.

Guatemala was a living aura: the colors, the people, and the vividness of life. If, like a child, she could craft her own auras, cut them from scraps of paper and magazine pictures to create a collage of those hazy spells, they would all recall a little of Guatemala.

Mischa looked down at her backpack holding her Guatemalan *huipil*, pottery, tattered Post-its of quotes, laptop, and the last two orange vials of anti-convulsants. There were perhaps ten—no, maybe eleven—seizures in Guatemala. The numbers were so sterile, so hopeless. She remembered the bizarre details of some seizures and would go over them; like an art collector of miniaturist paintings, she looked through her tiny cabinet of curiosities. Strangely, they were among the enjoyable memories of her time there. She tried to quickly pack the recollection away before the sequence arrived at the moment of the headache and those feelings of anger, fear, and hopelessness. She preferred to bring her thoughts to an abrupt halt before they got to that point.

She looked out the window to see a plane coming to a stop on the tarmac. Airport workers rolled metal stairs to the exit door. A random lot of passengers filed off the plane, and Mischa tried to guess their identities and purpose—as tourists, businessmen, hikers, diplomats, relatives, or expatriates. She looked down at her ticket and repeated "Heathrow" over and over to convince herself that she really was leaving.

15.   THE TENNIS COURT

THE BUS DRIVER HANDED MISCHA HER SUITCASES. Still jet-lagged from the flight, she stared ahead at Parker's Piece and looked down at the map the history faculty secretary had e-mailed her. The bus stop for all the shuttles between Cambridge and Heathrow was only four streets away from her new accommodations. She thought this lucky coincidence was a good omen.

For the first two months Mischa lived in a state of profound culture shock. She had left a place of sun, yellow dust, green banana trees, and people in the streets dressed in brilliant colors. In England during autumn, the sky was gray, the wind was freezing, and people dressed in black and brown. The sharp bursts of wind that pierced the tooth chipped in Guatemala were a painful reminder that she had come from an average daily temperature of eighty degrees Fahrenheit to one of thirty degrees.

With the change of location to Cambridge, she hoped that she might have fewer seizures. There was no medical reason to make her remotely believe it was possible. It was the belief that in a new place, there were new chances and opportunity for changes. At least she hoped. Seizures in close succession drained her emotional reserves. When she had fewer, she could forget them, and with simple denial, capture a few months of freedom before she was dragged back to reality.

Cambridge was a cluster of castles, cathedrals, and manor houses squeezed together in a few square miles. The thirty-one colleges were built by royals, nobles, and aristocrats over eight hundred years and comprised the University of Cambridge. Many were grand enough to deserve a moat or acres of woodland separating them from the world, but were built within a few hundred feet of each other. It was easier to be invisible in Cambridge; she was one among thousands of students. Not like in Guatemala, where she was one among fifty incestuous expatriate twenty-somethings.

She wanted to share Cambridge with her father and have him show her the town as he knew it—his pubs, bookshops, and the tea house where he first tasted hot cross buns. When they were dating in Chile, Mischa's mother had surprised him by serving him a batch of homemade hot cross buns. He joked that she had cast a spell over him with her cooking, like a magical character from Latin American literature. After they were married, she religiously baked hot cross buns once a month. In Mischa's phone calls to her father, she tried to tempt him with the prospect of authentic hot cross buns and persuade him to come to Cambridge. She had tried everything: telling him she was homesick, saying that she needed encouragement on her thesis, pleading that she missed him.

"Dad, don't you want to come back? It's been more than thirty years. We could have so much fun."

"Mischa, I'm so busy with conferences, and I took on another class this semester. I can't get away. After all, someone's got to pay for your education. Enjoy yourself. I don't have to show you Cambridge." His tone clearly conveyed his anticipation of concluding the conversation.

Richard had finished his PhD at twenty-seven and earned a fellowship to Cambridge. He had been there only a few days when he met a Chilean on the same fellowship, Tito Alvarez. They ended up sharing a flat together. Tito recommended that Richard come back to Chile with him for a month after the fellowship program ended. Young and unencumbered, Richard Dunn took him up on his offer. After Tito introduced him to his sister's friend, Cristina, Richard decided to stay a little longer, and eventually found a job with the University of Santiago. After one year he had saved enough money to purchase a diamond ring and he asked Cristina to marry him.

Following another failed conversation with her father, Mischa drank a consolatory cup of tea in the kitchen. She looked down at her hands cradling the mug for warmth and noticed her nails. They were too long; she needed to cut them. She remembered her father's nails and how he tore them in the days before her mother's funeral, in the emergency room when she had her first seizure, and that night in Chile, when Mrs. Alvarez came and cried about Tito's disappearance. Now she understood. It was clear. It wasn't her. He didn't want to be near the memories of Tito. Mischa ended her efforts to persuade him to visit her. She could not save her father from his grief for Tito or her mother. She had come to Cambridge for escape and adventure, as much as for a graduate degree that could get her a job. She was going to enjoy it.

In many ways, Cambridge was more exotic than Guatemala. Despite growing up in the United States, Mischa felt at home in Latin American culture. Whether it was Southern or Central, there were vast similarities in Latin America. She came to Cambridge presuming similarities between the United States and the United Kingdom, but the mass of differences, one after another, left her confused.

In the UK, Mischa felt as if she had been transported to a place where there was a sheet of glass between her and everyone else. Conversation with the British was the most difficult. Mischa was accustomed to a rhythm of relay in conversation; someone made a point, another reaffirmed and made his or her point. It could be as simple as "yeah," "uh-huh," or "I see what you mean." In Latin America, hands danced and touched, words splashed, and voices rose to emphasize, and never was there a lull in conversation. Pauses were perceived as expressions of disinterest. In America it wasn't as chaotic, but there was still that constant volley of words, someone telling a story, or making encouraging comments for the other person to continue speaking, and interruptions were common occurrences.

But in England it was far different. The English did not talk with their hands, they did not raise their voices in public, and worst of all, they did not interrupt. Mischa found herself talking and talking, waiting for an English student to dive and swim into the conversation so that she could take a breath. But they didn't come in; they stood there, quietly, waiting for her to finish. The need for air would finally bring her to a stop. They would utter a few sentences, and like a child who wants to dive into paddling pool Mischa would dive in with a comment and expect them to continue. But like adults who do not want to dive into a paddling pool with a child, the British would pause and wait for her to finish her comment. It was confusing, for her as much as for them. It was irritating, for her as much as for them. Then there was the word "sorry." It seemed to lose all sincerity in this country, as people apologized for the most mundane, trivial actions and for events for which they were not even responsible. Another idiosyncrasy was the query by others if she was Canadian. When she asked a few people why they would presume that, they said that even if they think a person is more likely to be American than Canadian, it was more polite to suggest Canadian, so as not to offend the potential Canadian. Commonwealth politics were lost on Mischa. The monarchy was a mystery.

Why would sixty million people choose to continue with a dynastic tax burden of the royal family? Why not give the prime minister a palace and sell off the rest of the castles and estates?

There were six English students and Mischa in the student house on 81 Warkworth Street. Since they were usually preoccupied with their research, boyfriends, girlfriends, and pub mates, there was little interaction among them except in the kitchen. If the polite silence in a British conversation was confusing, the quiet in the shared kitchen was inexplicable. In Mischa's life, kitchens were places of noise and rich smells and shared food. But in Cambridge the kitchen was a hushed place. Even when two or three people were preparing their meals, conversations consisted of "Excuse me," "Sorry," and "Are you done with the microwave?"

Inhabitants concentrated on averting their eyes and dancing the kitchen minuet as they tried to avoid collision. A baked potato (a.k.a jacket potato in British English) smothered with baked beans and cheddar cheese was the food staple for students. A fifty-pound bag of potatoes, which sat in the corner, was purchased by one of the housemates who had collected money from the others. It was a witness to the pale form of social interaction at 81 Warkworth Street.

The first time Mischa truly comprehended that England was her new home was in her fifth week. She brought her radio into the kitchen to accompany her as she washed dishes. It was one a.m. and Radio 4 was broadcasting the daily shipping forecasts. Before the shipping forecasts there are two minutes of a lilting melody "Sailing By," something akin to elevator music that evokes a swaying ship and seagulls flying in the distance. After the music, a lone announcer reports on the shipping forecasts. After five minutes of conveying information on the stride of the winds and waves, the announcer quips a polite and quick "good night," followed immediately by trumpets, cymbals, and drums pouring forth in a brief rendition of "God Save the Queen." Even a foreigner has the instinct to recognize that at one a.m., on BBC Radio 4, a person experiences a truly traditional British moment.

Occasionally, during bouts of homesickness, she would sing the lyrics of "My Country, 'Tis of Thee" to the music of "God Save the Queen." Mischa wondered how many Britons knew that an American in the 1800s had transposed the lyrics of their royalist anthem and turned it into a hymn to a federal republic. Would they appreciate it as early American irony or consider it the last gasp of British influence before slapstick and knock-knock jokes took over?

During the shipping forecasts there was a unique rhythm and pace to the announcer's reading of the forecasts, something like a gentle nanny repeating rules of table etiquette. There were familiar phrases. Mischa's favorite was "storms losing their identities." She imagined winds swirling and whirling themselves into the shape of that stressed cartoon figure in the Edvard Munch painting, *The Scream*, and wailing, "Who am I? What am I doing? What am I doing here?" At one a.m., before turning off the lights, the shipping forecast was the best lullaby. Like the calming tones of a Buddhist chant, the ritual comfort was all she sought. "Gales rising slowly...rising swiftly... five...point of Gibraltar...seventeen...the ten...Irish Sea...three...storms losing their identities over the North Sea...Dover...Hebrides."

For Mischa, the other British institutions that dominated Cambridge were less soothing and less appealing than the BBC shipping forecasts: the pub and Formal Hall. Socialization for students in Cambridge occurred through Formal Hall. It was the same as the practice in Oxford. Students and professors, members of their respective colleges, were required to "dress for dinner." It was weekly event. Attendance was voluntary but encouraged. The men wore suits and the women wore dresses, and both wore their scholars' gowns on top, the type of black gowns used for graduation ceremonies in the United States.

At these dinners, the students sat at dark English oak tables lined with candelabras. Kitchen staff served the various courses and poured the appropriate wines. The meals ended with cheese plates, fruits, and sherry. College elders, deans, professors, and fellows sat at the head table, while the members of the college, the students, would eat at the dining room tables arranged around the room. Among strangers, small talk was the height of conversation. Then again, sometimes dinner companions found a common interest and struck up a friendship, had an intellectual brainstorm, or ended up having a drink and more in their rooms.

If a person were forced to use only one word to explain the British psyche it would be irony. It was a lesson that was thrown in Mischa's face time and time again, outside and inside the classroom. British irony was a steady voice delivering an unexpected blow in a conversation. She learned to stay alert, for at any second a remark that seemed literal could be a facade. They called it irony, but Mischa considered it sarcasm.

Irony and sarcasm were common dishes in most Formal Hall dinners in Cambridge. When a sympathetic Briton met with an American's look of bewilderment, he or she ended the confusion with a phrase like, "I'm only joking." A less-than-sympathetic Briton remained stonily silent and stared until Americans took out a whip to flail themselves for their stupidity and failure to understand the "irony." A cruel Briton would continue, slapping the American with one sarcastic comment after another.

A polite conversation with ironic footnotes was like a lazy game of tennis played between friends on a sunny afternoon. One would gently hit the ball, the other would hit back, and the two would laugh at each other's quips. A conversation with irony on fierce display was like watching two competitors slamming serves and slicing backhands.

When Mischa arrived late to Formal Hall, she took the first seat she could find. The dinner companion to Mischa's left was in the midst of a raging flirtation with the woman beside him. Her dinner companion to her right had ginger hair—the British word for red. He wore cuff links engraved with the college's coat of arms. She had never met him before, but recognized the type immediately. Once he graduated, Cufflinks would wave his Cambridge degree throughout his life expecting respect as a consequence. He would be mystified and unsettled whenever he met someone who had graduated from a "lesser" institution and knew, or earned, more than him. He would gratefully rip open any invitation to an alumni gathering and RSVP "yes," and never miss the Oxford and Cambridge Boat Race on the Thames. Sitting across from him Mischa saw a familiar face. It was Hector, the treasurer and purchaser of the sack of potatoes at 81 Warkworth Street. She wasn't certain whether he had seen her, since he was studiously separating the gristle from the meat.

After Mischa introduced herself, Cufflinks commented on her American accent, which Mischa thought was a reasonable opening for a dinner conversation. He proceeded to give her a lecture on the difference between irony and sarcasm, and the Americans' lack of appreciation for both. When he finished, he smiled with self-satisfaction and looked over to Hector. When she saw him deliver a knowing wink to Hector, Mischa knew that Cufflinks had been practicing his backhand and he considered her the equivalent of the empty half of a tennis court.

"So, tell me, was our conversation ironic or sarcastic?" Mischa asked.

The red-headed boy was silent. Hector laughed in delight at Mischa's surprise attack on his patronizing compatriot and said, "My, the lady is dry. Why don't you pour her a sherry?" With the deference of a toast he tipped his glass in Mischa's direction.

"Oh, no, that's okay. I don't drink alcohol," she said. When she turned to look at Cufflinks, he was smiling like a Cheshire cat. Hector's face had the crestfallen look of a fan that had just seen his player lose the match. Mischa was flustered. "Ah, I get it. Dry sherry, dry wit. Ah, yes, I see."

"Don't worry, Mischa, it's fine." Hector picked up the water pitcher on the table. "May I refill your glass?"

The dinner companion looked to his other side for another source of entertainment, while Mischa and Hector continued talking and later walked back to 81 Warkworth Street. She had gone to bed late that night, having a cup of tea with him while he regaled her with stories of the absurd small talk he had suffered through at Formal Hall. Her first real conversation with a housemate, Hector, resulted in a monetary contribution toward the purchase of the next bag of potatoes. Now, she felt as if she belonged there.

16. THE CLASSROOM

AFTER MORNING LECTURES, MISCHA WOULD RETURN TO 81 WARKWORTH STREET FOR AN EARLY LUNCH. Coming up the steps from the kitchen on her way to the library one day, she heard Hector on the hallway phone and froze with surprise. He was speaking loudly. She looked around the corner. He was using his hands. He was speaking Spanish, and not high school Spanish. He spoke with the speed of a native. It must have been her imagination, but she felt a gust of warm wind. Hector felt himself being watched and looked over. Mischa blushed and hurried past him on her way out the front door.

From that afternoon on, the sound of steps on the staircase was sufficient cause for a visit the kitchen. Mischa had been doing that all day, in anticipation of finding Hector and then suffering the disappointment of realizing it was another housemate. Annoyed with herself, now on her seventh trip to the kitchen, she opened the kitchen door to finally find Hector. She greeted him with an air of affection that took him by surprise and he physically pulled back.

"So, how is it that you speak Spanish?" He was clearly alarmed that she would know such a personal fact. Mischa quickly explained that she had overheard him as she was on her way out and he was talking on the phone.

"My parents are Cuban," Hector replied curtly.

"I thought you were British. Your mail says Durham. It doesn't sound very Cuban."

"My grandfather emigrated from Ireland to Cuba. Then my parents emigrated from Cuba to the UK. I was born here. I am British."

"What was an Irishman doing in Cuba?" Mischa was nervous again. "Actually, don't answer that one. I forget, the Irish go everywhere. My dad is Irish American, and believe it or not, Bernardo O'Higgins is the name of a famous Chilean independence hero. My mom is—was—Chilean. So, tell me, what are Cubans doing in England?"

Hector was uninterested in the coincidence and irritated by her persistence to engage in a conversation about their origins. "There are planes and ships, and occasionally people move from here to there. Count my relatives among them."

Now, that was sarcastic. Mischa decided to continue despite his backhand and shot back. "I'm not asking for flight numbers." With a voice full of genuine curiosity, she repeated her inquiry. "Really, what brought them? What were the circumstances?"

Hector explained that when Fidel Castro came to power, his parents were idealists. They joined the cause, helped cut sugarcane in the fields, and went to rallies to cheer Castro in his speeches against Yankee Imperialism. A few years later, after hearing of executions and witnessing the imprisonment of friends, they lost their idealism. They realized that one dictator had just been replaced by another, only this one chose to wear fatigues and grow a beard.

"After one of my uncles, a Catholic priest, was imprisoned and executed, my parents decided to leave. European universities were still romancing the Cuban revolution and offered fellowships to attract Cuban scholars. My father was granted a fellowship at the University of Leeds. They left Cuba and never returned. I was born in Leeds."

"Do you have any brothers or sisters?" They still had not established an easy flow of conversation. But at least she was able to get him to talk.

Hector maintained eye contact with the box of tea bags. "I'm an only child."

"Isn't it ironic? Your parents left Cuba because of a Communist dictator. My family left Chile because of a Fascist dictator."

Hector didn't respond. She suggested that they speak Spanish. He was not enthused, but politely obliged.

Mischa couldn't understand why, despite their shared background, it was hard to talk. He was speaking Spanish, but he had a British manner of speech. He wasn't interrupting or using his hands. She gave him some leeway and reminded herself that not only was he British, but he was also a scientist. That would be enough to eclipse any Latin personality traits.

"Do your parents still live in Leeds?"

"My father is there. My mother has—or rather, had—cancer. She died last year."

"I'm sorry," said Mischa.

"Actually, it's harder for my dad than for me."

"I know what you mean. My mother died nearly eight years ago." Mischa paused in thought; she had never calculated the time that had passed. Her father had probably been counting the days. "My father still hasn't recovered."

"I don't think you ever do. You just decide to live on. Maybe it depends on whether you accept life as it is, or constantly rue the fact that your life is not the same." He took a last sip of tea and set his mug down in the sink. He looked at his watch. "*Perdóname*, you'll have to excuse me. I'm late for a lecture." He zipped up his fleece jacket. "Shall I see you later, Mischa? Sorry for the rush, we can share a cuppa when I'm not so rushed."

Such a dark conversation, but Mischa smiled uncontrollably at him, with her imperfect teeth on full display. Hector smiled back warmly and looked at her for a moment. With the barest hint of affection, he gave her a kiss on the cheek.

"*Hasta pronto*," he said, and turned to leave.

It was not a romantic kiss, rather the standard greeting and good-bye kiss in Latin America. It was the type a friend would give a friend or a brother would give his sister, but Mischa held her hand over her cheek, to keep it there just a little longer.

After that day, Hector was transformed in Mischa's eyes. His frame, which was lanky before, now became tall and commanding. She didn't see the awkward 1980s frames of his glasses that were so retro they were almost—only almost—fashionable, just his blue green eyes. Above all his physical features, Hector's hair was the measure of his character. Other students gelled their hair into spikes or moussed their bangs. They looked like boys at the seashore, their hair permanently swept awry by wind. Had there been a '50s revival, Hector would have been at the height of fashion. He kept a side part and wore his hair short and traditional. Faded T-shirts and worn jeans were his wardrobe staples, and sadly, for Mischa's tastes, his oxford shirts.

She could never bring herself to romanticize those oxford shirts. The ones that were clean and neat only reminded her of the ones she despised, with bullet-like sprays of black ink on the pocket. When he wore them he looked as if he had been in a shoot-out at the corral of Applied Mathematics and Theoretical Physics. He had an array of these shirts, only the ink-splotches differentiated them. The shade of the ink indicated the number of washes the shirt had survived and therefore the age of the splotch. The diameter of the splotch indicated how long he had gone completely unaware of the ink seeping into his shirt. There were more than a few of these shirts around the university. Mischa finally concluded there was a tribal element to this phenomenon. What the tattoo was for gang members, so was the ink-blotted shirt for scientists.

Despite the shirts her crush persisted, and so did her pursuit.

Sometimes they met on their way to class, when he was walking across Parker's Piece on his way back from the Department of Applied Mathematics and Theoretical Physics. She could recognize his shape from a distance and studied him as they neared each other. Other students wore backpacks, shoulder bags, and even carried briefcases, but Hector carried his books and pens in plastic grocery bags. As he approached her from a distance, she caught a glimpse of the boy who must have been calculating the arcs of missile paths for his homemade rocket while the other kids were playing football. Hector had a touch of the eccentric.

After a few weeks, of "spontaneous" appearances for a cup of tea when he did his laundry, Hector knocked at her door with his laundry in hand and offered to make her a cup of tea. Mischa was unaware that the invitation was not as casual as it appeared. Hector had come down repeatedly during the day but always returned to his room, with his dirty clothes, when he discovered that she was not there.

Sitting across from the washer and dryer, watching clothes swish back and forth, they realized that despite their completely different interests in history and science, they shared a nerdish habit in listening to BBC Radio 4 constantly. They talked about their favorite shows: *Desert Island Discs*, *The Strand*, and the strangely addictive *Gardeners' Question Time*. In that last program, sweet English ladies and kindly gentlemen, like petitioners to great oracles, queried an expert panel for solutions to problems with their *Helianthemum, Hedera helix, Tuplipa humili*, and other garden residents. A group of botanists and professional gardeners, absolute masters in their fields, so humble in their knowledge, responded with their diagnoses. The petitioners were in ecstasy when they discovered that their problem was minor and a solution was clear. Their utter despair was evident in their voice, when the panel responded that there was no hope and the plant must be uprooted. Even if a person lacked any knowledge of gardening, like Mischa and Hector, the near omniscience of the experts and the calm rhythm of the show—problem stated, problem solved, problem stated, problem solved—was an antidote to real life. In *Gardeners' Question Time* there was an answer to everything. *Beep-beep-beep* was the most irritating sound during Mischa's time in Cambridge. It was the signal that the dryer cycle was finished. Hector would take his clothes out, pack them into the hamper, say good night and walk upstairs.

One night as he did this, Mischa said, "There's a church across Parker's Piece, Our Lady and the English Martyrs. It has a Latin mass. Do you want to go this Sunday?"

"Our Lady and the English Martyrs?" Hector asked. "Where did that name come from?"

"You're the English Catholic, you should know. I guess that around the time that Henry was decapitating wives, England wasn't a safe place for Catholics. So, wanna go?"

Hector stopped folding and looked at her. "Mischa, are you asking me out?"

She was caught with her eyes wide open; the iconic deer-in-the-headlights. *Oh no, I am such a nerd. I am asking a guy out to church. Maybe if I say something sarcastic I won't look as stupid. What to say?*

"Why not? If communion doesn't fill us up, we could go out for dinner afterward. Mass is at six on Sunday." *Slightly heretical, but somewhat hip.* She hoped it sounded nonchalant, but wanted to hit her head against a door frame. *I thought Guatemala made me "cool," but no. I am still a nerd. I am hopeless and dysfunctional. I might as well be back at Mama MIA.*

Hector paused in thought. "Okay, just come by. I'll be waiting for you in my room."

He smiled and walked upstairs with his folded laundry in the hamper. She was taken aback. His reply was almost suggestive. She considered the deadpan delivery, the fact that his voice did not drop into a seductive lower register, the fact that he did not look at her differently. Was this flirtation for a British male? She wished she knew someone who could dissect this culture for her.

The next morning she lay in bed, half thinking about Hector and half listening to the radio. The Radio 4 Program, *Desert Island Discs*, was her looking glass into the British psyche. The format was ingenious. Mischa was jealous when Hector once described the announcer's voice as beguiling, but as she listened to the interviewer this morning she had to admit that he was right. Teasing and smoky, the announcer's voice was coy; she was an intellectual flirt who conversed easily with her guests, men or women, scholars, artists, actors, politicians, athletes, and authors. The guests chose music for the show that was particularly meaningful to them. These were the discs they would bring to a desert island. During the show the interviewer asked questions inspired by the music and then played an excerpt. The musical reverie lulled the guests into a state of intimacy. All of them lost their inhibitions, shed their protective layers of Britishness, and revealed details and emotions, seemingly forgetting that they were being broadcast to nine million listeners. Occasionally their voices cracked, yet they continued with their stalwart attempt to suppress their emotions. The announcer was sympathetic and often introduced the next disc during those moments, providing a musical interlude that allowed the guest to recover.

A twinge of memory, suggesting that she should be elsewhere, made Mischa look at her watch. *Oh my God. Brinkley's lecture! I'm late!* She ran, and jogged when she was out of breath, until she arrived at the end of the hallway. The faculty secretary gave her a sympathetic nod of encouragement to enter the classroom. Mischa kept her eyes downward as she opened the door slowly, in the hope of going unnoticed. She stepped into the room cautiously.

"Miss Dunn, so kind of you to join us today."

Mischa took a seat, knowing that this would not be a day to ask a question.

Professor Brinkley was brilliant, but brutal. He was nearly seventy, with waves of white hair. His timeless sky blue eyes offered a glimpse of what he must have looked like as a less-than-omniscient student. He wore tweed jackets, elegantly rumpled for lack of vanity. Though he was open to questions during the lecture, if he believed the question was foolish, he remained silent for fifteen seconds and then moved on with his lecture without addressing it. You could almost hear sighs of relief from students when he did provide an answer. Students whose questions met the quarter minute finally stopped asking. As the year progressed, the rising death toll of pompous and posturing questions led to a commensurate improvement in class discussion.

Mischa concentrated on taking notes, unwilling to look up at Professor Brinkley for fear. As she was writing, the lines of the paper seemed to melt together. The perfume worn by the girl seated next to her stung her nose. Mischa couldn't take her mind off the smell. *Is it a citrus fruit? Grapefruit, apricot, maybe lemon? Yes, lemon, with a soft wisp of mint.* The smell turned into a taste that was tangy, with a murmur of sweetness, and she could touch it and feel pinpricks that tingled. The tastes turned to music. She heard chimes, each one distinct, swaying in random directions that combined into a cacophony of delicate sounds, and then water; she felt waves of water surrounding her.

The state of fascination with the smells, taste, and sounds faded and transformed into a creeping fear. Her conscious mind returned, and for a split second and she was filled with dread knowing what was about to happen—the loss of control. She felt herself being pulled into a whirlpool and she screamed.

Though it seemed only a few seconds later, she was in the third stage of her headache, so she knew it had been a few hours. The girl with the perfume was next to her when Mischa awoke in the emergency room at Addenbrooke's Hospital.

"How are you?"

Mischa was embarrassed that she didn't remember her classmate's name, but she could blame it on the seizure. Now was not the time to place a new fact inside her head. She would ask her tomorrow.

"I'm guessing that I had a seizure."

"Yes. Sorry."

"It's not your fault. Don't say sorry. Why do the British apologize for everything?" *They do it all the time. Sorry for bumping into you; sorry we've run out of milk; sorry, but I was ahead of you in the cue; sorry that you had a seizure. Sorry means nothing in this country. She is nice enough to accompany me to the emergency room and I'm fuming about British speech habits. I should shut the hell up and stop being such a bitch.*

"Actually, I should say sorry. I didn't mean to be so curt. Really, thanks so much for coming here with me." Mischa closed her eyes and counted the weeks in her head. It had been almost ten weeks since her last seizure. After two months without one, Mischa was able to forget her epilepsy. She took her medicine every day, but it was a vacant habit, not a reminder. When she had seizures within less than two weeks of each other, she felt the constant dread of an animal sensing a predator ready to pounce. During these times, the slightest sign of nausea was a signal to begin sleeping on the floor surrounded by several pillows. Often she woke up alone in her room, with the type of headache that signaled a seizure had passed. Mischa was pleased that she had been able to avoid a public ruckus and the drama of an ambulance.

During that time every table corner was a knife, the floor was a sledge-hammer, and each step was a cliff. She would stop herself before she poured a drink into a glass and put it back to take out a plastic cup. She took elevators. She didn't stand as much, but looked for chairs or sat on the floor. If she was walking on concrete, she looked for a path over grass. She would not wear metal clips in her hair, but elastic bands. When she cooked she used the back burner. She still had a scar on her upper arm from one seizure, when she dropped a pot of boiling water as she fell. If it had been on the back burner, she thought it would have been harder to knock off the stove. She knew the measures were likely to be ineffective, but they gave her a feeling of control and to that end served their purpose. Her greatest fear was a fractured skull from a fall, or a hard blow that would result in something worse than her seizures. She would eventually force these thoughts out of her mind by forgetting or by coming to peace with the fact that if something did happen, it would be fate.

She mourned the seizures' return. They had started coming at night, so she could still function during the day and they didn't create such a stir. But she had one or two in the afternoon, when she was alone in the kitchen. She gave herself a few days to grieve and then move on. She had no idea why they had returned; her medication in Cambridge had been the same in Guatemala. Her neurologist in Cambridge was barely more than a resident, a "junior doctor" as they called them in Britain. He felt her derision and saw her as a patient without the sense to have her records at hand. The two of them had an unspoken agreement that they would keep their appointments to a few minutes. He would prescribe the pills, and she would say "thank you" and take the paper.

As Mischa lay in the emergency room, she realized it was the girl with the perfume who was talking to her. She could still smell the tang of citrus, only she didn't see it or hear it, so she knew it wasn't another aura.

"They say Addenbrooke's is the largest medical campus in Europe. That explains so many junior doctors in the emergency room. But don't get nervous, Mischa, this is Cambridge. They're probably the best, top of the class, A-levels, and all. Look at that doctor over there, the one with the red hair. He must be six foot or more. He's looking over right now. Pretend we're talking about something else."

Mischa didn't have to pretend to have heard the last fifteen minutes of conversation. It was a perfect segue to another topic.

"So…how did Professor Brinkley…um…react?"

"He was absolutely speechless. There was quite a bit of mayhem. The ambulance came and the medics could not get you down the steps. Fair enough. They didn't have accessibility building regulations in the sixteenth century. So, the department secretary, Mrs. Hariri, went through the classrooms and found two big rugby players. One of them took you down on his shoulder. He was fit, to say the least. He and his mate came over here after their class to see how you were. He's on the university rugby team. His name is…I forget. It'll come to me."

"I thought Professor Brinkley was made of sterner stuff."

"He's at Saint John's. That's it. He's a prop forward."

"Did you see the seizure—anything?"

"You screamed something, and then you fell. I tried to keep you from falling, but your head hit the chair, which explains your eye. I'm so sorry. You went a little blue, and then you were absolutely limp. The rugby player came in and carried you in his arms. He had absolutely vivid green eyes and blond curls. It could have been a scene from a movie."

"Thanks, but I'm not interested. I'm running after someone in my own college, actually, a housemate. I need to sleep. See if you can convince them to let me go. I don't want to stay overnight."

A few hours later, her classmate took Mischa home in a cab. When they came down to the kitchen, they found Hector trying to open a bottle of spaghetti sauce. The girl leaned over to Mischa and whispered, "Is this the one?"

Mischa nodded and took a seat on the sofa in the kitchen.

"Are you sure? Give me a day, I promise you I can find out the name of that gorgeous rugby player."

"No, that's the one," Mischa replied definitively. The girl left her side and introduced herself to Hector. Mischa was confused; there was no need for her to talk with him. *What is she doing?* Mischa wondered.

The girl with the perfume told him that Mischa had to be accompanied that night, in the event she had another seizure. Those were the doctor's instructions. She asked Hector if he would take over, since she had a previous engagement.

Mischa sat slumped and silent on the kitchen sofa. She felt the tenderness of her eye and her arms when she touched them. Her fingertips went over her mouth and she felt the edge of an inflamed cut lip. She could smell the girl's perfume on her fingertips. It was a faded scent, not citrus, but still fruity, and subtle, like the pale jade middle of a honeydew melon. She liked the smell now and breathed it in from her fingertips again. Mischa saw the drops of dried blood on her khakis. The headache weighed her down and she could feel her head leaning against the sofa, but she watched in admiration at her classmate's artful maneuvering. *I must be in a Jane Austen nightmare.* It was the modern-day equivalent of an eighteenth-century matron persuading a gentleman to ask a young lady to dance a quadrille. Only this was a kitchen, not an elegant ballroom, the gentleman had spaghetti sauce stains on his shirt, and the genteel lady was somewhat catatonic, in post-seizure recovery mode. Despite the differences, Mischa thought, even Miss Austen would have to admit that there were similar plot lines. Not wanting her presence to force an answer from the British-Cuban Mr. Darcy, Mischa staggered out of the kitchen to her room.

Once there, she looked through her CDs and stared at the stereo, trying to remember how it worked. When the music began, she walked toward her bed, but then heard a knock. She opened the door and Hector hugged her tightly, without saying a word. When Mischa pulled away, she gave him a kiss on the cheek.

"Thank you."

"No worries, I'll just pop up to get my laptop and stay here for the night and work."

When he left, she went to see herself in the mirror. She looked as if she had been in a street fight and lost. She returned to her bed to curl up in the blankets. Hector knocked lightly and let himself in. He sat on the floor and began his graceful tapping at the keyboard. Mischa was comforted by the soft light from his screen which reflected off the walls in the dark room. She fell asleep while Billie Holiday wept a song.

17. THE LAUNDRY ROOM

HE WAS WRITING BUT COULD NOT CONCENTRATE. How many times does she have these seizures? How long has she had them? He didn't have the right to ask such private questions. He wouldn't ask them, but he did wonder. Finally, he thought, and most importantly, how does she deal with them? Then the mind of the scientist answered the question. She would only be able to support the weight that she could tolerate. She must have built a way of life that would sustain these seizures. She had a structure in place. That's how she dealt with them. He answered his question, his curiosity abated, and his mind returned to work.

Two days later, on her way to class, Mischa bought a *Big Issue* magazine from a street vendor. Homeless people registered with a local distributor in town, and they earned income from the sale. "Street trade not street aid" was the publication's motto. When she gave the money to the vendor, he came over to her and whispered, "It's all about self-esteem."

"Pardon?" Mischa drew back, startled by the physical intimacy and confused by his words.

"It's all about self-esteem. My sister was beaten up. It took years, but she finally left him. You can too."

Mischa realized that he was looking at her black eye and the scrapes on her face. In horror, she realized that he thought she was a battered woman.

"Oh, no, no, that's not it. I'm epileptic. I got this black eye from falling down, when I hit the edge of the table. I cut myself, too," she explained openly, pointing to her eye and lip.

His eyes full of soft pity, he thought she was still at that stage of denial. His sister made so many excuses on behalf of that bloody bastard. He hoped this girl with the black eye would survive long enough to leave him before he killed her.

Despite her efforts to assure him that it was her epilepsy, he still had that look of sincere empathy. She gave him a few pounds and he handed her the magazine with a smile intended to cheer her.

Mischa knew it was a leap for the man to have even approached her with this suspicion, and beyond that, it was leap for him to share his past and offer her encouragement. She had never been so touched, yet so insulted. Here was a sincere expression of compassion, and yet such a terrible blow to her pride. How could anyone think that she would allow herself to be beaten? She walked down toward the city center, crying, angry with her seizures.

Hector checked in with her every day and knocked on her door with tea and chocolate biscuits. Their conversation would melt into Spanish. It was so much easier to speak with him inside her room. *Why have we never done this before?* she thought. Here he was, sitting on her bed, telling her stories. He wanted to delight her and make her laugh. He wanted to see Mischa again, the one he knew from the kitchen conversations, Formal Hall, and the washing machine. He wanted to see that smile.

"When people tell you that you're beautiful, they probably tell you it's your hair or your eyes, but for me it's your smile. I love it, Mischa. It's your most charming feature. In fact, it reminds me of my favorite place on earth." He stroked her cheek.

Mischa knew him by now. She was not so idiotic as to think he was fanning her with flattery. She prodded him for the punch line. "Out with it, Hector. You want me to ask, 'What is your favorite place on earth?'"

"Stonehenge."

Mischa needed a moment to absorb it. Then the image struck her—uneven rocks in strange formations. Mischa huffed, and then laughed hilariously and tackled him on the bed.

He was so happy to see that smile of crooked and uneven teeth. Finally, she was Mischa again. In the silence, with his arm around her, he asked, "Mischa, what is it like, having epilepsy?"

"Well," she began, and paused. "I don't really know what it's like not having epilepsy. I had my first seizure when I was fourteen. That's when everyone changes anyway. My change just included epilepsy." She went silent and spoke more to herself than to Hector. "I guess it's something of a presence in my life. It's strange. Sometimes it's like a stalker, a predator. Other times I feel as if it's more of a companion, even a mentor. It's part of me. But, that said, I don't like being called *epileptic*. I have epilepsy, but it's not what I am. I'm more than that. It's like being *disabled*. Some people would refer to my epilepsy as a disability, but I've never wanted to call it that."

"Why not?" he asked softly.

"It's limiting. I hate the word *disability*. I associate that prefix with words like *disrespect* or *disservice* or *disemboweled*."

Hector laughed and Mischa smiled. She wanted to break the tension. Hector was the first one with the courage to ask her this question, and he was the only person she would ever want to tell. She could hear her voice— so formal, clinical, and impersonal—but she had no other tone or vocabulary for talking about her seizures. She could not allow any emotions.

"I think a medical condition is an objective reality, so why does a word with a pejorative meaning need to be attached? I don't suggest verbal vigilantism against the word *disabled*. I just don't like to use it. I prefer to think of it in other terms. It's just there. It's a problem at times, but it's also me. It's difficult to separate."

Mischa was silent. She took a deep breath. Hector held her tightly, and she put her head on his chest and could hear his heartbeat. He kissed her and she softened. Mischa thought Hector's stoic and consistent kindness wasn't learned, but inherent. He had a decency that would not waver, no matter what the circumstances. Hector was noble. It was such an antiquated word, but so fitting. It described him entirely. She would never find someone like him again.

Unconsciously, she found herself forced into making the same decision that her father had made after graduate school. To be with Hector, she was going to try to stay in the UK, just as her father had stayed in Chile for her mother. She began applying for jobs in Britain. Her pen froze when she came to a disclosure section on job applications for revealing disabilities. *Why do they have to ask? Why do they have to know?* She would never have had to put that on a job application in the U.S. There was one saving grace in the phrasing of the question. So that she could honestly mark "no" for a disability. She wanted to kiss the British Member of Parliament or civil servant who must have insisted on the phrasing, which left a person with some dignity. It was always worded: "Do you consider yourself disabled?"

She wondered if, when she was hired, she would disclose her condition. Would they think she had been lying? How would she explain her whole philosophy on the word *disability* to a human resources officer who was wondering whether she had "lied" about any other facts on her CV? No matter how many disabled people she saw in the streets, she still could not afford to see herself as disabled. In the outside world that term was too damaging.

After receiving her degree, Mischa accelerated the ego-smashing job search, and after months, finally succumbed to the reality that she would not find a job in the UK. It was nothing she would attribute to prejudice; she had always checked "no" for the box on considering herself disabled. She wasn't qualified or there were people who were better qualified. It was just life. Hector was looming behind every reason to stay in the UK, yet he had made no promises to her. She forced herself to return to reality. She had to go back to the United States, get a job, pay off student loans, and start a career.

The week before she was scheduled to leave, Hector offered to take Mischa to the airport. That day, they didn't speak for the entire ride. She could only look out the window and think, whatever they had or didn't have, it was finished. *What a waste. Forget it. Forget him. Move on.*

When they arrived at Heathrow, Hector took Mischa to the ticket desk. They shared a coffee near the security gate, while they talked about the weather, the Concorde, and the lack of napkins. Mischa barely held herself back from standing up and shouting at him in the middle of the airport cafe. *Do you want to see me again? What are we? What were we? What are we going to do?*

It had been a romance built on a genuine friendship, and they had never pushed themselves to define the future. This was the moment, when she stood up to begin her walk to the security gates. *Make it short and quick, no scene, just say good-bye.*

Hector pulled a small box from a plastic grocery bag as she stood to pick up her backpack. "It's a good-bye present," he said, as he took the books out and handed a box wrapped with newspaper to Mischa. The wrapping didn't surprise her. She was appreciative, but assumed it was a box of chocolates and had already judged it a rather paltry gift. As she ripped the newspaper he explained, "I made the box. It's rosewood." The color was warm tea brown; it was smooth, sanded and polished, with small brass hinges. She opened it to find five shapes carved from wood.

Hector explained further, "These...um...I made from pine. That's an easier wood for...um...carving." He pointed to each of the different shapes. "This is a tetrahedron, that one is a hexahedron, that's an octahedron, this is a dodecahedron, and that one is an icosahedron. The names refer to the number of sides. The shapes, they're platonic solids, you see. All the faces, angles, and edges are congruent. They are the most elemental expressions...um...of beauty. I wanted to make something for you. I wanted...I wanted...to show...to show you...what I think of you." He looked at her nervously, fearfully biting his lip, wondering how she would react.

"Hector, when are you coming to visit me in Washington?" Mischa looked at him with tears in her eyes.

"I'll come whenever you want, on the condition that you visit me in the UK."

They hugged and kissed each other good-bye. Embarrassing tears ran down her cheeks as she walked through security and the sympathetic wardens waved her through.

18. THE COFFEE SHOP

March 1996

WHEN MISCHA RETURNED TO WASHINGTON, DC, SHE STAYED WITH HER FATHER WHILE SHE SEARCHED FOR A JOB. Professor Dunn was quiet and worked in his home office or library much of the day, without speaking. There was no classical music in the house the way there had been when Cristina was alive. He wanted it quiet and asked that music not be played. When she came in and surveyed the kitchen, she felt as if this was her territory and at least she could decide what to do with it. She threw all the frozen dinners in the trash and filled the refrigerator with fresh meat, fruits, and vegetables. She cooked all the dishes that her mother had made. Gradually her father livened. He began to talk to Mischa about his work, and they would take walks after dinner, the same routes that he took with Cristina when she was alive.

After job interviews, Mischa would call Sophie, sad and sullen. When Sophie's congressman lost his reelection, he went far beyond the remit of a typical politician to help his staffers find new jobs. Within a few months, Sophie found herself working at the prestigious Council for Foreign Affairs Analysis on the conference organization team. The giants of DC were the U.S. government agencies, international organizations, embassies, U.S. Congress, lobbyists, and contractors. Other giants, invisible to most people outside the Beltway, were the non-governmental organizations—think tanks, advocacy groups, and foundations. Think tanks employed policy wonks, academics, journalists, former government officials, economists, and lawyers to create reports, hold conferences, write op-eds, give testimony to Congress, and influence debate. They funded fellowships, and respected scholars could get their exposure to the real world sitting in DC, writing their books on sabbatical, hosting conferences, and providing policy analysis. Think tanks exploited bright young things looking for an unpaid internship in Washington, DC. Think tank boards of directors and staffs invited respected, like-minded journalists to join them, and their op-eds transmitted the thinking to the world. The big think tanks were the Council on Foreign Relations, the American Civil Liberties Union, the Urban Institute, CSIS, RAND, the Brookings Institute, the Heritage Foundation, the American Enterprise Institute, the National Democratic Institute, and the CATO Institute. They could be so influential that their very presence in the Washington policy debate changed the course of history. Think tanks were often the first draft architects of a change in policy. How would the U.S. military have developed after World War II without the RAND Corporation? Would Nixon have gone to China without the persuasion of the Council on Foreign Relations? What would the civil rights movement have been without the ACLU? Over trays of gyros and moussaka at Zorba's on Dupont Circle, Sophie tried to persuade Mischa to make the leap.

"Mischa, why don't you stop looking for a job in the hippie non-governmental sector? You weren't happy anyway. It was living nightmare at the Human Rights Advocacy Forum. Admit it. They were a bunch of bead-wearing hypocrites. If you refuse to remember it, I can do it for you. You'd like it at a think tank. You love researching and writing. That's most of what we do at the Council of Foreign Affairs Analysis. In fact, today I found out that they are setting up a Narcotics Policy Task Force. It's going to be cross-regional. I know they're going to need a Latin American analyst. The job is going to involve research and writing, policy analysis. You love that stuff. I was talking to our human resources assistant and she told me the announcement is coming out in two weeks."

"I don't know if I'd be welcome in the gentrified elite after being with 'bead-wearing hypocrites,' as you call them. But maybe schooling in Cambridge sterilized me. I could emphasize that experience and the time I worked as a researcher at the Woodrow Wilson Institute."

"Mischa, come on, we could be working at the same place! We might even be down the hall from each other and get sent to a conference together abroad! Can you imagine it? I'm planning one in Paris right now, before the UNESCO meetings."

"Sure, I'll apply. Why not? My ego has taken such a beating that it won't suffer much if I lose out on another job."

"Don't worry, Mischa. I'll coach you. Incidentally, although I'm not saying that Council employees have stepped out of *Vogue* and *GQ*, you do need to get a more professional look. You're not in a Guatemalan jungle or a classroom in Cambridge. Get rid of the jeans, the T-shirts, the sweatshirts, the baggy jackets. Oh, and every time your pant leg rides up I'm getting Cro-Magnon flashbacks. *Chica,* start shaving!"

"I suppose I should do my armpits as well."

"Oh God, I don't even want to hear it. You've gone all European on me. Don't tell me that you're not showering every day, or I'm going to puke."

"No comment."

"Okay. It's settled. Mischa, I can prep you for the interview. I'm also taking you shopping. You gotta dress L and D—that's low heels and dark colors. It's the unofficial uniform of the Washington, DC, female species. Women who wear high heels and too much color get treated like secretaries or cheerleaders. You'll also need a haircut. It should go just slightly past your shoulders. Those scraggly ends make you look like you're on your way to a Woodstock revival."

Three months later Mischa was in a congressional hearing, on her first assignment for the Latin American Team at the Council of Foreign Affairs Analysis. There was a buzz of electricity going into the Capitol for the first time, getting the security badge, and being directed to the Committee room to hear testimony on the trade talks with Latin America. Walking down the marbled halls and hearing the echoes of her low-heeled pumps, Mischa felt as if she had made it. She was an "insider" now; she wasn't just living in Washington, she was part of the scene; she was inside the Beltway. Mischa almost clapped with glee when the director gave her the assignment to cover the hearing. The senior analyst was out sick. There was a chance of a follow-up, perhaps doing the research for the op-ed piece the director was planning to write. This could be a chance to prove herself.

⌘ ⌘ ⌘

On her twelfth visit to Hector in Cambridge, which alternated with the eleven visits he had made to DC, they met at Heathrow. He beamed with the pride of accomplishment as he told her that two days ago he had received the letter to inform him that he had successfully finished his doctorate. She came back to his room and slept off her jet lag for the rest of the day. That evening, they walked across Parker's Piece to go to the Latin mass at Our Lady and the English Martyrs.

"Hector, it's been nearly four years of going back and forth. You have a degree and I have a job. Have you had any thoughts about the future, our future?"

"In what respect?"

"What are your thoughts about marriage?" Mischa stopped and looked at him.

He had walked on ahead a few steps and looked back. "Well, it sounds okay by me."

This wasn't the reaction she was looking for. She had hoped for something more effusive, perhaps even joyful. *I must not expect spontaneous outbursts of emotion. He's English. He's a physicist.*

When they returned to 81 Warkworth Street that night, he took her to his room. He stepped away from the bed to pick up a worn velvet box from the top of his bureau. He opened it and put a rose gold engagement ring with a rosette made of several tiny diamonds on her finger. It was the same ring his father had presented to his mother in Havana. He explained to her that she had popped the question twenty-four hours before he had planned to propose, in front of the washing machine. He had even planned his clothes out for the entire week so that he could afford to do his washing two days later than usual.

They decided to marry the following week at the church, and took accelerated marriage instruction from the priest at Our Lady and the English Martyrs. It was supposed to be a month-long course, but Mischa and Hector took him out for pizza and the priest counted it as the completion of the course. They married in a ceremony with just the priest, a parish secretary, and a witness from the Cambridge City Council.

For their wedding lunch, Mischa and Hector walked to their favorite coffeehouse across from Pembroke College. The feast consisted of two half baguettes with Gruyère, carrot coriander soup, white coffee, and poppy seed cake at Benz, Bayer, und Freunde. The shop was owned by two German men from Berlin, an unlikely pair of Anglophiles. In their avant-garde glasses, short haircuts, and colorful sweaters, they brought streusels, plum juice, zinfandel, and Bavarian rye bread to Cambridge. The walls of the coffee shop were warm scarlet and covered with museum posters. Mischa and Hector usually took the table underneath the poster announcing an exhibition that had occurred ten years ago at the British

Museum, which featured an Aztec mask covered with pieces of bright turquoise.

Hector had introduced Mischa to the shop when they were both studying in Cambridge. No one knew which one was Benz and which was Bayer. The presumption was that Benz and Bayer were a couple, but none of their patrons were interested in their private life. It was the perfect coffee shop for the isolationist scientists who occupied the buildings next door—the Department of Applied Mathematics and Theoretical Physics. The young men with glasses and splotches on their shirts, and their professors, merely older versions of the same, sat in corners and on stools within inches of each other, silently drinking their coffee with the complimentary cookie on the saucer or eating their baguettes. There was no interest in engaging in small talk with anyone, even a patron who came there regularly. The shop owners' genuine expression of disinterest in their patrons' lives was part of their success, a source of loyalty. For twenty years, the coffee shop was the most intellectually productive two hundred square feet in Cambridge. Students and professors munched and sipped while typing theses, solving theorems, writing algorithms, reading books, and reviewing conference papers.

Mischa appreciated Benz and Bayer's reactions to her seizures. She'd had three in the shop when she was a student and had never felt more comfortable than when she had them there. It was their matter-of-factness. There was no exaggerated sympathy. They closed off the area of the shop by draping a few checked tablecloths over chairs, and let her lie on the floor in silence under one of their warm woolen coats that smelled of roasted walnuts. When she was well enough to get up, one of them would drive her home and drop her off at her house as if they had just gone shopping. Very little conversation. All very perfunctory. At some point there was a name exchange, but she forgot which of the B's she was speaking to, and it was likely that he had forgotten her name as well. In any event, she knew that she could go into the shop the next day and there would be no question other than, "Vhat can I get für you today?"

After their ceremonial lunch at Benz, Bayer, und Freunde, Mischa and Hector took turns and called their fathers that evening, with both of them getting on the phone to talk to their new in-law for a few minutes. Mischa and Hector could hear the smiles in their voices. There was no regret that they had not been there or wishes for a big wedding party. They were both delighted to know that their child would not be alone in life.

When Mischa returned to Washington, her father met her at the airport. He had helped her move to her own apartment a few months before. With her father's assistance, and weekend trips to the mega-hardware stores, she began to paint and decorate the apartment. Hector packed up his things and left Cambridge a few weeks later and then stayed with his father for a little while. Five months after their wedding, Mischa and Hector began their married life together in a one-bedroom apartment at Dupont Circle in Washington, DC.

19. THE ASSEMBLY HALL

July 2001

HE PAUSED, AS IF WAITING FOR APPLAUSE. He was a nameless Washington nerd with that hurricane of confidence the young and ambitious bring to DC. Mischa chided herself for rolling her eyes as the five-foot-two policy wonk quoted his op-ed recently published in the *Washington Post*. She admitted she was probably envious. In his early thirties, he was already deputy director of a prestigious think tank.

DC was full of political prodigies. They were drawn to Washington like addicts to an opium den. In high schools across the nation, student government, debate, and chess clubs were littered with future policy wonks. They were the ones who were reading the *New York Times* and watching *Meet the Press* by the time they were fifteen. Ivy league degrees were stamps of approval and tickets to be a White House staffer, a congressional aide, a senator's senior adviser, or a program manager running development projects worth a few million dollars—and that was just a first job. There was so much power condensed into 68.3 square miles. Some of these policy wonks in the U.S. government, foundations, think tanks, advocacy groups, or lobbies made decisions with greater impact than those made by senior officials in third world countries. The proper word for less-developed nations was "emerging markets," but whatever the word, the vulgar truth was that a twenty-five-year-old policy wonk in Washington, DC, could wield more power than a cabinet minister in a small country.

Mischa watched him hold forth at the table, leaving no room for others to voice their opinions, and wondered if she was guilty of that type of behavior of a DC power nerd. Mischa knew she was not as bad as he was, and hoped she would never be the same. DC had the power to change a person very quickly. In two years, four years, six or eight years, you could be a far different person coming out of DC than coming in.

Each election brought new faces to town. The sudden burst of power and influence was mood altering for those coming to DC for the first time—even for seasoned professionals. Elections brought swarms of political appointees to government agencies as well as interns, staffers, and aides to senators, representatives, and presidents. They came to Washington with that fresh-faced look, like Jimmy Stewart in *Mr. Smith Goes to Washington*. It was possible to distinguish the people in their first few months in a job. No matter how old they were, if they were new to Washington, DC, they had a certain spring in their step and an innocent pride, not arrogance, in their carriage. Law firms, advocacy groups, defense contractors, think tanks, lobbyists, media agencies, and the U.S. government were always hiring, so there were new Washingtonians everywhere.

Regardless of whether a person was conservative or liberal, he or she first came to Washington as an optimistic idealist. The ones who stayed for the love of politics or power became realists. They stopped thinking that politics was a matter of good versus evil, but rather a choice of the lesser evil. Having that epiphany gave an idealist a dose of humility and respect, not disdain, for compromise. But you had to have the epiphany first; if not, you turned into a cynical idealist, most commonly referred to as a self-righteous bastard, and Washington was full of them. Mischa looked at the five-foot-two policy wonk. He wasn't a bastard yet, but it wouldn't be long.

She looked around the restaurant table at those who were not of her species of DC policy wonks. They were the more sophisticated, respected, and renowned authors, academics, advocacy group directors, and journalists from Canada, Latin America, and the Caribbean. They were all together in Quebec City and it was a night to relax. It was a few days prior to the hemispheric presidential summit. Many of them had followed the Counter-Narcotics Summit for the Americas for the last four years. The presidents and prime ministers were finally coming to sign an agreement on regional counter-narcotic policies and practices. They were going to pledge to implement a range of efforts on their own and together, to address demands, supplies, trafficking, customs procedures, criminal procedures, and social welfare programs for prevention and rehabilitation. For the last four years, non-governmental organizations had been following their diplomats to the negotiations in Miami, Tegucigalpa, Bogotá, La Paz, and Brasilia. They had been writing reports, publishing op-eds, holding conferences, and organizing protest rallies in hopes of influencing the final agreement. This was a night of relaxation; after tonight, for the rest of the week everyone would be living off adrenalin, caffeine, bravado, and fear of fiasco until the presidents and prime ministers signed the agreement on a table covered in green felt, in front of a wall of flags of the Americas and several potted plants.

Several leaders had agreed to meet with the non-governmental organizations. Therefore, the Canadian government had decided to host an official event during the two-day presidential summit, which they called the civil society consultations. In events like this the prejudice and class status within civil society came out. Equality as a virtue in humanity and in nation-states was a principle for which these groups fought, but among themselves, there was a belief that some representatives of civil society were just more equal than others. The more respected, established, and well-funded think tanks and advocacy groups were reluctant to be lumped in with the rest of civil society, some of whom they considered to be little more than neighborhood watch groups. Those elite advocacy groups and think tanks had hoped for more exclusive access to world leaders, but that was impossible. After all, thirty-four presidents and prime ministers meeting each other for forty-eight hours have an exponential number of priority meetings among themselves, in assembly, and with their own entourage. Wherever they were in the food chain, all the civil society representatives had to acknowledge that they were lucky to have the chance of a formal meeting.

Mischa looked around the table. The people from the slicker think tanks and advocacy groups dressed like the diplomats and moved smoothly through the events, as if they belonged there. People from the smaller, more grassroots advocacy groups of civil society usually wore an article of clothing or a small accessory from the countries whose human rights they were advocating—a purse made from traditional weaving, a necklace, a belt, or a scarf. Instead of briefcases they often used backpacks. Organic, fair-trade cotton shirts with wooden buttons were common. Another typical sight was the bracelets made of dirty cotton threads that had survived hikes through jungles and hot, sweaty days gathering signatures for petitions outside of shopping malls.

The elite think tanks and advocacy groups had talked among themselves and knew that their reputation and their future access to leaders and foreign ministries would be jeopardized if they did not engineer a smooth meeting. The fear was that the lower strata of civil society, those more inclined to wear Birkenstocks, would use the question-and-answer period to fire off their mouths at the world leaders, or burst in with placards while wearing protest T-shirts and take shameful advantage of the media presence. If that were to happen, those more equal than others had decided the night before in several private telephone conversations that they would walk out on their colleagues. They weren't going to drag their status in the mud. At a meeting of this caliber they had to make the others behave.

While the more equal than others members of civil society fretted about the consultations, the true aristocrats of civil society gave no thought of worry about their influence or reputation. They would always have access. In their retirement, even former presidents and prime ministers would want to sit on their boards of directors. These aristocrats of civil society were still .org in domain name, but were a class unto themselves: the foundations. Some of their directors and program officers had even made a rare appearance, coming to Quebec for the Counter-Narcotics Summit for the Americas consultations. They were curious as to what their million dollars in grants had accomplished and felt entitled to come out from the shadows.

Foundations were organizations established by well-meaning and/ or guilt-ridden wealthy individuals and corporations, for the purpose of improving the world. Their generic visions and broad mission statements justified the outlay of billions of dollars in grants toward health, democracy, entrepreneurship, peace, and social stability. Some had assets of one or ten or twenty billion dollars. Annual grants that amounted to millions could be just the skim of the interest earned on those assets in a few months. Before putting together a funding proposal, sleek annual reports of foundations were studied carefully by every NGO seeking potential cash. Those reports showcased what could be accomplished with creativity, persistence, good-will, and courage—but mostly with cash.

Despite the power of their pocket, the great majority of foundations did not seek the role of puppet master, but preferred to be fairy godmothers. With a sprinkling of fairy dust, a few grants here and there, they could make policy dreams come true. A grant of one million dollars could: fund an advocacy group's entire activities for two years, conduct several election observation missions, dig one thousand village wells, develop a curriculum for global human rights training of the military, educate a thousand literacy volunteers, fund a handful of academics to write a handful of books, and host one or two international conferences that found solutions for global problems—the standard goal of every international policy conference.

The Ford Foundation, the MacArthur Foundation, the Rockefeller Foundation, the Carnegie Endowment, and the Hewlett Foundation, just to name a few. Their program officers, who were approving and overseeing grants, were respected. Program officers showed themselves to civil society in rare events outside of the board meetings. They preferred to stay anonymous, sipping their wine at the reception. But, like celebrities who have been recognized, if someone caught sight of their badges a coterie of hopefuls for the next round of grants followed them around until the program officers had to excuse themselves, usually by finding a government official with no power over the purse strings, not another colleague in the foundation world.

In the policy world of civil society, a generalization that was more often true than not, was that the foundations had the money to fund change, the think tanks had the ideas for change, and the advocacy groups made change a reality.

At these spontaneous dinner parties at international conferences, when no event was planned the restaurants were last-minute recommendations from someone who knew the city from before or had asked a friend for a suggestion before they came. When people met, their patriotic pride demanded that the civil society representatives from the different countries bring bottles of their national wines, rums, tequilas, sherries, and whiskeys to share with everyone at the table. This was a time to chatter and joke, discuss grandiose geopolitical themes, disclose personal backgrounds, and share gossip. Controversial issues were left back at the hotel. It was a time to build relationships, for pundits to earn their insider credentials, and everyone to exchange cards with as many people as possible in as short a time span as possible.

The waiters had pushed together six tables to make one that seated thirty people. The most charismatic character had the power to hold everyone's attention. Whenever there was a pause in the conversation, everyone instinctively turned to listen to Francisco Le Cheval, who was holding court at one end of the table. He had served as spokesman for a Central American rebel force in the 1980s. Now he was part of that roaming herd of expatriates working as development assistance consultants, human rights organization directors, election observers, peacekeepers, and trainers. Mischa had met several of these types in Guatemala. Their salaries afforded them a good lifestyle in developing countries, with servants and nice houses or apartments. Regardless of their elite in-country status and comfortable lifestyles, they preferred to see themselves as people outside of the establishment and "with the people." Le Cheval had the misfortune to make a comment in a pause.

"It is like meeting an alien. I know I want to make love to her, but I don't know how."

People sat in silence for a few seconds, and then the entire table guffawed raucously as people at other tables stared. Le Cheval looked earnestly at his dining partners.

"What? What are you saying? I am but speaking the truth! It is a conundrum to be solved. I have the desire, but I don't know how. This is truth!"

A grad student at his side was working as a volunteer in a small NGO in Washington, DC, and soon would be heading to the UN Mission in Haiti. Le Cheval was enchanting her with his knowledge of the street gangs in Port au Prince, sprinkling his conversation with patois, and voicing ideals for peace, justice, and an end to the violence. Her eyelashes fluttered.

I think Le Cheval will know what to do tonight.

In addition to that night in the restaurant, several impromptu and organized meetings among the advocacy groups, think tanks, and foundations took place, and then the day of the civil society consultations with the presidents and prime ministers of the Americas finally arrived. Early that morning Mischa arrived at the assembly hall and looked around to make a quick assessment by scouting the delegations, analyzing body language, and noting the groups that were clustered. It was a good sign that even the most granola-laden NGOs were in jackets and skirts. They looked uncomfortable, the men with their ponytails braided neatly and the women with long dangling wire earrings who had tucked their Yoko Ono-length hair into thick, unruly buns. They had obviously made the attempt to look serious and had ditched the T-shirts and woven bags for those few hours. It was a good sign for the Council of Foreign Affairs Analysis and the others of its kind. The hoi polloi was going to behave.

⌘　⌘　⌘

The gavel struck and everyone took a chair. Mischa looked down at the agenda for the opening ceremony. There were eight speakers before the first break: three presidents, two prime ministers, the U.S. secretary of state, and the Brazilian foreign minister *Where is the coffee?* She would get some after the first speaker. *Now, who is it?* She fumbled with her agenda and looked at the names. *What language is this written in? French. No, wait, it's Hebrew.*

*That's Hebrew, isn't it, the way those letters are moving. Wait, where's the trans-
lated version? This is crazy. This is a meeting in...in...* Each of the sentences
turned into thin lines that grew thicker and thicker until they merged and
everything in front of her was black. *Oh no. No, not here, please, no.*

Mischa looked up. *Isn't that the director of the RAND Corporation's
Americas section? He's the one who slammed my report on the drug war as naive,
counter-productive, and overly focused on demand reduction strategies. Why is he
on the ceiling? Wait, no, why am I on the floor? Oh no. Oh God, it happened here.
Damn it.* Mischa closed her eyes. She didn't want the crowds or looks; she
wanted to fade to black.

When she woke up, she found Nathan staring at her from the corner
of the emergency cubicle. He was another Council analyst on the Americas
team who focused on the socio-economic effects of drug trafficking. His
shoulders were hunched and tense. Mischa saw that familiar look of panic
that belonged to a seizure witness. He had worked as a foreign correspondent in Colombia and other dangerous places, including border towns in
Mexico. *I would have thought he could have taken this all in stride. Then again,
context does influence a person's reaction to a crisis. If you're in Cartagena and you
hear a machine gun, it's another drive-by shooting, no surprise. If you're at an international conference and your colleague goes into severe convulsions, well, I guess it's
unexpected.*

"I guess I had a seizure."

"Yes, that appears to be the case."

She had told everyone in the office that she was epileptic, but she had not
had a seizure in the presence of any at the Council except Sophie, the secretary for the Americas team, and the Council receptionist. No one inquired
about her health and she was glad. *Now they'll probably remember.* Mischa had
been more than grateful to Sophie, who helped her keep her seizures unnoticed. At Sophie's request, the secretaries kept a special eye on Mischa. The
sound of a crash or a fall, sometimes an innocent consequence of clumsiness,
sent Sallie, the Americas team secretary, running into Mischa's office. After
a seizure, with the secretaries' help, Sophie would close Mischa's door and
watch over her while someone called Hector. Sophie would give excuses for
her for the rest of the day, saying that Mischa was in meetings, and would
have Mischa's calls redirected to her phone.

Mischa mulled over the consequences of this seizure. Was someone going to tell Sam, the director for the Americas team, that she was

overstressed? Would they blame this seizure on an imagined inability to handle pressure? She hated the implications. No matter where she was, she always worked 200 percent harder in the aftermath. Would she have to explain that she had seizures regardless of whether she was on vacation or at work? She had them as a lazy student. She had them while lying in a park, while at a party, and while asleep in bed on the weekend. She had them in different places, in different countries, at different times in her life, where there was pressure and no pressure, where there was stress and no stress. They just happened. *Why can't people understand? They just happen.*

Mischa could only hope that they would understand and that there would be no changes in her assignments, but that would be next week in Washington, DC. She returned her mind to the emergency room in this city. Still uncertain of where she was, at least she was certain that she was not in the United States.

"Nathan, who told you that I had a seizure?"

"Well, I was in the room, a few rows down. A Haitian diplomat was next to you. His sister is epileptic. He knew what to do, and the medics let me ride in the ambulance."

Diplomat? Haiti? Where am I?

"Nathan, don't be alarmed, this is normal for me. Where am I?"

"Saint Francis Hospital."

"Actually, my question refers to…well…which country am I in?"

"Oh…um…well, Mischa, you're here, in Quebec City. This is Canada. We're here, the Council, for the civil society consultations with hemispheric heads of state and government prior to the Counter-Narcotics Summit for the Americas."

"Oh, right, now I remember. So I had the seizure in the middle of the consultation?"

"Well, sort of. It was actually at the beginning of the consultation."

"Who was speaking when I had it?"

"The president of Colombia."

"Oh hell. Was she able to continue after that?"

"Don't worry about it, she's survived much worse. The chair decided to take a fifteen-minute recess and people had a cup of coffee."

Morbus comitalis. That was the name. It was in the binder he gave me. Mischa remembered the gift from Stanley, years ago, when she was a researcher at the Woodrow Wilson Institute. There was an article about epilepsy in

Ancient Rome. *Morbus comitalis*—the "disease of the assembly," the Latin term for epilepsy. The ancient Romans observed that seizures had the unfortunate effect of ending meetings and thereby delaying votes. While everyone else across time and continents named the condition for falling, jerking, or either godly or demonic possession, the imperial Romans made no reference to paranormal events. Their term reflected the mournful observation that their debates over the quality of the aqueducts, the costliness of their wars, or the scarcity of gladiators had been brought to sudden close. *Julius Caesar was an epileptic. Maybe I should point that out when people suggest that I can't handle the stress. If he could run an empire with seizures, then so could I. Perhaps that would come across as arrogant? Where did I put that binder?*

She looked up at the saline drip in her arm. She thought about making conversation to lighten the mood. *Why try? I don't think Nathan wants to talk about the Roman Empire.*

But Nathan broke the silence. "Mischa, did you have too much to drink?"

"Excuse me?"

"Did you have a little too much to drink when Sam took us out to the restaurant last night? My dad is a doctor. He thinks you probably got drunk and had a seizure the next day as a result."

She paused and took a deep breath. "Damn it, Nathan, I have epilepsy. I have seizures. I don't even drink. I can't afford to mix alcohol and anticonvulsants. What does your dad practice anyway?"

"He's a foot surgeon."

"Well then, tell him to stick with feet or brush up on his neurology before he makes a diagnosis like that."

She fell back on bed, relieved that it was at an incline. At an angle, her head did not suffer the impact of falling from an upright position. She had another cracking, slicing, splitting headache. This was what she hated most. It was not the blackouts. It was the aftermath. She imagined that her brain's cruel motive for these drawn-out, intense headaches was to force her to experience the entire seizure in slow motion as a penalty for her unconsciousness during the epic event. *When are they going to take this damn saline drip out of my arm?*

"So, I hear that we're epileptic," said a doctor, who had the forced smile of one trying to lighten the mood in an emergency room. It was well-intentioned, but it always irritated her. Mischa hadn't noticed him come in, but gathered herself to give him background.

"Yes. I have temporal lobe epilepsy. I have complex partial seizures that generalize into tonic-clonic. I have had the condition since I was fourteen. I'm currently being treated by Dr. Bradshaw at James Hotchkins in Baltimore."

"Very well, Ms. Dunn. After looking at the charts and speaking with you, I can tell that you are well on the road to full recovery. I will not keep you. I hear the future of the world lies in your hands." The doctor smiled at his own wit. "You can check out as soon as you have finished with these forms. Give me another ten minutes, please."

He looked to Nathan and said, "I assume that you will be taking her home, or rather, back to her hotel? I would prefer that she rest in her room all day—no more cocktails with diplomats, hee hee." He gave Nathan a knowing glance. Nathan nodded. Satisfied, the doctor left.

"I'm sorry," Mischa said. "I didn't mean to be so abrupt. Thank you for coming with me to the hospital and dealing with all of this. Let me take you to lunch when we get back to DC." *I shouldn't have told him that his dad is an idiot.*

When Mischa finally checked out of the hospital, Nathan took her back to the door of her hotel room and assured her that he would make the rounds of their delegation to tell everyone personally that she was fine.

When she entered her hotel room she looked at the extra-large king-size bed, so immaculately made that it was almost a work of art. A sprig of lavender was on the pillow and she could smell the scent of it from the sheets. The only time Mischa ever had made beds was when she was on a business trip. It pained her to disturb its tight, smooth, flat surface, but she had to sit down. She found her delegate badge, to which she had attached a card of her most important contacts in the other think tanks and advocacy groups, and all the cell phone numbers for the staffers on the Council. She pressed in a number.

"Sophie?"

"Mischa! I'm so happy to hear from you. I wanted to go with you. They didn't tell me until you were at the hospital. Nathan called and told me that he was taking care of you. *Chica*, how do you feel?"

"Everything is fine. I'm going to sleep it off tonight, but I need a favor. Please let me go to the follow-up negotiations tomorrow. This is so important. I can't let people think I've crawled back home in shame. I have to be there."

"Mischa, I would have asked you to sit in, no matter what. You never have to worry about that."

"*Abrazos*, Sophie. I'm going to sleep."

She woke up the next morning and her tongue was sore. Mischa looked at the pillow and there was blood, still a little red against the white cotton, which meant that the seizure had occurred in the last three to four hours. Had it been early last night, the stain would have been light brown. She could barely turn her head, it felt so heavy. *I must have had another seizure.* At least she was glad to be in the middle of a massive hotel bed. She looked at the sharp edges of the night tables on each side and counted her blessings that she had not ripped her face on one of the corners. Mischa reached over for the phone and called Sophie's cell phone. It was nine fifteen in the morning. She had already missed the staff eighty-thirty breakfast meeting. Sophie answered the phone after one ring.

"Hi, Sophie. It's Mischa."

"*Chica,* you don't sound too good."

"I had another seizure last night, or maybe it was early this morning."

"Another one? I thought you had only one at a time."

"It's unusual. I haven't had two seizures in twenty-four hours since I was fourteen."

"Sleep today, sleep. Don't come down to the follow-up meetings. The Council may be writing up its own report, so there's no need to negotiate with the rest of these NGOs. Sam and Nathan think the radicals are having a backlash after they were forced to behave themselves at the consultation. That's just a temperature reading from some of the conversations they had last night and over muffins and coffee this morning. Two directors from these no-name NGOs in Seattle and Vancouver went Woodstock on Sam for the Council's support of a military response to drug trafficking. Unless they tone it down, we may not sign on to the civil society consensus agreement and may do our own report. Anyway, that's the way things stand. I think you have time to relax."

"No, Sophie. I'll sleep until noon, but I have to be there. This isn't up for discussion. It's important for me to show my face. You have to know what this means to me—professionally and personally. This is my network of contacts and sources. I'll never see this many people working on narcotics strategy in one place again for a long time. There's not going to be a summit for another four years. I cannot NOT show up. Please, Sophie, please. Let me join you in the afternoon negotiations. I'll sleep this morning."

"Mischa, I will only call when we break for lunch at one o'clock. My condition is that you sleep the entire morning and turn your cell phone off until this afternoon. Promise me. Those are my terms."

"Yes, yes. I will. Thanks, Sophie. By the way, which suit should I wear this afternoon—my black one from Rome, the Max Mara, or the pinstripe from London, the Karen Millen?"

"Ah, Mischa, I love it when you're shallow. Now I know you're back to normal. Go for the pinstripe. I like the sleek tailoring. You look good when you're androgynous."

"Will do. *Abrazos*, Sophie."

Sophie folded her cell phone and took the nearest seat she could find in the lobby. She was worried. Mischa's epilepsy was worsening, but she would never suggest that to Mischa. Since they began to work in the same office suite a year ago, Sophie had been sneaking her out of the building after Mischa's seizures. She worried that if people saw too many of them, it would affect their perception of whether she could handle the pressure and travel to conferences. The invitations and opportunities to go to international conferences were awarded to senior officers at a tank; they were always allowed to travel. An analyst could come on occasion, but it was rare. Any event like this was a great opportunity to network or just put a finger in the air and find out which way the wind was blowing. Gatherings like these were research through osmosis.

Mischa slept, but made sure she had enough time to dress slowly and meticulously. People would not be back for the meetings until one thirty. She had to look in command of herself. She carefully did her hair with rollers and applied her makeup as if it were her wedding day. Usually she dashed out with only a touch of lipstick and eyeliner, but she used a little more today. After few spritzes of her tea rose perfume and adjustments to her skirt, along with a final check of her legs for any runs in her stockings, she picked up her briefcase and walked out of the room. With her Karen Millen suit, Ferragamo shoes, and her Coach briefcase, she hoped she looked like a woman in control, even though her head was still dizzy and the inside of her mouth felt raw. She took a deep breath and entered the elevator, thankful that she knew no one. She still needed the moments of its descent to pause and focus.

The meeting rooms radiated from a large common room and were stocked with coffee and tea, fruit, pastries, and savories to feed people wandering in and out of the negotiations. The need for food in these gatherings was underestimated by outsiders. Getting a cup of coffee could be a planned meeting to iron out a point that could not be discussed at the table in front of fellow conference participants. Commenting on the fruit could lead into a conversational swap of information and contacts. Generally, keeping your attention up throughout the day depended on keeping your sugar level constant and getting a psychological rest every now and then. Calming down after a confrontation could be justified by a glass or juice, instead of being interpreted as a walkout. Most importantly, a lack of food engendered grumpiness, a poor basis for a productive conference. Sophie had expounded her theories on the importance of food in the conference events she organized. Mischa looked at the substantial spread and mused how the access to good coffee, fruits, and muffins had more to do with reaching an international agreement than the shape of a table. She took her first sip of coffee and wished instead that she had chosen a glass of ice water. Her leftover headache made her regret her decision to come down this early. *Maybe I should have stayed up there for another half hour.*

"I hope you are recovered, Ms. Dunn."

When Mischa turned around, she saw the six-foot-four Dr. Schumann, RAND's director for the Americas research and intelligence team, staring down at her. The coffee's heat stewed the chewed insides of her mouth. She wanted to spit it back into the cup, but quickly swallowed instead.

"I am fine, thank you, sir."

"Yes. I realize you are under so much pressure. It all must be very difficult to handle."

"Not really, sir," Mischa replied. "I understand that you will be leaving RAND to join a lobby."

"Yes. Actually, it's a law firm, Ms. Dunn. Bloggins, Patent, and Winde."

"Don't they represent several Latin American governments that have come under criticism in RAND's recent reports on drug trafficking?"

"No, Ms. Dunn, they don't represent governments, they advise these governments on the inner workings of the Washington policy machine. Embassies represent governments. You should go back to graduate school and learn the difference." He turned around and walked away.

Mischa spoke, even though his back was turned to her. "Congratulations on your new job. I guess the highest bidder won."

The adrenalin rush that had enabled her to concentrate during the spontaneous exchange subsided, and in its absence the headache assaulted her with greater fury. She looked for a chair in an unseen corner. She had to pace herself. Every conversation would force her to act and look more alert than she actually felt.

When Mischa entered the room, a few conference participants looked up and stared. Others acknowledged her with a genuine smile and a welcome nod, while some whispered to their neighbors. Sophie sat directly behind the nameplate reading "Council of Foreign Affairs Analysis." The meeting was a parallel diplomatic event of the non-governmental world. These were 142 advocacy groups and think tanks from around the world trying to negotiate a consensus document they could present to the press in the aftermath of their consultations with the governments. If all 142 non-governmental organizations could come to a consensus, the document would have a better chance of influencing the action plan that the leaders would create in the follow-up to the summit. Their document might even frame the media's interpretation of the summit if they could get it out fast enough. There was motivation on all sides to come to an agreement.

Mischa sat next to Sophie, who pointed to the clause under discussion. A woman from a Caribbean think tank was speaking, and her lilting voice could lull anyone into fantasies of a beach with palm trees. *Concentrate. Concentrate. I have to concentrate.*

Every time Mischa left that room someone always came up to her. In post-seizure social encounters, Mischa learned to distinguish between those who were making a genuine inquiry about her health and those who enjoyed singling out her vulnerability. Before joining the Council, Mischa had had nearly eighteen years of experience in making these judgments.

To those who perceived the seizure as a sign of weakness, she tried to control herself from making passive-aggressive remarks; instead, she provided some bit of information about epilepsy before leaving the conversation. If the inquiry about her health was sincere, she would let them pace the conversation, assure them that she was not insulted by their questions, and allow their curiosity to run its course. In a conference like this, she had to take the inquiries and keep herself from getting too defensive. When she had the opportunity, she would introduce a topic for discussion where they could begin to deal with her like any other work colleague, not the one who had seizures. In her initial return after a seizure, this protocol was vital.

That afternoon, seated next to Sophie at the negotiating table, Mischa felt like a potted plant. She was grateful that Sophie understood how critical it was for Mischa to be at the table. It was not only for her own confidence, but for her effectiveness in future negotiations. Throughout the afternoon, Sophie made it look as if she were consulting Mischa. She would turn and point to a certain spot on the resolution. Mischa's advice was never as clear and precise as her usual standard, but this Kabuki theater act was important for her credibility. Sophie nodded seriously while other delegations looked on studiously.

Completely drained when she returned to her room at the Chateau Frontenac, Mischa immediately took off her heels and threw her blazer on the gilded armchair next to the window. The hotel stood on a cliff overlooking Quebec City. Mischa raked her mind to remember the name of the Alfred Hitchcock movie where she first saw its silhouette. She looked down from her window and thought how her mother would have loved the charm and elegance of this city. Perhaps she and her mother would have come here to a cafe. Perhaps it would have reminded her mother of her childhood in Paris, one of the posts where her father had served as the ambassador.

There was a knock on the door and Mischa opened it to find Sophie, visibly spent.

"Thank you for sitting by my side today." Sophie put her briefcase down, took off her heels, and walked over to one of the armchairs.

"I was useless. I needed to be there and you let me stay. I'm so grateful, Sophie."

She leaned over and kissed her on the cheek. Sophie was the perfect friend; she never pitied her, she was never frustrated, and she never pored over her medical issues. She just let Mischa get on with her life. She didn't broach the subject of seizures; she simply let Mischa talk, and if she did not, Sophie let it alone.

"Of course, Mischa, anytime. It's important for the delegation as much as it's important to you. I would never give anyone reason to doubt you."

"That means a lot to me." Mischa's eyes watered.

Sophie had to lighten the conservation. She surveyed the gilt antiques, the mirrors and brocades. "You know, I feel like I should be wearing a ball gown when I'm in these hotel rooms. I don't know how they do it. I always thought Louis XIV interior decorating was for gay men with a Cinderella complex, but these rooms are so elegant, I'm almost converted. I'm going to re-think my mid-century modern look."

"I feel like Marie Antoinette, only I'd like to have my head chopped off."

"I have some extra-strength aspirin if you need it."

"No, I've taken a few already. It's fine. The headaches fade eventually," she assured Sophie.

"Mischa, you know I love and care for you, but I'm going to ask. Why didn't you leave Washington a day early for this trip? You had two other seizures outside the country when we were on travel. We both concluded that you would operate better with a little more rest after traveling, a day before and a day after." Sophie knew this was a little harsh, but there was no better time to confront her. She couldn't let Mischa ignore her pleas again.

"Sophie, what would it look like if I asked to go to Buenos Aires or Miami a day before? There always is such last-minute stuff in DC before conferences. If I leave early, I miss out. I don't want preferential treatment. I don't want people thinking I'm not carrying my load."

"Mischa, you have to acknowledge your limitations. You cannot get off a plane and go into a meeting. Your body just doesn't work that way. Don't fight it. You can't push yourself like this. It's not rational and it's not reasonable. People know your work ethic. They know you wouldn't be trying to ease your load. Hell, if you come early, you can even do scouting for us. Work with your limitations, don't keep trying to deny and defy them. There, I've said it. I know you are mad at me, but I couldn't let this wait until we were back in DC. I would have probably just avoided it again."

"Yes, I am mad. But of all people, I would rather hear it from you. It's just hard for me to come to grips with it. I'll do something."

Sophie looked at her directly, and then paused with some trepidation before she spoke.

"How...how...do you do it, Mischa? How do you keep from being angry?" This was the deepest question Sophie had ever asked about her epilepsy.

"You either live your life with a bitter aftertaste or you spit it out."

"Do you ever resent that you don't have a normal life?" Sophie continued.

"Honestly, Sophie, if I could remove one word from the dictionary it would be *normal*. There is no such thing. I don't have an abnormal life. I don't even have a disabled life. I just have a different life." She could hear her voice rising. "Sophie, please don't take it personally. I'm not angry with you. It's just been a pet peeve of mine, that word *normal*."

"Don't worry, I understand," Sophie replied. She shifted in her seat, bit her lip, and began again. "As long as we're on the topic of normal and abnormal, perhaps I should reveal to you, my friend of, what is it now, nearly twenty-five years? I have a girlfriend."

At first Mischa thought Sophie must have meant to say boyfriend, but her face showed all the intensity of someone on the edge, waiting for a reaction. *Sophie really meant girlfriend.*

"Wow, Sophie. Well, I guess…um…when…did you meet her?"

"Mischa, go ahead and ask the real question: when did I know that I was gay?"

"But Sophie…you're…you're a Republican."

"If you want to list all the contradictions, then I'm a Republican, Catholic, Latina lesbian. What can I say? I support conservative fiscal policies, I go to mass every week, and as for my genes, well, *Latina soy*. I just happen to prefer girls." Sophie laughed.

"Uh-huh." It was a lot for Mischa to absorb. She was rewinding moments of their life together, trying to find anything that might have predicted this moment. Sophie allowed her a few minutes to mull over her thoughts. "So, when did you know?" Mischa asked, once she realized the irrelevance and futility of a memory search for early indicators of Sophie's homosexuality.

"I'm not sure. Maybe it was the first time I saw you in a hockey skirt." Mischa kept her face impassive as she went through the implications of various replies. Sophie enjoyed watching, but thought it kinder to relieve her. "Relax, Mischa, I'm kidding. Don't worry, you're not even my type."

Mischa laughed indignantly. "Hey, wait there, who the hell is your type?"

"She's at the Department of Justice. You might have met her, she said she remembers you. She works on international narcotics issues, trafficking in persons, and extradition. Her name is Janet."

"Janet Ellington?"

"Yes, that's the one."

"Yeah, I know her. I interviewed her for my report on links between drug trafficking and trafficking in persons. She's a senior lawyer at Justice. Hell, Sophie, she must be at least ten years older than you."

"So, I like older women. Janet is the vice chair for the Association of Gay Employees at the Department of Justice. We met at last year's Foreign Affairs Forecast conference. We started having lunch together, then we started meeting for dinner and over weekends, and, well, we're dating. We're pretty serious, actually. Meeting Janet has changed my life." Sophie leaned back in her chair and breathed a sigh of relief. "I found my peace. All those years spent trying to please my family, I ignored myself. I came out to my brothers and sister a few weeks ago. Those *machos* won't speak to me. My sister wants to reach out, but her macho-idiot husband thinks I'll infect his children with AIDS, and of course…"

Sophie stopped herself. Her voice, which had been slow and thoughtful, was now tinged with anger. "I'm sorry, I'm venting. I didn't mean to start that. That's a process I have to work out with my family by myself. Unconsciously, I must have waited until my parents passed away. Even with someone like Janet by my side, I would not have been able to survive their disapproval. After Mom died, I overcame the feeling that I was abnormal, and—"

Mischa finished her sentence. "Just accepted that you were different?"

"*Exactamente*, yes, that's it." Sophie smiled that her friend had finished her thought, just like the conversations they had at a cafeteria table in Mama MIA. They sat silently for a few minutes, one absorbing the new information revealed about her friend. "I better get back to work. I have to brief Sam I'll be in my room looking over my notes. I just wanted to come out of the closet and check that you were okay. Give me a ring if you need anything."

Mischa walked her to the door and hugged her once again. "Thanks, Sophie."

"Don't mention it—the thanks, I mean. In terms of the gay stuff, I am going to come out fully. I think I'll drop hints like, 'Sam, I'm going to bring my girlfriend to the Council's Christmas party this year.' Or maybe I should start wearing a tie." With a kiss on Mischa's cheek, she let herself out the door. "*Chica,* go to sleep. *AHORITA!* NOW!"

The week after they returned from Quebec Mischa took Nathan out to lunch. It was a tradition she began a few years ago. She always took the person who accompanied her after a seizure out to lunch. Later that day, Nathan came into her office with a book.

"I meant to give this to you at lunch, but I forgot. It's from my father."
He handed it to her and excused himself to get to a meeting. Mischa found
a letter enclosed.

Dear Ms. Dunn,

*When Nathan informed me that you had fully recovered, I
was very happy to hear it. I asked him to give you this book,* A
Leg to Stand On. *I thought you might find it informative and
insightful. The author is a famous neurologist, Oliver Sacks, who
has written several books that address, among other neurological
topics, epilepsy and migraines. I highly recommend those works and
I believe that you would find them interesting.*

I find this book to be his most profound piece of writing. In A
Leg to Stand On *he recounts his experience as a patient in the
aftermath of a serious accident for which he must undergo surgery
and intensive therapy. He gives a thoughtful and emotional analysis of the physician-patient relationship in all its complexities: its
follies, flaws, and realities. I recently re-read the book myself and
I thought you would find it interesting as well. I wish you success
and the best of health.*

Sincerely,

Dr. Stuart Burgess

Mischa could not feel more ashamed of herself for her comments about
Nathan's father in the emergency room. She wondered if Nathan had
relayed them to him in their full color. She closed the door to her office and
began to read.

20. THE REFUGEE CAMP

JANET ELLINGTON, SOPHIE'S GIRLFRIEND, WAS A SELF-POSSESSED AND
SELF-PROFESSED LESBIAN. Middle-aged, with teeth yellowed from nicotine, and long dusty brown hair, she wore loose jackets and kept a mas-
culine pose, with one hand in a trouser pocket at all times. She used her
known status as a homosexual to tease some of the men at the Department
of Justice. Sophie wanted Mischa to get better acquainted with Janet, so
she brought her to have lunch with Janet at the Department of Justice cafeteria. Over Styrofoam plates Janet explained her personal feminist crusade
to Mischa while Sophie looked at her adoringly. Janet was earnest.

"Mischa, I don't do it for mere amusement, though, yes, I admit that I
do enjoy myself. My primary purpose is to educate men and let them experience firsthand what women have survived in the workplace for decades."

She quoted lines from Simone de Beauvoir's *The Second Sex* and con-
structed articulate arguments to explain her motives. Mischa could not
sympathize with her feminist vigilantism, but she wished she could be
around when Janet meted out divine justice.

After lunch, Janet invited them up to her office and offered to give
Mischa a copy of the Department's latest public documents on trafficking,
the DOJ Annual Report to Congress and Assessment of U.S. Government
Activities to Combat Trafficking in Persons. When they stepped into the
elevator, a man in his early thirties was standing in the center. He moved
slightly to give them room. Janet considered him a useless pretty boy in
the department, whose opinion always seemed to coincide with the opinion
of the most senior person at a meeting. He also had the timing of a T.V.
studio audience and laughed on cue at his superiors' jokes. Janet's eyes were
gleaming with sarcastic delight. Mischa and Sophie looked on curiously.
The elevator started going up and Janet moved like a leopard around and
behind her colleague.

In a husky, sultry voice, she said, "Have I ever told you that you look
soooo hot?"

The young man avoided eye contact and stared up at the panel above the elevator door that indicated the passing floors. "Uh-uh. No. But thank you, Janet."

Leaning over his shoulder, she continued, "Really, every time I see you in the halls, I think you just get hotter and hotter."

The door opened and two other passengers scampered out, leaving only Janet, Mischa, Sophie, and Pretty Boy. The elevator doors closed and Janet circled him. "You are just sooo groovy." With a delicate flick of her finger the bottom of his tie flew up. "I love the tie."

Pretty Boy was standing firm but sweating. The doors opened and he rolled his eyes in relief. "Uh...good-bye, Janet," he said, as he escaped from the elevator.

The doors closed and the three of them exploded into schoolgirl laughter. Janet escorted them back down to the entrance and gave Sophie a light, romantic kiss on the lips, to the surprise of passing people in the lobby. Mischa reached over to shake Janet's hand good-bye like a proud father who approved his daughter's choice of a boyfriend.

"Nice to meet you. I hope we can all go out for dinner sometime. You should take it easy on the men here, especially that boy. You scared him."

"Hey, Mischa, a guy who dresses like that and looks like that is just asking for it." Janet gave two macho thrusts of her pelvis and pushed her elbows back twice before she turned around, laughing. She swaggered down the hallway with her yellow legal pad in one arm and her hand in her trouser pocket. Mischa could understand why Sophie loved Janet.

They waved down a taxi and leaped in. Both looked at their watches and realized they were late for the staff meeting on the preparations for the upcoming Foreign Affairs Forecast Conference. Sam was going to be furious.

The FAF, as the conference was known to Washington insiders, was the Council's big event of the year. It proved to the rest of Washington they had inside access, the power to convene first-class academics, cabinet ministers, diplomats, CEOs, and other movers and shakers from around the world. After a White House State Dinner and the White House Correspondents' Dinner, where the president of the United States was the keynote speaker, the FAF conference ticket was the hottest one in town.

Sophie's boss, Sam, who was chairing the meeting, gave them a glare as they walked in. They took the first seats they could find and looked at each other with a glint, knowing they had good seating for watching the main feature: Oscar Frost from accounting. People from offices came and went, some were absent for a while, meeting chairs changed, but Oscar was always there for the FAF meetings. Every year, he was there. He sat in the same chair with his back to the world wall map, and he always covered the Pacific Ocean. He always brought a one-liter bottle of carbonated Poland Spring water. These meetings lasted an hour and Oscar was as good as a clock. If you knew his ritual, you could tell the time. When he opened the bottle, the slight fizz signaled the start of the meeting. During the discussions he repeatedly chugged from the bottle. Half an hour later he would slurp the last few drops out.

Often, the irregulars would glance over, annoyed, before returning their attention to the discussion. Regardless of whether or not an impassioned debate was in progress, he plopped the bottle on the table and concentrated on slowly turning it around, ripping the paper label into a spiral ribbon. Mischa would, by that point, lose the thread of the discussion, hypnotized by his methodical discipline. Oscar finished by rolling the label into a tight scroll, depositing it in the bottle and twisting the top tightly. A brazen burp, which caught the attention of everyone, foreshadowed the conclusion of a meeting. In Oscar's pageant of the carbonated water bottle, progress toward a target was clear, something these FAF meetings sorely lacked.

"Do you think Oscar sees the absurdity of his water bottle habit?" Mischa asked Sophie, as they walked back to their offices.

"No, not at all. But I kinda like it. It's something to look forward to in those meetings, a framework for stability and order, a symbol of accomplishment. That bottle is a lighthouse, a beacon of hope, amid the waves of pointless discussion. Gotta go, *chica*. Got a hot date tonight and I want to finish up at work early."

Two weeks later Mischa walked over to Sophie's office to find her on the phone. She motioned to Mischa to take a seat, who sat fidgeting and looking annoyed for another ten minutes. After putting down the phone, Sophie picked up her legal pad and they headed to the Oscar Frost Show. "Damn it, Mischa, we are fifteen minutes late. Get a move on!" Mischa gave her an irritated look. *Hell, it's not my fault.* They jogged down the corridors and slid on the linoleum floor as they turned the corners. They slowed down at the door to the office suite and attempted to look official as they entered the conference room. Sophie and Mischa glanced at Oscar's bottle of Poland Spring Water to see that he had drunk a little more than 20 percent of the bottle. They received a disapproving stare from Sophie's boss. Both of them bowed their heads in bureaucratic apology and crept to seats at the back. This was the second time in a row they were late, and Sam was in full monologue mode while the rest scribbled.

"We're going to have to limit the invitations to three per embassy. For the more important countries we might be able to send them four, that should take care of the ambassador, the deputy, and two senior officers... smaller auditorium than last year. The renovations aren't finished on the main auditorium...who's taking care of the simultaneous interpretation? Use the same ones from last year for Arabic, but get rid of the French interpreters. They were so slow. Where were they from? The French ambassador complained about their accent. Who is giving the status report on the reception? Congress...who is taking care of dealing with the House and Senate Committees on Foreign Affairs? I know they always want a load of invitations for the underlings, but it's not happening this year. The senator, representative, and a senior aide, that's it." Oscar only had a third to go and the bottle was done, and the ripping rotation stage would begin. "I want to limit the number of lobbyists...not like last year...get the top ones because we can't avoid it, but we're not playing matchmaker to these hired guns. No one here should feel bullied into introducing them or answering their questions. If one of these mercenaries comes up to you, tell them you're busy. I don't want us associated with them or being seen as their intermediaries. They can find their own contacts." Oscar was now done drinking and the precision ripping had begun. He turned the bottle and delicately tore at the label and rolled it into a tight scroll. *Plip*, he dropped it into the bottle, where it fell on its side, absorbing the last drops of water. As he twisted the cap on the mouth of the bottle, Mischa could see the ridges at a delicate slant disappear as his fingers turned the cap at thirteen degrees, eleven degrees, nine degrees, five degrees, three degrees. Mischa felt herself twisting slowly. Ice picks began to pierce her tongue. She tried to take them out, but a tidal wave pushed her to the floor and a thousand shards of glass and light washed over her.

Mischa looked up. She realized that she was on the carpet in the hallway. A woman was sitting by her and medics were taking vital signs. As soon as one of them saw Mischa awaken he began asking questions.

"What is your name?"

"I don't know."

"Where are you?"

"I don't know."

"What day is it?"

"I don't know."

"What time is it?"

"I don't know."

"Who is the president of the United States?"

"I don't know."

With that, the medic said to the other, "Let her rest, she hasn't come to yet."

Oscar was still seated at the table in the conference room. The rest of the attendees had either returned to their offices or were next to Mischa. He looked at his empty bottle with the label scrolled inside and recalled his time in Zaire as a development assistance consultant. Red Cross had wanted a fast, on-the-ground assessment of needs and service delivery. All the people they had sent were saturated with work; they needed someone to write a comprehensive report within the next forty-eight hours reviewing the supplies, refugee numbers, camp conditions, medical needs, and means of transport. Oscar's friends at Oxfam recommended him, and at two a.m. a voice with a cut-glass British accent woke him up. The phone call was from Red Cross Headquarters in Geneva. Five hours later Oscar had contracted an interpreter and was driving a jeep to the border to visit a Rwandan refugee camp.

Oscar had been at the camp for more than seven hours, doing interviews with doctors as they were bandaging and trying to speak with refugees who looked able enough to speak through the interpreter, and there were too few of those. Oscar believed he deserved a chance to catch his breath. He hoped to escape the squalor for a ten-minute smoke. He quit smoking five years ago, but when he saw his interpreter with a pack he had to have one, and so he headed toward the entrance with a paper thin cylinder of sanity between his fingers. After taking his first drag he could see a bright-colored figure few hundred feet outside the entrance to the camp. Others coming in were walking with the help of friends, family, and other aid workers. It was a woman alone, carrying a boy on her back. As her face came into sight, he could not stand still any longer. He inhaled one last time, ground the butt into the dirt, and hurried out to her carry the child into the camp medical tent. The boy's head had been bludgeoned, and she had ripped her ragged yellow polka-dot dress to make a bandage. The cloth was still wet, soaked with blood. The child, Oscar thought, was five, maybe even older, but malnourished.

That tent, that bloody tent—the thought made him cringe at the conference table in an attempt shake off the memory, but his mind played it out against his will. He had never seen so much blood in his life as he saw in those two days. He took a plastic bottle of water from the box they kept in the corner of the room and brought it to the mother. She did not drink it, but instead washed her son's head. Her joy to see him regain consciousness as the water spilled across his lips was the only smile Oscar saw the entire week.

Oscar floated among the people with the interpreter. He had volunteered to visit the camp in order to provide a firsthand account for a cable back to Washington. The refugees in the camp were walking corpses. The aid workers, doctors, and nurses who had been there longest had that thousand-yard stare of disbelief. The ones who had recently arrived worked with a manic earnestness to drive away the demons of realizing the utter horror of their surroundings. Unspoken but understood, they all knew that they would carry a fragment of this madness within them for the rest of their lives.

That evening, Oscar saw a crowd in the corner of the camp, yelling and shouting. He ran toward it. People surrounded a cooking fire with the shadow of a shape inside. There was a smell of meat, but Oscar wondered where they could have found the meat to cook. The abnormal sight of a human leg, untouched by flames, jutting out from the fire was the first hint of the horror to follow. The putrid, sweet smell of burning flesh stung the air, unrecognizable at first and then unforgettable. People yelled and shouted at the fire. The woman in the yellow polka-dot dress was trying to drag the body out, but people grabbed and pulled at her violently to keep her from returning to the fire. Oscar took the leg, dragged the body out of the fire, and threw dirt on it to quell the flames. Unrecognizable but for the size, he knew it was her son. The mother's wailing was so strong that it soared above the manic shouting of the crowd.

Oscar shouted, "What happened? What is this? What happened?" The crowd ignored him and began to dissipate as if a sporting event had concluded. The interpreter followed individuals. He shouted angrily in

Kinyarwanda, "What happened? Who did this? What happened? Who did this?" and pointed at the heap of burned flesh. No one answered. They turned to walk away in soft mutters while the mother continued to wail. Like a drill sergeant, the interpreter began to stop and shout within inches of their face, "What happened?" No one responded. They ran away or defiantly pushed him out of their way. The interpreter ordered Oscar to get some water bottles to ensure better cooperation. Still in a state of shock, Oscar ran to the supply tent and returned to stand next to him with a six-pack of one-gallon bottles. The crowd returned and a spontaneous gaggle of voices shouted versions of events. The interpreter pointed to people to come out and talk to him. Oscar gave a bottle to each person who had spoken to the interpreter. As they walked away, the interpreter told Oscar what he could piece together from the different accounts. A boy had a seizure. Some of the refugees saw the seizure as an evil omen. They thought the boy was a devil. They threw him into the fire as he lay unconscious after the seizure. The woman at the fire was his mother. She had been waiting in the food line. Someone ran to get her, but it was too late. In shock and shame at the behavior of people in his own tribe, the interpreter could not look at Oscar, who was silent, still unable to grasp the reality of what had occurred.

Oscar walked in a direct line to the site of the cooking fire. The fury he felt was uncontainable and inexplicable, but his eyes conveyed the anger, and as they saw him walk to the site of the fire, the crowd parted and people moved out of his way. These were the same people who had barely escaped slaughter. Their arms and leg were hacked; the boys, the men, the women, and the girls had been gang-raped. Their bodies had been ripped, stabbed, and clubbed with machetes and hoes. The fortunate wounded among them had arrived in wheelbarrows, pushed by friends and relatives. Some were carried on backs. Others had hobbled and even crawled. He looked down at the black charred mass and saw the mother kissing the foot. Here they were, those same victims of inhumanity, throwing a child into the fire because he had a seizure?

The interpreter and Oscar wrapped the boy's crumpled body in plastic sheeting, the bright blue tarps used for makeshift shelters. Together with the mother, they carried the boy outside the camp. Oscar dug the grave to bury him while the interpreter consoled the mother, who wept and wailed.

The rest of the experience in that refugee camp was a monstrous collage without sense or reason. He completed the Red Cross report, sent it out and never read it again. He even sent Geneva his handwritten notes; he wanted no souvenirs. The complexity of terror, the evil of a hundred days, and the killing of eight hundred thousand people in Rwanda remained incomprehensible. The story of the mother and her son in the refugee camp was a contained memory with beginning and end. Out of respect for the survivors and his experience as an eyewitness to man's inhumanity to man, he knew that he could not and should not wipe out the experience entirely from his brain. That one anecdote which distilled the experience of the camp was like a thumb in a dike; it was a means of remembering what happened out of respect and restraining the random images, entombed in his subconscious, from leaping out in nightmares and flashbacks.

Oscar noticed the blood spots on the rug. He left the conference table to go to the office suite kitchen, where he filled an empty coffeepot with water and took a sponge from the sink. He tried to remember the girl's face. He had never noticed her before in these meetings; she was on one of the regional teams, probably an analyst. Who was she? He looked down at the spot of bloody spit that had come out of her mouth and began scrubbing.

Down the hallway, Mischa was still on the floor, but she had begun to recover. To the rest, she was still suffering from amnesia, but inside she was laughing, just slightly. *I must be in Washington.* She appreciated the absurdity that the truly critical question, used to assess whether or not she was fully conscious, was to name the president of the United States. When she first spoke she said the president's name and then hers. *My sarcasm is back, so my brain is back.* She smiled to herself, with her eyes closed and her head still, and continued lying on the floor.

Sophie was in the corner, helpless. She wanted to comfort Mischa, but was stopped by a wall of medics and emergency paraphernalia of oxygen tanks and medical bags. When Sophie returned to the conference room she saw Oscar scrubbing the floor and wondered what that weirdo was doing. There was no point in asking, she told herself, and she fumbled in Mischa's purse to find her cell phone. She located Hector's number in the cell phone's list of contacts and pressed to call. Before she had a chance to say anything, Hector spoke.

"Yes, yes, Mischa. I didn't forget. Tonight, six o'clock, at Kramerbooks."

"Hector, this isn't Mischa. It's Sophie. Mischa had a seizure—"

"Is she conscious? Where is she? When did it happen?"

"Well, it was a pretty big seizure. She was convulsing for about five minutes or something, maybe less. She hit her head against the table pretty hard, and I think she bit her tongue. There was some blood. I think she's coming to. The medics are with her. It happened about twenty minutes ago."

"I'm on my way. If I'm lucky with traffic, I can get there in fifteen minutes."

Sophie promised the medics that she would accompany Mischa until Hector picked her up. The building manager brought a wheelchair into the office suite. Mischa could tell that the manager didn't recognize her from a few months before, when she had broken her foot. The manager had refused to come up and meet her with a wheelchair because it wasn't a confirmed broken foot and he argued that he might need it for a real emergency. He had recommended that Mischa ask colleagues to help her down. After several minutes on the phone he allowed her to use the wheelchair. Now, here it was in front of her, and Mischa hadn't even asked for it.

The building manager and the others, even Sophie, kept insisting that she sit in the wheelchair to go down to the lobby to meet Hector. Mischa was tired of this scene, the mix of gestures that people made to make the epileptic feel better and gestures they made to make themselves feel better. This one was the latter. Mischa kept insisting that she could walk. They refused to listen to her. Unnaturally, people began to surround Mischa to persuade her to take the wheelchair. Exasperated, finally she shouted, "I am NOT—I repeat, NOT—getting into that chair! I am going to walk." She lifted herself off the ground and repeated in a normal voice. "I'm going to walk."

"Will you all just leave her alone!" Mischa looked behind and it was Oscar. He had heard the commotion and had come out of the conference room. "Let her alone. Let her walk." He understood Mischa's need for gentle dignity and stood next to her. He handed a coffeepot filled with soapy water to someone and put out his arm out so that Mischa could lean on him.

They took the elevator down to the lobby without saying a word. When Hector walked over from the car, Oscar was at her side. As Hector helped lower her into the passenger seat, she looked over as Oscar walked back to the lobby and regretted every vicious comment she had ever made about those water bottles.

⌘　⌘　⌘

Mischa sat slumped at the front of the car. The seat belt kept her head from falling on the dashboard. It was one of those small blessings, the consequence of a midday seizure, that Hector found a premium parking spot, right in front of their apartment building.

"Mischa, I think I'll get back to the office, since you'll be sleeping for the rest of the day. I'll get back around seven."

"No, Hector. Today you are going to come upstairs with me." Mischa clenched her teeth.

"Of course. That's why I parked."

He operates on another level. He can be so unaware. My very own blithe spirit.

In their first years together it came across as respect. He respected her by letting her deal with her own problem alone, without any intervention. He did not give her unsolicited advice. He did not patronize her. She could not pinpoint when she began to think it was indifference, not respect. She could not ascribe any meanness to him. She knew it wasn't in his character. Perhaps she wondered if she had grown needier and he had failed to see the change. Perhaps she failed to see it herself and he continued to act the way he always had.

"No, Hector. I'm saying that you are not only going to come up with me, but you will stay with me, for the rest of the day."

"Sure, Mischa," He looked at her, slightly worried and confused. He could sense a storm rising, but could not understand why. They had been commuting for four years between Cambridge and Washington. Their long-distance relationship was built on daily e-mails and phone calls, five day trips, and two-week vacations. Their long-distance relationship lasted longer than the time since they had been living together at Dupont Circle. Hector wondered how long it would take them to learn to live together. There were all these problems about which towels to use, how to organize the spices, whole or skimmed milk. It wasn't just her. He knew that he made unwanted demands such as taking weekend excursions into the suburbs to recycle their plastic and glass, washing whites with coloreds, insisting on expensive organic foods, and making constant arguments in favor of butter, not diet yellow paste substitute.

Mischa wondered if she had misunderstood Hector. She found it exhausting trying to draw out the feelings that she saw or imagined were there. His Latin nature was not as near the surface as she originally thought. Those extreme expressions of love, devotion, and hate had been calmed and cooled by his English upbringing. She reminded herself that further socialization and fraternization among scientists would have done little to nurture his Latin traits.

When Hector and Mischa arrived at the door, unbalanced by the feeling of tension, Hector fumbled clumsily with the lock. His eyes darted like a small woodland animal that had heard a twig break but had not yet determined the nature of the threat. Impatient, Mischa pushed him aside and twisted the key to open the door. She threw her coat on the floor and collapsed on the bed. He came in with an un-requested glass of water, which she drank gratefully. Again, another sincere gesture that muffled her anger for an instant. *If only Hector could do a hundred more gestures like that over the next thirty seconds.* If it were physically possible it could save him from the wave of anger that was gathering height, speed, and force. He stood there, expectant and nervous. He knew that she wanted to speak and she took a deep breath and began.

"Hector, after a seizure, I'm tired. It's exhausting, dealing with strangers. I want you. I want to come back and lay my head on your shoulder. I want to cry, but you're not here for me. You treat me as if I had tripped on a hose. I sleep and you leave or you listen to your music, or you take a walk, or you go to the gym. Sometimes after a seizure, I want life to go on as normal. But sometimes I need attention. But you don't know how to give it to me. I need you to ask me if I want a cold can of Diet Cherry Coke from the corner store. I need you to flutter and hover over me, just to show me that you're there. I don't want pity. I just want to know you're there. You have to be there. You have to be here."

Mischa thought it would take him days to comprehend this conversation. He would understand if it hurt; otherwise, he would file it in the back of his mind. She would make him remember so that he would not put it in a category with other disagreements. This was far different. She could hear her voice filling the room and the violent speed of her words surprised her. Confused and wounded, Hector's eyes watered, but she continued.

"You need me. But there are times when I have nothing to give. I have no affection. I cannot give you a kiss for a kiss, a hug for a hug. I cannot meet you halfway. I don't have the strength. I'm trapped in my own thoughts. I have my own worries. It may be days or weeks before I can come back to you and my life." She wished she could stop speaking. He looked like a child, sorry and bewildered. But she could not stop; she justified her rampage to herself. *This one explosion is better than a hundred passive-aggressive hints.*

Hector wished he could remain silent, but he had to tell her what had been bursting inside of him for months. Uninhibited, for the first time he shouted at her and his voice matched Mischa's volume.

"Mischa! I don't know how to deal with your epilepsy! After a seizure, when I try to comfort and pamper you, you push me away and scream at me. Other times you curl up in my arms. That same day, a few hours later, you attack me and tell me to go away! I don't know what to do! I'm paralyzed by fear that I might insult you or make you angry. I don't know what you want me to do. What is it? What is the right way to react? Tell me. I'll do it, but right now, I just don't know how."

"Hector," Mischa cried, and fell to the sofa sobbing, tears streaming down her face. "I don't know how! I just don't know! I don't. I don't." She held her head in her hands and said what she never knew she thought. "I've been alone with this for my whole life. It has just been me and my seizures. I've always dealt with my epilepsy alone. Just me. I go to bed with my epilepsy, I wake up with my epilepsy. But now you're there. You're here, in my life. I'm so scared that if you become part of what I need to recover, if I need you too much, then I'm not going to be able to take care of myself. I want you near. I want to let you catch me when I fall. But I have to be alone, because you won't always be there. It's not because you don't want to, but because you can't come where I need you, when I need you. I don't know. I just don't know."

She pressed her hands against her head to make the confusion go away. He sat next to her and held her close, stroking her hair, and gradually, she stopped crying, her breathing became regular, and she fell asleep in his arms.

21. THE CORNER STORE

A FEW HOURS LATER SHE AWOKE, UNAWARE OF HOW MUCH TIME HAD PASSED. Her headache had faded. She was still exhausted, but it was emotional, not physical. She recalled her meltdown and felt Hector's arm holding her. Hector stroked her cheek.

"Mischa, I am here. I always want to be here for you. You can choose when you want me near or not. Now I know. But you have to hear me out. I've let it go when you've said no before, but I'm going to ask again. Please, Mischa, get a medic-alert bracelet. It warns people that you have a medical condition. You wear it all the time, and you don't have to worry. When I'm not around, people will see the bracelet and know what—"

Mischa pushed him away and stood up. "Stop it! Stop it! No, Hector! No! I will not wear some kind of scarlet letter. I want to have my seizures and forget about them. I don't need some reminder handcuffed to my wrist telling me that I have epilepsy. I have it. It's fine. I have it. Everyone tries to get me to wear one. My parents, doctors, friends, and now you. I'm sick of it. I hate it. I don't want to." She walked away.

Hector was at a loss, once again. He regretted raising the issue. This was the wrong time. He should have waited. Why couldn't he have stopped? he thought.

"How about a cup of tea? Shall I make you a cuppa? No. Wait. Sorry, luv. Why don't I run to the corner store, Cherry Coke, right? Wait, that's a Diet Cherry Coke?" Mischa glared at him. "Well then...right then, luv. I'll only be a few minutes." Hector picked up his keys and closed the front door behind him.

When she heard the elevator doors shut, Mischa walked over to the CDs piled near the stereo. Hector had introduced her to British bands when they began to date. His favorites were The Smiths, The Cribs, and Joy Division, and they were Hector from three different sides.

The gently sarcastic Smiths were Hector's distinctly British sense of humor, eloquence, and irony set to song. The Cribs represented another side of Hector. They were an indie cult band from West Yorkshire, like him. As a student he had followed them around to hear their gigs in pubs and ratty clubs around Leeds. The Cribs had a strange electricity and sincere charm. They sounded like the early Beatles jamming in a garage with the Sex Pistols and Nirvana. And yet despite the testosterone-laden guitar riffs, there was a mellow tenderness to their music. Playing a Cribs CD was Hector's oblique invitation to the bedroom. If she had not responded by the third song, Mischa could count on his hands sliding around her waist, slowly pulling her away from whatever she was doing.

At first, Hector's admiration for Joy Division was inexplicable to Mischa. Their music didn't sound like his other CDs, and yet Joy Division was the only rock band accorded the status of sharing a shelf with his *Deutsche Grammophon* CD collection of the complete works of Johann Sebastian Bach, the counterpoint rock star for mathematicians and physicists. He often discussed Joy Division's song structure and lyrics when he played their music. He even compared the spare elegance of their songs to a well-written algorithm. Finally she understood that it was Hector's fierce intelligence that explained his taste for Joy Division as much as Bach. But Mischa refused to intellectualize Joy Division.

Hector gave her a Joy Division album, a few days after the seizure in Cambridge, when he had stayed overnight in her room, working on his laptop. He had stuttered at her door, turning the CD over and over in his hands. He admitted that it was an odd gift, but thought she might find the music interesting, since the lead singer and songwriter of the band had epilepsy and some of the songs referred to the condition. A few years later, Hector came to regret his gift. He developed a growing resentment of the band. Had it not been for Mischa rescuing their CDs from the trash, Joy Division would have been out of their lives, at least he thought.

She found the CD lodged somewhere between *Ella Fitzgerald Sings Cole Porter* and *Billie Holiday: The Commodore Master-Takes. No weepy ballads.* Right here, right now, she wanted to hear raw, articulate anger blasting from the CD player. She needed Joy Division for their fury. She wanted to hear that song. *After a seizure, Ian's the only one who understands.*

When others heard "She's Lost Control" they thought it was about someone seeing a woman have a seizure. But Mischa knew it meant more. The song was an intimate epiphany. It was an understanding that she shared with Ian Curtis, Joy Division's singer and songwriter. "She's Lost Control" relayed the terror and confusion of an epileptic as a witness to a seizure.

The intense empathy, fear, vulnerability, horror, and self-knowledge were laid out in five simple stanzas. Those same emotions surged years ago when she witnessed a man having a seizure in the subway. She thought her experience was unique and beyond words, until she heard that song.

Mischa pressed the "forward" button on the stereo until it arrived at "She's Lost Control." She was certain that Hector would be at the corner store by now. She knew that the people in the apartments above and below would be at work, so she turned the volume knob until it could go no further.

The immediate ferocity of the song's opening transmitted the shock from the unexpected experience of seeing a person suddenly fall to the ground in a seizure. The rapid, intense drumbeats were auditory adrenalin shots that alternated with ominous, heavy synthesized thuds of a jail door shutting closed. A sinister bass played a relentless, driving riff, and Ian Curtis's thunderous voice followed. He proclaimed more than he sang, so the guitar ripped the melody from his words. The chorus was carved into her memory the instant she heard it, "She's lost control again. She's lost control."

As the song approached its climax she sat with her hands pressing the sides of her skull tightly, as if to prevent it from cracking open. She took a deep breath, and then screamed a savage cry that merged seamlessly with the music. Exhausted, she leaned over to turn the stereo off. In the sudden silence she and the song left the room.

Curled underneath the covers of the bed, she felt her heart beating fast. Mischa pretended to be asleep to avoid speaking to Hector, but she underestimated her exhaustion. She was asleep within seconds.

Hector avoided each crack on the sidewalk on his way back from the corner store. It was a superstitious game from his childhood that returned when he was nervous. He recycled the questions in his head over and over. What had he done? What had he not done? What was he going to do? She had told him what she felt, but what was he supposed to do? What did she want him to do?

When Hector returned, he found Mischa's curved shape lying beneath the blankets. He switched off the lights and closed the bedroom door. The silence was depressing. He would play those jazz ballads that Mischa loved. Ella Fitzgerald singing Cole Porter was her favorite. He found the CD and pushed the button to open the CD drawer. He stared down at the CD that was already there. He would have smashed it with a hammer if he had one. He wished he had never told her about them. He wished he had never heard of them and he could amputate Joy Division from their lives.

Hector was familiar with the pattern. Mischa would play that CD endlessly and loudly for days. As if the gloom of that entire album were not enough, when that song began, she stopped whatever she was doing and sat in front of the stereo. Ian Curtis held her hostage and he was left to watch from another room. He could not touch her until that mood had passed. He knew the song's title, but over the years had forced himself to forget it. He hated Joy Division. He hated Ian Curtis. He hated that song.

22. THE WAITING ROOM

ON MISCHA'S FIRST AFTERNOON BACK AT THE COUNCIL OF FOREIGN AFFAIRS ANALYSIS, SOPHIE CAME INTO HER OFFICE FOR LUNCH. On their way to a deli on Connecticut Avenue, Sophie considered what to say. She knew that her approach was imperfect, and her instinct told her that Mischa would be insulted, but it was worth the attempt. She waited until they were back in the office to say what she had tried and failed to raise at lunch.

"Mischa, a few weeks ago I met one of Janet's friends from law school. She's a lawyer who has just been hired by United in Support of the Disabled with Epilepsy. It's a new organization, only a year old. It's more of a campaign, really. They just started up. I thought it was an incredible coincidence. It's a group of professionals from Rhode Island with some connection to epilepsy. They're not really planning to evolve into a big think tank or an advocacy group. They're pretty laser-like. They want amendments to the Americans with Disabilities Act to include people with epilepsy. Apparently people with epilepsy, diabetes, heart ailments, and other disabilities are not covered since they were considered only medical conditions and not in need of protection under disability rights. This group started in Providence, but they know they can't get anything done unless they have a toehold in DC. This lawyer, Sarah, was scouting out office space and she stayed with us. Well, you see, Sarah was asking me for advice about how to survive in the thick of it—working inside the Washington NGO scene—the whole mix of advocacy groups, think thanks, and foundations. I only put conferences together, I don't have a sense for it like you. To make a long story short, Janet and I thought that maybe you two should meet and they could use some help. Maybe, you could kind of volunteer, they need some—"

"My first and last piece of advice to them is that they need a new name, a better acronym. USDE sounds like an agricultural stamp for meat quality. But that's not for me to say. I don't want to get into the whole disabled rights world. I know that's what people call people like me, but I'm not one of them. I don't belong to an epilepsy support group. I don't read epilepsy blogs. I don't even read newsletters from epilepsy NGOs."

Most people would have pulled back, but Sophie was more assertive. This was her time to tell Mischa what she had been thinking for years.

"Lord knows, I admire your strength, but from everything I've experienced as an outsider, you cannot deny the need for community your whole life. You will eventually need people LIKE you. What's more, Mischa, is that you are a survivor and a fighter. You're strong. Maybe you owe it to others, to fight for people who can't fight for themselves. One day you may need someone to fight for you."

"Sophie, I hate that whole *survivor* and *fight* crap. That clichéd language is for anyone with…anything else different. I have epilepsy. I have it, I just have it, and I live with it. That's it. I'm not a survivor on a life raft. I'm not a Marine. I just HAVE it."

Mischa avoided looking at Sophie and stared at her computer screen, pretending to read a document. She could sense that Sophie was still there, so Mischa looked up briefly. "Thanks," she said, and returned her eyes to the computer screen to pretend again. Sophie waited a few more minutes and then walked away.

⌘ ⌘ ⌘

Mischa had planned to take the train to James Hotchkins University for her appointment, but Hector offered to drive her. The recent increase in seizures was unsettling. She always knew that her epilepsy frightened others, but now it was frightened her. Before, there were periods of increased seizures, but then there was a plateau that offered some respite. It gave her time to ready herself mentally for the next stage. Her epilepsy had worsened over these twenty years, but she had some months of rest and the change had been gradual. But now the rate of seizures had increased. There was so little recovery time. Before, she could be assured that after a seizure a bruise would eventually fade or a cut would heal before the next seizure. But now the scratches, scrapes, and bruises collected on her body. There was no plateau, and her denial of the threat to her life began to buckle. Even she was scared. Mischa wondered if she had reached her threshold for handling epilepsy, psychologically and physically. She felt as if she were going over a cliff.

They passed one door after another in the epileptology unit. Waiting for her doctor, Mischa saw the different patients. There was a woman with a beard. In another room was a middle-aged man who kept saying, "LA, LA, LO, LO, LA, LA, LO, LO." An older man was trying to calm him down so that he could hear the doctor, but the man continued with his loud and awkward song. She could hear a nurse talking about a thirty-three-year-old man who had just recovered from a seizure in the waiting room. He must have had them often, because he was wearing a helmet and had his sixty-year-old mother and father sitting next to him, worried and embarrassed. She wondered whether she was really one of them. She couldn't be. She felt guilty for her prejudice, but could not drive these feelings away.

Mischa had been seeing Dr. Bradshaw for three years. In her worst moods, she thought of him as little more than a drug dealer—changing medication, increasing dosages, changing medication. He belonged in an alleyway, not a hospital. People said he was a well-respected neurologist, she read his bio on the Web site, and the neurologist who had referred her felt he had done his best and Mischa deserved better, so he humbly recommended Dr. Bradshaw. Mischa needed to renew the prescription for the medication; on her first visit, it was the only reason she was there.

When she walked into one of the examination rooms, there were Post-its, clipboards, pens, and calendars with brand names of medications for neurological conditions. It was the pharmaceutical industrial complex. People were frightened of the military industrial complex and blamed it for the ills of the world, but Mischa blamed the pharmaceutical companies.

She had been through several neurologists over the course of twenty years, and all of their offices were infected with pharmaceutical company paraphernalia. Every so often, a news program or a documentary would talk about physicians being in the back pocket of the drug companies, but concern faded from the public's attention quickly. There were no protests. It wasn't obvious, like a nuclear missile. In one documentary she saw, they emptied out the conference briefcase that every participant received. They were filled with office supplies featuring the pharmaceutical company's logo or medication it was promoting.

Pharmaceutical companies invited doctors to conferences they held in Europe, the Caribbean, and spa resorts in the United States. They would wine and dine the doctors and sometimes pay minimal conference fees. It all would go down as work-related, so the doctors were not taking vacation time. The conference agendas were never too trying, perhaps two forty-five-minute presentations in the late morning, then catered lunch breaks, an optional cruise, swimming, and tour buses to take conference participants sightseeing. Some of the companies printed useful diagrams for doctors to post in their offices, with the name of the new medication being promoted modestly placed in the corner, but still there for the value of brand recognition. She had to admit the graphics were helpful. While Mischa waited for Dr. Bradshaw she often studied the temporal lobe, the part of her brain where the doctors claimed her seizures originated.

Dr. Bradshaw looked at her records thoughtfully for five minutes and asked what had happened since they last saw each other. She told him the seizures had increased significantly.

"There are times I'm having two seizures in a day. That only happened once before, when I first had seizures. It's happening more now than it has over the twenty or more years I've had epilepsy."

Dr. Bradshaw looked pensive. "I've said this before and you have said no, but I think the only solution you have left is brain surgery—a focal antero-medial temporal lobectomy—to stop these seizures. It is only by luck so far that you have avoided serious injury from your seizures. We've tried multiple trials of different anti-convulsants, yet we still don't have your seizures adequately controlled. Indeed, by your own admission, they seem to be worsening, if anything."

So there it was. After only ten minutes of consultation, barely a couple of questions from him and a few sentences out of her mouth in return, he had suggested brain surgery. He offered to schedule the MRI and neuropsychological tests for the next week so they could begin planning the operation. The doctor continued to speak, but Hector interrupted. So accustomed to being alone with a doctor, she had forgotten he was in the room. As he spoke, Hector's calm British demeanor gave way to a controlled rage that she had never seen. The British and the Latin in him finally seemed to fuse. He delivered methodological and rational arguments with passionate anger.

"So, Doctor, how much of my wife's brain do you propose to take?" Hector inquired.

"About two to four centimeters."

"How did you determine the amount, and where would you be taking it from?"

"It's a standard operation. We would have to determine where exactly, but she has complex partial seizures that originate in the temporal lobe, so it will be from that area."

"How can you be sure that you are taking it from the correct part? Over the course of twenty-five years she has had EEGs, MRIs, and CAT scans, and most of them have revealed nothing about the precise origin of her seizures—nothing more specific than the temporal lobe region, which is a rather large area. How would you determine where, exactly, you would take this? What was it, two or four centimeters? Or would three-point-five be more precise? Her seizures generalize rapidly. Is there a chance that they are originating elsewhere? In that case, even if you took out the correct—what was it?—two or four centimeters, she would *still* have seizures."

Mischa looked at Hector, startled. She didn't realize that he knew so much about her epilepsy. When did he learn all this?

"Well, I'm a neurologist. Your neurosurgeon would be able to answer those questions," Dr. Bradshaw replied.

Hector would not let go. "Dr. Bradshaw, you are Mischa's neurologist. You are the one recommending this invasive procedure for my wife and assuring her that it would be only two centimeters—oh, excuse me, maybe it's four. We're here. You are making a recommendation. I'm asking you to back your judgment with some evidence of intelligent consideration. No doubt you've had interaction with brain surgeons and patients who have chosen this route over the years. What are the risks and the side effects of taking out those two centimeters you talk about?"

"Well, the side effects are uncommon, even rare, but true, they can be serious. They include the small chance of paralysis of one side of your body, loss of part of your eyesight or some paralysis of your eye, infection, and loss of some of your verbal memory. People sometimes need to relearn to speak or use part of their bodies. There are always risks in an operation of this nature, but the primary goal is to stop the seizures, and with definitive surgery such as what we propose, there is a significant chance of preventing most of Mischa's seizures."

"A CHANCE at success? A chance? What is the rate of success and failure in these operations?"

"Well, that depends on a lot of factors, and again, is a question for your neurosurgeon."

"How do you define failure?"

"If the seizures don't stop," Dr. Bradshaw replied in monotone, staring at Hector directly.

"How do you define success?"

"If the seizures stop, or at least if most of them stop. If there is a significant decrease in seizure activity, then that is success." Dr. Bradshaw looked at Hector, irritated by his failure to recognize the obvious. The doctor's irritation mounted in response to Hector's barrage of questions. Dr. Bradshaw took a deep breath and reminded himself that he was not only director of the department, but he had also just received an award from the National Association of Epileptologists and Neurologists, and next week he would be attending the NAEN dinner in his honor—and this arrogant bastard, with no medical background, was sniping at him.

"Doctor, what about the lifestyle of the epileptic? Why does the definition of failure and success ignore this aspect? Your recommendation for brain surgery sounds like an amputation for a cut finger. You get rid of the problem with a sophisticated solution, while a patient's desire to be a complete human, with vital brain functions like memory, motor skills, coordination, and speech, is left by the wayside. This is all for the sake of achieving complete seizure control. Not only that, but you cannot even guarantee seizure control."

Mischa beamed with each verbal punch Hector delivered. She felt like the champion boxer's girlfriend on the sidelines. She wondered why she had never done this herself.

"Mr. Durham, I am an epileptologist, and my primary goal is to stop seizures. The majority of the complications I alluded to are only present in the short term. Complete recovery is more the norm. It is the neurosurgical team who would be able to answer your questions, as they deal with the complications and side effects, as well as with any rehabilitation that may be needed."

"Once again, Dr. Bradshaw, let me remind you that YOU are making a recommendation for your patient—my wife—and I imagine that YOU must do follow-up after surgery for YOUR patients who have made this decision before. I'm asking a very simple question. How long does it take to recover from an operation like this?"

Mischa was shocked at the volume of Hector's voice. She had never heard him speak this loudly, not even in their argument two weeks ago.

"It varies." Dr. Bradshaw continued to respond in a slow monotone. It was a standard tactic to defuse an emotional encounter with patients and bring them back under control.

"You are telling me that my wife might lose her memory, motor skills, and eyesight as a result of this surgery, and you have no sense of the scale and time for recovery? You can only tell us that 'it varies'? How many epileptics in the country choose brain surgery?" he asked.

"I don't know precisely. But antero-medial temporal resections are by far the most common type of surgery for epilepsy, and it has the best results."

"What is the level of severity of seizures and the length of time they have had epilepsy before they take this option of brain surgery?"

"I couldn't tell you."

"What are the treatments that epileptics undergo prior to deciding on brain surgery?"

"Well, it is based on different dosages of different medications. Some make changes to the diet."

"How many medications has my wife tried already?"

"I'm not sure." The doctor glared at Hector angrily.

"Well, she's been treated with fifteen different medications over the course of twenty-five years, with several variations on the dosage. How many anti-convulsant medications are out there?"

"Around fifty," the doctor answered.

"And you've concluded that the other thirty-five are likely to fail? On what basis have you made that decision? Mischa has been prescribed a few combinations of medications, so of course, there is an exponential factor to be considered in looking for the right mix. It's not just thirty-five, or even fifty. There are several alternatives, varied combinations at various dosages."

"Many of the drugs are from very similar classes, the same family so to speak, with different pharmacological properties and effects. If one doesn't work, it is unlikely the others would." The doctor appeared to be a little unsteady. "Also, monotherapy is the goal in creating a treatment program for an epileptic."

"Monotherapy? What does that mean?" Hector asked.

Bradshaw regained a modicum of authority in his voice. "The use of one anti-convulsant to treat a seizure disorder."

"Oh, that's convenient. It avoids confronting the exponential challenge of trying several combinations of drugs."

Mischa chuckled. That was the British side of Hector showing.

One after another, Hector continued with rapid-fire questions like a boxer; right hook, left hook, jab, jab, jab, on the chin, in the stomach, across the jaw. It was almost painful to see this eminent neurologist nervous and uncomfortable, but Mischa had to admit that she derived a perverse pleasure from witnessing this ego-bashing. For years she had been ignored by neurologists like Dr. Bradshaw, who gave her file a few minutes of review before they walked into the room to meet her. She thought of the people who had a hundred seizures or more a week. The extremes of epilepsy were the ones the neurologists found interesting. They were looking for walking-talking medical journal articles. Perhaps not even walking or talking, but nevertheless, interesting subjects for a paper. One neurologist had told her that she was a high-functioning epileptic. It came across as less of a compliment and more like an excuse for not continuing to try other medications and treatments. She wasn't much of a challenge or a mystery. Maybe she would have been more interesting if she had allowed doctors to open her brain. He could meet with all his friends in neurosurgery and review MRIs and CAT scans and EEGs, and then choose the spot on the skull where they would drill a hole, draw an arrow to the part of the brain they wanted to suction out, and then go for coffee.

Mischa thought of how often she had seen him over the last three years, and yet he had made no attempt to create a strategic plan to address her epilepsy. He just played it by ear when she came in. It was evident he had done no prior study. He just increased or decreased the dosage of the three medications and made intermittent recommendations of brain surgery. Mischa's commute to his Baltimore office was two hours. It lasted ten times longer than the time they had in consultation, which was usually ten to twenty minutes. Mischa spent more time in the waiting room than the doctor spent with her in the examination room. In his verbal offensive, Hector delivered his final punch.

"Doctor, I am a physicist. My work does not even approach the critical life-or-death issues that you address every day, but if I were to present any project for serious consideration I would have to have ready a range of facts, background information, calculations, and carefully thought-out scenarios for consideration. Not only do you blithely propose brain surgery for my wife, you fail to even get her approval or rejection before you begin scheduling arrangements. I don't know whether it's arrogance, folly, or both. You act as if you should not have to answer my questions, and when you deign to give an answer it falls woefully short of anything substantial. This entire consultation has been absolutely appalling."

It was the knockout punch. The doctor was down on the mat.

"Well, well, I may need to bone up on new techniques in neurosurgery, and I am a little behind on the current statistical data. On the brain surgery, you don't have to do it if you don't want to…"

As the doctor stuttered his excuses, Mischa's prizefighter stood up and gallantly offered his arm. They walked out.

Mischa took a few days off from work. Janet and Sophie dropped in for dinner the night they returned from Baltimore. Janet held up a bottle of Poland Spring carbonated water and laughed while Sophie gave Mischa flowers. While Hector made curry, Janet and Sophie giggled, held hands, and gazed at each other as they took turns telling anecdotes from their ski trip to Colorado.

Mischa never chose the brain surgery. After that appointment, she stopped going to Dr. Bradshaw and found another doctor in Washington, DC. She had the inevitable seizures, but one benefit of it was a thoughtful doctor at Georgetown University Hospital.

"Mischa, you're over thirty. I don't want to make a recommendation one way or another, but perhaps, if we're going to switch you to another medication, we should put you on an anti-convulsant that has been tested safe for pregnancy and moderately safe for breast-feeding. Do you want to try that drug?"

Mischa looked at Hector and nodded carefully. He nodded as well and reached for her hand. It seemed like a good decision.

23. THE TAXI

August 2003

SHE WAS LYING IN THE BACKSEAT OF A CAR. Her first sight was a ragged collection of fir-shaped air fresheners hanging from the rearview mirror. *There must be about fifteen of those things strung together. Aren't they supposed to be dark green? But these are red. Why don't people just stick with the classic—the ones that smell like Pine-Sol. It smells like I've been dropped into a vat of cheap strawberry ice cream.*

Through the front window, Mischa saw Hector give the cab driver a twenty-dollar bill without asking for change. The driver would not accept it and he backed away. But Hector came forward and folded the bill in his hand. Mischa's head was still spinning, but she began to remember that they had left Capitol Hill.

The ride to our house only costs about ten dollars. But there is Hector, a man who thinks a five-percent tip is excessive, giving a hundred percent. What did the driver do?

She had been sleeping there for a while. More than an hour. Slowly, random thoughts were succeeded by reasonable ones, and Mischa knew she had begun to recover. *I need to get out of this car and into my bed.* While speaking to the taxi driver, out of the corner of his eye, Hector saw her move slightly. He rushed to give her his hand to pull her up. She stood, but at five months pregnant, it was difficult.

Mischa slept until late morning the next day. After lunch she asked Hector to take her to a coffee shop and let her stay there for a while. He was nervous at the thought of Mischa by herself, but he obliged. Still apprehensive, he decided to drop her off, but park around the corner and read in the car. He could look in occasionally to see if she was all right, and then go back to the car without her seeing him. He had done this a few times now.

Mischa took naps at the coffee house occasionally. There was a huge plum purple velvet armchair. She would begin reading, only to find herself waking from a nap one hour or more later. Her naps at the coffee shop were more peaceful. At home, she took a nap in her bed and was reminded of one seizure or another. She would see the set of dishes with the Danish blue and white flowers and remember the saucer, the tea-cup, the bowl that had been broken when she dropped them during her seizures. She saw the chair that she had bumped her head against in another seizure. There in the corner was the small rip in the curtain she had pulled to keep herself from falling. But here in the coffee shop, she was free of those reminders, at least for now. She had not yet had a seizure in this place. She could walk in and think of nothing but coffee and cake, although now it was herbal tea and cake.

Mischa beamed when she saw Ella walk into the Mayorga Coffee Factory that day. She had come today hoping to find her. Ella was also pregnant and further along. After seeing each other a few times Mischa introduced herself one day. Randomly and coincidentally, they would meet with each other and sit for an hour or two trading updates on fetal weight, backaches, nausea, fashion, movies, chocolate bars, *Seinfeld* episodes, and then the deeper questions. They were unlinked by addresses, e-mails, phone numbers, spouses, or even last names. There was a freedom in that anonymity that allowed a frank exchange of hopes and fears.

The topic that most occupied them most was the "motherhood career plateau." They had coined the term over a slice of poppy seed cake. They knew they were both approaching it. No more climbing for professional success. They would do their jobs, without thought for promotion, while their male colleagues continued the climb. They wanted to be home to attend their children's soccer games, recitals, school plays, or dance classes. It would be worth it. But they knew it would be hard not to be envious of their male colleagues. The men never seemed emotionally torn by their dual roles as father and professional.

In Washington DC, one's profession could easily be everything. The town was filled with overachievers, both men and women, who had sacrificed everything for their career. A person had to make a conscious decision not to get swallowed into that mind-set. A professional woman who arrived in DC was an ambitious overachiever by virtue of being there. For some, alongside the career track came a second one, the motherhood track. How does that same overachiever define success in motherhood? Ella had her theory.

"Mischa, if you ask me, I think the first step is to depressurize. It's counter-intuitive to the type of alpha female indigenous to Washington DC, but seriously I think it's the way. You acknowledge that there is no model of success, no lessons learned, no strategy, just go with your gut, play it by ear, and cut yourself some slack. Getting into that frame of mind is probably just as important a milestone as all those measurements of fetal development. The problem is that we're not the focus, are we? Everyone is looking either inside or at our bellies."

Mischa and Ella reflected on how the delicate fifty-fifty split of housework between a childless couple was thrown off balance with a child. All documentation and anecdotal evidence from friends was conclusive. The woman—mother and wife—ended up doing most of it. That was the conversation on another day. They wondered how a woman faced the de facto increase in the housework burden, a career plateau, and raising a child, and not become embittered.

"I've given this some serious thought, Ella. To be honest, I think slobs make better mothers."

"Okay, Mischa, I'm game. Tell me, why do slobs make better mothers?"

"Well, it's logical. Think about it, what is the most common scolding by a mother? It's 'Clean up your room!' or, 'Oh no, what a mess you've made!' or, 'Your clothes are so dirty, throw them in the laundry!' A sloppy mother is just not going to care as much, and consequently will not be scolding her child as much as a neat mother. She's not going to be yelling or setting artificial goals like clean rooms. She's going to encourage a child not to care what other people think. After all, she doesn't mind that the house is a mess. A sloppy mother does not say, 'What will the neighbors think of us if you keep your toys scattered on the lawn like that?' There is a whole knock-on effect of not caring how neat your house is. I think it's a sign that a mother is setting real priorities for her child."

"So, is this your contribution to the assembled wisdom of child development: a sloppy mother is a better mother?"

"Yeah. Yeah, I think it is." Mischa considered the axiom smugly.

Ella laughed. "That's good to know, because my mom was a slob, I'm a slob, and if your theory is correct, then I am already a good mother. Now I can throw all those child development books away. Okay, Mischa, let's make a toast to sloppy motherhood."

Mischa heaved herself off the plum velvet armchair, and with her mug of herbal tea raised, she pronounced, "To sloppy mothers! No longer are we pariahs in a world of yummy mummies and alpha moms. Our failure to vacuum and maintain a clean kitchen surface is proof of our devotion of time to our children, not our house. Uh…let's see…no longer shall people equate a clean house with a good mother. Our time has come! Sloppy mothers of the world, unite!"

They clinked their herbal tea-filled mugs and Ella squealed with laughter. Even people with head-phone infested ears looked over in annoyance.

Mischa remembered these past conversations and smiled as she moved her papers and magazines to give Ella some space on the sofa in anticipation of another great conversation. Who knew where it would lead them? To decide on the role of women in society, to come up with a short list of the best movie directors, or to make some election forecasts. Some random thought would lead to an inspired discussion. After Ella had settled down with her herbal tea and cake on the table they exchanged the news since they had last met. After the initial small talk had calmed, in that first pause, Ella asked, "What is it like having epilepsy?"

It was unexpected, but it was not a surprise since everything was on the table whenever they talked. Mischa considered the question. It was one that she always heard circling in the background of other people's questions about epilepsy. It was never asked outright. That was, until Hector, and now Ella. But Mischa wanted to make sure it was the question.

"Well, my seizures start with an odd feeling, then it's lights out, waking up with a headache, and asking myself, 'Who am I? Where am I? Why am I here?'"

"Sounds like my honeymoon." Ella could make Mischa laugh in an instant. Once the schoolgirl giggles subsided, Ella clarified. "No, really, Mischa, it's not the seizures I'm asking about. What is it like having epilepsy as a part of your life?"

Mischa took a deep breath. *Yes, she was asking The Question.* Ella had not been in her life for very long, but she felt as comfortable to ask and Mischa felt at ease to answer.

"I have it, I live with it, I deal with it, and I move on." Mischa noticed that her response did not have the lyrical and hesitant voice of a soulful revelation. It was a direct statement about her life. It was exactly what she believed. Instantly she thought of incense. The smell was so vivid that fear gripped her, but then within seconds she realized that she did not feel the vertigo, the nausea, or the heat that foreshadowed her seizures. *It's only a memory.* The connection was still unclear, but before she could mull further, Ella pulled her back to the present.

"Mischa, have you ever thought how your life would be if you did not have epilepsy?"

"Nope. What is that phrase? 'That way, or this way, lies madness.' No, no. I do not, will not, ever have an answer to that question." That was not to say that Mischa had never considered the question, she had just never looked over the edge for the answer. The question, she thought—or rather, the answer to that question—would immobilize her.

"I think that to ask, 'What if' as an aspiration, like, 'What if I could fly?' is what makes a person achieve. That's a worthy frame of mind. But to ask 'What if?' out of regret and anger at your present status makes people see themselves as objects of fate, not movers. They focus on an imaginary past to derive an imaginary future. No reality, no matter how good, can compare with a person's fantasy of what life should be if it could be. It makes life more difficult, not to mention bitter. In that context, 'What if?' offers a limitless list of excuses for failure. People in that frame of mind dig themselves into holes of self-pity. Onlookers throw shovels of sympathy. What else can they do? The person gets buried in it."

Mischa shifted in her seat. She felt as if she were giving a university lecture, but there was no other way to discuss this. This cold vocabulary of reason gave her comfort. People expected an emotional waterfall when she spoke about her epilepsy, but it didn't happen. She wouldn't let it happen.

Mischa went on. "If you want me to get reflective, there are perhaps three discoveries that I would attribute to my epilepsy. It sounds pretentious, but I have found meaning in my life through my epilepsy. But it's not THE MEANING OF LIFE, like Monty Python."

"Monty what?" Ella asked.

"That's off topic, forget it. It sounds melodramatic, but a disability reminds a person of the act of survival. You deal with difficulty in life daily, sometimes hourly. You begin to wonder, you have to wonder at some point, why do I want to survive? What's the point? Imagine thinking that you might have died in that last seizure or that you may die in the next one."

"So what's the meaning of life, or rather, what is it you said, 'the meaning in your life'?" Ella asked.

"No drumrolls. This is just for me. It's my life, my meaning. It's simple. I have to make conscious decisions to be who I am and not submit to circumstances. I'm in charge of shaping my character. I have to become someone."

"What do you mean 'become someone'? Being important?"

"Oh God, no, I'm not suggesting celebrity, far from it. Being human is a real gift. Having the mind and free will to decide how to create yourself is a life project. There is meaning in shaping your own character. I don't know if I've become a better person over my lifetime, but I take responsibility for my character and my choices. I have not led a thoughtless life." Mischa took a sip of tea.

"Well, you're not alone. There are a few philosophers behind that idea. My favorite is—"

"Don't say it. Don't tell me the name. Allow me the self-delusion and self-satisfaction to think that I thought it up. Who knows, maybe I've derived all of this from a Chinese fortune cookie."

"And the other two?"

"What other two?" asked Mischa.

"You said there were three discoveries."

Mischa laughed. Ella was rigorously curious. "Okay, Ella, if you hold me to listing all three, you are setting me up to continue my monologue."

"No problem, Mischa. It's a big cup of tea and I have all afternoon. Go forth and expound."

"Well, the second one is the corollary to the Golden Rule. I would call it the Platinum Rule, but that sounds slightly heretical."

"Why not the Golden Corollary?"

"It sounds like a surgical term, but I suppose it will do."

"And the rule is?" Ella asked.

'Right, well, it seems pretty obvious, but it's not really. The Golden Rule is 'Do unto others as you would have them do unto you.' But I think that a better guide for action would be to "Do unto others, as they would like to have done unto themselves"—or, in modern-day speech, 'Treat others the way they want to be treated.' People with the best of intentions can be operating under the Golden Rule and cause irritation. It takes a little longer and it's a little harder, but sometimes you have to get into the skin of other people and consider the way they would want to be treated. Even then you might not get it right, but at least try to see the world from their perspective. For example, I have a colleague at work who is pregnant. I think she's in her seventh month. Last week, she asked me why I never asked how she was getting along with her pregnancy. She felt a little put off by my disinterest. I explained how I loathe hearing inquiries about my pregnancy at work. I get so defensive. The epilepsy and the tension is too much for hallway small talk. Because of my experience and my feelings I thought that the way to treat another woman's pregnancy with respect in the workplace was to treat it as a private matter for her alone and not for public discussion. But I guess if I had looked a little more closely and seen the crepe ribbon blue booties strung across her office and the sonogram pictures taped to her door, then I would have seen that she was begging to chat about her pregnancy. It's the happiest, most uncomplicated event in her life. For her it's just juggling baby-showers and choosing colors for the nursery."

"Mischa, you can't take the time and make the effort to get under everyone's skin and think about what they want. That's exhausting."

"Yeah, that's true, and frankly, I really didn't know her well so I never would have been interested to find out what she wanted. That's why the Golden Rule is a good default moral setting for dealing with everyone. But when you're dealing with someone who means a lot to you, about issues that are very important to him or her, then it's worthwhile taking into account the golden coronary—I mean, the Golden Corollary, as you so aptly named it. At least that has been my experience."

"And now for the third discovery?" Ella continued the inquisition.

"Don't I get a rest?"

"Nope, you're on a roll. Next time we meet, I promise I'll present my philosophical treatise on heaven and earth, but for now, let's keep it to one person at a time. Come on, Mischa, out with it. What is the third discovery?"

"No drumrolls please, though it does sound melodramatic. It's compassion. I think it's the core of what it means to be human. It is rare, but it exists and I can attest to it. I have found it in the most unexpected places, in the weirdest people and the strangest situations, and I am continually and gratefully amazed. Some very trustworthy, honest, and generous people have run as soon as they've seen a seizure. I've met dishonest bastards, womanizers, alcoholics, egotists, weirdoes, snobs, and sluts, and they've stopped their day or night to help me. When I had a seizure, they were there, caring for me, with nothing to gain."

"Why do you think that is?" Ella asked.

"I'm not quite sure. Perhaps someone who has an open wound in his or her life identifies with vulnerability in another's life."

"But can't you find kindness in people who don't have anything wrong with their lives?"

"That's it! That's the difference I hadn't figured out. Precisely, Ella. You can find 'kindness,' but compassion is deeper. You can be kind and be considered a 'good person' by society for knowing your manners or adhering to a religious code of ethics. But that doesn't mean that you are compassionate. Kindness might be the measure of a person's morality, but morality is a pale reflection of genuine compassion. I think compassion is often found in dark places, in tragic situations. Tragedy plays some part in creating compassion, and maybe even wisdom."

"But, Mischa, there's a lot of evidence that after a tragedy people can turn violent, bitter, angry, and apathetic. Like, think of the cycle of abuse—sexual, drug, alcohol, domestic—a lot of people who do it have had it done to them. They're not compassionate. They repeat the hurt and the violence on others and sometimes on themselves. They self-destruct with drugs or other addictions, even suicide."

"Yes, that's one reaction to tragedy, and I don't know whether it's nature, divine intervention, or just luck, but some take the alternative path. They break the cycle and develop an unusual depth of empathy. They wonder who else might feel the same way as they feel and how they would want to be treated in that situation, even one that is different from their own but nevertheless tragic. Religion, philosophy, or a code of ethics cannot teach that empathy. Perhaps tragedy that results in empathy is the real source compassion. I think empathy in action is compassion."

"So who is the better person? Someone who is kind or someone who is compassionate?"

"I don't really think one is better than the other. Rather, they each have their uses in the world. I think kind people keep the peace and order in society, they keep it working. But evil is inevitable. Why? That's another discussion, but when overwhelming evil or misfortune does arrive in an individual's life—or on a broad scale such as rape, genocide, a war, or a car accident—then kindness is not enough. People who are merely kind may not have the strength or the will to confront evil and misfortune. Confronting overwhelming odds to rebuild lives or a world depends on the compassionate. Think of people rebuilding their lives after 9/11 or those in New Orleans after Hurricane Katrina. I think it depends on people who have the strength of character and, I know it's strange to say, an understanding of the moral complexities necessary to restore life after it has met with evil and disorder."

"You're losing me. Moral complexities?"

"It's an ability to comprehend a choice between greater and lesser evils. Not deluding yourself into thinking that you or people like you make choices that are good over choices that are bad. There's no choice between good and bad. I think compassionate people can deal with the messiness of human behavior. They acknowledge that bad people can do good and good people can do bad. Also, understanding that intelligent people can make wrong decisions and people considered 'dumb,' with no education and no degree, can be a source of wisdom. They look for the best in both, judging actions rather than their appearance or the category that society given them.

"I think the compassionate derive solutions from their observations and experiences and come to peace with an evil that has occurred by not dwelling on revenge but on a better future. After all, forgiveness is part of the territory of compassion. It comes after one is hurt—psychologically, emotionally, or physically. A person with compassion can draw out the best in others and themselves, and rebuild. They can move on with life after a tragedy.

"I think compassionate people are wise. They see the big picture and the small picture, and are not trapped and immobilized by social conventions of what is good or bad or what people will think of them. The tragedy in their lives inoculates them, to some extent, from that virus of 'what will people think of me?' They are less interested in others' opinions and that's a freedom that cannot be underestimated. We're all born wise, but so much in the world obscures that. So much gets in the way: looks, job, status, income, just the business and momentum of daily life. Then a tragedy hits and it clears the unnecessary clutter in life. Everything stops for a moment and a person is forced to look at himself or herself in an empty room. They are given the opportunity to see inside and draw from a well of wisdom and strength that they might have never known they had. They have an opportunity to learn empathy. Everybody has wisdom, strength, and empathy, but not everyone draws it out. I think tragedy often does that. A person would never wish for the tragedy, but there can be a kind of transformation that results. There is an awfulness to it, but also a form of grace.

"I remember a quote that Robert F. Kennedy used when he had to inform an audience that Martin Luther King had just been assassinated. Police were expecting race riots all over the country that night. It was already known that the assassin was a white man. RFK was on a campaign stop and he delivered the news to an audience that was largely African American, in Indianapolis. I remember seeing the footage of the event in a documentary. Robert F. Kennedy had a microphone in his hand and was speaking to a crowd assembled outside. When he announced what had happened there was wailing, crying, and shouting. He called for calm. He started by telling the crowd that he knew what it was like to have someone that he loved killed, and noted that his brother had been killed by a white man. He quoted a piece of literature, I can't remember where it is from, but I've always associated this quote with Robert Kennedy: 'In our sleep, pain which we cannot forget falls drop by drop upon the heart until, in our own despair, against our will, comes wisdom through the awful grace of God.' I think that explains the transformative nature of tragedy better than I could. It can go either way. In some cities that night there were riots after King's assassination was announced. In that city, in that crowd, that night, where RFK gave that speech, there were no riots. I think many people took the path of self-reflection and found wisdom, strength, and compassion as a result."

Mischa took a breath and realized that she must have been on a monologue for more than a half hour. "Gosh, Ella, I'm boring you. I can hear myself. I'm sounding like a philosophy professor. I can get so pedantic."

"No, Mischa, not at all. This is a break from all that pregnancy talk. I get sick of the constant discussions over natural versus Cesarean; breast milk versus formula; blah, blah, blah. Philosophy was my major. I miss these types of conversations. But I really miss the joints I was smoking when I had these conversations. I don't suppose you have any on you?" She laughed.

"ELLA!" Mischa replied "Yet, I must admit it's a relief to hear a pregnant woman even joke about doing something unhealthy. I'm sick of all this herbal tea. You know what? I'm going for an espresso. I'm going to do it. The baby will probably be jumping around for the next few hours, but what the hell, a little exercise would do it some good. I'll be back in a sec."

Mischa went to the espresso bar and waited as the barista put together an espresso with a sliver of lemon rind on the edge. She lumbered back to the couch. "By the way, Ella, I'll have you know this is just a single, not a double espresso."

"But of course, I would not have expected anything less responsible. Okay, Mischa, back to the beanbag and lava lamp talk. You say that there are two paths in response to tragedy: bitterness, anger, and violence, or compassion. But what about the people who deny the existence of tragedy in their lives?"

"Hmm…I hadn't thought of that. Well, maybe that's the third alternative, another consequence of tragedy. I guess it's a lost opportunity to develop compassion, but I would never condemn that person. They owe no one. Surviving tragedy without resorting to anger is difficult enough. After all, to each his own survival. I'm just rambling. I really don't know quite how to express myself. It still remains a mystery to me."

"But I think I understand," Ella responded softly, and wiped a tear away.

Mischa did not see her; she was still trying to untangle her thoughts as she sipped her espresso. Ella had offered Mischa the first opportunity to understand what she had learned about her epilepsy. Mischa felt comfortable in the anonymity of a coffee shop with this amicable stranger-friend. They had still not exchanged last names or numbers.

"Ella, at the risk of sounding simplistic, cruel, and shallow, if you really want to know how I deal with my epilepsy, the secret is optimism with a dash of denial. Make that a few tablespoons of denial. People underestimate the value of denial. A person needs to get on with life. I'm not suggesting denial as a central tenet of existence, but in moderation, like salt, alcohol, or caffeine, I highly recommend it." Mischa gulped the last bit of her espresso. "I know, I know. I've been talking about compassionate people who are aware of their own vulnerabilities, and now I recommend denial. Take this as an admission that I am not a compassionate person. God, I have to eat some chocolate. I know I have something in here." Mischa rummaged through her purse.

Ella turned from the window to look at her and laughed. "So, Mischa, you think psychiatrists' offices should have signs on their doors like, 'Too much self-awareness can kill you'?"

Mischa found the half-eaten Snickers bar and smiled gleefully before she ripped into it.

"Yeah, why not? Or how about, 'Know thyself—but not too much.' Instead of those sappy corporate motivational posters with pictures of sunsets and waterfalls, I would like to see that saying on a poster with a picture of the Rodin statue—*The Thinker*—about to fall off a cliff. The type of therapist who would put that in her waiting room is the type I would visit."

They laughed, and Ella took a bite of her poppy seed cake while Mischa ate the Snickers bar with zest.

"Mischa, my mother died when I was about four years old. She had epilepsy."

Mischa put her hand on her own pregnant belly and a look of horror crossed her face.

"No, no, no, Mischa. Please don't misunderstand. It wasn't related to her epilepsy. It was something else entirely different. It was cancer." Ella was apologetic.

Mischa could feel herself breathe again. She asked Ella, "Do you remember your mother?"

"I remember the lullaby she sang to me. Years later I heard the melody again and discovered it was 'Mack the Knife.' My mother only knew the words to one peculiar version. It was from an Ella Fitzgerald live concert CD, when the singer forgot the words and improvised the lyrics. It's a jazz cult classic. Strange choice for a lullaby, when you think about it, but the melody must have been comforting, because it stayed with me. In fact, Ella is not my real name. I chose Ella as my nickname. My father told me I did that when I was three. He said I convinced my mother to allow me to have a nickname by telling her that if she liked Ella Fitzgerald, she'd like having a daughter named Ella.

"I remember that my mother laughed a lot. My father said that even her eyes smiled. She was hugely affectionate. She clapped at every minor achievement, like when I buttoned up my coat by myself for the first time or put my shoes on the right feet." Ella paused. "Then again, sometimes I wonder if my imagination is filling in those painful gaps. I always asked my father for stories about her." She bit her lip and broke the sadness for a moment with a low laugh.

Mischa could see that Ella was searching for another memory. Ella stared at a wall; she had long since stopped talking to Mischa. She was talking to herself out loud.

"I even remember the smell of her tea rose perfume."

"So that's what I smell, when it's not chamomile tea?" Mischa asked.

"Yes, it's strange. I only started wearing her perfume once I became pregnant. It's from a bottle that she left for me."

Whatever scent of sadness that might have hung in the air after their conversation about epilepsy was overwhelmed by Ella's heartache. Mischa thought to tell her about her own mother's death, but stopped herself to allow Ella to talk.

"I've never explained it to myself, but I share your attitude. You live with it, you deal with it, you move on. My father was wonderful and— oops, the baby kicked! Feel." Ella put Mischa's hand on her belly. "Did you feel her?"

Ella blossomed into joy. Just a minute ago there was such sorrow, but now Ella was smiling and giggling. Mischa looked at her face and wished she could have put Ella's bliss in a bottle.

"Wow! She kicked again, oh, and again!"

"Have you two chosen a name yet?" Mischa asked, grateful the mood had lightened.

"Yup, I knew it would be the name I wanted. My husband had to witness eight months of morning sickness, vomiting bouts, backaches, and fatigue to make that concession, but I knew he would."

Mischa told her that she didn't know whether they would have a boy or a girl. Hector wanted it to be a surprise. They never really wanted to know. They were prepared for any type of child, disabled or not, of any gender. They would love the child, and there was nothing else to hope for, just the birth of a child. And if that child did not survive the pregnancy, well, that was a thought they never considered. The word *miscarriage* was never spoken, not by them nor the doctor. Unspoken, but shared, they each believed they had no right to favor a gender or hope for the health of the child. That was a luxury for other people. They just wanted a child together. By battling over the baby's name, Hector and Mischa found normalcy in the pregnancy. It was almost a relief, and they had good-natured fun in gently ridiculing the other's choice. In this small way, they thrived, behaving like every other expectant couple. Their final compromise was that if, twenty-four hours after the baby's birth, there was still no agreement on a name, they would flip a coin and the winner would choose the name.

"That's what my parents did. My dad won the coin toss. That's how a Chilean American ended up with my non-nonsensical Russian name. He's a professor of Russian literature. We'll probably choose family names, a great-grandparent's or a parent's. I would like to name her after my mother, but I'm willing to consider other names. However, I don't want a new age, cosmic like name like Wind, Apple, Rainbow, Fallopian, or Tornado."

"Mischa, have you ever thought about the advice you would want to give your child?"

"Hector and I are so confused by the child development books. We've stopped reading them."

"Well, uh, that's…" Ella tried to explain. "No, Mischa, that's not what I mean. Let me see, how should I put it? Have you thought about what you would want to leave your child? Perhaps a letter of ideas, thoughts, advice? My mother left me with few things: a collection of short stories she had written, a bottle of perfume, a book, some CDs, and some other personal stuff. My father gave them to me when I was eighteen. I treasure them. I'm already composing a letter to my daughter in case anything should happen to me in labor, or anytime during her childhood. If I am still alive, I will give it to her before she goes off to college. If not, then at least I will have transmitted some life lessons, things I would have wanted to teach her had I lived."

"Aren't we being a bit morbid?" Mischa asked.

"No. I'm being a realist." Ella looked at her angrily,

Mischa felt chastened, ashamed. "I'm sorry, Ella. That was thoughtless, forgive me."

"Don't worry, Mischa. Admittedly, I can sometimes be too dark. When your mother dies when you're four years old it leaves a mark." Ella glanced at her watch. "Can you believe it? We've been here for three hours! I have to get home. I'll see you again. Good luck—I hope the nausea disappears." She gave Mischa a kiss on the cheek and waddled out the door.

That was their last conversation. Mischa returned to the coffee shop over the next few months but never saw Ella again. Dejected, Mischa presumed that Ella must have given birth and found herself adrift in post-natal chaos.

At Mischa and Hector's bi-weekly appointment, Dr. Carter asked, "Anything new?" He was barely over five feet tall, round-faced and round-bellied, with a white beard. If he were wearing a little red cap, a yellow shirt, and blue shorts, he could have been stuck in a garden, so Mischa and Hector decided to call him the Gnome.

"Well, she had a seizure," Hector reported, and Mischa nodded in confirmation.

"You WHAT!?" exclaimed the Gnome.

"I had a seizure. I did tell you I was epileptic when we first came here," said Mischa calmly.

"Yes, yes, Mischa. I know you are epileptic! You have to report these seizures as soon as they happen. You should be coming into the emergency room! What did you do?"

"I went to sleep after it. I just slept until the next day."

"Did you lose any oxygen during the seizure?"

Mischa looked to Hector, and he nodded. "Well, she did turn a little blue," Hector replied calmly.

The Gnome began to yell at them again. "Don't you understand? If she goes blue, the baby goes blue! Who do the two of you think you are? What are you doing? You call me whenever she has a seizure. She has to come to the emergency room. Immediately! Call me from the ambulance and have them page me immediately. I don't ever want to have to tell you this again. You should both know better. This is about the baby."

The rest of the appointment went well, relatively. The Gnome was angry, but he had delivered his message and hoped the two would realize their irresponsibility. Hector and Mischa walked out of his office like chastened puppies. In retrospect, they were ashamed. Their reaction was out of place and irresponsible; the doctor was entirely correct.

24. THE NURSERY

November 2003

HECTOR WALKED TENTATIVELY INTO THE BEDROOM WITH A SMALL BOX. Mischa saw the box in his hand and was surprised and pleased. The traditional jewelry gift from the husband usually came after delivery, not before, but she could accept a break in tradition. Would it be the classic diamond stud earrings? Perhaps a ring? Mischa liked antique jewelry and Hector had good taste. Perhaps a small brooch? Bubbly and smiling, she put her book down and moved over as he sat down next to her on the bed. When he spoke, Mischa heard a tone in his voice that instinctively made her heart fall.

"Mischa, I know you didn't want one, but please, for me…for the baby…please, I would like you…beg you…to wear this."

He opened the small navy blue box and inside was a thin stainless steel link bracelet. At the center of the bracelet was a medallion with the universal medical emblem—a snake encircling a winged staff between the words "Medic Alert." It looked like a soldier's dog tag. The morbid similarity of purpose made her hate it even more. Hector took it in his hand and showed her the other side.

> *Mischa Petra Dunn*
> *Epilepsy*
> *ID 25353675*
> *In a medical emergency call collect*
> *for patient information: 209-634-4872*

Hector saw her face transform from delight to dejection, but he continued because he knew that he must. Softly, he said, "Mischa, please consider the baby. It's not just you anymore. It's also me. I don't want to lose you. I don't want to lose the baby. I want to know that when you are alone, people will treat you appropriately. They'll know what to do, immediately. There won't be guessing. Every minute of time when you have seizure is precious.

There can't be a waste of time while medics try to figure out what's wrong. They need to know, and this bracelet will tell them. It will tell strangers. Don't you remember, some people thought you were drunk or drugged up when you had a seizure? If they don't see this bracelet, they'll leave you alone. I want to be there, but there are times when I'm just not around. We know that. This bracelet is a way of you dealing with it, yourself, in the event that I'm not nearby."

She picked up the bracelet and looked at it for a minute. She had never seen one this close. She had seen medic-alert bracelets. Often in a cashier's line when a customer was removing cash from a wallet she would see a bracelet would swing from the wrist. At meetings she had caught them when she looked down. They lay like worms on the wrists of the people wearing them. There were posters in waiting rooms, urging patients to order one at a discount if they had a heart condition, diabetes, asthma, nut allergies, and a myriad of other conditions. There were no good reasons not to wear a medic-alert bracelet. She had just avoided it for years. For whatever reason, she was too exhausted to psychoanalyze her motives now. The bracelet was looking up expectantly from its small box.

"Help me put it on," she said, defeated.

Hector started to put it around her wrist, but stopped. He took her hand and placed the bracelet curled in the cup of her palm. "You decide. You decide, if or when, you want to wear it. You can put it on by yourself." Hector kissed her and stood up. In forced cheeriness he offered to make dinner. "How about jacket potatoes with beans and lashings of cheddar cheese?"

"Yeah, that would be great. Who says the British can't cook?" She gave a forced smile.

Exasperated, Hector trudged down the steps to the kitchen. It's true, Hector thought, she has the right to decide how to deal with her epilepsy. But this is a new episode of life, their life. She has to take down that wall, he thought. That need to accept her limitations is colliding against all that self-sufficiency, stoicism, and denial. We have to build a life that allows her to accept her limitations. She's got to do it. He would have to be careful, but he would be persistent, because he had a right as well. He would be the father. That was, if the child were born. But that consequence was too tragic to consider and he swept the thought away as he searched for tinfoil.

For the rest of the pregnancy, Mischa and Hector rushed to the emergency room after each seizure. She had four in nine months. Each was a tragedy, for its unknown effect on the unborn child. However, the seizures were less frequent than before. But it was hard to see it as an improvement when she looked down at her belly to think of the effects of the oxygen loss and the medicine. The Gnome had warned them that the oxygen loss could result in brain damage to the fetus, and might have already.

No matter what, no matter what condition, no matter what they discovered, Hector and Mischa decided the baby was theirs and would be loved. They said no to all the tests. They didn't want to know. Every time she was in the emergency room, on a bed, staring up at the lights and then looking down at the dome of her belly, she felt the painful stab of guilt. When they put oxygen masks on her and rushed her down corridors into emergency rooms, Hector's eyes were dry but filled with such pain that she wished he would just cry. She knew they contained hours of tears. Inside those curtained cubicles, he could only hold her hand. Sometimes she was conscious but could not speak; often she chose not to speak. She wanted to be alone in her exhaustion and despair. After all, what was there to say? Mischa would try to remember something to make her laugh inside. Something funny and happy. During those moments in the emergency ward, she thought about the night she found out that she was pregnant. It was the night of choir practice.

One of Hector's office workers sang in a community choir of Chinese Americans, which was preparing for a performance of Handel's *Messiah* for Christmas. Several of the original choir members had dropped out and the organizers could not encourage anybody else to join. Hector's colleague explained that the choir had already hired a professional choirmaster and was now stuck with him and his exorbitant fee to pay. They were hoping that the performance would cover it and raise funds for the Chinese Community Center. It was too late to cancel and they were desperately seeking new choir members, Asian or not. They were even offering to pay minimum wage to newcomers to cover their hours spent at choir practice. Hector convinced Mischa to do it for fun. *What the hell. Why not?* They could probably get a few hundred dollars out of the whole experience. So they found themselves committed to eight p.m. choir practice, twice a week for seven months.

It was a few weeks into their new life with the Arlington Chinese Community Choir that Mischa felt all the signs. She asked Hector to stop at a pharmacy and buy a pregnancy test. While she read the instructions Hector sped down the Beltway. If they were late they would face the wrath of the choirmaster's enforcer, who they called "Chairman Mao." Hector stayed outside the door of the ladies' room thumping his hands against the wall with the drumbeats of a Cribs song running through his head. He heard Mischa squeal and she leapt out the door waving the plastic stick with the plus sign. They hugged and jumped and clapped until Chairman Mao found them in the hallway and demanded their return to the auditorium.

On the drive home from choir practice, they talked about names, the nursery, and the day and way to tell their fathers. Without discussion, they decided that they didn't want to know whether the baby was a girl or a boy.

"But, Hector, I don't want to refer to the baby as 'it' for nine months. We need a working title."

"Why not Handel?" Hector suggested.

"That's it! For the next nine months we are the parents of Handel—but that's just our name, let's not tell anyone else. This is just between us."

"You got it, love," he said, as he leaned over to kiss her at the stoplight.

They waited two more months to tell their fathers. Mischa didn't tell the office until she was further along. The doctor forced her to recognize that she would be physically unable to return to work immediately after the birth. Because of her epilepsy and the sleepless nights in the early months, he made it clear that he would require a longer maternity leave. When she turned in a request to stay home for six months, the human resources officer was surprised and wanted to confirm the time. Three months was the average length of time that a DC woman took for maternity leave.

Mischa left work a few weeks before her due date. She had a simple schedule. She stayed in bed—reading, sleeping, reading, watching movies, sleeping, listening to music, sleeping, looking at fashion magazines, and eating Nutella from a jar. When she was feeling social, she took a taxi to Mayorga Coffee Factory. Outside of Hector's bi-hourly calls, most of her social interactions depended on telephone calls from her father and her friends, and choir practice two nights a week. She could always count on regular calls from Sophie for gossip and old times' sake, and Janet called to share jokes. The cell phone on the night table would ring and Mischa would hear Janet's smoky voice.

"Hello, my dearest, how are you doing?"

"Hey, Janet!"

"I doff my hat to thee, you earth mothers, vessels of human reproduction. Not only could I not endure the very act of procreation, but seeing you all waddle around puts me in state of awe. You'll never guess what happened this morning."

"Don't keep me in suspense."

"A woman's water broke during a meeting. GUSH. It all came out. My God, you should have seen the faces of the men. Oy vey. There were two other women there. Calm and collected, ordered all the nitwits out. Including me. It was pretty comical. It was like some pioneer log cabin, where the women do women things, like get hot water and clean sheets, and the men stay in the barn and freak out. Until that carpet gets replaced we're meeting elsewhere. So, that was my procreative adventure. How about you?"

"Enduring a standard-issue pregnancy, with the exception of an epileptic fit every now and then."

Janet knew that keeping her voice emotionless, without pity, was the most compassionate response. Mischa didn't want pity, no matter how heartfelt. Alone in her office, with the door shut, Janet's emotions translated to her body. Her head fell in her hand and she closed her eyes in empathy, to keep the tears still. Janet kept her voice controlled and steady.

"Have you had one recently?"

"Yes, last week."

"Are they happening more or less often than before your pregnancy?"

"Good question, Janet. I was thinking about that just today. If you look at the trend, then actually, my seizures have decreased during my pregnancy. But, it's hard not to see a seizure as an aberration in the natural order. What can I say? Before, I just had the seizures, but now there's more, so much more, at stake. Anyway, talk to me, tell me something funny. Make me forget."

"Well, the reason I called was to tell you about the United in Support of Disabled with Epilepsy. Didn't you help them write up their strategic policy plan with Sarah, the lawyer we introduced you to?"

"Yeah. I don't think Hector had a weekend alone with me for about five weeks. She came over every Saturday morning and we brainstormed ideas for the campaign to amend the Americans with Disabilities Act. In fact, we finished it up about a week before I left the Council on maternity leave. Anyway, What about it?"

"Well, it looks like they're working through the plan. I saw Sarah yesterday. The *Washington Post* is doing a feature story on the campaign. Apparently, they've already got about a hundred and thirty representatives and about twenty senators supporting language that they would offer to amend the ADA. Also, they started up an alliance of NGOs to write up recommendations for the ADA. They've created this network of NGOs advocating for inclusion of medical conditions such as heart ailments and diabetes. Next month they are hosting a nationwide civil society consultation and several members of Congress have agreed to serve as co-hosts. Hey, Mischa, is it my imagination or does that sound eerily familiar to the Counter-Narcotics Summit for the Americas and their civil society consultations?"

"I thought if it worked in foreign affairs, it might have a chance at domestic policy. Who knows, maybe the whole idea was inspired by divine intervention. Didn't Sophie tell you that I had a seizure at the opening ceremony of the civil society consultations, during the speech by the president of Colombia?"

"Ah, yes, I remember. Is that the time you told that guy who sits across from your office that his dad should be a foot surgeon or something?"

"Nathan? Oh, gosh, I felt bad about that."

"Well, anyway, congratulations, Mischa. We told you USDE wasn't going to be some kind of pity group. You've done something that's going to have a real impact on people's lives. They're on their way to change law. You've come a long way, baby."

"Janet, you made my day."

"Well, let's see where they go. Once that's done, I'm going to get you working on a campaign to repeal 'Don't Ask, Don't Tell.' By the way, how's the pregnancy going?"

"It is not as easy as it was in the first seven months. I'm starting to vomit, there's dizziness, and I'm in the bathroom every fifteen minutes."

"That's what I've heard from my sisters-in-law. I've got two nephews and three nieces, so I've probably heard over forty months' worth of complaints. Also, Sophie just e-mailed me, she wants to drop by tomorrow and bring you some dinner. Do you want a gyro from Zorba's or some chili dogs and fries from Ben's Chili Bowl?"

"How about all of it?"

"You got it, and we can finish it up with your favorite dessert, strawberry buttercream from Cakelove."

"Could you throw in their coconut cake, too? I'm starting to get cravings. Hey, Janet, I'm sorry, but I've got to go to the bathroom again."

"Not a problem. Just do it."

Sooner than they thought came the Arlington Chinese Community Choir's performance of Handel's *Messiah*. As she had grown larger, Mischa had received several unsolicited touches from the women at choir practice. She felt like a fertility rock star; women just wanted to have physical contact with her pregnant belly, no matter how brief. Mischa could never understand the phenomenon of strangers touching pregnant women's bellies, with or without the permission of the bellied one. It happened so often that Mischa concluded it was a strange primal urge among women. A pregnant belly was treated like a talisman and by touching it, women hoped that their wishes for a child or a grandchild would become a reality.

The choir had rented an auditorium in a public high school. The halls were gaily festooned with Christmas trees and gold tinsel garlands. Posters of six-foot elves with basketballs lined the women's locker room where mostly Asian women pulled, zipped, tugged, and yanked themselves into the cheap emerald green taffeta gowns for the performance. The fifty women, from the ages of twenty to seventy, looked like lost bridesmaids at a cheap wedding. One of the matrons came over to her to check if Mischa had put everything on correctly. She looked her up and down approvingly.

"No jewelry, take off."

"It's not jewelry, it's a medic-alert bracelet," replied Mischa.

In that uninhibited manner of Asian matrons, she grabbed Mischa's wrist, examined the bracelet, and then walked away.

When Mischa came out of the dressing room, she found Hector in an emerald tie and vest standing by himself. Looking like lost ushers in their ill-fitting suits, several other men were milling around the water cooler and conducting their vocal exercises. Mischa wondered what the audience members were going to think when the curtains drew back for the performance of the Arlington Chinese Community Choir. There were more than twenty non-Chinese members of the choir: African Americans, Caucasians, and Hispanics. Mischa's father was attending a conference in New York so he couldn't be at the performance, but Sophie would be coming.

Once Mischa had parted the sea of choir members who came forward to touch her belly, she took her seat on the bar stool that she used during choir practice. From the audience it looked like she was standing. The choirmaster approved it easily; he was still down by four from the ideal number of people for a choir of the *Messiah*, and he needed Hector and Mischa. The performance went smoothly. The only notable event was that the choirmaster was visibly distracted by the soprano's décolletage, which seemed to go down to about three inches above her belly button. His back was to the audience, so only the choir saw his stares and occasional mistakes in directing whenever the soprano turned toward him.

After the performance, Sophie came up to Mischa with two paper shopping bags with the familiar shape of a pig printed on them.

"Mischa, that was GREAT! Janet's on a business trip, but I've got a present for you—a blast from the past. I went all the way to Virginia for this. Guess what I have here for missy and the baby!"

"Oh my gosh, Sophie, you didn't! Oh wow. Hallelujah!" Mischa could smell it; she looked inside—it was barbecue! "Sophie, oh my gosh! Ribs, hush puppies, peach iced tea, biscuits, extra sauce, and corn bread pudding! Oh, Sophie, thanks so much!"

"This isn't entirely generous on my part. I was thinking that we would drive to your house, put it in the oven and have a real Southern barbecue!"

In the car, the smell was enticing, but Sophie and Mischa both knew it would be better hot, so they talked about barbecue on the ride home. Sophie reminded Mischa that Pig in a Pit was the place she had recommended to take the Southern priest to when she was working in the Human Rights Advocacy Forum. After that night, Mischa was converted to Southern barbecue and they went there regularly. Father…Father…Mischa couldn't remember his name. It was fifteen years ago. Was it really that long ago?

Sophie went through all of their favorite dishes. "Remember how you loved the pulled-pork sandwiches? I have one of those in the bag. I asked them to pack the bun separately from the meat so it wouldn't turn to mush. Remember the bone-sucking specials they had? We ordered them all the time. Remember there was one month where we went every week and gained about ten pounds? I think we slowed down a little after that. Oh yeah! Remember the 'Better than Sex Spareribs'? I've got a whole rack of them in the bag—you loved them."

Sophie continued tallying the amount of pork and beef they had eaten during those three years. They concluded that they had probably savored the ribs of fifty pigs. Sophie loved the chicken wings, "Volcanic Buffaloes." She calculated that she had probably eaten the wings of two hundred chickens. Hector's vegetarianism betrayed him with uncontrollable cringes as he drove the car. Mischa looked over, but didn't care. *He can eat his tofu and rice—I'm having barbecue tonight.*

When they came in the house, Sophie ran to the kitchen to unpack the bag and Mischa waddled in behind her. While they waited on the meat and corn bread pudding, they picked at the hush puppies and dipped them in the sauce. Sophie brought five little tubs of her favorite, the Tangy Sweet Spice. She also brought along two experimental sauces—Poquito Mojito and Big Mama's Sauce.

Pig in a Pit offered a hundred barbecue sauces to choose from that were kept on shelves along a wall—an homage to the secret ingredient of good barbecue, the sauce. While you waited for your order, you could fill little plastic tubs with the chosen sauce. Sophie and Mischa made a pact to go through all one hundred. They were never sure that they did it, but they always took tubs of their favorite sauces and two sauces they had never tried before. All the bottle labels were legitimate pieces of folk art. The spicier sauces had sadistic, though poetic, names like "This is Gonna Hurt" or "Come to Mama Cuz You Deserve a Whippin'."

They took their seats at the dining room table amid the paper bags, the aluminum foil, the boxes, and the plastic tubs. The tangy vinegar tomato sauce on the pulled pork melted into the hamburger buns and Mischa's mouth. She could taste the hickory smoke tickling the ribs, which were dripping with sauce. Hector looked on with slight disgust as he saw them tearing meat from the bones, licking their fingers gleefully, and barely making conversation beyond "mmm," "wow," and "this is FAN-TAS-TIC."

While it might have looked primitive and chaotic to Hector, there was a method to Mischa's gluttony. When she had too much meat and sauce, she would grab a buttery biscuit or a spoon of corn bread pudding, a bite of crunchy of coleslaw, and a chaser of peach iced tea, and then the cycle would begin again—meat, biscuit, corn bread pudding, slaw, iced tea; meat, biscuit, corn bread pudding. Handel was happy because Mischa felt the baby kicking. As Mischa stood up to get more iced tea, she felt something wet and sat down in a daze. Hector came over to kiss Mischa on top of her head, not her lips, which were dripping with barbecue sauce.

"Mischa, are you okay? Mischa? Mischa?" Hector asked.

"No, Hector, I think my water broke."

Sophie sat in shock, with a corn cob caught in her teeth. Hector ran to the phone and called the Gnome, who told him to take Mischa to the hospital immediately. It was three weeks before her due date. Sophie offered to come with them. Hector declined, and Sophie looked relieved and promised to clean up the mess.

As Mischa started up the stairs, Hector asked, "Mischa, what are you doing?"

"I'm going up to brush my teeth. I stink of barbecue."

"Are you daft? Luv, come down, now. I have some mints in the car. Sophie, throw me some of those lemon wipes that came with that…stuff. I'm going to start the car. I'll pull it around and meet you outside."

"Okay, Hector," said Mischa. It was best to be docile and practical, no need to argue over the inconsequential in the midst of the extraordinary. Mischa had to admit that she was impressed with Hector's powers of observation for having noticed the wipes in that sea of wrinkled foil wrappers, plastic tubs of sauces, and bones. Then again, it was probably the only item he could recognize. *Okay, where's that overnight bag. Where's the car? Where's Hector?*

When they arrived at the first stoplight, they looked at each other, and Hector was smiling as he asked, "Do you think that next time we leave the hospital we're going to be holding our very own little human?"

"Yes." She smiled and motioned for him to drive on, since the light had turned green.

As they passed the city blocks, she thought, *thank God this is a Caesarian. Who are these women who want natural childbirth? Not Mischa. I will arrive at the hospital, I will be given an epidural, the lights will go out, I will wake up, and BINGO! A baby!* She had no desire for a midwife in beads chanting prayers to Mother Earth while she wailed in natural childbirth.

"Inject me now" was the only directive she would give. But the lights never went out. She was fully conscious while the obstetrician and his colleagues discussed a recent football game and their vacation plans. It was tempting to interrupt them with, "Perhaps we could focus on the task at hand?"

But she had seen enough medical TV sit-coms like *M*A*S*H** and had come to respect small talk as a form of profound concentration. She hoped that was true and not merely the reflection of the screenwriters' desire for witty banter. She kept her place on the operating table and let them follow their routine, however strange. Mischa felt nothing below her shoulders as she looked up at Hector, who stood behind her head. His face transformed by the second, showing curiosity, shock, horror, and fear. After a few minutes she decided to stare at the ceiling. She determined that things must be going as planned, since the doctors were still discussing the qualities of a quarterback and his chances of being traded, so she stared at the ceiling until she heard a cry.

"It's a girl!" the Gnome said with glee.

Oh God. Oh my God. Everything I ever did to my mother is going to come back to haunt me.

While Mischa was still on the operating table she turned her neck to see her baby in a clear plastic crib next to the operating table. For minutes, as she saw her crying a few feet away from her, Mischa craned her neck to say, "You are so incredible. You are so incredible." She said it over and over to her baby. When the nurses put her in the wheelchair, Hector picked up the baby, and once Mischa was settled, he passed the baby to her, wrapped in soft white cotton blankets with blue and pink stripes. Mischa was in state of spiritual awe when she saw her baby turn her neck and instinctively find her breast to suck.

While in post-op, Hector and Mischa decided to go ahead with the coin toss. Mischa won, or at least she thought she won. After the sight in the operating room, Hector thought it a small concession to let Mischa name the baby.

The next day Sophie called. "*Chica*, my lovely *chica*, Mischa. How ARE you? Boy or girl?"

"I'm fine. Tired, of course. She's a girl!"

"Who won, Hector or you?"

"Isabel Sofia Durham. The middle name is for you, Sophie."

There was silence on the other end, and then soft but audible crying. "Mischa, Mischa…What can I say? My gosh. It's such an honor. I—"

"Sophie, it's such a small gesture. I cannot tell you how much I love you for everything you are, for everything you have ever done."

Sophie sniffed and wiped her tears away to find her voice amid so much emotion. "I guess this means I'm going to have to remember her birthday."

Mischa laughed, happy that they had both recovered from what was probably the most emotionally raw moment since Quebec City. "Sophie, this also means that you will not be getting away with stuffed animals for presents. She will be expecting an envelope from Auntie Sophie, which I will promptly deposit into her college fund."

"Promise." Sophie said, laughing still.

"*Chica*, I'm exhausted. *Necesito dormir.* Gotta get some rest. Please come tomorrow. But promise me that you'll bring me barbecue. Otherwise, I'll name her after some character from a Russian novel, like Zhivago. Isabel Zhivago Durham. That will be your fault."

"You are really milking this, Mischa. *Abrazos, chica mía.*"

Later that day Mischa had a seizure. Hector was with her and shouted for help. By the time the nurses arrived, the seizure was over, but they gave Mischa an injection of Valium to prevent status epilepticus. Despite all of Hector's pleas that her instructions were that she not be given that injection, he was ignored. The baby was safely asleep in her crib in the midst of the frenzy, and a few minutes later, Hector looked over to her, then to Mischa and back. When Mischa finally awoke, Hector told her what had happened.

Mischa's room was at the end of the hall; the nurses' station was over two hundred yards away. She asked to be put closer to the station, but the nurses ignored her. Then she told the soft-spoken Southern neurologist to place her closer to the station.

"I really don't think I could do that," he replied in a matter-of-fact bureaucratic tone.

Mischa could hear her voice rise to demonic levels as she shouted, "I am not asking. I am not suggesting. I am saying, PUT ME CLOSER to the nurse's station! I said NOW! I want to be moved now!"

Having known Mischa for a little over a year, he had not expected this reaction. Nevertheless, as a neurologist he was prepared for these occasional frantic outbursts by his patients. It was best to remain calm. He supposed he could move her closer to the station.

Mischa could tell from the fearful look that she was going to get another room. He would probably save face with the nurses with an eye roll to show that he was reluctantly conceding to this hysterical woman to avoid any temper tantrums; otherwise, he would not have done it. If Mischa were younger, maybe she might have cared what they thought, maybe she would have been more polite, maybe she would have thought the doctor knew best. But she was now a mother and they were not going to endanger her or her baby.

Once the doctor left to speak to the nurses, Mischa thought of Ella and wondered what had happened to her and her baby, and what they might be doing. *Ella would understand me*, Mischa thought. Mischa never saw Ella again at the Mayorga Coffee Factory, though she later wheeled in there a few times with Isabel in the stroller. She wished they had exchanged numbers, but they had just depended on these random but frequent meetings. They never even gave their last names to each other; they simply had an instant familiarity and intimacy. They didn't go through the formal efforts to have done what she would have done to begin a friendship. Mischa thought that perhaps Ella never really sought to make their friendship more than the occasional meeting and it was not an oversight.

The Gnome was very happy with Isabel. He did a few tests on her and then gave her over to the care of a glamorous Latin pediatrician with a Miss Universe hairstyle of gold blonde hair teased and sprayed, red glossy lips, and two-and-a-half-inch heels. She probably wore three-inch stilettos after work. Mischa and Hector liked her; during their appointments she spoke in that rush of Caribbean Spanish that barely ended a word or a sentence without beginning the new one. The doctor suggested rubbing rum on Isabel's gums when she began teething, but qualified this advice, saying it was a tradition among her people, but not necessarily one they might feel comfortable doing. Mischa was tempted and Hector admitted that his parents had done the same, but he refused that route in the end, so they used Orajel.

Mischa continued to crave barbecue, and Sophie brought it to her every two weeks while she was nursing Isabel. After Mischa ate barbecue, Isabel sucked significantly more vigorously and left Mischa with tender nipples. She thought it must have been the sauce coming through the breast milk. Post-pregnancy, her favorite barbecue sauce from Pig in a Pit was "Poquito Mojito," which was based on that drink of choice among the DC "single-rati" at the time: rum, mint, and lime juice. Mischa found that Isabel always slept a little longer after she had barbecue.

25. THE BEDROOM

March 2004

SHE FELT A TERRIFYING STILLNESS INSIDE HER. She was in a room. She felt the floor beneath her, cool to her cheek. She tried to raise her head, but it was too heavy and fell like a hammer. When her cheek struck the floor, the sudden impact made her more aware. *What's that sound? What's that screaming?* She began to form the barest comprehension of what was happening. The raw sting from the gash inside her mouth made her more alert and she began to feel panic. She had to understand. The source of the sound was a few feet above her. *It's a baby. It's a crying baby.* Then panic exploded inside her. *That's MY baby!* Mischa bit the inside of her mouth to concentrate. She knew that the more pain she felt, the more alert she would become. She tried to lift herself up again and steadied herself on her hands and knees to keep her head in the air. Blood and saliva fell in threads from her mouth as she crawled around the bed. Her knee landed on a pebble and the sudden jab gave her another jolt of pain and consciousness. She pushed the blankets and pillows on the floor toward the bed and then lifted them to encircle the baby lying on the mattress, the baby whose name she could not remember, but she knew was hers.

Mischa could see a cell phone on a night table and crawled over to it. She stared at the phone in her hand. *How do I use this?* She shut her eyes to remember. She bit her cheek and blood oozed from the corner of her mouth. Mischa pressed one number, then the next, and the next.

"Hello?" Hector was unaware of the bedlam on the other end. His fear escalated when he heard a baby crying in the background, but no response from the caller. "Hello? Hello? Mischa? Mischa! Is that you? Mischa?"

"The baby is okay. The baby is fine. I just…I just…just had a seizure. Come home. Come fast."

"I'll be there." He shut the cell phone and ran down the hallway and through the parking lot amid curious stares.

Isabel cried for her mother's arms while Mischa wept at the side of the bed. She reached out to touch her baby, but drew back her hand in fear, and again her head fell to the floor. Lying there she began to hum an Ella Fitzgerald song that had the comforting sway of a lullaby. Mischa lifted herself to kneel at the side of the bed and hummed to her baby. Isabel stopped crying and looked over at her mother and began to giggle. The lyrics slowly returned to Mischa's memory and she began to sing. Tears ran down Mischa's face, but she smiled when Isabel smiled. Mischa heard the door chime, and within seconds Hector had run up the steps. He picked up Isabel from the bed and Mischa crumpled into a ball on the floor.

"Just hold her, Hector. I'm fine."

Hector bent down and kissed Mischa on the top of her head. She was curled on the floor like a snail in its shell. Mischa cried silently behind her veil of black hair, so that Hector and Isabel could not see. Isabel's little head bobbed sweetly and calmly, a baby of four months still trying to keep her head straight. Isabel stared in disbelief at her father who had suddenly appeared, and then her wide green eyes looked quizzically at her mother on the floor. Isabel wondered why there was no music.

That night Isabel fell asleep in Hector's arms after finishing her bottle. Beside him, Mischa lay on their bed, with her back to them. Though she was still, Mischa's mind was racing. She thought of past seizures. She thought about how she had survived all of them. She counted them and stopped at two hundred. She decided that she didn't want to know anymore. *Over two hundred. Over two hundred seizures in my lifetime.* She had moved on. After some it was easy. After others it was hard. She could even forget many of them. But now, after Isabel was born, every single seizure had the emotional impact of twenty. It was taking longer to recover after a seizure, psychologically.

Over two decades, Mischa had built a way of life with her epilepsy. She would not and did not recognize her vulnerability. That was essential. Now, it was different. She could not ignore it. She had to face it and force herself to think of tragic possibilities in order to avoid them. She had to consider each scenario. She was putting Isabel at risk with each seizure, if not physically, then potentially leaving a motherless child if she fell down the stairs or into the path of a moving car.

In the past she had attributed a power of transfiguration to her epilepsy. It built character, her character. *Maybe that was a delusion, but at least it was a form of self-preservation.* Overcoming obstacles and solving problems, epilepsy had made her. She had even developed a strange affection for these seizures—her seizures. But whatever framework she thought she had built seemed more of a facade, an obstruction that she had to tear down. Denial was no longer an option. Epilepsy was now a disability. It was one that physically endangered her own child. The seizures were no longer objects of fascination and challenge, but predators, objects of anger, evil and disgust. *But the seizures are still my seizures. They're still me.*

When they went to bed that night, Mischa stared at the darkness, unable to sleep. She recalled a phrase that had stood out in her sporadic research: "three generations of imbeciles is enough." Her brain kept repeating and repeating that phrase. She could not understand why. Then a stab of memory placed it. It was a quote from a U.S. Supreme Court case. She found it in the binder of collected articles on epilepsy. He had given it to her as a gift. *What was his name? The professor, the classics scholar I dated. Gosh, I can't remember his name.*

Mischa began to pull her thumb away from its nail with the edge of another nail as she tried to remember the details of the case. It was about a woman with epilepsy who had been raped and had given birth to a daughter who was suspected of being "retarded." No sensitivities then, the phrases "developmentally delayed" or "learning disability" were not yet created. The woman's mother also had epilepsy. In the courtroom an expert testified that the child, the third generation, also showed signs of "mental retardation." To confirm its right to sterilize the woman with epilepsy, to prevent her from having another child, the state of Virginia brought this case to the Supreme Court. It was in the late 1920s. Supreme Court Justice Oliver Wendell Holmes wrote the ruling, confirming Virginia's right to sterilize the female epileptic. For fifty years it was common practice to sterilize women with epilepsy. It was unlawful for an epileptic to have a child in the state of Virginia until 1979. *And here we are—Hector, Isabel, and me—in a house only ten miles from Virginia.* Mischa tried to remember the woman's name.

"Carrie," she said softly. The highly respected Justice Holmes justified the law with the argument that "three generations of imbeciles is enough."

Years ago, when Mischa first read that phrase, it burned in her mind for its blatant injustice. Oliver Wendell Holmes was revered for his wise interpretation of the Constitution. She had never heard of this ruling before she picked up that binder. American heroes are rarely depicted with their contradictions. His ardent support of eugenics was deliberately downplayed by history books and not even mentioned in school texts. It was a topic left for obscure conference papers by iconoclast academics. She was astounded and angered when she first read about that case. But now, she thought, it seemed a searing revelation. She understood his arguments. They even seemed reasonable. *Maybe I didn't have a right to have a child.*

Mischa wondered how she could have allowed herself to be left alone. *Left alone with Isabel?* How could she have denied these risks? They were obvious. Was this the same stupidity or pride that led to her failure to report her first seizure to the obstetrician? *How could I have let this happen?*

Hector was also awake in bed. Their backs were to each other, but he could feel that she was still awake. Her breathing wasn't deep and measured. She was tense and too still. They could not talk. Not tonight. They had lived through enough tonight. Mischa had been through hell and back. Hector could barely comprehend the terror. His mind was dizzy with the tragic consequences of innumerable "what ifs." When that landscape of potential disaster was too vast to contemplate he steadied himself with the phrase "it could have been worse." It was a peculiar chant, instinctive to survivors of tragedies. The phrase had the power to calm and anesthetize, so that he could think about their future, free of anger and frantic fear.

Only Isabel seemed unscathed by the night's events. She had giggled and gurgled, but otherwise stayed sweetly quiet for the rest of the evening. She was accommodating and did not demand a new game or a new toy, but calmly allowed Hector to go about his business regardless of whether or not he gave her attention. He wondered if Isabel had sensed their utter emotional exhaustion and their need for some respite. Now Isabel was calmly asleep in her crib.

Hector implicitly respected Mischa's decisions on how to deal with her epilepsy and never questioned her judgment. He caught her when she fell, stayed by her when she woke up, and when she could stand, comforted her, holding her in his arms and putting her head on his shoulder. But now, Hector thought, he couldn't trust her alone. The very person he loved most was a threat to the only other person he loved. He didn't know how to comfort Mischa tonight; she was beaten. Her seizures were so much more a part of their lives now. It hadn't been this way before. Now she cried and screamed at him more often. She had more seizures, and the weight of them, on her and on them, was heavy. He wondered when it would all return to normal. He just wanted things to be back to normal. When would life be normal again?

From that night on, Mischa decided she must be accompanied at all times. She knew that when Isabel turned five months old, she would return to work and Isabel would be safe at day care. At night Hector would always be there with Mischa and Isabel. For the remaining months of maternity leave, Mischa's father agreed to stay with her until Hector returned from work. Her father would have to be near Mischa at all times. Before these visits, Mischa's exchanges with her father over the last ten years had descended to little more than a trade of logistical arrangements: what time she would arrive for dinner, when she would meet him at the airport, her flight numbers to the UK, and updates on his conferences. Now, for the first time in years, Mischa had conversations with her father. Many of these were tutorials in Russian literature, yet she felt the comfort of a father reading his little daughter fairy tales. He began his stories with a summary of the plot. Once he was done, he put the work in its historical context. He moved into a character-by-character analysis. He examined the writing and interpretations behind each scene. It seemed as if he could find the meaning of life in each dacha, carriage, crinkle of silk, snowstorm, and Russian aristocrat. There were moments when she was bored, but she welcomed his company. They had not talked like this for years. He was joyful about the topic and curious about what she thought of their conversations, since they meant so much to him.

"Mischa, why haven't you read any Russian literature? You've had access to my library your whole life."

"I guess it seemed like your field, your territory. I wanted something of my own. I picked up enough about it from random conversations and your dinners with colleagues, but I was never drawn to it. But, Dad, these conversations are making it come alive. I've really enjoyed them, so consider this my delayed appreciation of Russian literature."

Mischa had started to tune him out and fall asleep; the room was hot, and she realized that if her father saw her attention wander his feelings would be hurt. To show him that she was focused and listening, she had to make a thoughtful comment and be quick about it.

"Dad, how many Russian writers have we gone through during these weeks?"

"Well, I think I've discussed the same ones I take up in my introductory class. Bunin, Pasternak, Solzhenitsyn, Chekhov, Gogol, Lermontov, Merezhkovsky, Pushkin, Rand, and Tolstoy."

"So, shall we do Dostoyevsky? He's the only one I could add to the list. Wasn't he the author of some groundbreaking book, *Crime and Punishment*? I had to do a book report on it in high school, but I got away with speed-reading and jumping to conclusions. I wrote the book report the night before. Can you believe I got an A? Now you can tell me the real story."

"Mischa, no! You didn't do that with Dostoyevsky! I have eleven translations of *Crime and Punishment* in my library at home. I taught an entire course on his works. He's my favorite author. I've published papers on him. Oh, really, Mischa, please tell me it isn't true."

"I thought the main character was dull and redundant. I think the plot boiled down to: guy meets old woman, guy kills old woman, guy feels bad about killing old woman. *Punto*. It was too much fiction. I prefer nonfiction."

"But, Mischa, every piece of writing is fiction, even your supposed nonfiction. Ideas are a matter of interpretation. There is no pure objectivity. No one has ownership of the truth. Nonfiction as a genre is a presumption and deceitful, for it fails to acknowledge its subjectivity."

"Fine, Dad, okay, okay. That's what you say. For class today, why not go ahead and make up for my crime. So, who was Dostoyevsky and what did he write?"

"Mischa, did you know he was epileptic?"

"What?"

"Yes, he suffered from seizures most of his life. I've published a few papers on Dostoyevsky's epilepsy and its influence on his writing."

Why am I angry?

"Dad, why didn't you tell me this before?"

"He led a tormented life. He was self-destructive and depressed. The epilepsy was a great burden for him. If you can believe it, his epilepsy was even less severe than yours. But you, Mischa, have led such a fulfilling life. You haven't let it define you. I am so proud of you. Why would I want to expose you to his interpretation of that sickness?"

THAT sickness?

"Dad, it's called epilepsy. It's me. It's not *that*. He had epilepsy. That is a fact. It would have been nice to have known your opinion of how I was dealing with this condition. Your failure to discuss anything about my epilepsy defined you and Mom so completely. I never knew what you thought. I was not going to beg for your help or your opinion. You never offered it. When Mom was alive, all I remember is getting chocolate cakes and *pastel de papas* after every seizure—at least the ones you knew about."

"Your mother always felt guilty that it was her fault. I don't think she ever could deal with it. That's my guess. I always felt guilty that I let the fever get so high when you were three years old and you had that first seizure. She said a rosary every morning for you and she went to six a.m. mass every Friday to pray for you. We felt guilty, but we didn't know what to do. When you look back at it, I guess that explains why she prayed and made comfort food and I wrote and did research. I don't know what to tell you. We never spoke about it, not even between the two of us."

"Dad, all that I sensed was shame and disinterest. I was a scar on her image of what she wanted me to be and less likely to get a husband. She never even tried to talk about it! When she picked me up at the hospital or from school, she didn't say a word to me, not a single word, on the ride home or in waiting rooms—absolute silence all the time. I have had epilepsy for twenty-five years of my life. You do research, you write about it. Your favorite author has epilepsy and you don't tell me? You don't even talk to me about my epilepsy. The only exchange that happens after I have had a seizure is when you ask me, 'Did you take your medication?' And, oh, I forgot, 'You've had a seizure,' whenever I regained consciousness! Why didn't you tell me you wrote these papers? I have epilepsy, that is a fact. So why not talk to me about that fact? Is this that blur between fiction and nonfiction? Why didn't you ever tell me about your papers?"

"I don't know. I don't know. Mischa, please, please know I love you. Your mother loved you. It's just, it's just that, there's no instruction manual for parents when a child...when a child...is born...different or if... if...your child has a disabling illness or a serious medical condition. It's so overwhelming. I know it's even more overwhelming for you, I don't pretend that it's worse for us. It's just that you try to do right by your child, but every situation is unique. Each child is unique. We knew that you were proud, we never pitied you. We knew that pity would have destroyed you. We tried to follow you and what you thought you needed—what you wanted. Whether it was confronting Sister Alice on your own, or going on as before, or changing neurologists at the drop of a hat. We let you lead us. We thought you wanted to be in control. We had no idea what we were doing. I still don't know. I know I admire what you have done. I don't know whether we or whether I helped or not. I just don't know. We didn't know what to do. But we always—your mother always, I always—loved you, and frankly, we admired you, and whatever we did or did not do, we never meant to hurt you. Mischa I don't know. I just don't know." Richard bit his lip and paused in thought.

"There must be a prayer to God for a parent to ask 'Why did you have to do this to my child? Why couldn't you have given ME the illness instead?' If it were possible to transfer your epilepsy to me, I would take it in an instant. There's guilt and so much longing to bear the burden of what your child is suffering through, but it's physically impossible to take it from you. So you wonder, after each seizure, 'Why couldn't God have just let this happen to me, not to you, Mischa. Why couldn't I be the one with epilepsy instead of you?' Your mom felt the same way, so intensely. What could we do?"

Mischa let the discussion lie. It was too much to expect to discuss twenty-five years in the two hours before Hector was expected home. Also, why would she want to upset Isabel, who was blissfully sucking at her breast, with her tiny spiderweb of blue, purple, and pink veins showing through her eyelids and stars sparkling around her head?

WAAAH! Waaaaaaaaah! Waaaaaah! WAAAAAAH!

Isabel was crying. Mischa was on the ground, and she turned her head to see her father. He looked anxious and nervous holding Isabel, sitting on the sofa, trying to comfort the baby.

"What? What? What! No! Not again! No! NO!" Mischa wailed.

Her father tried to soothe her. "Mischa, don't worry, I took her from your arms before you…well, you could have, might have, dropped her. You had a seizure."

Mischa tried to get up, but she fell to her knees, her head was too heavy. Her rage and grief bound her to the floor where she lay sobbing.

⌘　⌘　⌘

That night Hector returned early. Mischa heard the door chimes ring when her father left without a good-bye. The family stayed in their bed.

Hector held Mischa in one arm and Isabel in the other, until the two fell asleep. Tears crept quietly down his cheeks and Mischa felt them drop on her head while she lay still on his chest.

When morning came, Hector gave Mischa a kiss, stroked her hair, and went downstairs to prepare a bottle for Isabel while they waited for Mischa's father.

Mischa heard the door chimes and knew her father had arrived. When Hector came upstairs and put Isabel back in her crib, she had already fallen asleep after her morning bottle. He walked to their bedroom to kiss his wife good-bye.

"Mischa, why not check the answering machine? You've received another three calls from Dr. Bradshaw's nurse this week. She is doing some research project. Who knows? We might learn something new."

"Hector, she probably just wants to convince me to drill a hole into my skull. I'm not returning her calls. I don't want anything to do with Dr. Bradshaw anymore."

"Do whatever you think is right." He gave her another kiss on her forehead, then walked down the stairs, greeted her father, and thanked him quickly. Mischa head the door chimes ring sadly as he closed the door behind him.

26. THE DOOR

A WEEK PASSED, AND FOR THE SAKE OF SANITY, MISCHA TURNED HERSELF NUMB. She knew that her feelings would return, but for now there was comfort in feeling nothing. Mischa would stare and think of nothing. She would sleep and think of nothing. Survival demanded this stage. To consider the repercussions, the risks, the possibilities, the danger, and the damage would have driven her insane with guilt and fear.

During those times, when she washed the dishes, she would turn the water on so hot that it would steam from the faucet. Like her father with his nails, the hot water that scalded her gradually allowed her to feel in control of the pain. At first, it would hurt, but she would continue to keep her hands in the running water until they turned red. The next time she washed the dishes she could take the heat a little longer. Within a few months she could withstand temperatures that were near boiling, and her hands were covered in a callus so that when she accidentally pricked a finger on a needle or a thorn it did not bleed.

Mischa's father would sit across her and give Isabel her bottle, and occasionally Mischa would let herself hold Isabel, but her father was always next to her. Even her baby noticed the difference and was quieter than usual. She slowly tried to return, tried to remove the thoughts that would drive her crazy if she let them stay and run round and round in her brain. They would leave gradually, only when she began to replace that haphazard anguish with problems. Once she recognized small problems her brain thought about solutions. They began with inconsequential questions and challenges, such as trying to open a Hershey's Kiss without ripping the foil. She would drink from plastic cups all the time, in case she had a seizure and her teeth bit down on the glass. She would only cook on the back burners, in case she had a seizure and frying oil or boiling water would fall on her. She would never walk down the stairs alone, in case she had a seizure and tumbled down. She would never take Isabel down the stairs. Her father should be within two feet of her when she held Isabel.

Despite these rules and solutions, she could sometimes accept the fact that she was not in control. But there was one thought that never left Mischa's mind, the fear that Isabel might carry, within her, Mischa's epilepsy. The neurologists always told Mischa that there was only a remote 3 percent chance that the baby would be epileptic. Three percent. For someone inside that 3 percent, life was far different. There was a chance, but in a medical journal article that number was low an inconsequential statistical probability. Three percent was a number continued to churn around her mind. It did not matter whether the chances were low or high, what if Isabel was inside that three percent?

When Mischa began to return to herself, she would nurse Isabel again and hold her longer, though her father never left her alone. Mischa looked at Isabel through her tunnel of long hair, where it was just the two of them. Isabel grabbed at her strands and smiled as she pulled them. Mischa sometimes cried, and Isabel would catch Mischa's tears in her hands and giggle.

The daily phone calls from friends helped her forget on occasion. But when Sophie called, she could not hold back, and in seconds she would tell her friend what was really in her mind. One morning, the cell phone on the night table rang a few seconds after she heard the chimes. That meant that Hector had left and her father had come.

"Hello! How are you? It's Sophie. I'm stuck in traffic and thought I'd check in on you and *la princesa*. Did I wake you up?"

"I had a seizure last week. I was holding Isabel. My father grabbed her from me. He probably saved her life."

"Mischa, what can I say?"

"Don't worry, there really isn't anything to say. You've done enough. You let me say it out loud for the first time. At least I've admitted it. Look, I've got to go. Thanks for calling, Sophie."

"Okay. I'll call you later. But, Mischa, you shouldn't blame yourself. You didn't do anything wrong, it just happened. *Abrazos*."

As she put the phone down her father came up the stairs, and then knocked on the bedroom door.

"How are we today?"

"A little groggy. I don't know if it is the seizure, the medication, or having a three-month-old baby who isn't sleeping through the night."

Her father was silent, sad, and uncomfortable.

"Dad, I'm just going to stay here in bed. Isabel's asleep in her crib in the nursery. It's probably the only time I can get some sleep."

"Sure, Mischa, I'll go down and read the paper. I've brought you something."

"Really, what?"

Whenever her parents had brought her a surprise, no matter how old she was, she returned to the emotional state of an eight-year-old, with her eyes lighting up in hopes of a new toy, a new dress, chocolate, or a trip to Krispy Kreme.

"I was going through your mother's things last night. Here are a few collected odds and ends, like her favorite scarves, her rosary, a bottle of her tea rose perfume, and jewelry. Remember this box, Mischa? This is where she kept her favorite purse. Do you remember it?'

Mischa nodded when she saw the round apricot box with the creamy silk cord that lay languidly on the side of the box. She remembered being in the boutique, standing at her mother's elbow and staring at the reflection of her face in the gleaming display case as she paid for the purse.

"I always kidded her about that purse. I could not believe how much it cost. Where would you like me to put all of this?"

He looked around their room that had books lying on the floor alongside mismatched shoes. There were dirty clothes in the corner, lying next to folded clothes in a hamper.

"Just put it on the bed. I'll find a place for it later." Mischa spoke in a monotone.

He took a breath. "I need to start cleaning out the house. I've delayed that task for far too long. I've been thinking about getting an apartment. Anyway, I didn't want to forget. But here's something else." He put a thick folder stuffed with papers at the foot of the bed and walked over to Mischa to give her a grocery bag. "Here are the papers I published on Dostoyevsky, and this is a copy of *The Idiot*. No translation is perfect, but this is my favorite one. In *The Idiot*, the main character, Prince Myshkin, has epilepsy. I think this novel offers the most comprehensive treatment of the condition in all of Dostoyevsky's writings. Another character is in *The Brothers Karamazov*. Those are the most famous, but there are others in 'The Lodging Woman,' *The Insulted and Injured*, and *The Possessed*. But I thought it would be best to start with *The Idiot*, so I brought this translation for you. It's yours now."

In the midst of the morning's discomfort, here, safely ensconced in the topic of Russian literature, he felt protected from the tension and anger that Mischa radiated. He explained how the book contained descriptions of the Prince's auras and Dostoyevsky's thoughts on epilepsy. When Mischa had the first seizure in the library and told the doctor in the emergency room about her premonition, her father remembered those excerpts where Dostoyevsky described the moments before his seizure.

"When you stayed overnight at the hospital, I couldn't go to sleep. I re-read *The Idiot*. It was this translation, in fact, it might even have been this book. Here, I've marked the pages that have the passages on Prince Myshkin's auras and other points where Dostoyevsky refers to epilepsy."

"Thanks, Dad. Thank you." She leaned over to kiss his cheek and take the book and the manila folder filled with photocopies. She opened it, as if to verify its contents, and then laid it beside her. When her father finally left the room, Mischa opened the book to read one of the marked passages.

> *"He fell to thinking, among other things, about his epilepsy. Just before the fits, the ones that occurred when he was awake, there was a stage, amidst the sadness, the anxiety and darkness of soul, when his brain would suddenly catch fire. It was as if his life-force were condensed into one extraordinary feeling, an impulse. His sense of life and self-awareness, which flashed like lightening, was magnified. His mind and heart blazed with an extraordinary light. His agitation, all his doubts and worries, were placated at once. There was tranquility. It was a moment filled with serenity and harmony; joy and hope; with reason and purpose. However, he had no more than a glimpse of that infinity and it lasted only a moment. That moment occurred before that ultimate second, when the fit itself began. That ultimate second was, of course, unbearable."*

Mischa had never felt the romantic intensity of that ecstasy. It seemed exaggerated; then again, it was his epilepsy, and perhaps his seizures did put him in a state of rapture. The confused and compressed sense of time was familiar. His fascination with light during a seizure and the realization that these seizures were a glimpse of a beyond were also recognizable. In the last line she read, "*It was dullness, darkness of soul, and idiocy that stood before me as the clear consequence of these 'highest' moments.*"

Those words stabbed with recognition. That despair and fear of permanent brain damage, the loss of awareness, memory, and the seizures' devastation of brain's ability to perform its most basic functions. The side effects of the medication, the physical falls during the seizures, the terrifying momentum of worsening seizures, the destruction of synapses and gray cells from each seizure, or the brain damage from oxygen lost to the brain when the seizure goes for a few more seconds more than the brain can handle without oxygen. All of this could result in the loss of the most important organ to any human being, the organ that made a being feel human. It was a possibility, for an epileptic, that lay just around the corner, always.

She looked through the book at the other marked pages, and then on the back, inside the cover, she found a column of her father's handwriting. His slim cursive was not as smooth as she remembered. Uncharacteristically, there were no edits or strikes, but the jagged lines told how his hand must have trembled when he wrote those words. She thought at first that it was a draft outline for an academic journal article. Mischa read the words slowly and closely.

> *We were speaking at the door on unimportant topics.*
> *She turned her eyes and they stayed still.*
> *I did not understand when she stuttered.*
> *She halted and I saw the smear;*
>
> > *blood on the door, a few days later.*
>
> *We hoped that night of dread, of lifelessness had passed.*
> *We dealt with fear.*
> *We wished its end.*
> *We cleaned the door, but it was there;*
>
> > *blood on the door, a few days later.*
>
> *She stood and her eyes stayed still.*
>
> > *She looked to her umbrella.*

She took drops of rain with her thumb.
She wiped the blood but it stayed.
She took her thumb to her tongue.
She wiped the blood and it was gone.
Her heart, a wound ripped;
Her face, a wail etched;
Her eyes, a glass about to break;
Then I saw her kiss the spot, where it had been;

the blood on the door.

Mischa remembered the seizure at the door. It was few days before she left for college. She had been walking to the front door after some last-minute shopping for her dorm room. Her mother had just shut the trunk. That was the last sound Mischa remembered. Later, when Mischa asked what had happened to her lip, her mother explained how she tried to catch her, but did not arrive in time. She told Mischa that her head hit the doorknob and knocked her teeth against her lips. That was the seizure that left the little curl in her lip that had hovered over her crooked tooth ever since. Staring at the poem Mischa began to sob. She could not understand why, now, more than fifteen years later, she was crawling between the sheets to cry under the covers.

When she awoke, still exhausted, a few hours later, she saw *The Idiot* facedown on the bed and closed. Mischa picked it up to find a place to put it in the room. At the foot of the bed was the apricot-colored box that once held her mother's prized purse. When she removed the top, a wave of her mother's tea rose perfume surged toward her. She inhaled and a hundred memories seared her mind. She placed the book inside and pushed the box under the bed.

Later that afternoon, she prepared grilled cheese sandwiches while her father tickled Isabel and giggled with her as she lay on pillows on a quilt. The kitchen phone rang.

"Hello, Ms. Dunn?"

"Yes?"

"My name is Victoria Achebe. I'm working on a research project at James Hotchkins University for Dr. Bradshaw."

"Oh, yes. You've left some messages."

"We're calling all his female patients to see whether they would qualify and be interested in being part of a study of women with epilepsy."

"I'm a former patient. I'm not currently being treated by Dr. Bradshaw."

"Yes, I have that on record, but we're trying to get as many people to participate in the study as possible, so I thought I would also contact his former patients."

"I'm guessing that it's quite a long list."

"Yes…ahem…let me first ask you three questions to see whether you would qualify for our study. When did your seizures begin?"

"When I was fourteen."

"Are your periods regular?"

"Well, now they are, but they've gone back and forth. They've been regular and irregular throughout my life. I have trends."

"How many seizures do you have a year?"

"Gosh, that's hard. I usually count them according to places where I've been, stages in my life, like college or my time in Guatemala. Let me see. If I had to say by year, maybe…let me see…roughly…between fifteen to eighteen a year. The absolutely lowest was four during my pregnancy, but then again, that's only nine months. It has varied over the years—it was as low as ten, then it came up to more than eighteen at their height. But since I've had my baby, I think it might have been eight or so. I've had two seizures in a day a few times, including the day I was first diagnosed, and then once when I was on a business trip. That's also increased. The rate of my seizures has increased dramatically since I gave birth. It's only been five months, and if it continues at this rate it will be another high."

"You would qualify to be in our study."

"Why?"

"The number of seizures that you have a year is in the range of the number of a woman's annual menses and you have temporal lobe epilepsy."

"Wait just a second. Wait." Mischa left the kitchen to sit at the dining room table and absorb the information. Instantaneously, she realized that this was the most important medical conversation she had ever had about her epilepsy. "Are you saying that there is a connection between my menstrual cycle and my seizures?"

"Potentially. There is a condition called Catamenial Epilepsy among women. The seizures are provoked by hormonal levels in a woman's body.

Dr. Bradshaw is participating in a study with several other universities to look at this connection more closely and develop a potential new treatment. That's what we would be testing in this study. It's a trial."

Her father yelled from the living room, asking if something was burning.

"Just a second, Ms. Achebe." Covering the phone and raising her voice, she replied, "It's the sandwiches, Dad! I'm turning off the grill." Then Mischa returned to the phone call. "Excuse me, Ms. Achebe? Sorry about that. My God, oh my God! I cannot believe this. Can I be part of the therapy? When do you start?"

"Well, Ms. Dunn, if you could come in next week, I would like to explain the study in more depth and draw some blood. Over the course of six months, we would like you to log your seizures and your menses."

"Will I receive hormone therapy?"

"Not necessarily. This is a double-blind study. After six months of charting you, we will provide a drug, but I could not determine whether you would be in the control group taking the placebo, or the one taking the experimental drug. The nature of a blind study is that the test subjects— and even the monitors, including myself—do not know who is taking the drug, to ensure objectivity. But look at it this way, regardless of what category you may be in, we are collecting information that is useful for hormone therapy. We will be comparing hormone levels with seizure frequency. This would be useful background for any neurologist who would be willing to explore this treatment option with you, if you do have this condition."

"If I come in next week, can I see Dr. Bradshaw?"

"Certainly, I'll make an appointment. Let me call you back with a time and we can meet before your appointment with him."

Mischa started to make a new set of three grilled cheese sandwiches. She took the spatula to scrape the blackened butter off the pan. She would not be able to speak for another hour as her mind thought back through twenty-five years.

When Hector returned, he began cooking dinner while her father played with Isabel. She still could not speak about her conversation with the nurse. It was too much to understand all at once. Too many thoughts of causes and consequences crowded her mind at the same time. She told Hector after dinner and he was speechless. How could this man have suggested brain surgery for Mischa when this alternative therapy was available?

Mischa sat Googling for any information about catamenial epilepsy. There was too much adrenalin running through her body and she could not sleep.

> *Catamenial is a derivation of the Greek katamenia and means monthly. It is synonymous with seizures associated with the menstrual cycle... Ancient writings have associated epileptic attacks to the phases of the moon, from where the word "lunacy" is derived, and epilepsy was viewed as an indicator... A woman's menstrual cycle is the result of a complex interaction of hypothalamic, pituitary, and ovarian hormones...the prevalence of Catamenial Epilepsy varies from 10% to 72%... Epileptic women are not often diagnosed with the condition but treated with anti-convulsants... Catamenial Epilepsy appears to be related to a relative lack of progesterone during the luteal phase...not the amount of progesterone, but rather the ratio of progesterone to estrogen that results in the seizures... Researchers are using a variety of hormonal treatments in conjunction with anti-convulsants to control more adequately seizures that result from the condition of Catamenial Epilepsy... Some women are currently being treated with progesterone lozenges... Others who have been diagnosed have been treated with specific oral contraceptives...vital not to self medicate...still determining forms of treatment...experimental...trials under way.*

Mischa had never blogged, but now she searched them out. She didn't find the whining she expected, but practical exchanges among epileptics and the caretakers of them.

> *He won't prescribe it, but she heard from a friend about an unusual birth control; not the pill type or an IUV. It's common in Europe, but they rarely give it out here. You need a medical procedure... My daughter is 16 and can have anywhere between five to six seizures a day or two before her period begins. I have given her a progesterone patch. I use one for my menopause. My daughter doesn't have seizures anymore...gone for years without any kind of diagnosis, he never made the link. I never made the link until my menses became regular...must measure the basal body temperature to begin*

observation…if you ask me the prejudice against women has made this condition relatively unknown. We have it and we take pills, but in the 20th century and earlier women were institutionalized and sent to asylums… I don't think there is enough progesterone in cream to work. What books would you recommend?…This has ruined her life; I don't have a job, I don't…I would love to hear from other women about what you are doing…why don't neurologists look into this condition more closely…this is the breast cancer of the neurological conditions—women died of breast cancer and no one noticed until it became a movement. Catamenial Epilepsy is being ignored just like breast cancer. It's not as widespread so we don't have the strength of a movement…neurologists prefer to crack open brains… There should be a protocol of questions that they ask any woman who has epilepsy about seizure frequency and when it began…hormonal treatments are conducted by some neurologists, they are not all bad…I've been seizure free for 8 months now…I think it has something to do with my menopause…

Over the next few days, Mischa would overhear her father playing and laughing with Isabel in the other room as she hunched over the computer and focused on the monitor to read more information about catamenial epilepsy. She wanted to hit herself for being so blind to her own body, but she knew she wasn't regular. She couldn't have timed herself. The seizures she remembered were every time of the month.

Why, why, why would doctors have not even mentioned the possibility? Every neurologist had at least read the fact that her seizures had started at fourteen, and obviously she was a woman. Wasn't that enough for them? Over the course of twenty-five years, why not consider, even suggest, the possibility of catamenial epilepsy? Why had this word never made an appearance in even one of the appointments? She knew she would have asked for clarification if it had been mentioned, even casually. She always stopped someone when he or she said a word she did not understand. That was a lifetime habit.

She wondered if she should hate herself for the delay in realizing that she had this form of epilepsy, and therefore the chance at some alternative form of treatment without so many side effects. She had developed the epilepsy before the Internet; she had done her primitive research through encyclopedias. But once told it was a lifetime condition, she had simply assumed she would live with it and had stopped reading. To search for a cure for what she was told was incurable would have been a waste of time. What was most important, she thought, was building a life despite the disability. That's what she had done.

In those few days, Mischa expressed a random spectrum of emotions: excitement, confusion, rage, and calm. Hector remained alert to these shifts; he joined her in the happiness of a potential new treatment, and let her be alone when she wanted to think those angry thoughts. When he saw that dark cloud descend, he would take Isabel somewhere to play and Mischa would sit on her bed and meditate, trying to make her anger fade. *All those doctors, all those years, all those pills.* The phrase repeated in her mind like a stanza at the end of every new stream of thought.

Mischa knew that her rage had its rightful place and that this was a time to feel it. She could see that it was not yet destructive; it had not yet eaten at her. That point was near, and she knew that if she did not let go, the bitterness and the consideration of the exponential "what ifs" would overwhelm her.

Hector took Thursday off and drove her to Baltimore, where they arrived in time for lunch in Little Italy. They passed the university bookshop by accident, and decided to go in and see if her neurologist had published a book. There were hundreds of copies of a heavy, thick book that would have taken inches on any medical student's shelf. She wanted to see if he had anything on the link between menstrual cycle and epilepsy. Mischa was incredulous when she looked at the table of contents and found an entire chapter devoted to catamenial epilepsy. She paid the $140 for the book, still lost in thought. Hector let her alone, carrying Isabel, who smiled with her eyes and her mouth, so excited by the fresh air and the new surroundings.

When they arrived at the Research and Development Department, Mischa went to the receptionist to ask for the nurse, Ms. Achebe, and she came out quickly.

"Ms. Dunn, it's nice to meet you. Thank you so much for agreeing to participate in the study."

"Thank you for being so persistent. I never returned your calls because I thought it was one of Dr. Bradshaw's attempts to persuade me to choose brain surgery. I cannot tell you what your call meant to me. You explained in five minutes what every neurologist has failed to suggest to me in twenty-five years."

"I'm so glad I was able to help, Ms. Dunn. I really hope this leads to better seizure control. Let me tell you about the study. I know you have an appointment with Dr. Bradshaw in thirty minutes. I'll walk you over to that part of the hospital."

The nurse explained the study in detail and gave Mischa a binder of background information and charts for her to use over the next eight months. After Mischa signed papers agreeing to participate, the nurse drew Mischa's blood and then took them to the main hospital building and the Neurology Department's waiting room.

When Mischa's name was called, she stood up quietly. Hector started to stand, but she wanted to do this alone. Isabel was quiet and curious, bobbing her head and laughing. Hector gave Mischa a kiss and she followed the nurse to an examination room to await the doctor.

After fifteen minutes, Dr. Bradshaw swept in. When he looked over to the table, his face showed his surprise. Mischa thought, *He didn't even look at the medical records for the next patient before he came in. It was just a folder from his in-box. Had he read the name, he would have expected me. He wouldn't have that startled look on his face.*

A faint memory came to Dr. Bradshaw. It warned him that the last visit with this person, whoever she was, had not been a pleasant one. He came forward to shake her hand, still searching to remember the circumstances of when they met. He looked nervous, but focused.

While the doctor was flipping through papers in the record and looking down at the folder, Mischa felt like a hit man as she took the book out of the plastic bag. After years of being tamed and numbed by hopeless prescriptions, the accidental discovery of the possible cause of her seizures, even if only a potential, but nevertheless an alternative route, gave her a savage confidence. She wanted him to feel her sound and taste her fury.

"Dr. Bradshaw, you wrote a book like THIS and yet you recommended BRAIN SURGERY?" She held the book to her chest, with her two hands gripping its sides. "You didn't log my seizures, you didn't even consider catamenial epilepsy, you didn't explore options, you only gave me drugs and suggested a lobotomy!"

She slammed the book on the examination table and stood up. "I came here for three years. THREE YEARS! You wrote a book specializing on women with epilepsy FOUR years ago. YOU KNOW about catamenial epilepsy but you never—NEVER—suggested that as a reason for my seizures. Now you get some goddamn research grant and need some goddamn guinea pigs and THAT'S how I find out?"

Dr. Bradshaw's anger mounted. He took a deep breath and thought that this was just one of those hysterical patients. It was best to remain calm. He closed the door so that the nurses would not hear, and put the clipboard on the metal counter in the event that he would need to deal with her, should this verbal attack turn physical.

"You wrote a chapter on hormonal treatments, and you NEVER took into consideration that it might be hormones causing MY seizures? You never considered hormonal therapy or offered it as an option? You just prescribed and prescribed and prescribed these damn anti-convulsants that GRIND my brain and STEAL my memory? I traveled for two hours to Baltimore, and YOU gave me ten minutes in your office. ALL you did was increase my dosage and switch me to another medication—pills with names that you have on your Post-its, your calendars, and your GODDAMN pens! I only found out for the first time that this might be the diagnosis for my epilepsy because one of your researchers called me."

Dr. Bradshaw calmed himself with the thought that every so often there was a desperate patient; you came across them in neurology. It wasn't like the psychiatric ward, but there were outbursts. You had to be prepared for these types. There was more rage among these patients, unfettered reactions. They just had to get it out of their system. Today it was him; she would probably be yelling at her husband tomorrow and her work colleagues the next day. It was normal. Again, maybe it was a side effect of her present medication. But she was no longer his patient. There was no use in interrupting or justifying; it was best to stay calm while she ranted. To sympathize would only stoke the fire; he had to remain cool, emotionless.

"THREE questions. It was only three questions. THREE questions! That was all you had to ask. When did my seizures begin? How many seizures do I have annually? What type of seizures do I have? My seizures began in puberty. On average, I've had around fifteen to twenty seizures a year throughout my lifetime. That's within the range for someone with catamenial epilepsy. I am a woman and I have temporal lobe epilepsy. That's the most likely profile for a person with catamenial epilepsy. These facts are all in my records, and they were right in front of you for about ten minutes every three months for the three years that I was your patient. How could you have overlooked a diagnosis of catamenial epilepsy? You didn't even look at my records before I came into your office, that's why. Your failure to give my case any thoughtful consideration was utterly irresponsible."

Mischa looked at her watch, took a breath, and said in a calm voice, "I would call you a jackass and a fool if I could, but that would be rude." She took a deeper breath. Now was the time to compose herself. "I hope I didn't take up too much of your time." She put the book back in the bag and shook his hand on the way out.

Doctor Bradshaw closed the door and bit his upper lip. Perhaps, he thought, he should have considered a diagnosis of bipolar disorder with this woman. The outburst was probably a side effect of her new medication. He wondered which medication it might be, but that was just professional curiosity.

In any event, he reminded himself, she was no longer his patient. He thought it was a good thing that they were still able to get her to participate in the study, since the department could use the research funds. He tried to remember the requisite number of subjects needed to test the new drug treatment. He would have to check with Ms. Achebe, who was coordinating the study for the university. If he remembered correctly, they needed only five more subjects to qualify for the grant.

A nurse knocked on the door and poked her head in to tell him that his next patient was going to be late, but there were others in the waiting room he could see beforehand.

"I'll be out in few minutes. Whoever it is, just put the records on the chair in my office."

Once Isabel was asleep that night and her father had left, Mischa told Hector about her Internet research. "Hector, I want to visit this doctor in Atlanta, Georgia. I called her office and they have an opening on Monday, someone canceled. I found a flight. We can stay overnight and leave after the appointment. I know this is strange, but I've got to take every option. It's the first time I have ever had hope. I need to do something."

They were in Atlanta, but could have been in Baltimore, Bethesda, Providence, or Washington, since the waiting rooms in neurology departments were all the same: people with obviously tragic cases—severe learning disabilities and neurodegenerative diseases—sitting next to people who didn't appear to have anything wrong with them. The ones in the second group always looked around the room curiously. They wondered if they really belonged in this crowd, with the other people there. They wondered why they were in the same waiting room. They wondered if they were going to be like the others one day. They wondered if the world saw them in the same way they saw those people.

"Dunn. Mischa Dunn?"

Hector gave her a kiss for good luck and she kissed Isabel's cheek. She was taken to a room where the nurse took her weight and blood pressure. The doctor breezed in, smiling. She looked like the picture on the university Web site; tall, thin, with short red hair in a Princess Diana-style haircut.

"So, Mischa, tell me about yourself. Why are you here?"

"I am part of a study being conducted by a coalition of universities, perhaps Emersen is taking part in it. Anyway, I am a case of delayed serendipity. It seems that there could be a relationship between my period and my seizures, at least a strong enough possibility to have qualified me to be part of this study. I discovered that you are a specialist in hormonal treatment. Once I'm done with the study, I would like to start working with you and wean myself off these anti-convulsants. The side effects have been debilitating—everything from fatigue and memory loss to a lack of alertness. And I wonder if I have mood shifts."

"Now, you are forty-five with three children, expecting your fourth, is that right?"

"No, I'm thirty-six with one child." Mischa looked down to her belly to see if she really had gained that much weight. She had forgotten to mention that weight gain might be another side effect.

"Oh, right. Sorry, I'm confusing you with the woman I saw last month. She has long black hair as well and also brought her baby and husband. Right. Let's see."

"I brought my medical records, but actually I sent a copy electronically to your assistant a week ago. The secretary said she had put them on file so you could review them before we met."

"Yes, um, I see. Well, here they are. Well, let me see. Now, these seizures began after the baby, is it?"

"No, my epilepsy was diagnosed when I was fourteen. I have temporal lobe epilepsy with complex partial seizures that generalize rapidly. They have increased in frequency since Isabel, my daughter, was born."

"What type of seizures? What is the frequency?"

"Well, I'm having tonic-clonic seizures, sometimes twice a day, and I'm having them more often, a few in a month. Before, it might have been eight or ten in a year. It's now about fourteen and this year is only half through. Why is it, if it is linked to my menstrual cycle, that I would have had only eight or ten before? Why am I now having two or three a day?"

"If it is catamenial epilepsy, you would need to log your seizures and your menses for a while to draw that link conclusively. The seizures are linked to your hormone levels. You do not ovulate every month. Your hormonal levels will not always reach the point that might provoke a seizure. Maybe your hormone levels before you had a baby were more inconsistent. The frequency and consistency of your seizures is a sign that your hormones have changed since you gave birth, which is affecting your seizure threshold. From the evidence you give, it is lowering it, making it easier for you to have seizures.

"Currently among female epileptics, the figure is that anywhere from thirty percent to forty percent are aware that their epilepsy is catamenial. Because the effect of hormones on the brain is new—I should say, relatively new—it's not a condition that is commonly considered. Also, birth control, irregular menstrual cycles, sex life, breast-feeding, and pregnancy all have an effect on a woman's menstrual cycle, and hence the pattern is difficult to recognize. On top of this, I'm guessing that your medication has changed at different points in your development. That would also distort the pattern of seizures and make the link difficult to recognize. Finally, as if it isn't more difficult already, the time that a woman who is diagnosed with catamenial epilepsy is susceptible to seizures can be a few days before or after the period, even up to ten days either way. Again, another reason why this might go unnoticed for years."

Mischa felt somewhat relieved that she had not been completely clueless; there had been reasons why she never saw the link. Even so, she wanted to bang her head against a door. She thought, *Still, I should have done more research.*

"Anyway, before we make a definitive conclusion, you will have to do some careful observation of your menses and discharges and your seizure activity. Correlate it to symptoms such as headaches, bloating, breast tenderness, and irritability. You will be keeping a special calendar. The logging will require some tests as well, such as ovulation. We'll review the medication you're taking and try to make sure we have a sense of how much control it is exercising over your seizures. I would not advise you to change your medication before you have logged your seizures for a few months under the present medication. Do you take birth control, Mischa?"

"No. If I did, would I have had fewer seizures?" Mischa held her breath, hoping that the answer would not be yes. This would be another reason to bang her head against the door. She didn't want to take the Pill; just another thing to pop in her mouth, as she had done throughout her life. She hated pills, and THE Pill fell into that group, so she had ignored it. The doctor didn't hesitate, which Mischa saw as a good sign.

"No, not necessarily. It might have made your seizures worse, in fact. In some cases birth control has decreased seizures. It depends on the birth control, and the level and ratio of progesterone and estrogen in your body. This is not official treatment for catamenial epilepsy. It has been done informally, experimentally. Maybe if you were on birth control the link would have been more obvious. It's really hard to tell. Again, it's that thirty percent to forty percent phenomenon. Catamenial epilepsy is not commonly diagnosed. There are so many intervening factors. The preferred treatment still remains anti-convulsants and brain surgery. Anyway, back to the issue at hand."

"Which birth control would you recommend?" Mischa was anxious, excited, and on the edge of her seat.

"I would not suggest birth control as treatment. I think you would have to remain on anti-convulsants for a while and then go through a series of options for hormonal treatments. But this would require some close observation and frequent appointments. But of course, you have to finish the study first, which will take about eight months, if I remember correctly. Another colleague of mine is in charge of our participation in the study." The doctor wanted to move the appointment along, but could tell that Mischa was one of those conversational patients.

"I have been hitting myself over the head for not noticing the link. I've never even bought a copy of *Our Bodies, Ourselves*. I've even thrown some blame on my time in a Catholic girls' school."

"Well, you're part of a large group of women. Not even *Our Bodies, Ourselves* has devoted much attention to catamenial epilepsy, so you're not alone. I think I saw a weak allusion—two sentences—in the last version I checked."

"How is it that I have temporal lobe epilepsy and catamenial epilepsy?"

"Temporal lobe epilepsy describes the physical origin of your seizures and helps to describe aspects of them. Catamenial epilepsy is the term to describe the reason, the larger framework for the cause of these seizures. Some people have epilepsy due to a brain tumor or another lesion. If it is determined that you have catamenial epilepsy, then the way to describe your condition is that you have catamenial epilepsy with seizures originating in the temporal lobe."

The doctor stood up. "Well, Mischa, while I'm flattered that you came all the way down from Seattle, I would suggest that perhaps you should be treated there."

"I came from Washington, DC."

"Oh, yes. Let's see. Well, you're lucky. There is a neurologist who specializes in hormonal therapy in Arlington, Virginia. In fact, I saw him speaking at a medical conference last week. His name is Jaromir Pavlov. Leave me your e-mail and I'll get a nurse to send you his contact information. You might want to save yourself the money on plane tickets. Well, I think that's about it. Do you have any questions? Thanks for coming, and have a good trip back."

It was a twenty-minute visit to a neurologist. She had taken a three-hour plane trip with her husband and daughter to get to it, but this one was worth it. The doctor had confused her with another patient and had not looked at her records, but Mischa could not bear her typical grudge against doctors because she was finally given the information she sought.

On the flight home, Mischa could not help thinking that perhaps her flippant denial might have been to blame and made her unaware. All she wanted to do throughout her life was to forget her seizures. But if one of her neurologists—how many had there been? There were more than twelve; she could not count them all. If just one of them had even mentioned the term or explored the possibility, she would have jumped at the chance to try this. After trying one drug after another, they always ended with brain surgery and she stopped trusting them.

Maybe, she wondered, if she had been a little more aware of her disability; if she had just admitted to it herself and studied herself more closely, maybe she would have noticed sooner. But then, what kind of life would she have led if she focused on her seizures all the time? So much of dealing with and living with epilepsy was trying to forget that it was there. It was her approach and it had worked for her.

Ironically, it was a blind study sponsored by a pharmaceutical company that brought her closer to the information—the pharmaceutical industrial complex that she despised. After a few months, she would either be given a placebo or the new drug. So, as much as she blamed the pharmaceutical complex, it was business interests that brought her closest to a diagnosis, not a neurologist. *The irony of it all*, she observed. Irony was such a great way to distance yourself from disappointment and to explain life. It made life look like an art form and made it easier to see the humor of living. Perhaps it was Hector's influence on her way of thinking. For all his Latin genes, he still had a British outlook.

They arrived back in Washington, DC, late that night. Isabel seemed made for traveling, but perhaps she sensed the tension and chose not to make a fuss. Tranquil and happy, she frequently smiled and gurgled loudly when they made funny faces and tickled her. Mischa had left her e-mail address with a nurse in the Emersen University Neurology Department, but didn't wait for the e-mail that never came. She Googled Dr. Jaromir Pavlov's contact information and called his office on Wednesday to set up an appointment for next week as a new patient.

Mischa's outlook began to change; she felt more positive, but was tentative. She had to brace herself that perhaps she wouldn't gain complete seizure control. It wasn't a promise—just a more effective treatment, one that would be tailored to the cause of her seizures. She did not fantasize about a seizure-free life or a return of her memory. The lost would still be lost. But while she celebrated the potential for better management of the seizures, one thought had never left her since she gave birth: the thought that she might have left Isabel with a cruel inheritance. It was at the back of her mind, a thought that would interrupt a common everyday task and make her pause. She would mentally push it away to make room for the positive, and consoled herself with a solution that, if it ever happened to Isabel, at least she would not have to wait twenty-five years. Mischa would do the research, and if Isabel wanted to forget after each seizure she could, but Mischa would find the neurologists and question them. Isabel would know that Mischa would catch her if she fell, but she still hoped that Isabel would never have to see that word, the word that Mischa saw in the emergency room the day she began her life with her seizures.

27. THE DINING ROOM

July 2021

November 1, 2007

Dear Ella,

I asked your father to give you this letter before you left for college. I don't know where you are as you read this, but I know where I am. If I can count my blessings, one of them was having the time to consider what to leave you before I passed away.

For the last year, your father and I knew that the cancer was getting worse. The tests confirmed it and I lived through a movie cliché, the scene where a doctor tells a patient, "You only have a few weeks left." I should have screamed "Cut!" but my sense of humor failed me. It has been eighty-two hours since the doctor left me with that prognosis.

Perhaps I had an unconscious sense of a deadline because I began this project long before that conversation. Originally, I thought to write a collection of life lessons I would have taught you. But when I read over that letter it sounded so pedantic, self-righteous, and saccharine. True, I was pedantic and self-righteous, as your father can . attest, but I was never saccharine, so I ripped it up.

Again, I was left with the question of what to leave you and the answer came by accident.

One day I became manic. I grabbed bits of paper and scribbled paragraphs and phrases as soon as they occurred to me. I found myself possessed, literally. Those scraps of paper became the stories that I collected inside this box. It's the same one my father used to pass my mother's keepsakes to me, years after her death. When you open it, I wonder if it will still smell of tea rose. That was how it smelled when he gave me this box. The bottle of my mother's perfume had leaked. I'm leaving the rest with you and this time the bottle is tightly sealed. Underneath the perfume you'll find a few other items and then the stories.

The stories began as a mental exercise. Originally, I thought my writing was meant to amuse me, dispel my anger, and occupy my time during the treatment. But when I read over these collected scraps of paper, it became clear that these stories were meant to be my gift to you.

The stories are about places where I've had seizures. I marked important events and changes in my life with certain seizures. They were unusual and unwanted milestones, but they were there.

Admittedly, this collection of stories is an egotistical gift, but one day you may want to know me. If so, these stories will provide you with a version of who I think I was. Epilepsy helped shaped me, though I constantly resisted that reality. But even with the impact of my epilepsy and the undeniable reality of this cancer, I still believe that my decisions made me, not my circumstances. These stories will show you the more important decisions in my life, good and bad. You can be the judge of which was which.

Had I survived, perhaps over the course of our lives together I would have shared these stories with you on a walk or in a coffee shop. That's a sickeningly saccharine thought, but I'm going to allow myself one. In fact story number 23, "The Taxi" includes an imaginary conversation with you. I should warn you that remnants of my pedantic letter echo throughout, but I think the story is palatable.

By the time you read this letter you will be well on your way to becoming the wise, strong, and compassionate individual that I hoped you would be. Your father will undoubtedly raise you to be so, but he will not be the only one responsible. You were born with character. I knew you would develop into someone I would admire when I awoke after a seizure to find you calmly stroking my hair. You were only three years old. Your intelligence, confidence and compassion were so apparent, so early on.

One of my favorite stories was about your nickname. One day you announced that you were no longer Isabel: "My name is Ella, just like the lady who sings." You wanted a shorter name, like the other kids, and you must have heard that name whenever I asked your father to play some music. I've included a few Ella Fitzgerald CDs in this box. My favorite album was Ella Fitzgerald Sings the Cole Porter Songbook. But there's also a CD of her from a live concert where she sings "Mack the Knife." It was the only song that calmed you as a baby. It became our eccentric lullaby. Perhaps your father will explain the wooden box filled with geometric shapes. If he prefers not to, then respect his privacy. Just know that it was a gift from him and it meant a lot to me.

When I pass away you will be nearly four years old. I can barely write that sentence, the realization is so painful. Right now, my greatest fear is the sense of abandonment that you may feel throughout your life. I hope that you remember and understand that an illness, so far beyond my control, took me away. Nothing else could have made me leave you. Please know that I am there. I am still with you. I have loved you and do love you. Perhaps, through these stories, I can find a place in your life.

Yours,

Mischa

Acknowledgments

MOM AND DAD, NO ONE COULD HAVE TOLD YOU WHAT TO DO, AND YET YOU GAVE ME FREEDOM AND INDEPENDENCE WHEN I DEMANDED IT AND TOOK ME BACK WITH GRACE AND WITHOUT QUESTION WHEN I NEEDED YOU. It wasn't easy for you. I am grateful that throughout my life you trusted my judgment, stood by me, and made me the cockeyed optimist that I am.

Kathleen, thank you for coming down from New York when I was in GWU. Margot, thank you for seeking out advice on my behalf. Tom, you were my first editor, and saw the manuscript when I had no idea where I was going, but you encouraged me with messages from your laptop on a sunny porch, somewhere in Brazil; thank you. Tanya, when I was in a haze from writing until three in the morning you let the children play at your house, though you had been writing your dissertation until four in the morning. I am grateful for your friendship and the luck that brought us together as neighbors; thank you. Margarita, you were there after several seizures, you tutored me and entrusted me with career opportunities to prove myself. You were a guardian angel in more ways than one; thank you. Sibyl Ruth, your thoughtful critiques were harsh and invaluable; thank you. Natalie and Terri, your comments and edits made me believe that I might have written something worth reading; thank you. Catwoman, the sharp-sighted copy editor, and the entire CreateSpace team, thank you for your dedication and professionalism in bringing the novel to print. BBC Radio 4, for a stay-at-home mom your programs *Book at Bedtime*, *Book of the Week*, *A Good Read*, *The Strand*, and *Open Book* were creative writing tutorials as much as they were lifelines; thank you. Miss Aurelia Anna Baier, thank you for your work on the cover, the brainstorming sessions, and the brainstorms that you drew. I loved working with you.

QCL and Oleius, words cannot describe what I feel and think, but you must know by now.

FOR FURTHER INFORMATION

≈

WEB SITES

www.epilepsymoms.com	EpilepsyMoms
www.purpleday.org	Cassidy Megan's brainchild: to make March 26 "Purple Day," as a means to increase epilepsy awareness
www.coping-with-epilepsy.com	Coping with Epilepsy
www.akfus.org	The Anita Kaufman Foundation
www.ilae-epilepsy.org	International League Against Epilepsy
www.aesnet.org	American Epilepsy Society
www.charliefoundation.org	The Charlie Foundation
www.ninds.nih.gov	National Institute of Neurological Disorders and Stroke
www.epilepsyfoundation.org	Epilepsy Foundation of America
www.cure.org	Citizens United for Research in Epilepsy
www.ibe-epilepsy.org	International Bureau for Epilepsy
www.epilepsycongress.org	The portal for IBE and ILAE congresses worldwide
www.sudep.org	Epilepsy Bereaved
www.who.int	World Health Organization

COVENANTS AND LAWS

United Nations Convention on Rights of Persons with Disabilities (2006)
www.un.org/disability

Americans with Disabilities Act (1990) and ADA Amendments Act (2008)
www.ada.gov

BOOKS

Brizendine, Louann. *The Female Brain*. London: Bantam Books, 2007.

Curtis, Deborah. *Touching from a Distance*. London: Faber & Faber, 2001.

Devinsky, Orrin. *Epilepsy: Patient and Family Guide*. Demos Health: 3rd edition, 2007.

Dostoyevsky, Fyodor. *The Idiot*. Translated by Richard Pevear and Larissa Volokhonsky. New York: Vintage Classics, 2001.

Ettinger, Alan B., and Orrin Devinsky. *Managing Epilepsy and Co-Existing Disorders*. Woburn: Butterworth-Heinemen, 2002.

Fadiman, Anne. *The Spirit Catches You and You Fall Down*. New York: Farrar, Straus & Giroux, 1997.

Hippocrates. *Hippocratic Writings*. Chapters: On the Sacred Disease, On Diseases of Women, On Diseases of Young Women. Translated by Chadwick, J., W. N. Mann, I. M. Lonie, and E. J. Withington. London: Penguin, 2005.

Kossoff, E.H., Freeman, J., Turner Z., Rubenstein, J. Ketogenic *Diets: Treatments for Epilepsy and Other Disorders*. New York: Demos Medical Publishing, 3rd edition, 2000.

LaPlante, Eve. *Seized: Temporal Lobe Epilepsy as a Medical, Historical, and Artistic Phenomenon*. Lincoln: iUniverse, 2000.

Legato, Marianne J. *Eve's Rib*. New York: Harmony Books, 2002.

Murphy, Patricia A. *Treating Epilepsy Naturally*. Chicago: Keats Publishing, 2002.

Norsigian, J., H. Stephenson, and K. Zeldes, editors. *Our Bodies, Ourselves: A New Edition for a New Era*. Boston: Boston Women's Health Book Collective, 2005.

Ounsted, C., J. Lindsay, and P. Richards. *Temporal Lobe Epilepsy: A Biographical Study 1948–1986*. London: Mac Keith Press, 1987.

Ramachandran, V. S., and Sandra Blakeslee. *Phantoms in the Brain*. New York: Quill, 1998.

Redmond, Geoffrey. *It's Your Hormones*. New York: Regan/HarperCollins, 2005.

Richard, Adrienne, and Joel Reiter. *Epilepsy: A New Approach*. New York: Prentice Hall Press, 1990.

Sacks, Oliver. *A Leg to Stand On*. London: Picador, 1991.

Sacks, Oliver. *The Man Who Mistook His Wife for a Hat*. London: Picador, 1985.

Sacks, Oliver. *Migraine*. London: Picador, 1993.

Schmidt, Dieter and Schachter, Editors, 2nd edition. *Puzzling Cases of Epilepsy*. Amsterdam: Elsevier/Academic Press, 2008.

Temkin, Owsei. *The Falling Sickness: A History of Epilepsy from the Greeks to the Beginnings of Modern Neurology*. Baltimore: Johns Hopkins University Press, 1971.

Trombley, Stephen. *All That Summer She Was Mad: Virginia Woolf: Female Victim of Male Medicine*. New York: Continuum, 1982.

PERIODICALS

All of these publications can be subscribed to via the Web site of the International League Against Epilepsy, www.ilae-epilepsy.org.

Epigraph: The official newsletter of the International League Against Epilepsy. Published twice yearly.

Epilepsia: The leading source for current clinical and research results on all aspects of epilepsy, and the official journal of the International League Against Epilepsy.

Epilepsies: Reports on advances in the treatment of epilepsy.

Epilepsy & Behavior: An international journal uniquely devoted to the dissemination of the most current information available on the behavioral aspects of seizures and epilepsy.

Epilepsy Research: A journal comprised of high-quality articles in both experimental and clinical epileptology. It is intended to provide a forum for the many disciplines involved.

Epileptic Disorders: A journal devoted primarily to the clinical aspects of epilepsies and related disorders.

Seizure – European Journal of Epilepsy: An international journal providing a forum for the publication of papers on all topics related to epilepsy and seizure disorders.

ARTICLES

Arida, R. M., E. A. Cavalheiro, A. C. da Silva, and F. A. Scorza. "Physical Activity and Epilepsy: Proven and Predicted Benefits." *Sports Med.* 38, no. 7 (2008): 607–615.

Commission on Epidemiology and Prognosis, International League Against Epilepsy. "Guidelines for Epidemiologic Studies on Epilepsy." *Epilepsia* 34, no. 4 (1993): 592–6.

Duncan S, Read CL, Brodie MJ. "How common is catamenial epilepsy?". *Epilepsia* 34 (5): 827–31. (1993)

El-Khayat HA, Soliman NA, Tomoum HY, Omran MA, El-Wakad AS, Shatla RH. "Reproductive hormonal changes and catamenial pattern in adolescent females with epilepsy". *Epilepsia* 49 (9): 1619–26. (2008)
278

Fisher, R., W. van Emde Boas, W. Blume, C. Elger, P. Genton, P. Lee, and J. Engel. "Epileptic Seizures and Epilepsy: Definitions Proposed By the International League Against Epilepsy (ILAE) and the International Bureau for Epilepsy (IBE)." *Epilepsia* 46, no. 4 (2005): 470–2.

Gouldman, P., and J. Smith. "People with Epilepsy and the Joy of Flying: Is There Discrimination?" *Epilepsy & Behavior* 15 (2008): 483–497.

Herzog A.G.,Klein P, Ransil BJ. "Three Patterns of Catamenial Epilepsy." *Epilepsia* 38, (no. 10)1082-8.(1997)

Herzog AG,. "Catamenial epilepsy: Definition, prevalence, pathophysiology and treatment". *Seizure* 17 (2): 151–9. (2008)

Hitiris, N., R. Mohanraj, J. Norrie, and M. J. Brodie. "Mortality in Epilepsy." *Epilepsy Behavior* 10, no. 3 (2007): 363–376.

Hirtz, D., D. J. Thurman, K. Gwinn-Hardy, M. Mohamed, A. R. Chaudhuri, and R. Zalutsky. "How Common Are the 'Common' Neurologic Disorders?" *Neurology* 68, no. 5 (January 30, 2007): 326–37.

Neal, E.J., Chaffe H., Schwartz R.H., Lawson, M., Edwards, N. Fitzsimmons, G., Whitney, A., Cross J.H., "The Ketogenic Diet in the treatment of childhood epilepsy: a randomised controlled trial." *Lancet*, Vol. 7, Issue 6, (2008) 500-506.

Rociszewska D. "Menopause in women and its effects on epilepsy". *Neurol Neurochir Pol* 12 (3): 315–19. (1978)

Sander, J. W. "The Epidemiology of Epilepsy Revisited." *Current Opinion Neurology* 16, no. 2 (2003): 165–70.

Made in the USA
San Bernardino, CA
15 January 2015